Note on the Author

Ellen McCarthy is the author of *Guarding Maggie* and *Guilt Ridden*, also published by Poolbeg Press. She is married and, together with her husband, has travelled extensively in South America, Central America and Europe. She lives in Waterford City.

More information on this author is available at www.ellenmccarthy.ie

ALSO BY ELLEN McCARTHY

Guarding Maggie

Guilt Ridden

ACKNOWLEDGEMENTS

As always thank you to my husband, family and friends for always being there.

To Poolbeg Press for their faith and support – Paula Campbell, Niamh Fitzgerald, Sarah Ormston, David Prendergast – and a big thank you to Gaye Shortland for her editorial skills.

Thank you to everybody at Gregory and Company, especially Jane Gregory for taking a chance on me and to Stephanie Glencross for her guidance.

And to Paul O'Brien, Jason Byrne, Kevin O'Connell & Co, Clarissa Byrne, Pat White and Anne McAuliffe in Eason's Dungarvan, The Book Centre in Waterford and Waterford Libraries – city and county. You all know why.

And to all the booksellers and book buyers out there, you keep me going.

To Ann, Jacinta and John

Burn for burn, wound for wound,
stripe for stripe.

EXODUS 21:25

PART I

BOSTON, OCTOBER 1992

The Driver

A searing pain was starting its retreat to a dull throb, allowing him to finally open his eyes and focus them. All he could see was a shattered windscreen smeared with a film of red blood. The wipers were still rhythmically crossing the screen, scratching a little as they tore across the cracked glass. The headlights were fixed on the bushes behind a gnarled tree that was embedded in the centre of the car's grill, the front of the car wrapped around the trunk of the tree with the bonnet crumpled and pushed back. Steam hissed up through the shredded metal. He could see the icy rain, a little heavier now, illuminated in the lights, but beyond their glow all was darkness and he had no idea where he was. An eerie groaning was coming from somewhere in the front of the car as the scarred metal protested against the indignities it had just suffered. The radio was still on. He remembered a rock station coming to life as he'd started the car – now its heavy beat was vibrating in the confined space.

3

His chest felt tight and constricted against the steering wheel, which was pushed in over the driver's seat. The pain rose up through his chest and neck. The wheel had cracked or broken something. He reached for the radio to turn it off but he was still strapped into his safety belt and he couldn't get to it.

For a moment he stared at a streak of blood on the windscreen. The lines of the spider-print of broken glass started at a central point on the passenger side. The blood was spread on that area. His neck hurt but the blood couldn't be his. He was pinned in too tightly by the safety belt to move, even now when he wanted to. He raised his gloved hands, holding them above the invasive steering wheel. There was no blood on them and they had good range of motion. Wherever he was wounded, it hadn't affected them. His eyes were drawn back to the blood.

His harsh breathing was audible now, mixed with the sound of the wipers and the thumping music. He tried to turn his head but the pain caused him to black out briefly.

Once more he came to and this time the pain had lessened. The world outside was starting to turn a dull grey. The tree embedded in the front of the car mocked him, its branches stretched towards him for a macabre embrace. As the fog in his brain lifted, he tore his eyes away from the outside world and back to the blood on the screen.

He hadn't been alone in the car. He searched his memory. Who was with him?

He'd been at a bar. He'd walked out, seen a car unlocked and found the keys inside. It had seemed like a good idea to open the car and sit inside. A light rain had started, slowly melting the ice and turning the car park to

4

a cold slippery slush. There would have been no public transport at that time. Anyway, he'd left the bar when his money ran out so he'd had nothing left for a taxi.

He'd started the car. Looking around him to see who was watching, he'd slowly backed out of the parking space and driven with caution out of the car park. If he kept his head and didn't go above a normal driving speed it was unlikely anyone would notice the dark sedan leaving.

At first he just wanted a lift home. His new friends were still inside and he didn't want to wait for the buses to start running again. He wasn't even sure if he was on a bus route. When he'd arrived the positions of bus stops hadn't been uppermost in his mind. A couple of guys he had met in an earlier bar were going there so he'd just tagged along. He didn't know for sure what was in the area. It wasn't a place where sane people normally went. He'd seen that instantly but his driver wasn't someone who'd appreciate him rejecting his choice of pub.

He drove on, enjoying the purr of the engine and the feel of the gearstick under his hand. He hadn't driven a stick shift since he'd left Ireland.

Then he saw her standing at the side of the road. She was like a vision, in a light coat. Nobody walked out here. You drove or took a cab but you never walked and yet this beautiful girl was walking on the grass verge with her pink coat flapping around her long legs. How could he waste such an opportunity? He had a hunk of purring metal under his butt and he didn't want to go home. This was his last night and this girl was his goodbye gift.

Back in the present moment, without turning his head he stretched out his left hand. Through the thickness of the leather glove he could feel the soft presence of her body.

5

Painfully he turned his head, unprepared for the wide-open blue eyes, still bright even in death, staring into his own. Her beautiful face was snow white, her hair stuck to it in thick jelly-like clumps which held tenaciously to the congealed blood that caked it.

In his mind he saw her blue eyes crinkled in anger but then they smiled as she sat into the passenger seat.

"Are you going into town?" Her voice was soft.

His eyes locked on to a dark glob of blood setting above the dead girl's eyelid. He let his tears run unchecked down his cheeks. He could feel their salty taste on his dry lips. He couldn't remember if she'd ever told him her name.

Adrenaline was starting to spread slowly through his veins. He didn't know how long he'd been there but he knew that soon someone would find them. Then he would be in a lot of trouble. He'd stolen this car and now he had the body of a girl whom he didn't even know lying beside him in the front seat.

He looked in the rear-view mirror. He wasn't cut and he was wearing his woollen hat. He looked again at his gloved hands. Moving almost on autopilot he opened his safety belt and tried to open the driver's door. It was buckled. He stretched his hand down and found the lever to push back his seat. He found it but it worked too freely. The sudden push backwards sent waves of pain up into his neck. He waited until they subsided. Now that he had more room he used his right arm to exert more force on the door. It creaked open, sending a shower of shattered glass onto the ground.

Hurting all over he got out and stepped away, looking the car over as he did. It was a write-off. He couldn't remember the impact. He might have hit his head on the side window. His right temple was throbbing. The passenger side of the car was wedged against another tree. A tree had sliced off the wing on his side but, luckily for him, it hadn't prevented his door from opening. There was an overpowering stench from the fuel which had seeped from the tank and was pooling somewhere underneath the car. It was a miracle the whole thing hadn't already burned with both of them in it.

He walked towards the front of the car so he could see her more clearly. Tears trickled down his face as he looked at her eyes staring out across the road, as though they were trying to see the life that she'd just left behind. She wasn't wearing a safety belt. He could see it still hanging behind her.

Slowly he removed a book of matches from his pocket and struck one. Holding it up he watched it burn itself out, sizzling in the morning rain. Then he took another, struck it and before he could change his mind flipped it under the car. Instantly a hiss started and then a swoosh as the fuel under the car ignited. The ground underneath was still relatively dry. He stepped back, walked to a safe distance and watched the car as flames licked over it and then it exploded into a fireball that he was sure must be visible for miles. The Rolling Stones "Sympathy for the Devil" was still playing as the car burned. The destructive force of the licking flames hadn't reached its wiring yet.

As he looked around, sniffing back tears, he thought he recognised the road he was on. If he was right, he was only a few miles from public transport and safety. Keeping to the sweeping shadows of the trees as they blew in the early-morning wind, he made himself as invisible as he could in *the dawn gloom as he left. People didn't walk here and he didn't wish to be pulled over by the police. In his mind he could see her beautiful face melting like a wax doll's in the ferocious heat. That memory stayed with him for the rest of his life.*

CHAPTER 1

Mel sat in the car, her trembling hands grasping the steering wheel for control. Her breath was coming in rasping gasps as she steeled herself to enter the station. The effort was causing dizziness and a blurring of her vision. How she managed to drive here she couldn't imagine. Thinking back over the journey she found that she couldn't remember a single turn in the road. It was as though she ran, climbed into her car and was transferred by some time warp to this spot. The blood had almost dried by now but there had been a lot of it. Her hands were covered and it was still a bit tacky as she gripped the wheel. There was probably a lot on her clothes too. She could smell its acrid pungency. What would they think in there when she walked in, in this state? There would be a lot of confusion.

If this were a television programme set in New York she would walk in the door and men would immediately surround her with drawn weapons. At first she probably wouldn't be able to understand them because the shock would make them all speak at once but then after a couple of seconds they would become more confident and coherent and then the words would stand out. "On your knees!" – "Hands behind your head!" or whatever they said in those shows.

Mel absently ran her blood-soaked hands through her dark wavy hair and looked at the blue globe with "*Garda*" written on it. They weren't very observant. She'd been here for a while now, illegally parked in front of a Garda Station and no one was coming to move her on. Well, here goes, she thought as she stepped out of the car, leaving it parked exactly where it was. Let one of them move it for her.

Mel walked up the steps to the station door, took a deep breath and stepped inside as though she were stepping onto a Broadway stage for a show. *Ta-daa!* She felt like bowing.

The lobby was empty. The desk was unmanned with the glass shutters pulled shut. There was, however, a camera mounted high on the wall. She stood in the centre of the room, looking around, wondering how long it would take them to come and find her. Minutes ticked by and nothing happened. She shifted from foot to foot with the tension inside her building.

There was a button on the wall to the left of the customer-service counter. Mel pressed this and waited. Time ticked on. She placed her finger on the button and let it rest there. Still nothing happened. She was getting angry. They were ignoring her. She wondered, if she turned and left now, could she use that as a defence? "Your Honour, I tried to turn myself in but they wouldn't answer the doorbell." Biting her lip, she stood looking around her. Nobody came to meet her.

One last time she placed her finger on the button and then she held her bloodstained hands up, palms visible, so the camera above her could see them. But what if it held black and white film? They would think some wino with dirty hands was standing downstairs playing silly beggars.

Mel stood there like that for a few minutes, which felt like hours. But she stayed still as granite like one of those performance-art idiots on Grafton Street in Dublin.

A door burst open in front of her and three officers came through and stood there. They seemed to be in shock. There was no shouting and no brandishing of weapons. They just stood there looking at the slightly built woman in the bloodstained shirt.

Mel hadn't looked at her face but it too was covered in cast-off blood. She lowered her hands but didn't withdraw them. She held them out straight like she wanted them to take them. Still none of them spoke and they certainly weren't going to touch the proffered hands.

Finally a female officer stepped forward and, holding Mel's elbow, guided her through the doors. The other officers stepped aside to let them pass and then fell quietly into step behind. The room into which she was led was bare except for a table and a few chairs. The female officer indicated a chair to her. Mel tried to pull it back so that she could sit down but it was fixed to the floor. She sat into it and looked around her. The walls were a neutral cream and the floor was tiled. A reinforced window faced the outside somewhere but Mel couldn't see where – it was too high up.

"My name is Detective Emer Doyle." The female officer spoke softly, as if still unsure whether she was dealing with a victim or a criminal. She turned and indicated a heavy man, with hair greying at the temples and receding at the front, who had just come in. "This is Detective Walter Carroll."

He nodded but his face didn't seem like one that embraced emotional outbursts too often.

Mel stared straight ahead but remained mute.

The two detectives sat opposite her.

"What is your name?" Detective Doyle asked.

A younger officer stood off to the side just inside the door, no doubt ready to pounce if Mel became violent. His counterpart stood at the back of the room. There was a pair of eyes fixed on her from every angle. She wondered what they were expecting her to do.

"Where are you from?"

Mel was having a problem deciding where to start so she ignored the questions and quietly gathered her thoughts.

"Has there been a car accident?"

Melanie shook her head.

"Did you hit an animal on the road?"

"No."

"Have you been hurt? We'll be getting a doctor here shortly to get you checked over."

"Does he speak?" Mel turned her head to look at the young officer near the door. He stoically stood with his back to the wall, avoiding any eye contact with her.

Detective Doyle laughed while Detective Carroll remained impassive.

"Yes," she said, "but this is between you, me and Detective Carroll. Forget about him."

"I'm sure he's not deaf," Mel said.

Emer Doyle smiled. "He's not deaf but he is discreet. Anything said in here will stay in here."

"Really!" Mel said. "So if I said I just killed somebody you'd say well done and go back to what you were doing?"

"No, I'm afraid not."

"'I'm afraid not!'" Mel raised her eyebrows. "Then don't treat me like an idiot."

"Sorry. Have you killed somebody?"

Mel stared into space. Emer Doyle was direct. Mel wasn't trying to obstruct the enquiry but she really didn't know what to say to that.

"At this point I need to advise you of your rights," said Emer. "You are not obliged to say anything unless you wish to do so but anything you say may be taken down in writing and may be used in evidence."

Silence from Melanie.

"Do you understand that? If you speak to us you might implicate yourself in a crime." Silence.

"You can speak to a solicitor."

More silence.

"Right," said Detective Carroll abruptly. "Before we start we need you to empty your pockets for us."

Mel stood and obediently showed them that she had no pockets in the leggings and sweatshirt she normally wore in bed.

"We need to search you." Again Walter spoke but Emer was the one who searched her for hidden weapons or needles.

Finally satisfied that there were none they allowed her to sit back down.

"Okay," said Emer Doyle firmly, "before we continue we need to know if there is somebody else injured or needing our help out there."

"No. Nobody you can help."

"Okay," said Emer. "You speak when you're ready and tell us what happened."

"I'm wondering where to start." Mel finally met Emer's gaze.

"Take your time."

Mel sat for a few minutes formulating her thoughts. Was she a victim or something darker she didn't want to consider yet? Perhaps they would tell her when her story was done. Mel wasn't sure herself what had happened over the past few months. Either way she needed to trust this detective. She took a deep breath and started to speak. At least now she could look back on events with accuracy. As the words flowed, she saw Detective Doyle start writing.

CHAPTER 2

I suppose it started when I got the news about Ryan. By the time I heard, he'd been missing for almost a week. I was distraught. I'd been sitting at our home in Raven, a small village about ten miles from Bantry, eating the previous evening's leftover food for a late lunch with a glass of wine, when the phone rang. I rushed to the hall because the battery was flat in the kitchen phone.

A deep male voice with a strong southern American accent spoke to me.

"Is this Melanie Yeats?"

"Yes."

"I'm afraid I have some bad news for you."

I sat on the bottom step of the staircase and chewed on my knuckle, a habit I'd had since I was a child.

"Yes?" My legs felt weak and, despite the fact that I was sitting, my knees were starting to shake. I was terrified of what this news was going to be.

"It's about Ryan." For a moment I couldn't catch my

breath. Ryan was my boyfriend. We'd been living together for three months after a whirlwind romance. I'd only met him a couple of weeks before that but we knew it was right from the beginning. I braced myself for what this news would be.

I should have asked the caller for his name then but he had thrown me with the mention of bad news. My stomach felt like it was full of ice water and a flapping sound had started in my ears. I couldn't speak. Silence filled the hall until the caller continued.

"He's missing."

"Missing?"

"Yes. He went diving in Caye Caulker in Belize on Friday and he hasn't been seen since."

"Caye Caulker – diving on Friday?" My mind refused to work quickly. "Ryan's not in Belize."

"He is. Or at least he was."

"This is Tuesday," I continued on as though I were talking to myself. "Ryan is coming home tonight." I'd been planning our dinner for that night. I'd bought some fresh fish. Ryan loves fish.

"Miss Yeats. I don't think he will be. Ryan is missing. He went out on a dive trip on Friday in Caye Caulker. It was a one-day trip. He signed on for the trip just before they left and completed the dive – but he wasn't on the boat when they reached the dock afterwards. People remembered seeing him during the dive but nobody remembered him on the way back in to land. He just seems to have disappeared." He paused for a moment to let the words sink in.

"Disappeared?"

"Yes."

I was confused.

"Ryan is still missing?" I couldn't believe what I'd been told.

"He is. He'd been staying at The Split guesthouse on the island. He went out with a group who were diving the Blue Hole."

This must be a sick practical joke.

Ryan did dive. He told me that it was a passion of his. I remembered a conversation we'd once had about going to Belize. He told me it was his favourite place in the world. Ryan said when he was out on the water the problems of the world all fell into perspective and he was at peace. I asked him why he needed peace and he'd reached for me, smiling sweetly, and kissed me gently on the lips. "We all need peace, Mel." He didn't elaborate and I didn't probe. I never was one to probe.

I stared at the receiver of the phone as though I'd be able to see through to the other end if I stared hard enough.

"Who are you?"

The phone was dead in my hands.

This was ridiculous. Ryan was in South Africa visiting a contact centre there. He'd been having trouble with his mobile before he went so I hadn't been able to contact him since Wednesday. But he'd called me. He rang me on Friday morning. I leaned against the wall. That must have been shortly before he went out on that boat. I hadn't been worried because this was what he did and what he had always done since we met. He travelled a lot for work and I'd never had any reason to question where he went. Why would he tell me he was going to South Africa and instead go on a dive trip to Belize? Why did it take this stranger five days to contact me? All these questions swirled in my head and I couldn't think straight.

I picked up the phone and rang the number I used to contact Ryan at work.

"*The number you have dialled has been disconnected*," an automated voice said. Bewildered, I rang directory inquiries and got the number for Ryan's company. I asked to speak to the human resources manager.

"Who will I say is calling?"

"Melanie Yeats. I'm trying to find my partner Ryan Lester. He works for your company."

I impatiently twisted a thread on the hem of my sweatshirt while I waited. Finally a woman's voice spoke.

"This is Cora Lennon. I'm the human resources manager. Who did you say you wanted to speak to?"

"Ryan Lester."

I could hear computer keys clicking in the background.

"I'm afraid he doesn't work for us."

Once more shock rendered me dumb.

"Miss Yeats?" she prompted me.

"Ryan Lester? My boyfriend."

The line went quiet and I thought I'd lost the connection.

"I'm afraid, Miss Yeats," the embarrassed woman tried to break the news gently, "Mr Lester doesn't work here and never has."

"He's the manager of contact centres abroad. Maybe you don't have much reason to speak to him."

By now the woman was getting annoyed. "I can assure

you, whatever lofty position this man told you he had here, if he worked for us I'd know of him. He doesn't work for us."

"I'm sorry. I must have made a mistake."

I hung up the phone without speaking another word.

Where had I been calling when I used the old number? A man claiming to be Ryan's PA always answered. He was friendly and even took the time for a little small talk. Ryan was rarely there. He would usually have been "in a meeting" or "just stepped out for a minute, Melanie".

The quietness in the big old house settled around me. The hall I was sitting in had lofty ceilings and a large open stairwell so I could feel cold empty space all around. I was used to the emptiness of Raven House. Even though Ryan was away a lot, knowing he was in my life and thinking of me made me feel very secure. I used the time alone to read and just relax into my new life.

But now the silence seemed to have thickened and taken form. I imagined if I stretched my hand towards it I would feel it solidly pressing against me. Shadows crept into the hall. A knot formed in my gut.

What did all this mean? I wondered what should I do.

Mel looked at the small group of officers assembled around her as though they could tell her what she should have done.

They were listening without sound or comment. Even the statue by the door had glanced in her direction until he caught her looking back at him. She hoped they had nothing on for the night because this story would keep them all there until morning. Detective Doyle studied her with quiet concentration. A short bobbed hairstyle gave her a fragile appearance. It framed her small features but she had a steely stare in her blue eyes whenever they locked onto Melanie's. Mel knew she was closely analysing everything she said.

Emer Doyle spoke first. "You said your name is Melanie. May I call you Melanie?"

Mel nodded.

"Has somebody hurt you, Melanie?"

Mel shook her head. "The blood isn't mine."

"Whose blood is it?"

"I can't say yet."

"Have you hurt somebody else, Melanie?"

"I don't think so." Mel frowned slightly and ran the palm of her hand along the tabletop as though she were cleaning crumbs off it.

"I need to advise you again that you are not obliged to say anything unless you wish to do so but anything you say may be taken down in writing and may be used in evidence." Emer had already cautioned her. But she wanted to be doubly sure that the vacant-looking girl sitting opposite her was listening.

Mel listened again to the caution. "May be taken down in writing?" She raised her eyebrows. "You've been scribbling away since I started talking."

Emer Doyle didn't speak.

Mel asked, "Can I continue with my story?"

"Do you understand your rights, Melanie? You can ask for a solicitor."

"I'm fine. I've told you I understand."

"Melanie, I must ask you again. Is someone else in need of medical attention? Is anyone in danger?"

"No. Can I go on?"

"Sure," Emer said softly.

"Thank you." Mel took up her story again. She could feel the tension in the room. They all wanted to hear the rest of her tale.

CHAPTER 3

Immediately after making the call to Ryan's company I called my dad in Galway. His silence surprised me. At first I wasn't even sure he'd understood what was happening.

"Dad?" I prompted a response from him.

"I'm thinking." There was another long pause. "We have to go out there and see what's happening. I'll make some calls this evening. I'll call you later when I've arranged our flights."

The phone went dead. He'd hung up.

I immediately set about gathering some things together and packing my bag, taking a moment to look up temperatures in Belize. When everything was ready I had nothing to do but sit and wait for the call from Dad. The call finally came a few hours later.

"Mel, I tried booking you on a flight from Cork to Dublin in the morning but the flight from Cork might not get in on time to make your flight out of Dublin. Can you manage to get to Dublin somehow?"

"Yes," I answered. "I'll drive."

"That's good. The flight from Dublin leaves at ten to twelve. The flight is about eight hours so we should be in Atlanta at quarter to four Atlanta time. You need to be at the airport two hours ahead of departure at least. Get petrol before you leave and take a map."

"Yes, Dad, I know." He always treated me like a child. "I have driven alone before."

He ignored my sarcasm and gave me the flight details.

"Okay. I'll meet you tomorrow." Again he abruptly hung up.

My father had always been like that. My mother died when I was a child. My world changed after that but in any case emotion was never one of my father's strong points. He missed my mother, I knew that, but he never talked about her. She didn't just die. It felt like she was forgotten, her memory buried with her body.

My brother Bobby was nearly a man by then and soon he moved away. Like me, he was closer to my mother than my father and when she died any ties he had to our home were severed. Bobby moved to study in America and then to Australia for work so we never spent much time together. When I was a child he was closer to being a father to me than my real father was. But too much time had passed. I couldn't turn to him in a crisis.

After the phone call with Dad I replaced the receiver and made my final preparations for leaving. Then I went out to my car. It would be easier to make the drive to Dublin that night. It was still fairly early, not yet nine. At that time of night there wasn't a lot of traffic so I knew I'd be there by about one o'clock. I had no hotel reservation but on the way I called the Radisson Airport hotel and was relieved that they had a vacancy.

I felt numb with fear as I set off.

Since the call to Ryan's company my brain had feverishly sought reasons as to why he might have lied to me. But how could I find a reason? The company said they'd never heard of him. He'd never worked there in any capacity. How could he be in the Caribbean? Was he there on holiday? Why did he tell me he would be in South Africa? Each question just led to another question with no answers forthcoming.

After about four hours on the road I parked my car in the hotel car park and walked to reception. I couldn't remember any part of the journey. Tears were welling up inside but I refused to let them fall.

Still on autopilot I checked in and ordered a wake-up call for the morning.

I walked upstairs and found myself in a nondescript room. I crawled into bed physically exhausted but my mind was on overdrive.

That night I barely slept and was awake long before my wake-up call. The room price I'd been quoted didn't include breakfast so I avoided the crowded dining room which was full of business travellers and took the hotel shuttle straight to the airport.

I dragged my trolley bag behind me from the shuttle stop, its little hard plastic wheels hopping off the concrete, making a terrible racket. Once inside the airport terminal and officially started on my journey my anxiety levels increased steadily, elevated even more by the bustling shouting crowds around me. After the quietness of my home the noise seemed ear-splitting.

The airport seemed particularly crowded with

holidaymakers that morning. I had to push my way through couples saying goodbye to each other and parents waving goodbye to their beloved children.

At last I got checked in, got my boarding card and then went upstairs to the dining area. It was quite full and there was a long line for the hot counter so I just bought a croissant and coffee. There was a small table near the railing right in a corner so I sat there. I always liked to sit where nobody could sit behind me, if possible.

I felt the minutes slowly tick by, letting my anxious eyes flick around the airport lounge. I watched happy travellers go towards security, smiles on faces full of anticipation. Very few of them looked anything like I felt.

Once I'd finished my coffee restlessness took over. I picked up my phone. Dad was normally early. I wondered where he was. There were no texts or missed calls.

I was toying with the idea of another coffee when a text came through.

On my way. Got delayed. Go through to the departure gate.

I made my way through the crowd towards security. People were piling up as a man argued about taking off his shoes. I fidgeted, toying with the idea of telling him to cop on and just take them off. Finally he got the message. I passed through the X-ray without incident and then made my way to the gate. By now the knot in my stomach had tightened its grip. My teeth and cheekbones were aching from clenching them tightly.

I waited for Dad at the gate. It was still early but I couldn't help glancing at the board in case I missed the flight. Relieved, I saw his small shape walking quickly down the corridor. For a man in his late sixties he could still move.

Dad had been the head of security for an insurance firm in Galway when I was growing up so I trusted him implicitly to know what to do in an emergency but for the first time in my life I saw Eoin Yeats at a loss. He sat down by my side and handed me a coffee he'd picked up for me on the way. But he didn't speak beyond his initial "You got here" which I thought didn't need verbal clarification. He seemed loath or unable to start a conversation. He sat rigidly in the chair, his narrow pinched face looking beyond my shoulder. I waited for him to hold me or speak softly to me but he didn't move. His eyes stayed glued to the scene behind me.

Finally I sat back in my chair. This was going to be a long journey if he didn't speak at all. My dad's eyes were dull and void of sparkle, with his mouth straight and unable to form a smile. But that was how he usually was, so I hadn't expected more from him that day. He had few friends and I never remember him talking about hobbies or interests. He just quietly went about his business or occasionally erupted in anger. Finally he spoke.

"Mel, let me get this straight. He disappeared on a dive trip to Belize when you thought he was in South Africa on business. He has never worked in the company he told you he worked in. You've no idea what is happening."

"Umm," I nodded.

"Oh my God." Dad's cheek sucked in to form a deep hollow and I could see a twitching muscle just under his ear. He only did this when he was extremely angry. "Dad. I'm so sorry." I alternated between shame and fear. Ever since I could remember that had been my reaction when I felt I'd disappointed my dad: shame that I was a failure and fear that I would never do any better.

My father's questions confirmed for me that my life was indeed a sham, a façade that was crumbling in front of my eyes.

"You gave up your job and moved down there to Bantry with a stranger."

I nodded.

"How could you be so stupid?"

"I'm not stupid!" The sharpness of my response shocked us both.

I didn't trust myself to speak after that so for a few minutes we just sat there in silence.

Finally, ignoring my earlier outburst, Dad continued talking. "So what do you have without him? You have no job." His words dripped with sarcasm.

I shook my head. There was no point in arguing with him as he would just stop for a while and then continue on once he gathered his thoughts again.

"Are you sure he even owned that house?"

"I think so. Ryan bought it before I met him."

Dad looked at me. He couldn't believe his ears.

"You have no documentary evidence of any ownership of that house, do you?"

"No."

"Do you have any paperwork, receipts, bank statements or anything that would prove who he is?"

I bit my lip and said nothing.

"Do you?"

"No!" I shot back.

I suddenly realised every transaction I'd ever seen Ryan carry out was in cash. There was a safe in our bedroom that was always stocked with large amounts of cash for expenses. It was hidden in the bottom of the wardrobe in our room. I suppose that should have triggered an alarm for me. People don't usually keep that much cash at home. But we lived in the country quite a distance from the nearest bank so I thought it was just for convenience's sake. There were no cheques written, no credit cards used and I'd never seen any paperwork on the house or for utilities. Now, alarm bells were ringing loudly in my head. It looked like he'd been avoiding a paper trail.

"Oh God!" Dad looked like he wanted to squeeze the life out of his coffee cup.

I shrank further back into my chair. I decided Dad could talk to God all he wanted and I'd stay out of the conversation. Maybe God could come up with a satisfactory answer for him.

At last our flight was called. We got up and gathered our things. It was time to start our journey properly, see if the love of my life was really lying deep in the Caribbean.

We snaked our way through the crowd. Towards what, we didn't know.

CHAPTER 4

Atlanta was the North American Delta hub so from there we could catch a flight directly to Belize City. There was no easy way to get there and we knew there would be no good news once we arrived.

Each stage of the trip passed in a blur. Dad led the way and prompted me for my passport or reminded me to pick up my bag whenever I left it down just as though I were a dependent child again.

During my working life I'd been a manager in a large call centre. Work was one of the first things Ryan and I had in common. During our first conversation we traded stories about our jobs and I knew by his face that he was impressed. I was a senior manager – I had worked my way up internally – and had been promoted at each step based on my intelligence, capability and social skills. It was all there in the reviews I got every year. I was the real deal at work. They respected me. I was going places. But after I met Ryan things changed. It was a slow process and at first I didn't notice the changes.

Ryan was softly spoken and gentle. He told me stories of his travels and talked about his job. His job – that was a lie for a start. I listened to his soft reassurances about how he would take care of me, I felt his arms protectively around me and I assumed we'd be together forever. I gave up my job because I had the perfect man and now I had no job and no man. Somehow he had disarmed me and left me helpless. I was like an invertebrate depending on an external corporate or masculine shell to keep me functioning. I was afraid to move in case I just caved in.

As Dad was late checking in and the flight was fully booked we couldn't get two seats together. The plane was a large Boeing 767. I got a middle seat in the centre row. I hated that. Even on a couch or in the cinema I hated sitting between other people. It was going to be eight hours of my worst nightmare but I was glad not to have eight hours of Dad frowning every time I looked at him or periodically saying "Oh God!". Even being wedged between strangers was preferable to that.

As soon as we arrived in Atlanta Dad immediately headed for the baggage claim. The airport was huge. We took an internal train, a conveyer belt down a long hall and a flight of stairs before we finally got there. I trailed behind all the way. Then as we arrived at the carousel I finally plucked up the courage to speak.

"Dad."

"Yes." He didn't even turn to look at me.

"Why are we claiming our luggage? Is there not a follow-on flight?"

"Yes. Tomorrow morning. Delta has one direct flight to

Belize City every week. We covered all that at the airport. We fly out in the morning. There is a non-stop flight at eleven forty-five. We're staying at an airport hotel tonight."

He was too annoyed to speak to me any more. I didn't blame him. Typically I'd remembered none of that earlier conversation.

Dad led the way outside. Just a short walk away a line snaked along the footpath as people stood behind signs dotted along the path, waiting for the shuttle buses to take them to their hotels. We stood in the line for the Hilton Hotel. I wouldn't have even thought about accommodation but at some point Dad had checked availability and booked us a room and even researched where we would find the shuttle. Maybe he'd told me all about it at some stage over the last ten hours. But I didn't remember.

That night we ate and slept with no more than a dozen words spoken between us.

When we got to Belize City we made our way through baggage claim towards the exit. As we did an onslaught of taxi drivers came our way touting for fares. Dad spoke in his few words of Spanish, negotiating a price to get us from the airport to the boat terminal where we could catch a boat out to the Cayes.

I had picked up a small guidebook earlier at the airport and it was now gripped tightly in my hands. The islands were a Mecca for water-sports enthusiasts. Ryan was an avid and experienced diver. He must have been because, according to the book, you had to be, to dive the Blue Hole. You had to have documentary evidence to prove your diving proficiency. So at least he must have had documentary evidence for that, unlike his employment. For that much I was relieved.

The taxi dropped us on a bustling street. I took my bag from the driver.

Whirling on the spot to get my bearings, I looked around. I couldn't see the ocean. This was supposed to be a dock. Dad was disappearing into a low building across the street. Quickly I followed him. Straight away a slew of people came at me, selling island tours. I sidestepped them as I entered the building and followed my father towards an information counter. Dad turned, pointing to a bank of chairs.

"Sit there and I'll get the tickets."

Too tired to argue with him I did that. I gathered the bags protectively in front of me and sat down watching the crowds mill around me. My father stood in line for the counter, his eyes fixed firmly ahead with the lines of his face still deeply etched with a worried frown. Was he more upset at my stupidity or his own for not realising earlier that Ryan wasn't all he seemed?

Despite the dark shadow hanging over me, I couldn't help but be affected positively by the air of festivity in the terminal. People moved about and gathered, laughing and joking, anticipating the paradise island they were all aiming for. I looked at my leather trolley bag and compared it to the luggage of a woman sitting beside me. Everything she carried was in a black bin liner. Two children travelled with her. I'd never seen such a display of sisterly affection in my life. The little girl lay flat on her belly on the elder sister's stretched body. The back of the elder sister's head lay on her mother's knee. The little girl was kissing her sister's cheek while the bigger girl stroked the hair back off the little girl's face. They loved each other with an abandon that I'd never seen in Irish children. Looking around me, all the native Belizeans attended to each other in a similar fashion.

I thought of the amount of time I'd spent in my life depressed, alone and putting it all down to weight gain or some other issue blown entirely out of proportion. Here size, colour or economics didn't seem to be a factor in happiness. The people had an inner glow that seemed innate and separate from any outside factors. I could see why Ryan came here.

Knowing now how little I could depend on Ryan's words or intentions, I suddenly viewed my partner with a complete suspicion that left no room for any kind of reasonable doubt. Though my heart was breaking for my loss, I had to admit to myself that this man had lied to me. He had probably never told me a word of truth.

Dad came back and handed me my passport. He gave me a heavy metal tag that obviously served as a boarding card.

"Come on, Mel, we need to go through there." He pointed to a doorway thronged with people. Again he walked off and left me to follow behind with my luggage.

The room we entered was similar to the one we had just left but now everyone faced forward. I watched a group of men taking luggage and announcing the next boats leaving the terminal. We handed our bags to the baggage clerk and stood back in a line, waiting to walk through to the dock and board the boat.

Now I could clearly see a sliver of the beautiful Caribbean ocean through the doorway we would soon exit. The terminal was built lengthways along the ocean side.

After the long flight the previous day my back hurt but I stood straight with my eyes firmly fixed forward. A little ache didn't seem so important. Soon I would find out Ryan's fate.

The crowd surged forward and pushed us through to the dock. Dad held my hand to steady me. He'd never been to Belize before so, despite what might lie in wait for us on the island, he was determined to get a good seat and see some scenery.

I stepped awkwardly off the dock and nearly slipped. A smiling black man in blue mirror-shades and mid-calf beige shorts held out his hand to help me. I accepted this spontaneous show of support gratefully. It was the first kindness extended towards me in days.

Dad was in front again when I boarded. He was aiming for the open back of the boat. When I reached him he was sitting with both hands flat down on the seat on either side of him, keeping me a place. I stood beside him until he lifted one hand to give me room to sit but he didn't meet my gaze. The boat had bench seats right around the sides. There was also a large square in the middle with a quantity of seats around its perimeter.

The woman with the little girls I'd seen earlier walked by. The little one put her hand on my knee and looked into my face, smiling. I got an uncontrollable urge to pick her up and hold her but I was afraid they would throw me off the boat for inappropriate behaviour.

As soon as the boat was full, the crew untied the rope from huge iron rings embedded in the dock. Then they threw the tethering rope onto the boat and jumped on. We were on our way.

At first I couldn't see where we were going but I could

see out through the back of the boat. The terminal was slipping further and further into the distance. The expanse of ocean between the dock and us was getting wider. The sun shone harshly down on the dock, burning its way into the wood, but it seemed to dance off the beautiful blue of the water, creating a sparkling array of diamonds on the crest of the waves.

I had no sunscreen on and the rays were burning against the exposed skin of my face but once more Dad came to the rescue. He handed me a tube of Factor-40 sunscreen, as if he'd read my mind. Gratefully I took it from him and applied it liberally, paying particular attention to my nose. Already I suspected it might be turning red. It always did.

The boat ate up the miles of ocean, bouncing over the waves and dipping into the troughs between them. I wished I could see what was coming up in front of us. As I thought this I looked across the boat towards a side window. A small sliver of green island had shimmered into view in the distance like a mirage. I fixed my eyes on it, thinking this must be it. This was where Ryan went without me. But as it got closer the boat seemed to be passing it by and moving on to somewhere else. There were obviously more islands out here than Caye Caulker.

Again the boat powered on and once more an island came into view with palm trees waving in the hot breeze. The island from here looked like a thin sliver of sand with a line of trees growing along its length. Then the houses came into view, huge houses completely at odds with the isolated look of the island. They seemed to be individual housing units with massive glass fronts and equal distance between them. I could see this wasn't a town. It was some sort of private luxury housing development. I wondered who boarded those massive glass fronts up when a hurricane blew in from the ocean and roared through their private little world. Nature had no respect for monetary might.

I felt the boat turning off its course and heading in towards land and then I saw the town. We were aiming towards a long pier cutting out into the water. A couple of boats were already there and people were arriving or leaving, dragging their trolley bags behind them or staggering under heavy rucksacks. Our boat pulled up lengthways along the end of the pier. The crew threw off the rope and a man on the pier tied it up.

"Caye Caulker! Wait for your luggage to be unloaded!" a voice with a strong accent boomed from further down the boat.

Three men sporting the boat-company logo "*Caye Caulker Water Taxi*" on their dark green T-shirts started unloading our bags and throwing them onto the pier. We surged forward, alighting quickly from the boat. We picked up our bags and began to pull them down the pier towards the town.

As we passed a tiny wooden bar built out on the pier a man, fully dressed, put down his bottle of beer, winked at me and dived fully clothed into the sea. I stopped for a moment, fascinated, as he swam a few feet out and then back. He climbed back onto the pier dripping wet and stood once more at the bar sipping his beer. He turned and caught me looking. I turned back, embarrassed, and followed Dad. Already I was seeing that this was a different world.

The town was a brightly coloured collection of wooden houses, mostly single-storey but with a few up to three storeys high, stretching along the beach front. Small streets stretched off the beach. I slouched along, terrified now of what I was going to find waiting for me.

"Cheer up, lady! There's no place here for sad faces!" an old black man shouted to me as I passed.

I frowned in reply and rushed after Dad.

"Slow down, lady! This is the Caribbean . . ." His voice faded into the distance as I finally set foot on the sands of Caye Caulker.

Dad had turned right at the end of the pier. I followed him along the beach until he got to a small office right on the sand. He pushed at the door-handle. The door opened with a sucking sound and a rush of cold air. We couldn't both fit in the confined space so he stood inside in front of a whirring fan while I stood outside in the searing heat. A kid on a bike cycled by and spoke to me.

"Apartment Four is empty!"

"Thanks!" I shouted back.

Dad emerged. "We're staying in Apartment Four."

"That kid just told me that. How did he know?" I pointed at the dreadlocked back of his head as he disappeared down the beach on his bike.

Dad looked at me as though I'd finally lost my marbles completely. Then he led me through a small gate to the right of the office, down a crazy-paving path and then up a flight of wooden stairs. We were on the third floor of a three-storey bright purple apartment block called the Rock Lobster. Above our heads a line of washing danced on the breeze, stretching outwards towards the blue ocean.

The apartment was two-roomed. There was a good-sized bedroom with an en suite bathroom and a sitting room with a futon and extra bedclothes.

Dad looked at the futon. "I'll sleep out here. Get ready and we'll go and find someone to give us some information."

I nodded, wondering what that information might be.

CHAPTER 5

I went into the bathroom and turned on the shower. There was plenty of hot water and the pressure wasn't too bad. When I had taken my shower and changed my clothes I came back out to the living room.

"Mel. I need to talk to you before we go anywhere."

My heart lurched. I didn't want a lecture. Yes, I deserved one but not yet. Anything Dad had to say I was already saying to myself. I sat on the armchair to his left and looked at the coffee table in front of him, unable to meet his eyes. Feeling stupid was awful – it was the most awful feeling imaginable – but being told I was stupid, actually hearing the words from someone I'd spent my whole life trying to impress, was too much for me.

"Mel, the day you called me I rang the Belizean authorities. I told you I would."

I nodded.

"I asked them about the tourist who had gone missing off Caye Caulker, asked them about Ryan. They told me they never heard of him. Yes, a man did go missing while out diving that day. He was American as far as they can say but his name wasn't Ryan Lester."

"So maybe it's all a hoax?" I looked hopefully at Dad. "Maybe the caller lied and Ryan really is in South Africa?"

"Do you think we'd be here for a hoax? I faxed a photograph of Ryan Lester to them. They said that he was the man who vanished but he wasn't using that name. He used the name Tony Foster. He didn't use an official dive group when he went out. He and a group of people from Germany hired their own guide and went on a private tour from a private boat. He wasn't reported missing immediately. The guide never came forward to say he was missing. It was some of the Germans who went to the owner of the dive shop the next day to enquire about the matter. The owner hadn't known about his guide's out-of-hours diving trip so he called the police. The Germans had taken photographs on the dive and gave one to the police, clearly showing Ryan amongst the group."

I couldn't take it all in. Maybe Ryan wasn't even his real name. He'd lied about his job, he'd lied about his destination and now maybe his name.

"I wonder who called me?" I spoke my thoughts out loud. "Why would this person need to tell me that Ryan Lester was missing? I mean, he knew that was the name I'd known him as and that I would be waiting for him."

"We might know if you'd asked," Dad answered in his usual brisk manner.

"I did ask." I was getting mightily sick of my dad's sarcasm. "He hung up."

"Well, he wasn't acting for anyone here, at least anybody that the authorities know of. They didn't have any reason to contact you. They didn't have any name down for next of kin. And you're not married to him. So you're not next of kin anyway."

"What can I do?" I asked, ignoring his comments on marriage.

"We are going to talk to some people who met him, meet with the police. I must shower." Dad got his toilet kit and robe and went to use the bathroom.

When the door clicked shut behind him I lay on the futon and buried my head in the pillow. I was alternating between anger and sadness. At this point I thought even if they did fish him out of the sea I didn't want him back. But I knew I was talking about the man he was turning out to be, not the one I thought I had.

Finally I heard the door open and Dad came back in. I straightened up.

"I'm ready, Dad."

"Okay." He tidied his things away and grabbed the key of the apartment. "Let's go."

I followed him like a dog through the door and into the bright sun. Together we walked down the wooden stairs to the beach below.

As before Dad didn't direct me: he just started walking and I followed. After about five minutes on the beach we turned down a side street into the little town and walked for a block, then turned right and walked for a few more minutes, passing brightly painted wooden houses. Then we came to an area where the island seemed to disappear into a churning chasm of water and then reappear again on the other side.

"What is this?" I looked at the area where the island disappeared into the water, through the dangling doorway which was the only piece left of an old bar. The rest of the building appeared to have gone with the missing chunk of the island.

"It's called 'The Split'. A hurricane hit the island some time back and this portion of the island was swept away and obviously most of this bar went with it."

I stepped to the edge and looked through the doorway into the powerful current.

Dad had obviously come this far just for a look at the famous split. He doubled back on his tracks and walked about three minutes back the way we'd come. I assumed he knew where he was going. He certainly hadn't bothered to tell me. The guesthouse Ryan had stayed at stood on the side of the street. *"The Split Guesthouse"* was written in ornate lettering on the pillar of the gate. Dad opened the gate and walked inside and then down the path to the front door. I followed him. The house was wooden and single storey. The building was narrow but it stretched way back from the street to where I couldn't quite see.

Dad was already knocking on the door by the time I reached his side. He must have done a lot of phoning before he left Ireland. I'd just assumed that he would take care of everything and he had, as always. I wondered, if he were not so dependable, would I be in this mess today? I knew that I'd never had to develop survival skills. Dad had always been there for me in the past and I'd mistakenly assumed that Ryan would always be with me in the future: Now I needed to reassess and learn to care for myself.

Finally the door opened. A heavy woman stood there, probably in her seventies. Her face split into a welcoming smile and she gestured us both inside.

"Are you Rita, the owner?" Dad asked.

"I am. Come in, please, and take a seat."

"I'm Eoin Yeats and this is my daughter Melanie. I called you from Ireland about your missing guest. Mel was his . . ." He faltered over what Ryan was. "He was her . . ." His lip curled slightly as he spoke, "They lived together." Finally he'd found something he was satisfied with.

"Yes." Rita seemed a little confused. "Please take a seat." She indicated a small rattan couch.

"No. Thank you. We can't stay long." Dad was brisk as usual. "We'd like to see his room and his things if we can, please."

"Are you sure – a cool drink maybe?"

"No, honestly. Just his things, please."

She instinctively stood in front of the doorway leading into the interior of the house. "I'm sorry, Mr Yeats. I'm afraid his brother already took his property away. He came here on Saturday to pay for the room and collect the luggage."

"His brother! What was his name?" I gasped the words at her.

Frowning, she turned to me. "He said his name was Mr Gary Foster. I had no reason not to give him his brother's bags." She spoke defensively.

"Of course not," Dad said.

"Did you speak to my boyfriend at all?" I asked, wondering if this woman knew more of the truth of Ryan's life than I did.

"Speak to him?" She seemed baffled by what I meant.

"Did he talk about why he was here or where he was from?"

"Wouldn't you know that?"

A good question, I thought, watching her lined old face

43

trying to figure us out. "I wondered what he talked about during his last days." I put as much sadness into my expression as I could.

Her face softened at that. "Oh. He told me he always loved to be near the ocean – that he'd never dream of living anywhere else. But I didn't talk much with him. Just small talk, you know, while I served breakfast."

"Did he mention Ireland?"

"No." She seemed puzzled by my lack of knowledge of the man I claimed to be close to. "He was American. He said he came from Boston."

"Boston!" The more I learned, the more confused I was becoming.

"What about the brother?" asked my father. "Did he leave a forwarding address? A telephone number?"

"No." She shook her head, looking worried. "There was no need. He paid in cash so our business was finished."

"Can we see his room?" I stepped forward, trying not to show my impatience. Perhaps something there would give me more information.

"I'm afraid it was thoroughly cleaned this morning. We already have other guests staying there. I'm sorry but there isn't anything else I can do for you. You must speak with Mr Foster."

"Rita," my father held out a photograph of Ryan, "is this Tony Foster?"

She frowned and looked at the photograph. "Yes. But he was dressed more casually in shorts and a T-shirt when he was here."

Dad spoke again. "Was there a strong family resemblance, do you think, between the two Fosters?"

"No. There was no resemblance at all. Gary Foster was smaller – maybe five ten. There would have been quite an age gap too. He was older with dark hair going grey at the temples. He had dark eyes and dark skin. He looked Italian."

I thought about Ryan. He looked Scandinavian, not Italian. He was very tall, six three he told me once as I stood in front of him and laid my head against his chest. I liked to do that. I could hear his heart. I would look up and his blue eyes would look deeply into mine. He always seemed to be looking into my soul. For some reason rerunning that image in my brain made me squirm. In hindsight I didn't see the look of a lover. I saw someone examining me like a specimen in a bottle. Was that just imagination born of the situation in which I'd found myself?

I reached my hand out to Rita. "Thank you, Rita, for your time. We're staying at the Rock Lobster if you think of anything else."

"I'm sorry." Rita held my hand and smiled tenderly.

"Thank you."

Dad walked off again as soon as we left. This time we walked back to our apartment and then almost the same distance in the opposite direction. We came to a wooden shack with a sign saying *White Sands* in bold letters. As we got there a sharp downpour started, landing large stinging drops onto my skin. In seconds the pitted white sandy road was full of pools that looked like spilt milk.

The door of the shack was locked and a sign hung on the latch. "*Gone fishing*". A smiley face with dreadlocks was painted beside it.

"Humorous," Dad said with no trace of humour at all.

"How did you know where these places were?" I had been dying to know since we got there.

"I asked while I was booking the apartment." He spoke carefully and simply like he was speaking to a slow child.

"Oh." I lapsed back into silence, my eyes drawn to a hermit crab sidling quickly across the wet street.

"I want coffee." Dad walked away again. This time he just crossed the street and climbed a set of wooden stairs to a first-floor coffee shop overlooking the shack so we couldn't miss the owner when he got back.

We sat in silence by the wooden railing at the front of the shop. A lizard about a foot long ran across the railing in front of our table but I was so numb I didn't even flinch. Despite the rain it was very hot. The lizard ran up the side of the shop and alighted on the tin roof of a smaller shed next door. He sat there, raising two feet at a time to keep them off the burning tin, one front and one back – it was quite a balancing act. I wondered how every living creature had evolved a system to protect itself, except for me.

Finally, after sitting there for close to an hour, we saw a thin dreadlocked man come down the street on his bike and park it by the shack. He took a key from his pocket and opened the door. He walked in, leaving the door open behind him. We jumped up and Dad paid the bill. Then we walked back down the stairs and crossed the street, following the man inside.

It took a moment to adjust our eyes to the gloom after the brightness of the sun.

"Hello!" a cheery voice boomed at us inside the small space. "How can I help you?"

"My name is Eoin Yeats and this is my daughter

Melanie. We're making enquiries about the man who went missing from your dive shop last week."

"No. Not missing from my dive shop. No. That is not the truth. No." He said no a few more times and continuously shook his head.

"We were led to believe that it was from here." Dad was starting to lose his patience.

"No," he said again. "Those people went out on a trip with a casual employee on his own boat without my knowledge and one of them didn't come back. I knew nothing about it. That employee, he didn't tell me he lost a diver. Then he left too."

"He's left? Where did he go?" I was starting to shake.

"I don't know. He didn't even wait for his wages. Some tourists who had been with the group came to me and said that they lost a diver on the trip. He said they panicked, they searched and then they came back without him. My employee, he said to them that he would go straight back out after he had gathered help and find the man. That was Friday. They came to me Saturday evening and asked about the man. I said, 'What man?' They told me the story and asked to speak to my employee. I said I hadn't seen him since Friday. They go to the police and get everyone looking for the man and now I cannot take out tours until this is sorted. Who are you?" he ended abruptly, suddenly remembering that neither of us had told him what relationship we had to the missing man. He halted his speech as he waited for our answer.

"The missing man is my daughter's friend." Now Dad seemed to have decided on Ryan being my friend.

"I do not even know his name but the tourists said it was Tony. My employee did not keep a file. It was an illegal dive. It was done without the paperwork. I do not know if these names were correct. You need to go to the police and find out if they have found anything. I am as in the dark as anyone. Now, is there anything else I can help you with?"

"No," Dad said. "Thank you."

We left.

"This is ridiculous," Dad fumed.

A morbid curiosity had replaced the despair I'd been feeling since the caller told me Ryan was missing. I was going to get very angry and soon. I could feel it. Ryan had lied to me. He was gone and I couldn't do anything about it. I needed to know what had happened.

By now we were at the police station. It was a small station in another wooden building. Dad walked in and introduced us. An officer immediately came to talk to us.

"Mr Yeats." He extended his hand and shook it. "My name is Joe Ramírez. You are here concerning our disappeared American?"

"Yes. We are. My daughter was married to him." Dad was now hoping my being married to Ryan might get me more information.

"My condolences." Ramírez looked kindly at me.

"Thank you."

The police officer opened a file that was already sitting on his desk and started talking. The file seemed to be a prop because he didn't actually refer to the pages.

"I will tell you what we know. An employee at the White Sands dive school took out an illegal group without permission last week on Friday. The people there couldn't get out to the Blue Hole by regular group because they didn't have their PADI licences completed. This individual, the tour guide, was from the mainland and has since left the island. We don't know where he went. The owner's records are patchy." He smiled. The causal employee was more casual than the dive-shop owner led us to believe. "The group went out later than we recommend and they lost an American. The others were German. The guide brought the Germans back and deposited them on the island. He promised them he would contact the authorities and they would start a search. He didn't. He refuelled his boat and left the island. We do not know where he went. We have sent out requests for information to stations in Belize City but it is not uncommon for people to disappear in a city that size. There is a very high crime rate and resources are stretched. This man is just a person of interest for questioning. We don't even know if he has committed a crime. That was on Friday. The Germans decided to check on Saturday to see what happened. Neither the police nor the owner of the dive shop knew anything about the incident. The Germans have since left the country of Belize and gone home. The owner of the shop never saw the American. But the owner of the guesthouse where he stayed remembered him of course. His brother, Mr Gary Foster, came on Saturday before the alarm was raised, paid for the room and took the bags of Mr Foster. He never made himself known to the police and appears to be no longer on the island either. We have no idea of where he might have stayed while he was here. We searched the islands and the water for the body. There are underground caverns around the island but yet you would expect to find some trace of him so we are wondering now if this man could have made himself deliberately disappear. It is unusual for divers to disappear without any body parts being found." He looked from one face to another.

The police had no more information for us so we left and returned to our apartment. Neither of us uttered a word on the way back. I could picture us from the point of view of the cheerful islanders as this little area of darkness moving around their world. My heart and limbs were heavy as I trudged along behind my dad.

Dad's first cousin Bill Yeats was a police officer in New York. Dad thought he might be able to help. Family was sacred in Ireland but it was even more so amongst the Irish in New York. So he placed a call to him from the apartment.

I'd recalled as much information as I could for him regarding Ryan's family from what I could remember Ryan telling me. It wasn't much. A mention of a relative living in New York near Central Park. And a mention of Cape Cod. Dad passed it on to Bill.

After his search, Bill found that there was indeed a Mrs Lester living near Central Park but she had no children of her own and certainly didn't have a family member named Ryan living in Ireland. There was also a Lester living in Cape Cod but the story was the same. This elderly gentleman had never had a relative named Ryan and none of his family had ever set foot in Ireland. It seemed that this Tony Foster had taken a phone book and at random picked two names in his chosen locations to appease a cursory examination by my family.

We stayed on the island for a few more days but there was no sign of the man I'd called my partner or his brother. When we had done all we could and found ourselves no wiser than when we'd arrived, Dad decided it was time to leave.

As I stood on the pier, about to board the boat back to the mainland, I thought about what I had learned. During his time there Ryan didn't mention his life in Ireland. He had told me he came from New York and now it appears he was probably from Boston. He told Rita he loved the ocean. At least that part of our stories was consistent. Ryan told her he never wanted to leave the ocean – well, now he'd probably never have to. Lies upon lies were what Ryan Lester left for me. I was worried too about the caller. How did he know that Ryan was in an accident when he wasn't even out under the name Ryan Lester? And how did this person find me? Then I thought, could he have hurt Ryan? Was I in danger too? He had my number. Of course I'm not stupid – in a little place at the back of my mind I had to consider that perhaps Ryan was alive, had staged his death and disappeared for reasons of his own.

Detective Emer Doyle was considering all options. Ryan still being alive was only one of them. That morning she'd dragged herself out of bed. Her work life recently had been less than challenging. Her own relationship had recently ended and her life had been on hold while she tried to get over it. Emer had been seriously thinking of a complete career change or maybe even just a career break and getting a change of scenery. But from the moment Melanie Yeats walked into her lobby with bloodstained hands she knew this case would be memorable. It could break her out of this backwater and maybe get her back to Dublin or, if not, into Cork City. This girl hadn't hit a dog on the road or something simple like that. Emer sensed this was going to be much bigger. Perhaps she'd killed this Ryan Lester and was setting herself up for an insanity plea.

Emer looked at Melanie. She met her gaze without flickering but there was no aggression there. There was a vacancy about her. Emer was wondering if she'd taken something. The doctor would find that out later. Her eyes were a little recessed with large dark circles underneath, ominous against her pale skin, like someone who was deeply stressed and very tired.

"Melanie."

Mel lifted her chin and pulled her arms protectively around herself when Emer spoke.

"Have you hurt someone?"

Mel looked away.

"Melanie, if someone is hurt then you must tell us."

"Where did the other one go?" Mel ignored the question. She'd suddenly noticed the empty chair. Until then she had been engrossed in thinking about telling her story.

"He just stepped outside."

Mel nodded. She wondered how long she had been speaking. "Will I go on?"

"Not yet." Emer knew she wasn't getting anywhere with her questions. "Excuse me, Mel. I'll be back in a minute."

Emer found Walter Carroll outside.

"Walter, did that story sound odd to you?"

"Everything about her sounds odd to me."

"Yeah. Me too. Do you know anything about this Raven House?"

"No." He shook his head.

"Do a quick check on it – who owns it – get someone to find out if Melanie really lives there and if she's alone there. If somebody is injured we need to get inside. Get people out there to look around."

"Will do. Anything else?"

"Not yet. Let me know what you learn." Emer was about to re-enter the room when Walter spoke.

"Do you think it's all a fairy tale?" he asked.

She turned. "I don't know but there's something off about her." Her heart gave a little thud. This could be national headlines by tomorrow.

Emer halted again at the interview-room door and instead went to check on the crime-scene technicians who had been notified. They needed to get a move on. She wanted them to take Mel's clothes for analysis and take samples of the blood on her hands for DNA testing.

Mel turned to the young Guard by the door, the only one in the room now, but he still wouldn't look at her. She wasn't in the mood for small talk either – she just wanted to tell her story. So she sat and examined the grain in the table as the time ticked away.

The door opened again and Detective Doyle returned.

"Melanie."

"Yes."

"We need to do some tests." The male officer immediately left the room and two female crime-scene technicians wearing protective clothing entered.

"Now, Melanie," Detective Doyle said softly, "we have to take your clothes and take some DNA samples. We're not going to hurt you. It will be all over in a moment. I'll stay with you. Is that okay?"

Mel nodded.

The crime-scene technicians placed a white plastic sheet

on the ground and asked Melanie to step into the centre of it. Trembling visibly, she did as she was told.

"Now, Melanie, I need to ask you to remove all your clothes, please," said Detective Doyle.

Another officer held a sheet in front of her to give her privacy.

Detective Doyle used her now-gloved hands to open a large clear plastic bag. "Hand me your clothes one piece at a time and I'll put them in here." She smiled, trying to calm Mel down.

Mel removed each piece and handed them over as requested. They handed her some clothes to put on instead.

Once Mel was dressed again one of the technicians took a couple of DNA kits out of a box. She used one to take a sample of blood from Mel's hands.

"Do you mind?" She indicated towards Mel's mouth. "We won't hurt you."

Mel obediently opened her mouth and allowed the technician to take a DNA sample from her. The technicians worked like zombies, mechanically doing their business but never meeting her gaze. The swabs were placed in a box. Then they took scrapings from under her nails.

Next, one technician held a sheet of paper behind Mel's back, at the base of her neck. The other gently combed Mel's hair onto the paper. The first then folded the paper like an envelope and packed that away.

When they had finished taking what they needed and were gathering their equipment together, Emer Doyle spoke to Mel.

"Before we continue, Melanie, take these." She handed

Melanie wet wipes for her hands. When she'd cleaned them thoroughly Emer held out a plastic bag for her to put the soiled wipes into. Then she guided Melanie to the door and allowed her to sterilise her hands at the hand-sanitizer dispenser.

Then she led her back to the table.

"Do you want a drink? We can get you tea, coffee or a soft drink."

"Can I have some water, please?"

"Sure you can. Just a moment." She gestured to the young male officer who had just come back into the room after the crime-scene officers left.

He went outside, returning a minute later with a paper cup of water, Detective Carroll in his wake.

"Now, Melanie, you sit back down and continue on with your story." Detective Doyle smiled encouragingly at her.

"Thank you."

Mel started speaking immediately. She desperately wanted to get her story out while it was still straight in her head. She needed these detectives to tell her what her story meant.

Emer Doyle watched her as she began to speak. Mel's eyes turned inwards to somewhere no-one was privy to. Her voice dropped and she frowned occasionally like she was pulling things out of her memory that even she couldn't understand, fragments of thoughts and memories like sheets of paper somebody had asked her to read out loud.

Chapter 6

The flight arrived back into Dublin Airport on time. My father said a hurried goodbye and left.

I was drained after my trip. Once I was back in Raven I could try to figure out who Ryan Lester really was but now it was eleven o'clock in the morning and my stomach was growling for food. I was very tired. I decided to check into the hotel and travel home the next day. But after my lunch and a double espresso I got a new lease of life. As the strong coffee hit my central nervous system I decided against staying and instead went to my car.

I remembered all the warnings about driving when you were tired but between the caffeine and the open window I thought I'd be okay. As a last resort, if I got too tired, I'd stop for a short nap.

I was fine for the first three hours but after that I could hardly keep my eyes open so I stopped at a pub for another coffee. My car was parked in the corner of the pub car park so once I came back outside I thought I would just put my seat back for a few minutes and nap. The minutes turned into hours and by the time I woke it was late afternoon.

I felt free of my father's accusing expression. I was glad I was going home. Now that I was on the road and nearly there I felt fine.

As the car headed south-west a gentle rain started to fall and stayed with me all the way. The deeper I got into the countryside the narrower the roads became and the higher the hedges. I felt as though I were travelling through arteries to get back to the heart of my world. A heart that had stopped beating the night I got the call to say that Ryan was missing. The leaves had fallen now and the trees stretched their dead limbs across the road, pointing at me as I passed.

The journey from Dublin was faster than I'd expected. It normally took about five hours but today there was hardly any traffic. As I approached the end of my drive it was almost dark but I could still make out the looming dark shape of the house above me. I swept through the tall gates which were always left open and drove up the steep drive. I stopped about halfway up. The house seemed to reach over from its perch to look down on me sitting in my car. There was something brooding about the great house standing there, like it had seen many stories over the years but yet was still recording, quietly, the lives of those who came and went through its majestic front door. Each of them was just an entry in the diary of the great house.

I drove slowly up the rest of the drive. Raven House was a three-storey mansion with the outbuildings hidden around the back.

As I reached the turning area in front I had the uneasy feeling that the house had settled back onto its foundations and was now waiting for me to step into its centre. Was it a protector, I wondered, or did it sit there attracting pain to itself to fulfil some sort of macabre curiosity?

I parked the car right in front of the door. Normally I would have driven it around the back to the stables – that was where Ryan always insisted that we park. The rest of the drive swept around widely, lined by massively overgrown rhododendron bushes stretching fifteen feet into the air. Behind that, acres of woodland extended to the side and around the back of the property. The drive and the stable yard felt very isolated at night. I didn't like the darkness back there.

I got out of the car and walked up to the front door. I stood for a minute thinking. Had Ryan been in hiding here? Did he park the car out the back because it wasn't visible there?

My key ring had a little light attached to it so I used this to illuminate the lock while I inserted the key. I had a creepy feeling like someone was watching me. I stepped back and looked at the rows of windows facing down on me. They were all dark and silent, void of life or movement. Chiding myself for my silliness I pushed open the door and stepped into the dark porch, closing the door behind me.

Still that creepy feeling wouldn't leave me. I opened the inside door and entered the large hall. My footsteps echoed across its tiled width and high up into its plastered ceiling. I crossed the hall and entered my sitting room. It was small and warmly furnished. In there I felt secure and safe. In the old days this had been a breakfast room, according to Ryan. The family ate there and then the lady of the house used the front area of the room, where there still was a desk close to the window, to sit and catch up on her correspondence. In the evening the family would eat in the dining room across the hall and then gather in the big drawing room adjoining it. Now the breakfast room was my room. Being smaller than the drawing room it was easier to heat and was quite cosy.

I flicked the switch to turn on the light but nothing happened. Damn, I thought. The bulb must have blown. I walked across the room, avoiding the coffee table by memory, towards the standard lamp in the corner.

The room was dark except for a weak ray of moonlight coming through the window. I only used that room in the evenings. By day it was quite dark because of a large oak tree, which spread its branches across the lawn in front of the window, a window that was deeply set in the thick old stone wall. At night, however, the room came alive with a bright wood fire reflecting off the cream walls and bouncing merrily on the red accessories I had strewn around. This room was my sanctuary. I turned on the lamp, which to my relief worked, and looked around me. The room was exactly as it had looked the night before I left. As I gazed around appraisingly I ran my hand along my bookshelf, touching the covers of the many paperbacks lined up there.

I was quite hungry after my long drive. I walked back out to the hall, opened another door further down it and stepped into the huge kitchen. As in the hall earlier, my footsteps echoed around the room. My heels tapped on the slate tiles while the heavy appliances stood sentry around me.

The dark kitchen was full of corners which seemed to whisper their secrets to me as I walked around, yet try as I might I couldn't quite grasp what they were saying. I flicked on the light and watched a dark and dangerous space transform into my well-known and loved kitchen.

This was the place where I'd cooked for and taken care of Ryan, a place where we'd planned together. In a few years I'd wanted this kitchen to be full of children and life. I'd wanted laughter and tantrums echoing through the doorways.

I looked at the stool where Ryan usually sat. I felt uncomfortable. Ryan. I used to have to call his name to bring him back to me. His mind was absent and sometimes it would take him a moment or two to turn those blue eyes back to me. Often I would lay my hand on his arm to get his attention when calling didn't work. Now his distant moments took on a new significance. Ryan's mind really was somewhere else.

I suddenly got angry. The memories seemed like echoes of an old movie, not real scenes replaying in my head.

At this stage I no longer felt that Ryan Lester, the man I had loved, belonged in this bright and cheerful kitchen. He was darkness now. Once more I flicked off the light and stood looking at the alien landscape left after its glow vanished. This was where that man belonged, here in the shadows. The thought brought back the fingers of fear that the bright light had momentarily banished. I felt a chill as I had outside the front door earlier. I crossed the room and looked at the door which was open into the darkened hall. Hadn't I closed that? I stood in the doorway looking out. The house was quiet.

I turned back into the kitchen and went to the wine rack. I chose a nice Pinot Noir. Opening the drawer underneath, I took out a chrome-plated corkscrew. I switched on the light over the kitchen island in the centre of the room. Two high stools stood by its side. This was where Ryan and I ate breakfast each morning though sometimes, if he was away, I liked to take my coffee out to the front doorstep and look across the gardens and meadows towards the river in the distance.

I poured a large glass of wine. I sat there for what seemed like minutes but as I lifted the bottle to pour some more wine into my glass I realised it was empty. Incredulously I shook the bottle but it was indeed empty. I didn't even feel drunk. I wondered if I should eat something. I got off my stool and walked to the fridge.

I opened the door of the freezer and saw a range of healthy homemade frozen meals that Ryan insisted I keep in there. In my memory I could hear him telling me that there would often be times when I'd be too tired to cook and I might be tempted to eat fattening junk food. I could almost feel his hands pinching my waist to emphasise how far my efforts had taken me.

When we met first back in Galway I was bigger than I am now. I was nearly a stone heavier. I'm only five foot three so it made a huge difference when I lost the weight. Ryan was such an encouragement. He helped me with eating plans and exercise. As I thought back I suddenly felt an aching doubt. What seemed like concern back then now seemed more like systematic control. He pointed out my flaws, making me feel bad about myself, and then helped me mend them, making me feel grateful. It bonded me to him. I was broken until Ryan fixed me and brought me to Raven House. But maybe I hadn't needed fixing in the first place?

That first night, the night I'd met him, I'd been to my

book club with a friend and we'd stepped into a bar afterwards. We usually just had a glass of wine and then went straight home but for some reason that night I wanted a second glass. My friend Alma didn't want another as she still had a half-full glass. We argued about it and finally she agreed to take another just to shut me up. I walked to the counter and there he stood watching me. He was the most handsome man I had ever seen. His fair hair was cropped tightly and his blue eyes seemed even brighter against his tanned skin. I didn't even attempt to talk to him. I looked up into his face as I pushed around him to get to the bar and then just as quickly looked away. But he sought me out. Ryan Lester pursued me. I should have known that didn't make sense. I wore my hair long and straight then with no make-up. Eyes slid by me but no-one ever looked at me for very long.

I took a meal out of the freezer and placed it in the microwave. It was a rice concoction mixed with salmon and vegetables that I'd invented myself. I opened another bottle of wine and went back to my stool. Despite my situation I ate the food and drank the wine.

Another hour passed and by then I was quite drunk. I knew I was going to have trouble staying on my perch so I took the remainder of my bottle and, forgetting my glass, went back to my sitting room, obediently turning off the light in the kitchen as I went. Ryan hated unnecessary lights left on. As I left I closed the heavy door behind me, leaving the ghostly Ryan Lester to his shadowy kitchen.

I sank into the deep soft cushions on my couch and faced the cold empty fireplace. As I took a large swig out of the wine bottle the phone rang in the hall. I put down the bottle and jumped up suddenly, falling over the coffee table and banging my arm painfully. I sat back down and rubbed it and then I hauled myself unsteadily to my feet.

I flung open the door and stepped into the dark hall. Without turning on the light I picked up the phone from the hall table.

"Hello." My voice was surprisingly steady, considering the rest of me.

"Hello."

Immediately I recognised the voice. Its deep southern American tones sobered me instantly.

"Miss Yeats."

I felt as though he were mocking me. "What do you want now? Who are you?" I frowned into the darkness.

"That doesn't matter. I wanted to see how you fared in Belize." His voice had a singsong quality to it.

"What business is it of yours?"

"Ryan is my business. I've been searching for him for a long time."

"Why?" Suddenly I was starting to see why Ryan had disappeared. He wasn't leaving me. He was running away from this person.

"I'll tell you when the time is right. Did you find any information on his disappearance?"

"You know more than I do. I presume it was you who removed his bags from his guesthouse, *Mr Foster*."

"I will find him, Melanie."

"What did he do to you?" I was holding a humming phone in my hand and he was gone.

For a moment I thought, if I found Ryan, then maybe I'd hand him over to this caller. Bursts of anger came and went. Stumbling slightly, I turned off all the downstairs lights and climbed the stairs to my room.

As I went upstairs I had a thought. Ryan used to live here until a couple of weeks ago. Perhaps he cut some spare keys. Any of the previous occupants could have keys. I would need to look at the locks and see how I could tighten security. There could be any number of people out there with keys who could walk in at any time.

CHAPTER 7

The next morning I opened my eyes and groaned loudly. My head was splitting and a shaft of sunlight was shining directly into my eyes through a slit in the shutters. I hadn't shut them properly. I wasn't used to this much alcohol. I knew I was just lying there hiding. The sun in my eyes was annoying me – no wonder Ryan insisted on keeping the shutters closed. That thought made me pause. He was fastidious about closing the shutters in the sitting room and here in the bedroom. I realised that if we didn't do this the lights in those windows would be visible for miles. The more I thought about it the more obvious it was to me that Ryan had been hiding our presence in the house as much as possible.

Dragging myself across the room I went to my bathroom and stood in my shower. I soaped myself four times, trying to deep-cleanse my pores and perhaps help cure my hangover, running my situation through my brain. Nobody ever came to the house. We hadn't had any visitors since I'd moved here. The only person who ever climbed that hill was a deliveryman named Keith Byrne from the village. Perhaps I should ask him if he'd noticed anything strange about Ryan. But I was worried about who I could trust.

Wrapped in a thick cotton bath towel I stood in my dressing room deciding on what to wear. I felt empty looking over my clothes. Most were bright and inappropriate for a woman who'd just tragically lost her boyfriend. I looked at myself in the mirror. I was drawn and pale. My eyes had darker circles than usual, probably because they were soaked in red wine. I smoothed my hands over my hips and could feel my bones. I liked that. When I put my jeans on they stretched across my narrow hips, the dark material making me look even thinner. That was how Ryan liked me. He had definite ideas about everything. My hair should be jaw-length to play up its dark waviness – it had been straight and limp until Ryan encouraged me to cut it. My body should be as svelte as possible, my clothes classic. I even wore make-up now during the day though he insisted on muted natural tones. I was nothing like the girl he'd met in Galway but the transformation suited me. I gulped. Perhaps that was the idea. To spend any time with me he had to make me more palatable to his tastes.

In the kitchen I put on a pot of coffee and placed a muffin in the microwave. Then I sat daydreaming on my high stool. The microwave dinged behind me as my muffin finished heating. I walked over, took it out, poured my coffee and went outside to the front doorstep. The sun shone brightly for so late in the year. On a day like this I knew I would never again find a home as beautiful as this.

For just three months I had been a princess in my own country mansion.

I had thought this was going to be my home for the rest of my life. There was nothing permanent for me now. I knew I should find out more about the house and my situation but I was scared. I didn't want to face reality yet, didn't want to see the final remnants of my life crumble away. But I had to do something. I'd procrastinated enough. When my breakfast was finished I went back to the kitchen and placed my dishes in the sink, then walked back out to the hall. My bag and keys were sitting on the centre table. I picked them up and took an umbrella from the stand by the door, went out and locked the front door behind me. I needed to get out of the house for a while.

The hill down from the house was steep so the drive crossed over and back across the hill to reduce the gradient. I hadn't been there yet for a freeze but I suspected that if I stayed in Raven House there would be a time when I might have to abandon my car at the bottom and walk up to the house. That time would be soon. It was approaching the middle of November and already very cold.

Bantry was about ten miles from Raven House. The drive didn't take too long. As I drove into the town along the sea wall I could see the white caps of the waves to my left and the town stretching out in front of me. Built into a cleft in the landscape, part of the town is built high above the rest leaving some of the streets narrow and steep. I parked my car near to the square and made my way to the sea wall.

I walked along it feeling the spray of the ocean on my face. I kept walking until I reached the end of the pier and then I leant across the wall, looking into the water. Ryan loved the ocean and never wanted to leave it. Once more his landlady's words came back to me. How ironic if he'd died in it.

I turned around and saw a bench a few feet a way. I walked over and sat there as the cold sea air whipped around me until my ears, nose and lips were numb. When I couldn't take the cold any longer I decided to go and get a hot drink somewhere so I could thaw out.

There was a pub on the corner of the street where I'd parked my car. I went in there and ordered a coffee. I drank it sitting at a window table looking out onto the wintry street.

I was twenty-eight. I'd always had a plan ever since I was a little girl. I wanted to be a young wife and a young mother and I thought Ryan could give me all that. But he'd made me no promises. Looking back now I'd built my dreams on hopes and certainly nothing more concrete than that. If I'd had more time, would I have made such a huge decision as moving in with him? Would I have insisted on more reassurances from him or was I totally blinded by love? Would I have insisted on getting more information from him about his family and his life? Perhaps not. It was more than just a case of eleventh-hour nerves as I faced mid-life – the need to find a husband before the dreaded clock started ticking. No! I wanted the handsome man, the wealthy man, the educated man and the cultured man. I wanted the best. I woke up everyday thinking "This is the day when Ryan will tell me he wants to spend the rest of his life with me". Now what was going to happen?

I was worse off than before. I had no job. I was too

scared to check the situation with our house. Did he really own it? Now that he was gone I would have to move out. We hadn't been together very long and perhaps his family would want to sell the house. The elusive family I'd never even met. I didn't have any rights over his estate and I doubt he'd made a will with me in it. What an idiot I was moving in with him and giving up my job!

I shook the coffee remains around the bottom of my mug. I'd jumped into this of my own free will based on a shadowy promise. How stupid could one woman be? Of course I'd wanted children. I thought, now that I'd found the perfect man and we had the perfect home, that weddings and babies were the next steps. That didn't make me stupid, did it, I reasoned. Surely that made me normal?

I could hear the sympathetic, condescending tones in my head as people would secretly laugh at my silliness.

I bent over, holding my stomach. I often suffered from stomach-ache when I was upset. Trying to collect my thoughts, I decided to have a drink. I made my way back across to the counter, ordered a gin and tonic and then went back to my window. I was hidden from the interior of the pub by an overstuffed rack of hanging coats.

The recent numbness was starting to wear off but already I wished it wasn't, as the pain it had been masking was taking my breath away, literally. I knew it was a panic attack but I couldn't breathe. It was like a great weight was sitting on my chest compressing my lungs and causing my heart to palpitate from lack of oxygen.

I had to get out for some fresh air so I threw back the last of the gin, grabbed my coat off the rack by my seat and in doing so knocked a bundle of coats on top of myself.

Swearing under my breath I clumsily threw them back up whereupon they promptly fell down the other side and onto the floor. The barman was walking in my direction so I swung about and quickly returned to the street.

CHAPTER 8

I had to get to Cork City. There was just one person I could turn to. I walked along the now drizzly street, to where I'd parked my car. I manoeuvred the car out of its tight space.

It was going to take at least an hour and a half to get to Cork. The roads were busy and the conditions dangerous due to the heavy rain of recent days so the trip took longer than I'd anticipated. Small areas of flooding lay in the troughs of the narrow hilly roads making them treacherous.

The day was darkening as I approached Cork. My friend was a solicitor so I drove to his office and parked my car as close to the building as I could get. If anyone could help me he could.

I wouldn't need an appointment but I still should have called. I had a mobile and it had been a long journey with ample time to call ahead but I wanted to speak to him now and didn't want to be fobbed off by an over-zealous PA.

Hugh and I had known each other in school and in recent months we'd renewed our friendship. It was shortly after I moved to Raven House and I was feeling very alone. I tried explaining this loneliness to Ryan but he had a way of turning it around on me and making me feel ungrateful. He would ask if he'd done something wrong or if our home wasn't good enough. Gradually I stopped struggling against my environment and blended in. Most of what we needed was delivered to the house and we rarely went out, but one day when Ryan was away I decided to drive to Cork and do some shopping. On Patrick Street I bumped into Hugh. We hadn't spoken since school but we'd been close then. Hugh went to the local Christian Brother's school. I went to the convent school but we met on our lunch breaks and walked home together afterwards. We were inseparable until we left school and were a couple briefly that summer, then gradually grew apart.

That day we went for coffee and talked for hours. Later, on Ryan's return, I told him about the meeting but immediately I knew he was jealous and didn't approve. I felt like destiny had given me back my friendship with Hugh. Ryan didn't like the idea much so I hid it from him. That was my only act of rebellion. After that first meeting I managed to meet up with Hugh about once a month and it was nice having someone familiar living not too far away. Because of his job he often had meetings outside Cork so sometimes I didn't have to drive too far for our lunches.

I breezed in the door of his office and crossed the small floor space pitted with creaking sagging floorboards. Hugh wasn't in the top percentile of legal firms in the town, but he'd been to law school and was smart.

Hugh's PA sat behind a wide desk that looked like an

old school principal's desk. It was grooved and chipped from years of knocks and use. I could picture a large principal with a sagging gut bursting from his striped shirt slaming a stick across its wooden surface, burning his anger into the desk's grain.

The desk belonged to a different species of worker now. A young man with a large smile greeted me.

"Hello. Can I see Hugh Curtis please?"

"Who will I say is calling?"

"Melanie Yeats."

He picked up the phone on his desk, buzzed the inner sanctum that I knew was through that door, to the right of the desk, a door with visible handprints all around the handle. Was I noticing these little details because I'd spent the last few months living in a manor?

"Go on through, Miss Yeats."

"Thank you." I continued my journey and stepped through the inner office door.

Hugh crossed the floor to meet me. He was just a year older than I was but his hair was speckled with grey. He had a lean physique and a pair of the palest blue eyes, like pools of ice under a winter sun.

"Hello, Melanie." He always used my full name.

"Hugh."

He hugged me tightly and moved me a little away from him so he could have a proper look.

"You look thin and pale. Are you okay?"

I could feel my chin quivering. Hugh didn't speak. He turned and led me to his desk and handed me a box of tissues. I sat down, blew my nose loudly and attempted to gather myself together. Finally I sniffed loudly and looked into his concerned eyes.

73

He smiled at me, waiting for me to explain.

"I'm so sorry, Hugh, for bursting in like this."

"Hey! You know I'm always here."

"Are you?"

"Of course." He sounded a bit weary.

I made a mental note to ask him later if there was something bothering him. But first I took a deep breath and told him about Ryan, the recent happenings. Every time I heard these words they sounded more ridiculous.

"You must think I'm an idiot." I examined his face as I spoke, searching for the confirmation of the harsh judgement I was heaping on myself.

"Of course not."

I knew he was being kind. "You know what everyone says. If it looks too good to be true it probably is. I'm so embarrassed."

"First thing we need to do is find out if his name is really Ryan Lester, Tony Foster or something else entirely."

"How do we do that?" My brain was creaking slowly into action.

"Have you gone to the Guards?"

"No."

"Why not?"

"He's not in Ireland. He disappeared in Belize."

"You need to register him as a missing person and let the Guards put an international search for him in place. He may have done this before. He might be flagged on a list someplace."

I hadn't even thought of that. Anyone who used an assumed name and invented his job could have done anything in his life.

"Why did I have to get involved with him?"

He seemed uncomfortable as he answered, "I don't know. We'll find him first and ask him. Are you feeling better?"

"A little." I smiled. My tears had dried. Then I became serious again. "A man phoned my house a couple of times. The first time to tell me Ryan was missing and the second time to find out if I found out anything when I travelled to Belize. He scares me. I don't know how he knew about Ryan or how he knows my number."

"Don't panic but, please, Melanie, go to the police."

Once I'd calmed down he offered to get me some coffee but I wanted to leave. I didn't open up like this very often and I was exhausted. I needed to be by myself and think. I promised to call him.

He looked at me, his brow lined with worry. "Please do, Melanie. That house is an isolated place. You don't know what this caller has in mind for you."

In less than two hours I was back in Raven. I stopped in the village at a petrol station and filled up my car. As I was pumping the fuel my eyes wandered around the road. It was a quiet village and tonight with the bad weather it was practically deserted. I noticed a car parked across the street by the junction leading to my house. Somebody was inside. I knew the person inside was watching me. I couldn't see him because the streetlight on that side was too far from the car but I could see the outline. He was turned towards me. I kept watching the car as I put the cap back on the tank and walked inside to pay. When I came out the car was gone.

It was just a short drive back to the house but I kept watching in my rear-view mirror, still spooked by the car's presence earlier, wondering if it was anything to do with my caller.

When I got home and turned up my driveway, once more I got the feeling that the house was watching me. I could almost see the walls expanding and contracting as the house rhythmically breathed while it watched my approach. As my lights swept across the front of the structure they flashed against the dark glass of the house. I had to blink. It was as though the house was blinking back at me. I wondered was it relieved I was back.

I stepped out of the car and my feet crunched into the gravel by the door. I stood by the car and let my eyes wander around the property, trying to see through the gloom what had first attracted Ryan to this house. All I could see were the shadows and pockets of darkness that surrounded it.

I turned to the car again, pressed the button on the car keys and heard the familiar thunk as the lock engaged. Then I heard a sound in the gravel behind me. Before I could turn around, a heavy body pressed against me, pinning me to the side of the car. I realised it was a man as a large leather-gloved hand gripped the lower part of my face, stopping me from twisting around or calling out. As I tried to shout all I could manage were a few yips through his clenched fingers.

The weight of his body was crushing my ribs into the metal of the car. With his free hand he dug his fingers deeply into the flesh of my left thigh, pressing our bodies more closely together. I could feel his face pushed into the hair at the nape of my`head. We held this position as the seconds ticked by. I tried struggling but it was no use so I let my body relax, waiting for an opportunity to act.

Finally the hand he'd been holding my leg with released its grip and started to move up and around my body. As he started running it across my abdomen, panic took over and I started to struggle again. It was futile. He was far too strong.

I could feel his heart beating against my back and smell his breath. He'd been eating garlic. Finally he grabbed the back of my head, twisted my head sideways and ran his tongue along my cheek before pushing me to the ground.

Everything went black.

I opened my eyes. I knew it couldn't have been too long since I fell because I could hear the engine still ticking and as I pulled myself up by the side of the car I could feel the bonnet was still warm. I leaned against the car and closed my eyes and groaned. I was okay. I thought I had just blacked out from fear.

Disoriented when I tried to move, I had to sit on the gravel again. I looked around me. It was totally dark. Somebody was really trying to frighten me. It had to be the caller. I thought about the caller and "the mugger" and in my head they were interchanging and becoming one person. And Ryan's disappearance: how did that fit in?

This time Mel noticed as Walter Carroll left the room while she was speaking. Detective Doyle, however, never took her eyes off her face.

Mel paused. "Do you want me to wait for him?"

"No, Melanie, you can continue – that's fine. Would you like another drink first?"

"Yes. Please. Can I have tea?"

"Of course."

Walter returned and nodded to Emer Doyle. She stood up.

"Excuse me, Melanie, for a minute. I'm going to go and see about your tea. We might even find you some biscuits."

"Thank you."

"Will I wait for you?"

"Yes. Do. I won't be long."

Mel looked up at the face of Detective Walter Carroll as he sat in the seat closest to her and smiled. He nodded but tried not to meet her gaze. He was not the most communicative.

She looked down. She felt odd sitting there in some stranger's clothes. They'd given her a sweatshirt and jeans but the room was getting quite cold and she was starting to shiver. It could be stress. Mel was worried and she always shivered when she was upset.

It would help a lot if they let her finish her story because as she said it all out loud it helped her to process things. It was sort of like she was wrapped in a cocoon. But telling her story was helping her to unwrap the truth and letting her stand back from it all and see what was happening.

Right now her memories were like blobs of colour in front of her eyes. She could clearly see them but she couldn't see the big picture those tiny pieces formed. One day she would be able to stand back and it would all come fully into focus. Bits of her life were tantalisingly out of reach. Mel feared she mightn't like what she saw. But for now it helped to see her story reflected in the face of Detective Doyle.

Emer interrupted her thoughts. She had just returned and had a cup of tea with her and a plate of biscuits.

"Here you go, Melanie." She handed her the cup. "Please continue. You still haven't told us where all that blood came from. I need to ask you again: should we be looking for somebody injured?" She looked closely at Melanie's face as she spoke. "Has somebody died?"

Mel sipped her tea and bit into a biscuit, not meeting Emer's gaze. She knew she was bringing the memories of what happened to the surface. Suddenly she didn't think she wanted to.

CHAPTER 9

That night I checked every door in the house to make sure they were locked tightly. I was terrified. I knew I should call the police. But what would they do in that type of situation? Look for clues, take a look around and then tell me "there's not much to go on, Melanie, but call us if anything else happens". I decided to cut the bullshit and just look for clues myself and keep my eyes open. I read the papers. Rapists and murderers getting away with their crimes or serving ridiculously short sentences. I imagined a prowler would get way with a caution, if even that. I didn't even have a bruise on me and there were no witnesses.

I hadn't seen his face. He'd never spoken to me so I had no idea what he sounded like. Then I thought about his hands. His hands were large, he was very strong and I thought he was tall – I couldn't be sure but he was definitely taller than I was, but then who wasn't? He seemed well built. So I thought he might have been tall and muscular with large hands. Oh, he also ate garlic. Gosh, I thought sarcastically, with that much information I really should go to the police – they'd have him in no time.

Before I went to my room I went back and rechecked all the doors.

When I was in my bedroom I looked at my door. It had a key so I could lock it. But I'd watched too many mystery movies. There were ways through locked doors. I didn't want to sleep here unless I had more protection than that. For want of a better plan I jammed a chair under the handle. At the very least this would give me a chance to react if anyone tried to come into the room. What would I do if they did? I walked to the dressing room and looked at that door. It had a key too. That was my plan. If someone tried to get through the bedroom door I would run to the dressing room and lock myself inside. And then what? I didn't want to think about it.

I also placed a large pair of scissors by the bed along with my mobile phone. If the door rattled I would grab the phone and scissors and run to the dressing room. I would lock the door behind me and call for help. Finally, satisfied that I could keep myself safe, or at least safer, I climbed into bed.

The next morning I brought my coffee out to the front step so I could look down into the valley below. When I'd finished I was going to get a number and call a locksmith. There wasn't anyone who did that in Raven so it would have to be somebody in Bantry. As I stood there listening to the sounds of the morning my mobile phone rang. I dug it out of my back pocket and flipped it open.

"Hello."

"Have you searched the house?"

"What?" I looked at the phone but it was an unknown number. "Hello?"

But silence greeted me. The caller had hung up. How did he get my mobile number? A knot of fear was growing.

I looked down the hill.

Of course I should have searched the house before then but it hadn't ever dawned on me to do that. But I would now, search it from top to bottom and the outhouses too. Now, with this plan in place, I was nervous about going inside. I shifted my feet in the gravel and looked at the door. Somewhere behind it might lie the secret implied by this caller. He had put the locksmith out of my head for a while.

Again Mel was interrupted as a female Guard came in and whispered something to Emer.

Emer nodded and stood up. "Melanie, we need to take you to another room – our medical suite – so the doctor can have a look at you."

Mel rose and Emer guided her out of the room and into another just across the corridor.

A man in his sixties stood there.

Emer turned to Mel. "Melanie, this is Doctor Hanley. He's going to make sure you're okay. Is that all right?"

Mel nodded.

"Hello, Melanie."

"Hello."

"I'll just check you over and then I'll come back with you and stay while you tell the rest of your story."

Mel nodded.

He checked Mel's heart rate, pulse, looked at her eyes, her throat and took a couple of blood tests. Then he checked her reflexes. He got her to walk a straight line, catch a ball thrown to her at different angles and at different speeds. He gently felt her cheekbone where a dark bruise lay and worked his fingers softly along the bridge and sides of her nose. Then he got her to sit down.

"How do you feel, Melanie?"

"I feel fine."

"Do you feel any dizziness or pain?"

"I'm tired and my cheek hurts."

The doctor made some notes, filling in details on a form before speaking to her again.

"The good news, Melanie, is I don't think your nose is broken but you have quite severe bruising. Can you tell us what happened to your cheek? It would help me to figure out how to treat you." He smiled in a coaxing fashion.

Mel smiled back patiently. "It's not the right time yet."

"It would be helpful for later, Melanie, to answer any questions we put to you," Emer said, adding, "Not answering might make it seem as though you've got something to hide."

Mel ignored that. "Am I okay to carry on?"

"Sure. If you understand what I just said."

"I do."

"Okay."

They went back to the interrogation room where Melanie settled back into her original chair. The doctor who'd come with them sat away to the side.

"Go ahead, Melanie," said Emer. She guessed that even Mel wasn't sure of where this story was going. It would unfold in its own time.

They all waited for her to continue.

Just as Mel was about to start speaking again, she stopped herself and turned to the doctor. "Why did you take blood tests?" She seemed more interested than frightened.

"I need to check in case you're under the influence of drugs or alcohol. We also had to do a physical check just in case you were unwell or injured."

"Okay." Mel sat there, looking suddenly bewildered and lost.

She'd wound down a little since she'd come in and Detective Doyle was getting worried about her because it was getting quite late.

"Melanie, do you really want to continue with your story right now?"

"Yes." She brightened up a little.

"We can take a break if you like?"

"No!" Mel spoke sharply.

"Okay. We'll continue on."

Detective Doyle sat back and Mel started talking again.

CHAPTER 10

I looked around the kitchen first as I washed my breakfast things, wondering about what the caller had said. I wouldn't need to search there. I knew every space within its walls. He wouldn't have put anything here or in my sitting room either. The rooms I used were so full of me that he wouldn't have risked putting anything in them. I was one of those people who were constantly arranging and cleaning. Nobody knew that better than Ryan. So that left the places I didn't go in the house.

When Ryan first took me to Raven House I fell in love with its solid elegance. It was beautiful. While not massive in scale it was massive in proportions. The staircase was oak and swept elegantly upwards to a stained-glass window on the first landing. I wandered around, with Ryan watching my reaction to it all. He loved it too and seemed very comfortable there. He seemed at one with the house.

That morning was cold and damp and he had lit a real

wood fire in the massive marble fireplace in the hall. I had felt its comforting warmth as soon as we entered. I suspected Ryan saw himself as a proper country gent.

Now, I wondered as I started my search what or who the caller was guiding me towards.

I thought about Ryan's study. If he had a secret this would be the most likely place for him to hide it. I rarely went in there. I crossed the hall and opened a door leading to the dining room. The room had a large window facing towards the side of the house but the window was greatly overgrown with ivy and other foliage waving across the windowpanes. It clearly was the family dining room at one point; a huge mahogany dining table stood in the centre of the room. Wood panelling surrounded the room on all sides going halfway up the walls. An ornate wooden desk stood in front of the window. I thought I would start there. I crossed to it and opened the drawers. The entire desk was empty. An old-style wooden filing cabinet stood off to the side of it. I opened each drawer and found them to be empty also. I couldn't believe my eyes. So what did he do every night when he came into his study to work? Doodle, twiddle his thumbs? I certainly couldn't see evidence of any work. There were a few books and A4 writing pads on the desk. Though hard-covered and officious-looking the books were crime fiction and when I opened the writing pads they were all empty. A cup full of perfectly sharpened pencils sat at the side of the desk. I looked behind the desk and immediately saw an Internet connection point in the wall but there was no computer. Ryan had a laptop. He'd taken it with him. I should have thought of that – if he were working, of course he would have his computer with him. Next to the desk was a selection of books but they were all paperback novels and of no interest to me then. Bewildered, I walked next door to the drawing room. Except for an overstuffed chintz three-piece suite there was nothing there and no reference to Ryan.

I returned to the kitchen and walked to the cupboard under the sink, withdrew a large flash-lamp and flipped the switch to ensure it was working. Next I was going to search the empty rooms upstairs. It was doubtful that there were functioning bulbs in all those rooms and I guessed the curtains or shutters might be closed. You should be prepared. I enjoyed adventure books when I was a kid and those kids always carried their flash-lamps.

Poised and ready now, I walked out to the hall and climbed the stairs. Apart from my bedroom, there were four large rooms on this floor that I'd barely entered since I'd moved in. But for a bed in one, they were all empty. No furniture and no heart. It had been slightly exhilarating to know I was surrounded by so much empty, abandoned space. Now my mind was filling that space with a dark presence I couldn't yet name.

Ryan and I had walked hand in hand through these rooms shortly after I moved in and he had listened with an indulgent smile on his face as I outlined all I would like to do with them. It was a fantasy house. Then, my fantasies were large country parties and some day tons of children. Now, my thoughts were on shadows and hidden eyes.

I walked along the length of the first-floor corridor and opened each door in turn. The curtains were closed. I crossed the floor to each window and pulled open the curtains but even with the sharp rays of the sun flooding the rooms they still remained empty of any reference to Ryan. All the furniture would have been heavy freestanding pieces, which were removed before Ryan moved in, so it was immediately obvious that the rooms were empty.

I closed the doors again and went back to my spot at the head of the stairs. Above me was the attic floor which had more guest bedrooms. These sat under the eaves and had dormer windows. Since they were mainly used as extra space the guest rooms only took up the front of the house while the back section, overlooking the stable yard, had originally housed servants. A solid wall, without doors, divided the two areas.

The secret must be up there.

So, with growing trepidation, I climbed the stairs. At the turn of the stairs a beautiful if dusty stained-glass window allowed timid rays of light to squeeze their way into the stairwell. As I walked on the carpet, dust was rising and I could see it suspended in the air through the shafts of light. As on the floor below I systematically went through each guest room but they were silent and empty.

Next I needed to turn my attention to the servant's quarters, but I couldn't get to them from here. This was the main house. The help lived in their own part of the house, which was reached from the kitchen side. The servants climbed the two flights to their quarters up a narrow staircase, rising from the pantry which I now used as my utility room. I made my way downstairs again.

I walked through the kitchen to the pantry. It was a long narrow room with three small windows built high in the wall. The stairs to the servants' quarters rose from here.

I stood at the foot of it and looked upwards. I could see a wall facing me where the stairs took a sharp right-hand turn. I could stand there all day fidgeting and shifting my weight from one foot to the other but I was unable to see around corners.

I'd explored the attics the week I moved in but there was nothing up there. Unless we turned the house into a hotel or took to hosting shooting parties I didn't feel the need to open up these rooms and furnish them. Nor did I ever go up there. I was a creature of habit and ritual. The presence of the servants' quarters just didn't factor into my daily habits of coffee and reading. There was no need to go wandering in those musty old rooms.

But the caller had sent me on this search and I had no idea what was waiting for me. So, plucking up my courage, I climbed the first section of stairs and peeped around the corner: nothing. Up above me the stairs ended in a closed door.

Feeling like a schoolchild stealing apples in a neighbour's garden I climbed the rest of the stairs and stood outside the door.

There wasn't a sound on the other side. Tentatively I reached out my hand and turned the old-fashioned, china doorknob. The door opened with a creak. I started to laugh, feeling as though I were in a Hitchcock movie. Any minute now Ryan would come charging at me in his mother's clothes and a wig, wielding a knife. I stepped onto the landing and looked down the length of the corridor.

Four doors opened off it. I walked along, opening each one. The first two rooms were completely empty and musty, their shutters not having been opened in ages. Any furniture had been removed a long time ago. The third one was a bathroom. I stood in the doorway but I could see there was nothing hidden in it either.

I was just about to leave the room when I noticed the smell of urine. I froze. I looked back into the room. The toilet seat was up. I crossed the room and looked into a toilet that shouldn't have been used in years. It was unflushed and had been used very recently. I whirled around, looking at all areas of the bathroom but nothing else looked as though it had been used in a long time.

I left the bathroom and turned my attention to the last door.

Immediately the beam of my lamp picked out a little cupboard to the left of where the bed would have been. It was built into the wall.

I crossed the bare floorboards to it. The small wooden door was painted a pale pastel blue, which at one time would have complemented the fussy floral-print wallpaper on the walls. Both were now layered in grime with a thin frosting of dust. I opened the door and looked inside. It was empty except for a couple of sheets of yellowing paper. I turned my flashlight on the paper.

It was a Green Shields Stamps catalogue. Written in pencil on the top of the front cover was the name *Imelda Connolly*. My grandmother had saved for and purchased nearly everything she ever had in her kitchen from this catalogue. I remembered the tiny green stamps that she placed in a stamp book every week. When she had a sufficient amount of stamps in the book she then went to the Green Shields Stamps shop and exchanged her book for whatever she was saving for at that time.

I turned the flashlight into the cupboard again and played its beam along the narrow wooden shelf and sure enough there was one of the tiny stamps nestling in the corner. A tiny green fragment of a dream lost in an old dark cupboard. I wondered what Imelda had been saving for. I looked back at the catalogue and turned over a sheet. Circled in pencil on one side was a lady's brush and comb set. With a sense of reverence I returned the pages to their little tomb.

Next, I shone my lamp around the floor. What I saw made my hands shake and my heart hammer in the gloomy space. There was something on the other side of the room. My footsteps rang out loudly as I stepped towards it across the wooden boards. A bedroll. There was a bedroll rolled up in the corner with a couple of blankets and a flat-looking pillow but no other sign of life in the room. At some point someone had slept here and if he were the one who used the bathroom then it couldn't have been too long ago. I bent down to examine it closer. It seemed relatively clean and wasn't layered in dust as it should have been if had lain there a long time.

Closing the doors behind me I quickly went back down to the kitchen. I leaned against the counter top trying to think of a solid reason why some unknown person had been using an old bathroom in my home. Of course there was no reason.

I should have gathered my things and run from the house but I didn't. Instead I turned the key in the outside of the door leading up to the servants' rooms and placed the key in a kitchen drawer.

I suddenly remembered the safe upstairs. I had the code. Ryan hadn't actually given it to me but I had seen him using it and memorised the number.

Then I thought: what if someone else knew the code and had emptied the safe? I ran up the stairs, arriving breathless on the landing. When the black spots cleared from before my eyes I ran to my room. I went straight to the wardrobe, inserted the code into the safe and, click, the door opened. Inside as usual was a stack of money. Again I knew I should have gone to the police. I wasn't sure if this money was legal or if I had a right to it but it was all I had. I took it out and counted it: six thousand euro. Now I decided to change the number. I sat for a moment on the ground trying to think of a sequence Ryan or anybody else wouldn't know. Then I keyed in the numbers and double-checked I'd done it correctly. Now I could still get at the cash. The safe was bolted to the ground so nobody could walk away with it and if they couldn't open the door then this money was mine until I figured out what I was going to do.

I went back to the kitchen and thought about the rest of the house. Perhaps a bedroll and unflushed toilet wasn't the big secret. Maybe there was something else hidden in this rambling house.

Doctor Hanley whispered to Detective Doyle. She listened, nodded and turned to Mel.

"Melanie? Is there anyone you want us to call?"

As soon as she'd asked the question Mel started to shake. She started scraping her knuckles on the desk. Her face turned from relatively soft lines to a frown of stress. Her colour started to rise.

"Melanie, are you okay?"

"I want to tell you my story. Then you can tell me if I'm okay."

"I think it would be better if we resumed tomorrow," Doctor Hanley said. He wanted to test her reaction to someone getting in the way of what she wanted to do.

Her voice rose sharply and she started rocking. "I want to tell my story now. *Now*."

"Okay, Melanie. Let's keep talking."

Immediately Mel calmed down and continued.

CHAPTER 11

From the kitchen I went into the scullery and out into the backyard which had a small walled kitchen garden beyond. I glanced into the small shed. Nothing there, just some old junk. I went back to the kitchen and walked down the flagged corridor which ran along at the back of the house, passing the door which opened into the hall. At the end of the corridor was the door leading out to the stable yard. I had decided to have a good look at the outbuildings. As I reached the door something started to niggle at the back of my mind. I paused, frowning, and looked back down the length of the corridor. Something didn't make sense.

I opened the back door and stepped onto the path, which extended through a small flower garden. This was the one area I'd nurtured since I'd moved in. It was a long narrow strip running part of the way along the back of the house and in it I'd sown a selection of old-style cottage garden flowers like hollyhocks, bluebells and flowering currant bushes. This was my patch. I'd planned the garden for a spring and summer display but now I probably wouldn't be there for that.

I was excited as things bloomed and faded with a promise to return. I loved the fleeting and the transitory. Somehow engineering nature to ensure constant supply cheapened life for me. It made my heart lift when I walked outside and saw the first daffodil of the season but walking into a filling-station forecourt and seeing imported blooms from "wherever" left me cold.

I crossed the narrow strip of garden and came to the stone wall, about four foot tall, that extended the length of the garden. I opened the iron gate which hung there. I was then in the stable yard. I turned and looked at the house standing behind me. Raven House stood solid and silent, wondering what its new occupant was up to.

The yard wasn't huge. While Raven House was a mansion to someone brought up in a three-bedroom semi-detached house, as far as mansions went it was modest. To my left a large archway led out to the drive that swept into the woodland and around to the front of the house. Straight ahead, a gateway led to the land behind which was now covered in trees and scrub. In the old days there were hundreds of acres going with the house but now there were just ten.

The stables themselves surrounded the yard on two and a half sides providing stabling for ten horses. Clutching my lamp tightly I walked to each of the stables and looked inside. Crumbling bridles hung in the boxes. Moulding hay lay decaying and blowing away on the wind which blew through the lofts. You could smell the dust as soon as your feet disturbed the hay on the ground. Rusting farm implements stood idle, just remnants now of a bygone age. I liked the quietness as I passed through the old buildings. It was obvious that whatever the caller was referring to wasn't there.

It was a chilly day and I hadn't brought a jacket with me so I returned to the house.

Crossing the yard I looked up at the attic area. I counted seven dormer windows. I frowned. There were just four doors off the servant's corridor upstairs and each room had just one small window looking out towards the back of the house. I rushed back inside, locking the door behind me and ran down the corridor. This was what was niggling me earlier. When I was going outside I knew that this corridor was too long for the attic floor upstairs. There was another set of rooms beyond the ones I had seen.

Grabbing the key from the drawer I opened the door and raced up the stairs. Once more I stood on the attic corridor. I listened but the rooms were silent. Just to be sure I took a peek into the room with the bedroll. It was empty as before. The toilet was as I'd found it previously. On a sudden whim I walked over, flushed it and put down the lid. I have no idea why I didn't do that the first time.

Standing now at the end of the corridor, I tapped the wall. It was wooden. I ran my hand along it but there were no openings anywhere. I went into the end room and examined the wall. It was solid also, offering no knowledge of what was on the other side.

I turned and ran back downstairs. I knew the attics were servants' quarters. I suspected the rooms I'd just come from used to house the women. Between housekeeping and kitchen staff there would have been at least three in times past: one cook, and probably a couple of maids. But where were the men housed? There had to have been some men, possibly a manservant or stable boy or a foreman for the farm.

The women's quarters obviously were close to the kitchen. The cook and her maids would be first down to the kitchen in the morning and it seemed likely that the men might be first to the yard. I guessed that the lady of the manor might want to keep the genders apart. The League of Decency wouldn't have wanted unregulated relations between the sexes in the household.

I stood in the corridor inside the stable-yard door and looked around. Apart from the door into the hall, the only doorway down this end of the house led into an old cloakroom. I opened it and walked inside. There were old household appliances stored there and a number of old coats covering fashions from many decades. Large piles of packing boxes were piled up at the back of the room. Then I spotted the top of a doorway behind them. It was probably a cupboard or an old coalhole but my curiosity was fired up now.

I heaved the boxes aside, piling them behind me by the wall and revealed the doorway. This door was hidden. Had Ryan hidden it or did they just pile rubbish in here, over the years gradually forgetting it existed?

I grasped the handle and turned it but the door held fast. It was locked. I ran my hand along the top of the frame and checked the wall around it in case there was somewhere to hide a key but I couldn't find one. Desperate now to see the other side of this door I went through every nook and cranny in the cloakroom but there was no key. Maybe the key was lost years ago.

I went back and looked more closely at the door. The

lock was new or at least less than a few years old. Had it been changed before Ryan moved in? I wondered if I really wanted to know what was in there.

As Mel paused, Emer Doyle seized the opportunity to ask her some questions.

"Melanie – you said you had nowhere else to go. I don't understand why you didn't go home to your father."

"Do you go running home to Daddy every time the going gets rough?"

"No. But I'm not sharing a large house with an unknown person and getting calls from people who don't identify themselves."

"Well, until you do you can't judge me." Mel stared obstinately at the table.

"That money could have been drug money or taken from a bank robbery," Emer continued, "but you continued to use it. Were you not afraid of consequences?"

"Of course. But what else could I do? I had no personal money. Thinking back, Ryan had ways of controlling me. He encouraged me to go online and order food rather than drive. 'It's just easier, darling.' He was the one who wanted me to leave my job and move down to Raven House with him. 'We can be together every day.' He moulded me."

"Why?"

"Can I finish my story?"

"In a minute. Just a few more questions."

Mel had no identification on her when she came into the station. She hadn't been carrying any car keys but couldn't possibly have walked from Raven.

Detective Doyle had sent an officer out on to the street earlier to search for a car Mel might have come in. It didn't take him long to find it. There was a Honda Civic parked illegally right outside the front door. The keys were covered in dry blood and still in the ignition and a mobile phone sat on the passenger seat.

They impounded the car and ran the number plates. A Cork solicitor named Hugh Curtis owned the car.

"Melanie."

"Yes."

"Why do you have Hugh Curtis's car?"

"I'll tell you when I get to the end of my story."

Emer saw she wasn't going to get any further with that question.

"Where did you work? Earlier, you said you worked. What was the name of the company?"

"What does that matter?" Mel frowned at the detective.

"It would just help us to get a clearer picture of what's going on."

"I don't see how."

"Can I have your address in Galway?"

Mel looked darkly from one to the other of the officers assembled around her. "I'm from an area of Galway called Mount Bank. Now can I get back to my story, please?"

"Okay, Melanie. Continue."

CHAPTER 12

I gave up trying to enter the locked room. I decided to sleep on it and try again the next day.

When I awoke I showered, dressed and went downstairs. I opened the fridge door and checked what food I had. There were a few packaged muffins. I heated one in the microwave and made a fresh pot of coffee. I was getting far too dependent on sugar.

Going out to the front doorstep I sat there, chewing thoughtfully. I could see over miles of land down the hill into the valley. It was going to be a stormy day. Already the howling wind was lashing the trees across my line of vision and the first fat drops of rain hit the house around me. No longer able to enjoy my view of the countryside, I decided to try again to get into the locked room. I knew that was where I would find the secret to which the caller was directing me.

I walked back to the kitchen, dumped my dishes in the sink and went back down the back corridor to the cloakroom. I examined the locked door closely. It was solid heavy timber. There was no way I could force my way through it so I turned my attention to the lock and the hinges. The hinges were on the other side of the door so there was nothing I could do with those. Getting in by way of the lock would be no easier. It was one of those heavy security locks that would be impossible to pick.

Maybe I could take it off, I thought. But where could I find tools? As far as I knew we didn't have many. I searched the cloakroom and found nothing. I went back to the kitchen but there was nothing there either. Racking my brains I thought back to the stables I'd visited yesterday. Was there something out there I could use to get through the door? I opened the back door to cross the yard but the rain hammered past me and the wind nearly blew the door out of my grip.

Not yet, I thought. Locking the door, I went back upstairs. I would do some tidying in my room while I waited for the weather to calm down.

The ceiling in the bedroom was at least twelve feet high and the room had windows on two sides. Light poured into it on a good day but today it hid under a grey shadow. The minute I walked in my heart got heavier and I felt tired. All the stress of the last week flooded me. I looked at the bed. A little nap wouldn't do me any harm. Fully clothed I crawled into bed and cradled my pillow as I felt my eyes closing.

Some time later, I sat bolt upright. The dream had been so real. My eyes darted around the room but nothing seemed to have been moved. A large seven-drawer chest stood tall and imposing against the far wall. In my dream Ryan had been in the room, opening his shirt and removing his cuff links. He placed them in one of the many little paper boxes he seemed to have stored in the top drawer of the chest and closed the drawer.

Ryan always referred to the chest of drawers as the "bureau" – he said that was what they called it in America. It was a massive piece of mahogany furniture, a symbol of a bygone era. The top drawers were too tall for me to even see into, so Ryan had used it exclusively. That might be where he would put the key. I jumped out of bed, forgetting how high it was and landed sprawled across the carpet. Winded for a moment, I paused and then picked myself up.

I dragged over the big chair I'd used to block the door the previous night. The top drawers were the most likely places that he would hide something he didn't want me to find. I hadn't thought about that earlier. I'd assumed the secret was something bigger than a key. In the top drawer were his little boxes. They were filled with trinkets, pieces of jewellery, cuff links, watches and even a few pieces of neck jewellery. I started laughing when I saw them. Ryan hated when I referred to them as necklaces. Quickly I shook off the memory. It only drew tears.

Then I opened the second drawer. Carefully I went into every corner, separating items of underwear and opening balled-up socks in case he put the key inside one. At first there seemed to be nothing there either.

Then, in the last ball of socks stuffed in a corner in the back, I found a key. It was a strange shape and quite new. Jumping off the chair I ran back downstairs to the cloakroom.

I inserted the key in the lock. The lock was in good condition and turned instantly. Almost at the point of throwing up with apprehension I pushed open the door. The caller had led me here for a reason. Ryan had hidden the key and kept this part of the house a secret, for a reason. Now, I was about to find out why.

The door opened into a dark stairwell. I'd forgotten my flash-lamp. There was no way I was exploring up there alone in the dark. I ran to the kitchen, got the lamp and a sharp vegetable knife in case I needed a weapon.

Once back in the cloakroom, I cautiously climbed the bare wooden steps and turned the corner of the staircase but came to a halt in front of a closed door at the top. I turned the handle. The door opened straight back, into another corridor almost completely in darkness except for the dim light shining from behind me. I switched on my lamp and shone it down the corridor. It seemed to be similar to the one I'd seen the previous day.

There were three doors on this corridor. I walked to the first door. This was a large room and completely empty.

The next door had frosted glass on the top in a fanlight so I guessed it was probably another bathroom. I opened the door. It was an old-style bathroom. A pull-chain toilet stood at one end with the lid down and an iron bath with claw feet stood to the side.

I moved to the next door. This must be it. I turned the china doorknob but this door held solid. On a hunch I put my hands up over the door and felt along the frame. No key. I shone my lamp down on the floor but there was nothing there either.

My head was spinning. I had to find what was in that room. I could go to the barn, see if there were tools or something heavy there, to break open the door. I went back again to the big bedroom. A pair of heavy wooden shutters covered the window leaving a slim chink of light into the room. I opened those to see if the rain had cleared at all. It hadn't. It was pounding off the window and the wind sounded as though it would come through the slates. I would just make lunch. It couldn't last forever.

Leaving the room, I noticed the key half-hanging out of the back of the lock. I passed through and out of habit closed the door behind me. As I closed it my hand rattled against another key in the outside of the door. Two keys! One was in the lock at the front and other was loosely placed in the back. My heart jumped. I knew one of these keys would open that door. I took the key from the inside first. It opened the door instantly. "Not so clever Ryan, are you?" I asked the silent corridor. I got no reply. I pushed open the door and entered the room. My eyes immediately saw Ryan's secret.

PART II

BOSTON, OCTOBER 1992

The Lover

Gordon Grant opened his eyes when he heard his mother's knocking. He saw the digital display on his clock. Five thirty – he'd been in bed since one. It had to be bad news.

"Gordon!" she shouted. "Bradley Renfield is on the phone for you. Take it in the hall."

"Okay!" he called back, dragging himself out of bed. He grabbed a sweatshirt and descended the stairs.

He picked up the phone.

"Hello."

"Gordon. Is Elizabeth there?" Bradley was in no mood for small talk.

"No. Of course not." He knew she wasn't, thought Gordon. "The last time I saw her was about midnight."

"She hasn't come home and she hasn't called." Bradley's voice held panic.

They both knew something was wrong and they both blamed Gordon though Bradley didn't know the full story.

The previous evening Lizzie and he had been at a cocktail party hosted by her aunt. The whole evening had been a disaster. It was a typical formal Renfield affair, deep-shag carpets and shallow conversation, each person trying to outdo the other with their grandkids' schools and their children's growing portfolios. Whether it was property or commodities these people were buying them up as fast as they went on the market.

Lizzie shone at these events. She was the other great asset to a family like that. All evening she twinkled and sparkled like a jewel in an exquisite old-world setting. Trained for these things since birth she had every man in the room wrapped around her delicate little finger. He wasn't stupid. His family were wealthy but they weren't rich by the Renfield standard. That evening it finally sank in that Lizzie was killing time, playing with her bit of rough until the time came to marry for the family. He couldn't bring that out in the open in case she agreed and ditched him ahead of schedule. Lizzie and he had things to do before that happened. But he was so angry that he had to find some way to vent his frustration.

Walking the perimeter of the room giving her dark looks wasn't helping his case and he knew it, but he couldn't rein himself in. Finally, he was proving to be a family embarrassment so Bradley had to come and have a word with him. It was noble of the big brother to step in but it wouldn't be seemly for the Renfield princess to air her dirty laundry in public so she watched out of the corner of her curled eyelashes while she batted them prettily at a Wall Street friend of the family.

Bradley ushered Gordon out to the great hall and held him there, calmly trying to talk him down, until Lizzie

*came smiling through the crowd to see what was going on.
By then Gordon had worked himself into a sweat. If Lizzie
was going to ditch him he'd given her ample reason. Not a
person in the room would argue with the girl needing to
rid herself of his dark presence. They probably wondered
what she was doing with him in the first place.*

*By the time they realised he was too wound up to calm
down, Bradley hissed at Lizzie to get him out of there.*

"I've had enough of him. Get rid of him."

*All three of them knew what he meant. Lizzie was to
break it off as soon as possible, stop embarrassing the
family and get herself one of those handsome, wealthy
studs roaming through her aunt's drawing room.*

*Lizzie was angry at having to leave the party early.
Gordon was angry because he knew this was the end.
There was no way now she could keep seeing him after an
ultimatum from Bradley. Lizzie was born to do the right
thing by the family. He was born for what he didn't know.
He wasn't conceived with a purpose.*

Once they drove off she started shouting at him.

*"You embarrassed me and yourself in front of my
family and all our friends!" She paused so the enormity of
his actions could sink in.*

*"You embarrassed yourself." Gordon spoke softly despite
the heat of the moment.*

It halted her.

Then she spoke again. "How did I do that?"

*"By prostituting yourself to the highest bidder while
you have a fiancé."*

"You dick!" Her voice was shrill.

*"Nice language from a princess." Gordon laughed. He
could clearly remember he laughed and when he looked at*

her, thinking perhaps she might see the funny side of it, he realised she was livid with rage.

"You are not my fiancé. That is all in your head." She laughed sarcastically.

"We talked about it," he protested. "You agreed that at Christmas we would announce our engagement." His voice was rising now.

She raised her left hand. "Nothing on my finger and no hope of you ever getting anything there."

Gordon grabbed her hand and held it so tightly he could feel her tiny bones crack. "That is my hand." He let it drop back on her lap. He knew they were empty words, just more posturing on his part. He'd never own any part of a Renfield.

Lizzie had a violent temper and nothing scared her. She turned and attacked him, grabbing his hair, punching him in the chest and biting his cheek hard.

"You total bastard, you embarrass me in front of my family and then you think you own me! You'll never marry me!" She punched him again in the ear.

Gordon stopped the car abruptly and leaned across her. "Get out of my car. Now."

"What?" She seemed surprised. The route he'd taken home was quicker but it went through an area that if he'd been thinking straight he wouldn't have wanted her walking in.

"Get out of my car." There was silence for a moment but he wasn't backing down.

"Fine." She got out of the car, her coat swinging, giving him one last look at her long legs.

Gordon drove off, tyres screeching, leaving lines of burnt rubber on the road. He accelerated and drove *blindly until the mist lifted and he'd calmed down. Though it had only been a couple of minutes since he'd driven away he'd covered quite a distance. He had to go back. He couldn't leave a twenty-year-old girl stranded there even if it was Lizzie Renfield.*

Driving back Gordon rehearsed all the things in his head that he was going to say to her to buy himself some more time in the Renfield circle. As he approached the place where he dropped her Gordon saw her walking on the sidewalk, her expression still thundering from their fight. He drove past and did a U-turn further down and drove back towards her. As he approached he saw a dark sedan stop to pick her up.

Elizabeth Renfield, the family trophy, pushed one leg seductively forward, showing the legs Gordon had been admiring just minutes before. He knew all her moves so well. She turned her head, slightly shaking back her hair and turned her face to the side. He knew that coy look that made his heart melt. Then, as she stepped into the car, he saw the smile, the mega-watt smile, which she used to turn on just for him.

Then Gordon knew he didn't want her. No amount of money and prestige could make him spend another minute of his life with that girl. Let the bum in the ten-year-old car have her. He'd had enough. Once more he accelerated away, a bold move he was to regret for the rest of my life.

CHAPTER 13

Ryan's secret was the only thing in the room. It was like a shrine displayed on a large corkboard, which took up almost two thirds of the wall. A small ottoman stood in front of it like a prayer kneeler. On shaky legs I walked to the stool and sat down. Carefully I took a couple of deep breaths to calm myself.

In the centre of the board hung a large photograph of the most beautiful girl I'd ever seen. She couldn't have been any more than twenty. Her features were small and delicate. Her eyes twinkled as though she were in the middle of some salacious gossip. I stood up and walked a little closer. Though her clothes, make-up and hair were classic and difficult to date, the photograph was obviously not taken recently. Her hair framed her face in sheets of gold. The face stared at me, boring holes into my soul, asking me why I had disturbed her space.

"Why did Ryan want you to himself?" I spoke out loud

and the sound of my voice echoing in the bare room frightened me.

I stood for a couple of moments in the eerie greyness of the room with the photograph highlighted by the beam of my torch. It seemed to make her blue eyes sparkle and the pale whiteness of her skin luminous in its glow. We sat like this in the gloom as the seconds ticked by. Then I spoke again.

"I want to know who you are."

I got no reply from the silent young woman so I stood and stepped closer. I ran the beam of my torch around the board. It was covered in smaller photographs and newspaper articles. Afraid of what I was going to discover I walked to the shutters and opened them wide, allowing as much light as possible through the grimy windows. A swathe of ivy waved across the windowpane, further adding to the dreariness of the little room.

Despite her wide smile, the mystery woman did little to ease the murkiness of her surroundings. Something about her sunshine appearance seemed wrong there, tragic, like someone took a sunbeam and condemned it to live in eternal darkness.

I now started to read the newspaper cuttings surrounding the image.

"Police are still searching for the driver of a car that spun out of control on a remote road in south Boston. The passenger in the car, twenty-year-old Elizabeth Renfield, appears to have died on impact. It is still not known why she was in the area and how she ended up a passenger in a stolen car."

"The body was badly burned but she was identified by dental records and X-rays."

"Foul play is now suspected in the death of Elizabeth Renfield. The charges have been upgraded to murder. It has been discovered that Elizabeth was in fact still alive when the car was burned and may perhaps have been saved if the driver called 911. The car she was riding in was stolen from the car park of the Chaser Bar in the early hours of October 13th 1992."

"Questions are still being asked about why Elizabeth Renfield was in a stolen car on the night of October 13th 1992. Her family deny their daughter had been drinking. Her boyfriend Gordon Grant left her earlier that night."

"Gordon Grant II had been dating Elizabeth since high school. They were expected to marry according to his parents, though an engagement had not been announced."

"The owner of the stolen car, in which Elizabeth Renfield was a passenger on the night of October 13th 1992, reported the car stolen at four thirty the next morning. The owner is a member of staff at The Chaser Bar. He had been on duty that night and was heading home when he noticed the theft of his car."

"Today was the tenth anniversary of the death of Elizabeth Renfield. No one has ever been charged

with her death. The owner of the car she was travelling in had a verified alibi. Elizabeth's boyfriend was also questioned as they had argued violently prior to her entering the other car. Mr Grant's face showed the physical marks of a struggle but he was later ruled out as a suspect. Numerous witnesses showed him in his own car at various points on his way home, eliminating him from the enquiry. It has since come to light that following the fight between the couple Mr Grant left Elizabeth alone on the road in the area where she subsequently died. Police traced as many people as possible who were drinking in the bar that night for questioning but though some remain as persons of interest, nobody was ever charged."

All photographs in the articles had been removed before Ryan had placed them on the wall. I wondered why. What was his interest in this girl and her story? Was he related to her? Had he known her? Was there something in the photographs which would lead to Ryan Lester? Ryan was older than I was. He could be the driver. Elizabeth was staring coolly at me from her perch in the centre of the board, waiting for me to figure it out. I spoke first.

"Did Ryan kill you? Did he steal that car and kill you? Has he been carrying this around since then? Is that why he ran away?" All my questions were answered by a deep silence with her arched eyebrows mocking my attempts.

I needed some answers. How do you find out about such an old case? I would try the Internet first.

Out of respect for Elizabeth, I quietly closed the

shutters again and left the room. Not knowing why I did it, I locked the door and returned the key to its hiding place.

I wondered if Ryan was running since that night. It would explain a lot of things.

While he walked the earth trying to come to terms with what he did to Elizabeth, did he pick up sad, lonely women like me and then move on again when things got too complicated?

Then I thought of the caller. That was why Ryan ran. This man was chasing him. Maybe he was a relative of Elizabeth's. Or her family could have hired him. Should I go to the police and tell them? Tell them what, I wondered. I found some pictures. What did that prove? They would just assume I was a woman scorned. My rambling thoughts went on and on.

I made my way back to the kitchen. After my morning in the attic I was starving. I decided on pasta for lunch. It was quick to prepare but it took an hour to eat it and sip my glass of wine. I was procrastinating. I knew that. I was terrified of maybe finding proof that I'd been sleeping with a man who could cold-bloodedly kill a girl and burn her body. What did that say about me if I didn't see it in him? What had I really seen and felt about Ryan? Did I ever suspect that he wasn't what he seemed?

I wanted to say no. I wanted to say that I'd never suspected for a moment that he wasn't everything he appeared to be, but I couldn't. There had certainly been many times when I had paused and thought there had to be a catch, but I didn't care. There were enough good things on the surface to stop me from asking too many hard questions about what might be lurking underneath.

Though he could be distant and often was, Ryan was animated when he talked about the things he loved – like the sea. His eyes sparkled as he talked and his hands were constantly moving. He was so alive. Now what was he?

Emer Doyle noticed that Mel's breathing was getting shallower and she was starting to pant.

"Melanie, are you okay?"

"Why did that officer just leave?"

The young one had stepped outside.

"He's just going out for a minute. It's nothing for you to worry about."

"He's checking on Elizabeth, isn't he?"

Emer wondered should she lie to Melanie or tell her the truth. Obviously the idea of him finding more information on Elizabeth Renfield was upsetting for her.

"Wait a moment, Melanie. I need to step outside and then we will continue with your story." She moved towards the door.

Mel stared sullenly after her.

Once outside the door Emer Doyle went looking for the other officer, Seán Walsh.

She found him in the office. "Seán?"

"Yes?"

"Do we have a search warrant for her house yet?"

"Not for Raven House, no. We can go out and have a look around but we haven't found anyone yet to sign the warrant."

"Have we traced any Yeats living in Galway?"

"We have an address. Someone is checking that out now."

"Right. Can you contact someone in Boston and ask them to check up on her story about Elizabeth Renfield?"

"Yes, boss."

He smiled and Emer made a face at him.

She turned and went back to the room.

Mel turned to look at her. "Has he found Elizabeth?"

"No."

"Well, I'm sure he will."

Just as Mel was about to get started again another officer entered the room and beckoned Emer back outside.

"Excuse me, Melanie."

"Take your time." Mel could feel irritation bubbling up inside her. She wanted to tell them what happened but they were breaking her concentration.

About fifteen minutes later Emer re-entered the room. Now she was sure that Melanie's story wasn't reliable. Melanie Yeats from Mount Bank in Galway hadn't had a full-time job in her adult life. She had never paid any tax.

That part at least could be discounted. Emer Doyle decided that if it took two days for Melanie Yeats to finish her story then she wasn't leaving this station until she got to the bottom of it. Emer hadn't been this excited about a case in a long time. Her usual caseload involved motoring offences and a few robberies. This was promising to be something very unusual.

"Go on, Melanie." She sat back down and listened as Mel continued her tale.

CHAPTER 14

I wondered if I could find out more about Elizabeth without giving people too much information. My father was the perfect person to ask but he was the last person in the world I wanted help from right then. I couldn't tell Dad that Ryan might have killed someone.

The storm was still raging outside. It was completely dark. The wind had whipped up to a gale and it savaged the sides of the house. I had an urge to go back upstairs and have another look at Elizabeth's shrine. I also had an urge to open a bottle of wine. The rack was starting to look a bit bare but there were still a few bottles left.

I picked a nice Cabernet Sauvignon, poured a glass and took a few sips. The only light on in the kitchen was the light over the hob. It barely spread its glow past the stove. The house creaked and sighed around me but it didn't feel empty. The barely controlled panic I'd carried with me since Ryan's death subsided once I'd had a drink. Should I worry about that? I shrugged the idea away. Did it matter where I got my comfort?

I'd been unconsciously pouring and sipping as I sat there and again I'd reached the bottom of a bottle. There were too many things to process, too much for me to face. The wine was just propping me up while I got my strength back. Drunks had years of hard labour put in lifting bottles before they had a problem. Wasn't that true? I had only been doing it for a couple of weeks; alcohol didn't take control that fast. It was just a comfort for now, a crutch.

I opened the second bottle and filled my glass again. Elizabeth might give me an answer to some of my questions. I grabbed my glass, held the bottle in my other hand and walked towards the corridor that led to the cloakroom. But I turned back and put down the bottle again to get my flash lamp. If a bulb blew I didn't want to be in Elizabeth's shrine without light. I held the lamp under my arm and grabbed the bottle again.

The corridor felt like the Bridge of Sighs as I walked along it. There was a deep sadness at the back of the house and in the attics that I didn't feel in other parts of the manor. Maybe it was the absence of my things or the dulling, peeling paint which spread its shadowy fingers across everything back there. I felt them now stretch towards me as I walked along the heavy grey flagstones. My mind wandered and scurried as I entered the cloakroom.

Immediately I felt something. Something was different. Carefully I laid down my bottle of wine and used the beam from my lamp to find the light switch and turn on the light.

As the light illuminated the dark room I saw the door to the attic standing open. I'd closed that when I came down earlier. If I went up to the attic someone could be waiting for me. If I went back out into the main house perhaps there was someone out there.

The cloakroom felt like a middle world, safe until proven otherwise. A bench sat against the wall covered in old newspapers. I grabbed my bottle and sat there.

I tried to steady my brain and think logically. I looked back at the outside door of the cloakroom. It had a key in the door. I could limit the danger. I could lock that door and if someone were in the corridor I would lock him out there in the main house. On unsteady feet I made my way to the door and turned the key before I went back and sat down. How long could someone upstairs stand in silence waiting for me?

I drank my wine straight from the bottle, forgetting the glass with my eyes fixed on the door to the servants' stairs. I'd wait them out. For an hour I sat there in the cold silence and not a sound could be heard from upstairs. Nobody could sit up there in silence for that long. Feeling confident now, I drained the last of my wine and walked to the door. I looked up into the stairwell and listened for anyone moving about above.

There was no sound. I stepped inside and stood on the bottom step, still nothing. I climbed the stairs and used the flash-lamp to search for the light switch on the landing. As I feared the bulb fizzled, the light glimmered briefly and then went out. Luckily for me I'd had enough common sense to carry my lamp.

I turned my attention to the door of the shrine. My breath faltered. The door was open. The key stood in the lock. I knew I'd locked that earlier and placed it back in the other door where it had been hidden.

Terrified, I screamed down the corridor. "Who's there?" There wasn't a sound except for the howling wind outside.

"I'm sick of this!" I shouted as I strode down the corridor.

I flung open the other doors but the rooms stood empty. I went back to Elizabeth's room and pushed the door inwards. This room was also exactly as it had been the last time I was up there. Elizabeth's beautiful face smirked at me in the glow of the flash-lamp.

"What happened, Elizabeth? What has it got to do with me?" I said softly.

Elizabeth's expression never changed.

Why did I care why Ryan kept this room? Perhaps it had nothing to do with his disappearance or me. Then I reminded myself that maybe this room had nothing to do with Ryan. The previous owners might have left it behind.

I gathered myself together and walked back downstairs. But approaching the door to the corridor, I found it difficult to breathe. There could be somebody else in the house with me right now. My legs gave way and I had to go back to the bench by the wall. Again I thought of how many sets of keys there could be floating around. People could be coming and going as they pleased. The house was large enough to hide any number of people.

I couldn't stay there, in the cloakroom, trapped between the attic and the rest of the house. I was swaying on the bench trying to reassure myself that I was being silly when I heard the footsteps on the flagged floor outside. A cold sweat was breaking out all over me. Locked away in the centre of this house I couldn't be further from humanity and with no means of communicating with the outside world. I'd brought my flash-lamp but not my phone.

The door was strong and solid but the lock could be old and rotten. Shaking convulsively with fear I ran to the foot of the attic stairs. If it came to it I could run up there, lock myself in, break the glass in the upstairs window and start screaming for help . . . but my screams would just blend with the screaming wind.

As my horrified eyes watched, the handle on the door started turning. I could hear the door rattle. I turned, ran up the stairs to Elizabeth's room, locking the door behind me. Listening intently I sat with the ghost of a long-dead girl, waiting for the owner of those footsteps to climb the stairs but the minutes turned into hours and nothing happened. Thoroughly exhausted and still under the influence of two bottles of wine I fell asleep in a bundle on the floor.

The cold woke me hours later with the weak face of a grey dawn peering through the cracks in the shutters above me. The house was silent. Stiff with cold, I stretched and listened but the house was quiet and still. The effects of the alcohol had worn off to some extent. I felt stupid. Maybe the alcohol caused me to see things last night.

There was no such thing as ghosts and no evidence of another human in the house with me. Standing up, I unlocked the door and stepped out into the corridor. The house was still deathly quiet. As I walked down the attic stairs my back prickled and tingled with the awareness that something or someone could be waiting for me. "Idiot," I whispered to myself.

Gaining confidence, I reached the bottom step. Then my heart thudded painfully into my ribs.

The outside door into the corridor stood wide open. The cloakroom was empty and no sound came from outside. I shook painfully. I walked towards the door and peered around the corner. The corridor was empty. I looked at the lock. The lock wasn't broken or tampered with. The key was in the lock on the outside exactly as if I casually opened the door and stepped into the cloakroom. But I knew I'd locked it last night.

CHAPTER 15

I wandered quietly in the early morning light, trying to see if anything looked amiss but nothing seemed to have been moved in the house.

The kitchen was comfortingly familiar as I sat down with my breakfast. I'd made toast spread thickly with marmalade and a pot of coffee. I was ravenously hungry, not having eaten since some time the day before. I couldn't even remember what I had eaten then. Now my stomach was too upset for anything heavy. I thought I'd try the toast first and see if it stayed down. The rain had stopped for now but the trees and bushes were laden with moisture. Drops were falling from the eaves and I could hear water running through the drains. The rain would probably start again soon.

The stress was getting to me. It had been a time of loss. I was consumed by it. I was like a hollow shell blowing like tumbleweed through the corridors of that empty house. My boyfriend was missing and I was alone and insecure. The house was lonely.

Having barely slept the previous night I was exhausted. Trying to maintain normality, I gathered my dishes into the sink, washed them and tidied the kitchen. If I kept my life and surroundings in order then the rest would fall into place. It would be a domino effect, the positives exerting the greater pressure, flattening all the bad things. My life could be a sea of calm and tranquillity.

When the kitchen was in order I climbed the stairs to my room. I ran my eyes over every space and surface in the room to ensure it hadn't been touched. Satisfied that it was safe to sleep, I locked the bedroom door. The stress of the last few days was really catching up on me. My chest was tight and I had a ringing in my ears.

I brushed my teeth in the bathroom, my eyes drawn to a bottle of Valium. Would it be safe, I wondered, to take that? Would I wake up if there were danger? I wanted oblivion. I needed to shut my eyes and disappear from this world for a while.

I struggled with the childproof lock on the drug bottle, dropping a bunch of the tablets into the sink. I gathered them together and put them back in the bottle. I kept one and filled a glass with water. Then I took a second and swallowed them both. Returning to my room I crawled into bed and sat back against the pillows. The alcohol from last night still hadn't totally left my system and coupled with the drugs it didn't take long for me to slip into a deep sleep.

My eyes opened quickly. I tried to focus on where I was. My head felt heavy and the bed was cold. Though I couldn't remember closing the shutters the room was in pitch darkness. I turned my head and looked towards my clock. The light was turned down low but I could still make out the time. It was eight thirty a.m. A whole day had gone by. It was yesterday morning when I'd got into bed. I turned on the light and went to the bathroom. A shower would wake me up.

As I entered the bathroom the sunlight hit me. The shutters were closed in my room blocking out its light but I hadn't closed the bathroom shutters. I stepped in the shower and attempted to wash away the cobwebs.

When I was dressed I unlocked my bedroom door and stepped out into the corridor. The house was silent. I was sober. The deep twitching was starting again. I needed a drink. If I didn't have one the fear escalated and gradually took hold until I believed the very walls were watching me and plotting my downfall.

I went downstairs to a freezing kitchen. I heated my second-last muffin and took my coffee with me into the sitting room. Tomorrow I was going to get a television. Ryan hadn't wanted one. It would be another distraction, another mind-numbing drug to help me shut out the world. I'd like to watch some morning television. Morning. I still couldn't get my head around the fact that I'd slept for almost twenty-four hours.

The food helped me. It warmed me and briefly helped me to calm down. Being in that house alone was like being buried alive. I tried to remember when I'd last spoken to someone. I was having difficulty even keeping the days straight.

After the third cup I heard the phone ringing on the other side of the room. This was a new sensation: fear of speaking to the outside world. Maybe the phone would just stop ringing and the world would forget about me. But the phone rang on and on. I got up and walked across the room. I grabbed the receiver and held it away from me as though it might bite. Then tentatively I held it to my ear. I opened my mouth to speak and for a moment I didn't recognise my own voice. It sounded hoarse and alien. It was the caller again. His American accent was unmistakable now.

"So you found the girl in the attic?" He paused, waiting for me to answer.

"Yes. How did you know that I'd found her?" Now I knew that the girl wasn't a legacy of the previous owner. Ryan must have known about her. Did this man know that I'd found Elizabeth because he'd been in my house?

I heard the little puff of air escaping though his nose as he smirked down the line at me. "I know. Why do you lock the door when you go up there?"

"Have you been in my house?" My voice shook.

Silence.

"Did you know Elizabeth?" I asked.

"I knew Ryan."

"Good for you. You're American?"

He ignored my question. "Have you been drinking, Melanie?"

"What?" How did he know I was drinking?

"I just wondered."

"Why? Why would you think I'd been drinking?"

"Melanie, haven't you got any friends or family?"

"I'm fine."

I could hear him smile again across the phone line. "I'm not sure about that."

"Why did you call me?"

"I just wanted to know what you thought of Elizabeth?"
He sounded genuinely interested.

"How do you know her?"

There was a long silence at the other end of the line.
"I'll tell you about that someday."

"How did Ryan know her?"

"He knew her very well." His voice was hard.

I wondered about his voice. How old was he? He had
the kind of voice which was difficult to age and an accent
that probably wasn't too difficult to fake.

"Are you looking for Ryan?"

"Yes." He sounded surprised at my question.

"What was Elizabeth to you?"

For a few moments he didn't speak. "Elizabeth loved
that house."

"How did she know this house?"

His voice broke as he answered. "I'll explain when I
can, Melanie."

"Can we meet?"

"You're going to see plenty of me soon."

Then I was holding a humming receiver. He'd hung up.

Elizabeth, the girl in the attic, knew the house. How
was that possible? She was American. But then Ryan was
American and he'd lived in this house.

I was twenty-eight years old. Elizabeth had been dead
for sixteen years. I was twelve when she died. How could
it have anything to do with me? And why would the caller
be seeing more of me soon? Now I was definitely going to
change the locks on the house. I ran my mind over the
various entry points. There was the front door, the back
door leading out to the stable yard and the door from the

130

scullery out to the backyard and kitchen garden. How could I possibly fix all those locks? And then there were the windows.

In order to get out of the house for a while I decided to go into Bantry to talk to a locksmith and find out more about the house. Maybe it had American connections.

The caller had pulled me out of my slump. He was trying to tell me something. Ryan had brought me there for a reason. Ryan, the caller, this house and Elizabeth were connected though I still couldn't see how.

Detective Doyle's phone buzzed and danced across the table. She picked it up and looked at the screen.

"Excuse me a minute, Melanie." She got up.

"Did you think I'd be less disturbed if they texted you instead of coming in and whispering in your ear?" Mel's eyes were narrow as she scrutinised the detective's face.

"It's nothing to worry about, Melanie," Emer answered absently while she read the words on the tiny screen.

"I'm not worried. Are you?"

"No, Melanie, I'm not." She didn't look at Mel – she just continued to read the message.

Emer saw that the more they examined Melanie's story the more agitated she was becoming. At first the detective thought she was setting herself up for an insanity plea but as time went on Mel seemed as confused as any of them. She looked away from the phone and watched the flickering emotions on Mel's face for a moment. There was definite anger visible from time to time but mostly she looked bewildered and a little stressed.

Imagine, she'd nearly swapped her shift today! She

didn't doubt for a minute that something very unusual was going on in the mind of the woman before her.

Without saying another word to Mel she left the room.

Seán Walsh was standing outside the door when she came out.

"Guess what?" he said.

"I have no idea. Surprise me."

"Her family own the house."

"Melanie's family?"

" No. Elizabeth's."

"Elizabeth's family own Raven House?"

"Yes. It was her mother's family home. Her grandmother died there about seven years ago. She was the last of the family to live in it. It's up for sale. It's been on the market for nearly a year."

"So why is Melanie Yeats in the house? Maybe this Ryan guy really did bring her there for a reason. Maybe he has something to do with Elizabeth. Can you see if you can find pictures of the boyfriend and brother? We can show those to Melanie and see if one of them is Ryan."

"Okay." Seán walked off.

Emer returned to her interrogation.

Once more Mel was anxious to continue. "Can I go on?"

"Sure." Emer glanced at the other officers. They were all as entranced as she was. She felt like a child listening to a bedtime story and she just couldn't tear herself away.

CHAPTER 16

In Bantry I parked almost in the same spot as the last day and walked across the town square and down the street to an estate agent. They mightn't be the ones who dealt with the house but they would probably have a good idea who did.

Of course I didn't have an appointment. I tried to sweet talk my way past the receptionist there but she wasn't having any of it.

"Miss Gill is in a meeting, Miss Yeats, and I'm afraid she can't be disturbed."

"I'll wait." I sat on the chair closest to the desk.

"She has another appointment straight afterwards." She frowned at me.

I smiled sweetly and picked up a magazine, flicking through the pages.

Ten minutes later a man left an office to the left of the desk. He stopped to speak to the receptionist and I immediately got up and entered through the doorway he'd just exited through.

133

"You can't do that!" The receptionist ran around the desk.

I was already in the room by then. I knew if there really was another appointment the clients hadn't arrived yet so I had a couple of minutes.

Miss Gill was sitting on her chair staring into space and jumped violently as I came charging through the door.

She frowned. "Can I help you?"

"I'm sorry, Miss Gill!" The flustered receptionist was just at my elbow.

"I just need two minutes," I interjected. "I need to know who owns Raven House."

"Do you want to buy it?"

"No. I just want to know who owns it."

"I just wondered why you're interested." Miss Gill paused. "Maybe I can offer some help if you wish to buy it. We're the agents for the house."

I smiled patiently. "The only help I need is the name of whoever owns the house."

"But. . ."

"Just the name. Please."

"That house is owned by someone in Boston."

"Who?" I was getting annoyed.

"I can't give you that information. If I can't help you with business I'd like you to leave."

"Thank you."

I took my leave from the confused estate agent and left the building.

Boston again. Elizabeth was from Boston. Thanks to our trip to Belize I knew Ryan was from Boston and now somebody in Boston owned Raven House. Did he really own it after all? I didn't know. I made my way back to the car. As I was unlocking it, I saw the library across the street. It gave me an idea. Raven House must be well known in the area. There was bound to be a history section in there. It might have a section on the local landed gentry.

I relocked the car and crossed the street. I pushed the library door open and stepped inside. It was quite small, but modern.

"Excuse me," I said to the library assistant.

"Yes?" he answered in hushed tones.

"Where could I find information on a local house named Raven Hill?"

"In our history room."

"Where's that?"

"It's locked. I'm afraid we're short-staffed today."

"I'll come back after lunch."

"We're closing for a half day today. I'm sorry."

"Thanks for nothing." I spoke a bit too loudly in the quiet space.

"You're welcome." He lowered his tones but the sarcasm was still evident.

Somehow that only further inflamed my temper.

"I just want to find out some information about a house." My voice rose.

"We're open all day tomorrow." He spoke with exaggerated patience and a slight frown.

"This is ridiculous!" I spun on my heel and almost fell over in front of the counter. I left.

Since I was out now I decided to stay out for lunch. I was starving. The pub on the corner had a board outside advertising a carvery lunch or soup and sandwiches.

There was a long queue for food snaking along the counter and towards the door. That was a good sign. The larger the crowd the more likely the food was going to be good. I doubted these people were gathered there by chance.

However I wasn't in the mood for elbow-to-elbow crowding. The pressure in my chest was building. I was verging on a panic attack. I was about to turn and leave when the chef spoke to me.

"What can I get you?"

I blinked. "Soup and a BLT, please."

He handed me a blue card with a number on it and smiled. "We'll drop it down to you."

"Thank you."

Too far now to turn back, I joined another queue for the cash register. My eyes darted nervously around trying to find a quiet table but they all seemed full. I put the money into the cashier's hand and I'm sure she noticed how my hand was starting to shake from temper and frustration. I had to sit down.

Gripping my bag I walked through the tables, looking for somewhere to sit that would give me a chance to calm down. Just as I was giving up hope a couple sitting at a small table to the back of the room stood up and put on their coats. I got there before the woman had picked up her bag. A girl had started moving that way from the cashier's desk.

I had just got myself settled when the waitress arrived with my order. The soup was potato and chorizo, piping hot and delicious. The sandwich was fresh homemade bread with herbs and filled with real bacon, lettuce and tomato. I had made a good choice of food and had a nice quiet corner to sit in. I held out my hand and saw that the shaking had stopped.

I was at the end of rush hour and gradually people were getting up and leaving. By the time I'd finished I was one of the only people left. The others had an hour-long window to eat while I could sit and sip my coffee all day. I had nothing to do indefinitely. Just as I was almost fully relaxed my mobile rang. I looked at the screen. An unknown number! Should I answer it? I pressed the button and said a faltering hello. It was the caller.

"Melanie. What did you find out? An estate agent and then the library – are we doing a little research?"

"How did you know?" I looked around me. There were still a couple of diners left in the pub but none of them were using a phone.

"I'm with you all the time, Melanie."

"Are *you* Ryan?" It suddenly seemed like a reasonable possibility.

He laughed. "No. Ryan is gone, Melanie."

I could hear traffic on the street. "What do you want with me?"

"Somebody has to pay for Elizabeth."

"What?"

He'd hung up.

Was I the one who was going to have to pay? I couldn't figure out what I could possibly have to do with it.

As I left the pub and made for the car, watching everyone I met on the street with a deep sense of suspicion, I completely forgot about the locksmith.

When I pulled out of my parking space and turned towards home, the rain fell again in big fat splotches across the windscreen. It gathered pace as I drove. This weather certainly wasn't helping my mood. Almost as soon as the rain started the wind followed close behind. I could feel the crosswinds in the steering wheel. I had to slow down a bit.

By the time I got home it was dark again. I felt like saluting the house as it stood there on its grassy pulpit looking down on me with its superior air.

"What are you trying to tell me?" I asked, looking up at the gaping windows. But the house was still and silent in the midst of the angry weather.

As I stopped, a van drove up behind me with its lights blindingly reflected in my rear-view mirror. I sat in the car, too scared to get out. I turned off my lights. The rain hammered off the roof and ran in rivers down the windscreen. The driver of the other vehicle stayed in the driver's seat but left the car light on.

I didn't know what to do. I looked around the car. I had no weapon. There was nothing I could use to defend myself. Then I remembered. I reached into the glove compartment and grabbed a spray bottle of window cleaner. If this person was dangerous I could spray this in his eyes and maybe get a chance to run away.

The rain seemed to be getting heavier. The sound of it on the roof filled my ears.

Beyond the rim of the other car's lights the yard was dark. I judged the distance from my car door to the porch door. It was only about six feet. The other car was twice that distance. I could get out and run for it. Once inside with the door locked I'd be safe.

There was nothing else I could do. I took my keys from my bag, opened my door, jumped out and ran to the porch. I heard the other car's door opening, which caused me to lose my grip on my keys. I fumbled with them but finally got the porch door open and ran inside, slamming it closed behind me.

Almost instantly I heard a sharp knock on the door. Too terrified to move I stood with my back against the door listening. Then a voice called out.

"Melanie, fuel delivery!"

I'd forgotten about my fuel order. We had a standing order every month for coal, briquettes and timber. I liked my open fires. Feeling stupid, I turned and opened the door. Keith the delivery guy stood there dripping wet, a big smile on his face. He worked at the filling station in the village. They had a coal yard attached at the side of the forecourt.

"Melanie, I'm sorry. Did I startle you?"

"Keith! I'm sorry."

"No. I'm sorry. I did frighten you?"

"You did a little."

"Sorry. Will I bring them around for you?"

"Yes. Please."

I heard him start his engine and drive around the back. He drove a small white delivery van with the station logo on the side. A couple of minutes later I heard him drive back and park outside the front door. I opened the door again and held it against the wind while I waited for him. He always came in for his money. I heard the door bang. I stepped aside and let him in.

He always stopped for a cuppa with Ryan and myself so I walked ahead of him to the kitchen, opening the doors as I went. I flicked on the light in the kitchen.

"Take a seat."

"Thanks." He smiled at me and walked to the counter.

I was glad of the company. "Can I make you some coffee?"

"Sure."

"Okay." I went about making the coffee and getting some nibbles ready.

He sat on the stool by the counter where I normally sat.

"Do you mind living up here by yourself?" He looked around the kitchen while he spoke.

"Not usually. I was just a bit rattled tonight. The rain and the dark, I suppose."

"Why are you here alone? Where's Mr Lester?"

I didn't want to answer that. "He's away. He travels as you know."

"It must be lonely here."

"It can be but I like my own company." This was turning into a desperate-housewives moment and I didn't like it.

I brought the coffee cups to the counter and sat on the next stool.

Straining for some topic of small talk, I started on the weather. "This wind and rain will never let up."

"No. It's been a rough few weeks."

"It's so cold and damp. You guys must be busy."

He smiled, sipping his coffee. "Someone always benefits from misfortune."

"I suppose they do . . ." My voice trailed away.

"What are you guys doing for Christmas this year?" Keith made another attempt at small talk.

"I don't know." I couldn't figure out what I would be doing next week.

Keith began to tell me about his plans for Christmas and New Year. I made some half-hearted comments in return.

Eventually there was a long silence and Keith guessed he had outstayed his welcome. Maybe I just wasn't built for company. He stood up, throwing back the last of his coffee, wearing his usual easy smile.

"Well. Thanks, Melanie, for the coffee."

"Let me show you out."

We walked to the front door. He lingered a moment but I looked at the door.

"Goodbye." He smiled at me, standing just a little too close, but I wouldn't meet his gaze.

"Goodbye."

He hesitated again for a moment on the doorstep. The rain was heavier now and was really pelting down. I knew I should suggest maybe he could wait another few minutes and I guessed that's what he was waiting for. Then, without looking back, he stepped into the yard and ran to his van.

I closed the door instantly but waited in the porch until I heard the van driving down the hill and into the distance. I didn't want to become known as the desperate woman in the big house.

I locked the door and was about to go back to the kitchen but decided first to double check the back door. I went through the door at the back of the hall and into the corridor.

The back door was tightly shut.

I turned around and looked down the corridor. It was empty. It stretched long, grey and silent towards the kitchen. I hated it there in that part of the house. There was something eerie about it. I never bothered pulling the curtains on the back windows. Now, with their hollow eyes, those windows watched the strange goings-on in their space.

Inside, the house was still and silent. Outside, the wind

whipped the rain against the windows. I was alone. The house listened and in my current state of mind it appeared to be mocking me. I wondered whether the owner of the bedroll had returned. As I allowed these thoughts into my mind, of course they multiplied and took hold.

CHAPTER 17

The phone rang. It sounded shrill and common in the quietness of the old house. It spurred me into action. I turned away from the dreary back corridor and ran out to the entrance hall which was in complete darkness. My hand instinctively reached for the phone on its table by the sitting-room door. There were four extensions in this house, three on the ground floor – in the kitchen, the entrance hall and the study – while upstairs there was one in the bedroom. As I gripped the handset I wondered if there was somebody in another room also reaching for a phone. Was somebody listening inside the house as I took a deep breath to say "Hello"? This thought consumed me so deeply it took a while for me to speak.

"Melanie, is that you?"

"Hugh!"

"Yes. I rang to see how you are."

"I'm fine. Thank you." My desperate dash to his office

seemed so long ago at that moment. But it had just been a couple of days.

"You sound a big vague. Are you tired?"

"I am." After each sentence I paused to see if there was any sound on the line. But there was nothing. No clicks or breathing or any of the sounds I imagined in my head. I was a fan of old noir movies.

"Do you want me to come and see you?"

He'd been talking while I was daydreaming.

"What?"

He laughed. "Are you listening to me?"

"Sorry, Hugh."

"Well. Do you?"

"Do I what?"

"Want me to come down and see you."

I definitely didn't want that. "No. Of course not. It's too far." I didn't want to explain why I was living in a house I didn't own and spending money that wasn't mine. It was too bizarre even for me to figure out.

"If you're sure."

"I am."

"What are you doing out there on your own?"

I'd known that would be his next question.

"I'm keeping busy."

"What could you have to do out there in that big house?"

What indeed, I thought. "Research."

"What are you researching?"

He was just being considerate.

"My next step. Whatever that will be." I picked at the edge of a sheet of wallpaper.

"You'll figure it out," he said.

"I suppose I will." I wanted so badly to reach out to him and tell him how lonely I was but I couldn't.

"You don't sound sure."

"I'm just confused."

"You're bound to be. Has there been any news of your Ryan?"

My voice broke slightly as I answered. "No news yet." Then I had a thought. "Hugh, can I ask you a favour?"

"Of course."

"There are a couple of things I'd like you to do for me."

Hugh was silent, waiting for me to go on and reveal my requests. I could imagine an unseen person gripping the phone tighter and holding their breath as I continued.

"Can you find out who in Boston owns this house?"

"Sure. So you don't think Ryan owns it?"

"I did. Now I'm not so sure."

"Why?"

"Suspicions. I wonder if maybe Ryan picked this house for a reason. And me for a reason."

Hugh fell silent for a moment. "Why?" he asked again.

"I don't know. I'll know more when I find who owns this house."

"Is that it?" Hugh was a little confused.

How could I explain the second request? "There's a girl I'd like some more information on too."

"Does she have something to do with Ryan as well?"

"I don't know."

"What's her name?"

"Elizabeth Renfield."

"Is she from Cork?"

"No. She's from Boston too." I gave him as much background information as I could on Elizabeth.

"What is she to you?" Hugh was obviously curious.

"Nothing. Her story just came up during my research and I wondered what happened to her. That's all."

Hugh knew that wasn't all but knew he wouldn't get any more information from me that night.

"Okay, Melanie. Sweet dreams. I'll call when I have news."

"Thank you, Hugh. Goodnight."

"Goodnight, Melanie."

Hugh hung up but I waited to hear if there was a click on the other end. I waited but nothing happened. Was the other person doing the same? I smiled at myself. There was nobody there with me except some old ghosts of Raven House past.

I was just leaving the hall to go to the kitchen when the phone rang again.

I thought it was Hugh ringing back.

It wasn't.

"Did you find out who owns your house?" came the American voice.

There was no need for formalities. We were quite familiar with each other by now.

"Somebody in Boston." I decided to be direct and see what he would say.

He laughed. "I know that. You need to dig a little deeper, I'm afraid."

"Is it Ryan?"

"No. Keep digging."

"I'm doing that. Why don't you do it yourself?" Why was I continuing my conversations with this person?

"I know already. I want you to figure it out."

"Why?" I was getting weary of the games.

"Keep digging."

Once more I held a humming phone. What did the ghosts make of that, I wondered? I hoped they made more sense of it than I did.

Hugh was a good solicitor and he'd always had a knack for turning up information. I trusted that he would find something interesting. Then maybe I would be able to find a link between Ryan, Elizabeth and Raven House.

CHAPTER 18

The next morning at ten thirty the ringing of the telephone wakened me from a peaceful night unpunctuated by dreams. Trying to banish sleep I reached slowly for the phone but I hit the side of it with my fingers and knocked it off the bedside table. It landed with a crash on the mat. "Shit!" I shouted with my eyes still glued shut.

"Hello?" I grabbed the receiver and held the phone suspended just off the floor.

"Mel – what's wrong?"

It was Dad.

"Dad. I'm sorry. I knocked over the phone."

"Were you asleep?"

Less than a dozen words and already he couldn't keep the accusing tone out of his voice.

"I'm not anymore."

He ignored my sarcasm and carried on. "Mel. They found a body."

148

My heart jumped in my chest and suddenly I was wide awake.

"They found him?"

"They don't know yet, Mel."

I tried to speak but I couldn't. Suddenly, the beautiful face of Ryan was replaced by the grotesque image of a rotting corpse.

"It's down to DNA and whatever they do."

"Forensic anthropology," I threw in.

"I suppose so." My father waited for me to speak but I said nothing more.

"DNA will be the only way to identify him," he said then.

"How long does that take?"

"I don't know. It will take a while."

"Why was his body in such bad shape?" I still couldn't get the image out of my head.

"Sharks. They ate parts of him."

"Dad, I need to go." I wasn't in the mood for Dad's plain speaking.

"Sorry, Melanie." To give him his due he did sound sorry.

"I've got to go, Dad." I hung up.

Each chapter of this awful story revealed more horrors. It was easier to keep the illusion of what I had in the back of my mind when I could still see Ryan's face and see him smile. The image faded and then returned only now, when it returned, it had taken the shape of a dripping corpse. My mind couldn't stop dwelling on the details. I knew now what they meant by "the devil was in the detail".

Was Ryan trying to stage his death and run or was it just an ill-timed accident? Whatever his motivation, I hoped the shark intervened after his death and not during.

Whoever he was, nobody deserved an end like that. But the thrashing terrified final moments of a fleeing man and a powerful shark took my breath away. It must have been quick but I couldn't imagine it could ever be quick enough.

I had watched enough *CSI* to know how a body was usually identified but in the case of Ryan Lester most of those avenues wouldn't work. Probably no facial recognition. Perhaps no fingerprints either. Unless he had broken ribs from a childhood accident or something like that there would be very little hope of medical records either. Having been in the water for two weeks and gnawed on, his bones would have quite a few postmortem injuries that would confuse the whole process. No, putting him back together would be like making a jigsaw puzzle.

I wanted to get out of the house. I would go for a walk. But I had no idea where to go. In all the time I'd lived there in Raven I'd never walked anywhere. I'd never been a walker at any stage of my life. In Galway I lived in a town with a bus stop practically outside the door and if I did have to go anywhere my dad drove me or I got a taxi. So my putting on and maintaining a few extra pounds wasn't any great mystery. Ryan had fixed that as soon as I moved to Raven. Down there in that big old house I was deprived of any influence except his. I was like a modern-day Eliza Doolittle. But I still had no idea why he bothered. Was I just a hobby, a toy to play with?

I wasn't in the mood for walking on the road so I thought I would explore the woods. Growing up in a town the great outdoors seemed like an alien landscape to me but I thought I would have a look at what was out there. I left by the back way without even glancing at the cloakroom door.

I crossed the stable yard and went through the gate opposite the house. As I closed the gate behind me I felt a tingle across my back. With my hand still on the lock of the gate my eyes were drawn to the back of the house and the attic windows.

The house seemed poised as though it had leaned forward slightly, waiting to see where I went. I wondered were the grounds and the wood really an extension of the house. Was there a hushed whisper spreading amongst the low walls and swaying trees keeping them all informed of where I was going? In answer a gust of wind swept along the side of the wall, which separated the yard from the wood. It blew through the leaves of the eucalyptus trees, which were planted along the line of the wall. As I looked up at them they turned their faces towards the house, firmly away from me. It was as though they were all in a huddle, gossiping together about the newcomer in their midst.

Leaving the house behind me, I walked deeper into the trees. It was overgrown out there. Fallen trees and bushes clogged the path. I felt as though it were virgin ground broken for the first time by my steps. However, there was a deep sense of peace out there despite my disruptive presence. I stopped and looked around. I normally had no emotional connection with nature but somehow that day I felt like I was led there. A calmness I hadn't felt for a long time was settling on my shoulders. It was like the little wood had been calling me.

The house could no longer be seen. From where I stood in the little copse, there wasn't a single man-made object visible. Even the path I'd walked in from seemed to have vanished. No sound could be heard either apart from the wind and the trees. I could be the only woman alive. An involuntary smile spread across my face. Out here the world and its problems seemed insignificant and irrelevant.

I pushed on through the greenery until I came to a tangle of bushes and briars too dense for me to break through no matter how hard I tried. They tugged at my clothes and scratched my skin. There didn't seem to be a way for me to get around it either. This was my boundary. It was as far as the house was willing to let me go.

Slowly I retraced my steps, unwilling yet to let go of the embrace of this little wood.

As I arrived the rain started up again. Even before I was through the yard gate it was lashing in great sheaths towards the ground. I broke into a run with my head down, towards the back door. Stumbling, I turned my key and went through the door locking it again behind me. As soon as I turned, the cloakroom door drew me towards it.

Feeling braver now I unlocked it and went inside, taking the key with me. Once I was inside I relocked the door behind me. The door leading to the attic steps was slightly open. I tried to remember if I had left it that way. I opened the door wider and climbed the stairs. I had to do that for my own peace of mind. I didn't want the attic to take on more significance than it deserved. It was just a room with some pictures in it.

Pushing open the door into the room I held my breath but I needn't have worried. Immediately I knew it was empty. I crossed to the shutters and pulled them open and the weak light fell on Elizabeth. Nothing had changed since the last time I'd stood there. It was unsettling to know that a tragedy that happened on the other side of the

Atlantic so many years ago was preserved right there in my home in the form of a shrine. Someone unseen but probably Ryan once worshipped in that attic at the feet of this girl and now there I was doing the exact same thing.

No, I'd done what I'd gone up there for. The attic was empty. I was alone.

Locking the door I went back downstairs and into the cloakroom. I unlocked that door and stepped out into the corridor and straight into Keith. I screamed loudly and Keith screamed louder still.

"Jesus, Melanie! I'm sorry."

"'*Jesus, Melanie.*' What are you doing in my house?"

"I knocked at the front door but I got no reply and then I got frightened that something was wrong."

"So you let yourself in!" I shouted. He'd given me such a fright.

"I was phoning for ages and you didn't answer."

"I was out for a walk."

"I'm really sorry." He did seem genuinely embarrassed.

"How did you get in?"

"The front door was open."

"It couldn't have been."

"It was."

"But I'm sure I locked it."

"It wasn't even shut. It was standing wide open."

I was horrified. I remembered letting Keith out the evening before and going straight through the house to the back door to check it was properly locked. Had I left the front door open since yesterday evening? Wouldn't I have felt a draught or wouldn't the wind have caused something to bang at some stage during the night?

Leaving a confused Keith still standing there, I went to

the front door. If that door had been open all night the hall would be swamped with water. There was a woven mat in the porch. That should be soaked in rainwater.

I stood in the hall. The mat was dry. There were no leaves blown into the corners. There wasn't a drop of water anywhere despite the heavy rains yesterday evening and last night. Was Keith lying to me? Or had there been someone here who had opened the front door and left it that way? Why would someone do that? Nothing made sense. The only thing I knew for sure was that I did not leave that door open and I hadn't been near the door all day. I knew that either Keith was lying or somebody had been there with me. Somebody was moving about my house with me.

"Are you okay?"

I jumped violently.

Keith had got impatient waiting for me.

"What's the matter?"

I lied. "I think this door may have blown open. I mustn't have locked it properly."

I looked at his face closely as I spoke. "I had coffee out there this morning but I was so sure I locked it."

He seemed sincere in his ignorance. "Don't worry about it, Melanie. Are you sure you're all right?"

"I am. Just stressed. It's okay. Why are you here?"

"I forgot to ask for money last night. Because you always pay cash the boss wasn't too happy with me."

"Oh. I'm sorry." I blushed despite myself because I knew why he'd forgotten and why I didn't remind him. "Come on. I'll go and get the money. Would you like a coffee?" I was just being polite and hoped he'd refuse.

"I'd love one, thanks," he smiled.

It was as though I was seeing his smile for the first time and I was convinced something was lurking behind those eyes that I hadn't yet met. It made me shiver.

I brushed the feeling aside. But something dark and almost tangible seemed to be in the hall with us.

I led the way to the kitchen, hyper-aware of Keith trailing behind me. I got the coffee jug and filled it at the sink.

As I bustled about I kept my eyes diverted from Keith. I didn't feel comfortable making eye contact with him. I placed a coffee and biscuits in front of him. Then I ran upstairs to get some money, still not looking at him. He had really frightened me. The coffee would keep him occupied until I got back.

Keith knew I'd expected him to be somebody else. At that moment I thought my ghosts had stepped out of the shadows and were standing in the corridor. In those seconds I knew he'd seen it on my face. Keith was now wondering who I had expected him to be.

Upstairs I quickly took the money from the safe and came back down, still feeling nervous. I wondered if he was checking if I was still alone and how much money I had lying around the house.

I walked back to the kitchen and put the money down near Keith on the counter. He let it lie where I put it.

"Why are you here alone if you are this scared?" he asked. His eyes were a light grey colour and searched mine intensely as he spoke. Though his words were cloaked in empathy I still sensed something cold in his expression.

What was he searching for on my face? I felt his scrutiny sharply.

His question was a good one and I didn't have a

satisfactory answer for it so I stayed silent. Ryan had brought me there. He had brought Elizabeth here too. Why had it been necessary for us all to be here? Time would tell.

Was Ryan the driver of the stolen car, the boyfriend or the brother? I was sure he'd been one of them. Why else would he be so connected to Elizabeth? But then who was the caller and why was he involved? He led me to where Ryan died and he led me to Elizabeth. If Ryan wasn't the driver of the car then maybe he was the boyfriend or the brother seeking revenge.

But why on earth did they include me? Was I just collateral damage? Did this person trace Ryan and find him with me? Was that why I was dragged into it? No. We were all there for a reason: Ryan, Elizabeth, the caller and me. The house was important too – I knew that though I didn't know why yet.

Each question led to another question and my head was throbbing. Keith had been watching me closely as thoughts flicked like shadows across my face.

"What is going on with you?"

"I don't know yet." I smiled.

He picked up the money I'd left on the counter and, without counting it, folded it and put it in his pocket. We walked to the door together and like the last time he stood close to me. I could feel his breath on my cheek.

"I'm sure it gets lonely up here sometimes."

I stepped back instantly and turned my head. "I'm in a relationship."

"But where is he?"

Something about the way he said it made me feel cold.

The wind and rain had whipped up again and leaves were swirling in the doorway as Keith stepped outside. He turned to speak but it was too wet to stand and talk. He smiled and leaned over, giving me a quick peck on the cheek before he ran for the car. I flinched, too shocked to react further. I just stood and watched him. I didn't feel comfortable around him. I knew Ryan had known him and seemed perfectly happy with him but I wasn't so sure. The rain was lashing the house again as he drove away.

Keith finding the door open earlier was still bothering me, and it was now compounded by his kiss, however fleeting. Did he really phone me? He only had the number for the landline so there was no way of knowing. As I stood there the phone rang. Tentatively I picked it up. A familiar voice filled the quiet space.

"Mel."

It was my brother Bobby.

"I'm in Cork. I don't want to drive down to that godforsaken place if you're not there."

His cheery voice was like a godsend, pushing all worries about Keith out of my head.

"I suppose I could break in," he went on.

I laughed. "There's no need for that."

"Great. I'll be down in less than two hours." He hung up.

Bobby was the spontaneous one of the family. The irresponsible one according to Dad though in my experience you got no kudos for responsibility either. I wondered if Dad had told him about Ryan. Bobby and Ryan had never met. When I met Ryan, Bobby was in Australia. As far as I knew he hadn't been home since then.

Bobby wasn't one for keeping in touch. Sometimes as I talked I wondered was he even listening or had he left the phone down and let me ramble on. Now he was coming here. I couldn't even remember the last time I'd seen my own brother.

Bobby was ten years older than I was but even in his thirties he'd lived like a student. He'd never married and shied away from all forms of responsibility. He led a basic lifestyle.

When I was a child Bobby was my hero, a flawed hero, but even then I'd barely known him. He was always out of the house – at football, in school or away at college. But when he was there he was all mine. When we were in the same space he couldn't take his eyes off me. I was his little sister and I knew he loved me but we often take for granted the ones we love the most, assuming they'll always be there. When I was little he told me stories and took me out in his car. I grew up feeling I was the most special little girl in the world but that all changed when he left for college.

Then things between him and Dad came to a crashing halt before I ever got the chance to get to know him as an adult. Bobby left Galway and now I was getting ready to meet someone I barely knew. Dad and I were a package deal. When Bobby fell out with Dad he let me go too. I didn't travel, Dad needed me and Bobby certainly wasn't coming home. As time moves on the gaps get wider and the distance between estranged family greater.

I wondered briefly where Bobby got my Raven number. Perhaps he got it from Dad. I guessed the only reason he was visiting me in person was because I was here without Dad. If I was at home I might have got a short phone call or an email.

Where was he going to sleep? I turned my mind back to practical matters. There was a bed in the room next to mine. There was no other furniture but he'd be okay.

There were plenty of bedclothes. Forgetting my fear of ghosts for a little while, I climbed the stairs and went to the airing cupboard in my bathroom. I pulled out some bedclothes and brought them in next door. They were frilly and pretty but he could put up with that too.

My life was simple. Bobby probably didn't know that. Maybe he still thought his little sister had taken a leap and landed in a gold mine.

I went back into my room and looked around. The furniture was too heavy to move. But there were two chairs in my room – I could take one in and he could use it as a bedside table. The room was cold but it was a little musty so I walked to the window and opened the shutters. Then I pulled up the sash and let the cold damp air in.

There were a couple of spare hot-water bottles downstairs. I didn't want him catching pneumonia on his first trip to my home. His only trip probably. It was doubtful that I'd be living here in another two years.

The house seemed once more to have changed its mood. It no longer seemed to be possessed of its usual gloom. There was an air of expectancy as though it too were waiting to see this new person coming to visit. On an impulse I placed my hand against the wall.

"Do you really feel these things or am I projecting my thoughts and fears onto you?" I got no answer.

Shaking away my whimsical thoughts, I went downstairs and got the hot-water bottles. While I waited for the kettle to boil I decided to organise food. I was hungry and men were always hungry in my experience. Pasta would be quick and simple. I chopped some vegetables and took a box of sieved tomatoes out of the cupboard. There was some bacon in the fridge. In twenty minutes I had a large dish of pasta ready. I took another look inside my fridge. I had some bread. That was plenty.

I filled the hot-water bottles and was just leaving the room when I remembered the wine. It would be nice to let a bottle breathe. I put the hot-water bottles down again and uncorked a Cabernet Sauvignon, then went to the pantry and brought out some more bottles to restock the rather bare wine rack. Now everything was ready.

Suddenly, I got a pang of fear. Bobby had never met this Melanie. The sister he left behind in Ireland was overweight and ate ready-meals. Was his relationship with me built on pity or love? There was never a time when he'd come to me for anything in particular but yet he checked in on me from time to time. Maybe I was his connection to his roots. He feared his father's reproach but there had never been anything to fear from me.

As I stood there ruminating on my family situation I realised the hot-water bottles would be cold. I picked them up again and carried them upstairs.

Just as soon as I'd placed them in the bed I heard a car approaching up the hill. I went to the window and looked out. It wasn't coming up after all. It was going by on the road below. The lights, barely visible over the high line of the hedgerow, disappeared down into the valley. I went back downstairs again.

Excitement was building. It would be so lovely to spend time with Bobby and talk. I loved hearing about his adventures. Maybe that was the difference between Dad and me. He saw the nomadic life as a gross failure but I saw it as an exciting alternative. Bobby lived and I waited. My whole life had been spent waiting.

The phone rang. I jumped and ran to it.

"Hello."

"Where the hell is this house? I'm driving around in the dark and I can't find it."

I started laughing. "What county are you in?"

"Very funny. West Cork. What's the name of the house?" His impatience and energy were evident even on a phone call.

"Raven House. Have you found Raven – the village?"

"I went through it five minutes ago."

"What road are you on now?"

"I don't know."

"Look, go back to Raven. You'll see a signpost for Glengarriff. Raven House is about quarter of a mile down that road. It's the third left."

"Right."

He'd hung up again. He always made me laugh the way he did that. He was more like my dad than he would ever care to admit.

Bobby would be here shortly. I poured myself a glass of wine and went into my sitting room.

The room was so cold. That was what I should have done straight away – lit the fire. But I had enough time. I put the glass on the table and built up a large fire. There was plenty of coal and briquettes already in. The fire was warming the room after only a couple of minutes and making it feel quite homely. I turned off the main light and lit a corner lamp instead. With its mellow glow and the warmth from the fire the room looked beautiful.

For some reason it was so important for me to get it all right. Bobby would have plenty of reason to pity me once I told him what was going on. Maybe I thought that by feeding his senses he wouldn't think too badly of me.

When I had finally sat down and taken a few sips of my wine, confident that the cracks were all nicely painted over, I heard a car approaching up the drive. This time there was no mistake as I heard it crunch to a halt outside the front door.

CHAPTER 19

Throwing the door open I ran outside and threw myself at the man who stepped from the car. As he was tall, the top of my head fitted under his chin. He wrapped his arms around me and held me close. I could feel the strength of his broad shoulders and I felt comforted. This was what I'd been aching for since I got the first phone call. I didn't want him to ever let me go. He pushed me back and looked me over top to toe.

"You've shrunk."

"Thanks. Are you saying I was a cow?"

"No. But you were a little bigger. The big brown eyes are the same – maybe a little sadder though. What's the matter, Mellie?"

That was one thing about Bobby; he always knew when I was sad. When I was a little girl he would come over to me and put his arms around me and ask, "What's the matter with my little girl?"

"I'm okay. Don't worry. I'll tell you all about it when we go inside. I made you dinner."

He started laughing. "You can't cook!"

"Don't laugh." I punched him in the arm. "I learned to cook. I didn't lose this much weight eating pizza."

"I suppose you didn't." He looked worried as he scrutinised my face.

"Stop looking at me like that."

"It's just strange. It's like I'm seeing somebody else."

My heart lurched. I was always so angst-ridden and Bobby loved to take care of me. I think that was our bond. Well, he shouldn't judge a book by its cover. I had just changed one set of issues for a whole bunch of others. Once I'd fed my brother, boy, did I have problems for him to sort through!

He pulled a rucksack out of the car, then looked up at the house. He whistled.

"Mellie, who did you rob to get into this house?"

"I don't know." I said it with such an air of truth in my voice that Bobby looked strangely at me. I just laughed. "Come on."

"Wow!" He stopped when he stepped into the hall. Just like I did the first day I stepped into the house, he stood in the centre of the room, looking up the stairs and craning his neck to look at the intricate plastered ceiling. He twirled, taking in the solid doors and the ornate limestone fireplace in the hall. "Wow!"

"There's more." I couldn't stop laughing. "Don't you have a home?"

"No." His tanned face was serious as his brown eyes took in every detail of his surroundings.

In the light I noticed Bobby seemed older, more worn

somehow. His hair was cropped short but I could see that the front was a little thinner and what remained was a little greyer. When I thought of Bobby and looked over the image of him I held in my heart he was young, vital and full of energy. This man in front of me now was being etched deeply by life. Something darker was fighting inside my beautiful brother and leaving its mark.

I wanted to examine him closely but there is something terrifying about the first time you see someone beloved being eroded like that. Like a beautiful house built on a cliff, little bits of Bobby were slowly falling away. For one terrifying moment I saw him in ten years' time without a home, family or roots, and I could feel pain flowing from him, see it swimming in his eyes – but mercifully the image faded and he walked away to the foot of the stairs, out of my reach.

I let it go for the moment. "This way. I'll show you upstairs later."

I led him through into the kitchen.

"Wow!" He looked around my vast kitchen in awe.

"It will be a long night if I get that reaction to everything you see. Sit there." I indicated the two stools by the counter. He dropped his bag, pulled out Ryan's stool and sat down.

Bobby swivelled on the chair taking in every detail of the room from floor to ceiling as I dished up our supper. I placed two large platefuls on the counter and poured two glasses of wine.

"Wow!" Bobby was still too mesmerised to say anything else.

"Eat."

"You can really cook, Mellie. I'm impressed."

"I learned when I met Ryan."

"I heard you moved in with someone. How did the old man take that?"

"Not well. Who told you?"

"Amanda."

"You're still in touch with the cousins then?" Amanda is our first cousin. She is the same age as Bobby and they had always been close.

"Yes. You're not?" Bobby was surprised because I had always stayed close to all the family. But meeting Ryan had ended that.

"I lost touch with a lot of people."

"Amanda told me that this Ryan has disappeared." Bobby spoke softly, concern evident in his voice.

"Yes. You know that Ryan was supposed to be wealthy?"

Bobby nodded.

"And that he's probably not called Ryan and nobody knows who he was or where he came from."

Bobby nodded again

"I'm such a fool. He offered all this. I fell for it."

"It's a lovely house."

Bobby knew I wasn't talking about the house. He knew I fell for the adventure. Ryan offered me excitement.

"A house that's owned by somebody in Boston and half-furnished."

"Amanda didn't hear that part or she would have told me."

"Does she know they found a body?"

"No."

I took a deep breath. "It was partially eaten by sharks."

He put down his fork with a frown. "It's him?"

"They don't know yet. They're testing DNA or something."

"Really?"

I nodded as I ate a mouthful of pasta.

He changed the subject. "You have a well-stocked wine rack."

"Restocked wine rack." I smirked. "I emptied it in less than a week."

He threw back his head and laughed. "I'm sure we'll knock back a few tonight."

"I'm sure we will." I paused for a minute. "I'm so glad you're here."

He held my hand. "Me too."

Two bowls of pasta later and Bobby was mopping up the last of his sauce with a hunk of fresh bread.

I watched him with pride. "I'm glad you enjoyed that."

"I did. It was great. You really have become a great cook."

Together we gathered the dishes and placed them in the dishwasher. I pulled another bottle from the rack and we carried it to my sitting room. The fire had died a little so I threw some more coal on it and stirred it up. Sparks rushed up the chimney.

Bobby was sitting sideways on the couch, waiting for me to sit down. He patted the seat next to him. I sat but I didn't like the look of concern on his face. I was in for some probing questions.

"So, Mellie. What are you going to do now?"

"I don't know." What else could I say?

"If this house is rented why are you still here? It's not your home."

"I don't know." I closed my eyes for a minute and listened to the crackling fire.

"You haven't thought this through, have you?"

"No." I had decided to take the honest approach. I changed the subject. "Where are you living?"

"Here and there." He shifted his weight on the chair, uncomfortable with my question.

"What do you mean here and there?" I wanted to be able to understand my brother better and he seemed evasive when it came to his own personal life.

"I travel all the time for work so I live on the road. I never bothered buying property."

"We're a fine pair, aren't we?" I reached and held his hand.

"A great source of pride to our father." He smiled but there was pain in his eyes.

"What do you do?" I knew he'd trained in engineering but his day-to-day life was a mystery.

"I design water systems in developing countries."

"Where do you travel to?" The room seemed deathly quiet as I waited for his answers.

"Anywhere I'm needed. I've had contracts recently in Iraq."

I jumped and my eyes opened wide. "Iraq. That's so dangerous."

"It is, but someone has to do it and the pay is very good."

"Doesn't anyone worry about you?" I knew nothing about his personal life.

"No."

I watched his face closely. For a moment he looked a lot younger. He seemed shy and ill at ease with personal questions.

"You don't have a girlfriend?" I had never met a girlfriend of his.

He shook his head. Bobby was a good-looking man. He was tall, broad-shouldered and very charming. I couldn't imagine him having girl trouble.

"Boyfriend?" I tried another angle.

He laughed. "No. No boyfriend either."

"So. No property, no partner and you don't see your family more than once or twice a year." My voice softened. "Why?"

"I want my life to be simple." He couldn't look me in the face and in that moment I felt, like an acute pain, the inner sadness that was my brother. Why was his life so empty? But prior to Ryan, had mine been any fuller? No. We were two empty people who should have been able to help each other.

"You must be loaded." I spoke without thinking.

"Why?"

"The simple life doesn't cost much unless you're a cocaine addict or a gambler."

"No drugs, no gambling, no property and no women – yes, my bank account is quite healthy. I could probably buy this house. Who owns it?"

"Somebody in Boston apparently. Ryan is from Boston too. I think. Perhaps when I find out who he really was I'll see his connection with this house." My voice trailed away.

"Why was Ryan here? I mean, he wasn't based here, was he?"

I suspected that Bobby was delving into my business so I would forget about his.

"No."

"You were just two people here alone. Why stay in such a large house?"

"I don't know." I had wondered that. We only lived in

a couple of rooms so we could have lived happily in a little house somewhere. I wouldn't have been so alone and Ryan wouldn't have had to travel to Cork Airport when he needed to travel abroad.

"You don't know much, do you?" Bobby smiled and squeezed my hand.

"Not much," I answered truthfully.

"We must change that." Bobby shook his head, looking into my face. "We must get you back in control."

I sat back in my chair and looked up at the ceiling. Uum, I thought. Control seemed very far away.

We sat together for another hour and finished a second bottle of wine. I was about to open a third one but Bobby stood up.

"No. I need to sleep. I'm just back from Afghanistan. Can I see my room?"

"Afghanistan?" I was shocked. One of these days if I didn't sort out my brother I was going to get another late-night call telling me he was dead.

"They need water too."

"I know they do but it's dangerous."

"Mam died at home." He tried to smile but the smile withered and died before it found purchase.

I nodded. Had my brother always been this complex? I suspected he probably had but I was always too self-absorbed to see it.

I slipped my arm into his and pulled him close. "Come on. I'll show you your room."

He picked up his bag, then I led him up the stairs and down the corridor.

"I gave you the room next to mine."

"That was sweet."

"It's the only other one with a bed."

"None of these rooms have furniture?" Bobby looked incredulous.

"None."

"Sis, didn't any of this seem weird to you?"

"Not at the time."

"He must have been gorgeous."

"He was. And I was fat." And stupid, I thought.

"You were never fat. You were a little overweight."

"You always saw me differently than everyone else did."

"Mellie, who are these 'everyone elses' you're always talking about?"

For a minute I wondered that too. Try as I might I couldn't remember actual words anyone had spoken, just assumptions on my part, funny looks or perhaps my imagination. Had I really spent my life trying to change because of my own inner dialogue? Had everyone else been totally unaware?

"I don't know that either. Is the room okay for you?"

"It's perfect. I like this house, Mellie."

"So do I. I wish it were mine. But you know I'm not sure the house likes me."

CHAPTER 20

I closed the door of Bobby's room and went back downstairs. I did a quick tidy-up, placed the fireguard in front of the fireplace, then I walked to the front door, double-checked that it was in fact locked tonight and not standing open. It was locked tightly.

Then despite my better judgement I went and checked the back door and the cloakroom. Everything was as I had left it earlier. I locked the cloakroom door and put the key up over it.

As I was about to make my way back upstairs I stood in the centre of the hall and listened. The house was silent and peaceful.

In my own room I closed the shutter and for the first time in a long time I didn't place a chair under the door. Bobby was nearby after all. As I snuggled down into my bed, gripping my hot-water bottle tightly I managed a happy smile. This had been a good evening. The first one I'd had in a long time.

Some time later I woke terrified. I tried to get up but I was trapped. A great weight was lying on top of me and I could feel its intense pressure on my body. Then I realised, as awareness returned, that a hand was clamped over my mouth. I tried to scream but the sounds were lost under the seal of the hand. Whoever it was on top of me was finding it hard to hold me and keep my mouth covered too as I wiggled about on the bed, so he felt around, took my pillow and pushed that into my face. Panic was building inside me as I tried to push him off me. Then I must have blacked out.

I woke again and sat up in bed, my heart pounding. It was daylight. My second pillow was on the floor and my bedclothes were wrapped up in knots. Had it been a nightmare? When I was a child I used to get them and I remembered how realistic they could be. I got out of bed, my body feeling heavy, and made my way to the bathroom. Going straight to the shower I turned on the water and sat on the toilet, waiting for the shower to warm up.

As I stood up my ribs hurt. I walked to the mirror and stood examining my reflection. A scream caught in my throat. A blue stain was spread across my ribcage and a series of scratches, angry and red, crisscrossed my throat. There had been someone in my room and I'd fought him until I'd blacked out. It had really happened.

I turned off the shower and got dressed.

Without waiting for Bobby to wake up I rushed outside to my car and drove to the doctor. I had no appointment but one look at my face convinced the receptionist that it was an emergency. She slipped me in just before the first patient of the day.

Immediately I started to shake.

"Are you okay, Miss Yeats?"

I explained what had happened and showed the doctor the bruises. The doctor examined me.

"You should involve the police and go to the hospital."

"No. No police."

"Please, Melanie. If there is DNA present then we will want to trace this person. I'll call the guards now. "

Finally I relented and allowed her to contact the police.

When I got back Bobby had gone out. His car was no longer parked where he'd left it last night. A police car had come back with me. I stood in the corridor and watched as they stripped the bedclothes from the bed and the crime-scene technicians went over the room.

I didn't tell them my brother was staying with me. I don't know why. I also didn't mention my worries about the house having a presence or that my boyfriend was missing. I didn't want them to think I was unstable but earlier at the station I did mention my mugger from outside the house. They took a statement.

I sat drinking a cup of coffee with an officer. Another officer entered the room.

"Miss Yeats, there is no evidence of a break-in. We've taken the bedclothes from the bed and thoroughly examined your room. We'll get back to you when we have more details."

"Thank you."

"We'll show ourselves out."

I watched them leave, unable to move.

Thirty minutes later Bobby came back. Immediately he saw my expression. "Mellie? What's going on?"

I gave him the whole story.

"You don't sound surprised," he said.

"No."

He looked distressed. "Has something like it happened here before?"

For a moment I was going to show him the shrine but decided against it. I didn't think it was relevant to this.

"Yes, something has." I told him about my mugger.

"God, Mel. Why did you stay here? It's so remote and way too big for you."

"I suppose I'm attached to it. I came here thinking Ryan owned it. It was to be our home."

"It was all a lie, Mel."

"I know."

Bobby frowned. "You've had a lot to deal with."

I nodded and then went quiet for a while before telling him about the caller.

Bobby sat with his head in his hands. "This man may have killed Ryan."

I was beginning to think that too. And it had something to do with Elizabeth's death.

"Mel, you've got to leave this house. I have enough money to get us a place in Bantry or Cork. You'd be safe then."

"No."

"What?"

"No. I need to be here until I sort myself out."

"You're crazy."

I jumped from my chair, my eyes blazing. "Don't you ever call me that!"

I turned and left the room, leaving a shocked and bewildered Bobby behind.

Alone, Bobby's face disappeared into the background.

Emer Doyle had a thought. "I'm sorry, Melanie. I need to step out for a moment."

"To check on my story?" Mel's eyes narrowed a little.

Emer smiled at her and left the room.

Again she went looking for Seán.

"We need to check on a possible assault reported by Melanie recently. The police records should be here and the doctor's surgery on Raven Road should have the medical records."

"Okay. Anything else?"

"Her brother's name is Bobby Yeats. Can we see if we can find out some more about him? She says he's a water engineer and he works abroad."

"Right."

She went back inside.

Melanie started again as soon as she sat down, not even asking this time if she should.

CHAPTER 21

The night after my attack Bobby slept on the couch in my dressing room. I placed a chair under the door handle this time but the night was uneventful.

Bobby was amazed that I had chosen to stay on. He'd spent hours trying to persuade me to leave but I wouldn't budge. Bit by bit he was getting more and more information out of me about the months leading up to everything. He could only put it down to shock. I'd lost my boyfriend. I was holding on by my fingertips, to the edge of a lie. He couldn't persuade me that it was all smoke and mirrors and that none of this wonderful mirage had ever existed.

"What do you expect to salvage from it all, Mel?"

I didn't know. But yet somehow I felt I should be there in Raven House.

Next morning we had breakfast in the kitchen with neither of us speaking. I felt Bobby was judging me for my stupidity. After breakfast we cleared up the kitchen.

"I have some things to do," Bobby said.

"Fine." I needed to get his accusing eyes off of me.

I watched Bobby climb the stairs to his room. I was sorry he'd come back now. If he'd stayed away I would have had my door blocked up and a weapon by my bed but I assumed that with my brother being next door I'd be safe. Depending on other people had never done me any good.

We spent most of the day apart, Bobby upstairs doing whatever he did while he floated around the world. I was downstairs in my sitting room reading. Families were strange units. They should be the closest people in the world but in my experience they seldom were. My father lived alone and bitter in Galway with the ghost of a dead wife and two children whom he'd never understood. My brother had no family, no home and a job that took him to war-torn places he passed through with no care for whether he lived or died. And here I was holed up in an old house with the shadow of a lost boyfriend, the shrine of a dead girl and a dark force I hadn't identified yet. The logic I'd been brought up with told me it was a dark human presence but then a little voice inside insisted it was the house.

An old place like that would have had many lives pass through its doors. Some would have been good and some would have been capable of hurting me.

As I sat there a car arriving outside broke into my thoughts. I walked cautiously to the front door. A Garda car was just coming to a halt outside. A female detective in her forties got out. She was tall and strongly built with a masculine walk. Beside her walked a male detective a few years younger and a couple of inches shorter.

"Miss Yeats, my name is Detective Roe."

"Yes."

"This is Detective Boland. Can we speak to you for a moment?"

"Sure. Come inside." I stepped back and let the detectives follow me to the kitchen.

"Do you want coffee? I was just going to put on a pot.

Both officers accepted. When we all had a cup and were seated, the woman detective continued. "The results of your rape kit have come back."

"Oh." My breath was coming in short gasps.

She looked uncomfortable as she spoke. "Melanie, there was no semen found in your kit and no trace of spermicide. The doctor found no discernible bruising in your vaginal area."

I couldn't catch my breath so I had to get up and walk around the room. I was afraid I was going to hyperventilate.

"Good," I finally managed to say. "That's good. So I wasn't raped."

"It doesn't look that way."

I was relieved about that at least.

The detective continued. "Melanie, there was no evidence of a break-in at all and beyond the bruising on your chest no evidence of an attack." Detective Roe looked upset.

"But my chest! You saw the bruising. You photographed it. I told you what happened."

"I know. We know you were injured."

"But you think I made it up?" I looked at the two faces. They were looking directly at me. Maybe they thought I was an attention-seeker.

Detective Roe's face was inscrutable. She knew I believed I'd been attacked and I certainly had injuries.

My hands were tightly gripped together, shutting off

their blood supply. I didn't see an attacker, I didn't hear a voice. I knew nothing because it was dark. I became unconscious during my ordeal and didn't wake up until morning. It was all adding up to being just a nightmare. Somehow Detective Roe believed that I had caused these injuries to myself in the middle of a bad dream.

She cleared her throat, obviously distressed. "There is something else."

I couldn't speak.

"The scratches on your neck and shoulders – you made those yourself. We took swabs from under your nails and it was your own blood and tissue under there."

Detective Boland, who hadn't spoken yet, turned to me. "Have you heard of sleep paralysis?"

I shook my head, wondering what they were accusing me of.

The detective went on. "If you suffer an episode of sleep paralysis you are in effect asleep and unable to move, though you are conscious of what's going on around you. It's very frightening. I've known people who've had it. It's probably where the incubus myth came from."

"You think I dreamt about having sex with a demon?" I almost spat the words at him.

He looked embarrassed and didn't answer.

"Besides, according to you," I went on, "there *was* nothing going on around me! And how do you explain the bruising if I was supposedly paralysed? I would hardly be trashing about and scratching myself. I wouldn't be able to move."

"Maybe it was just a regular nightmare," Detective Boland said.

I glared at him, unsure if he was being sarcastic.

Detective Roe pushed a card across the table to me. "This is the number of a counsellor. She's very good. I think she can help you."

I looked at the card but left it sitting on the counter. I was so embarrassed. I didn't know what was happening to me. Was it all imagination? Was it just an unfortunate list of coincidences – Ryan missing on a Caribbean island, the dreadful weather? I was depressed in that lonely old house. It must be stress.

Then I remembered.

"What about the person outside my house?" I'd mentioned it to them at the station. As soon as the words were out of my mouth I could see the disbelief on their faces.

"It is difficult to investigate that, Miss Yeats. You didn't come to us at the time."

"I had no evidence."

Detective Roe spoke gently. "So you can see our difficulty. Without any evidence what can we do?"

"Nothing, I suppose." I whispered the words.

Maybe Elizabeth's shrine had been in the attic for years. The owners of the house might know what its story was or perhaps a previous occupant set it up there.

They all thought I was dreaming or a self-mutilator. No matter what happened from then on, unless I had indisputable proof I couldn't go to anyone.

CHAPTER 22

Just after the police left I heard Bobby on the stairs. He was probably coming down to check up on me.

I couldn't face explaining to him that I'd imagined a night-time attack. I swiftly went through the door to the back corridor, closing it gently behind me, went out to the stable yard and through the gate to the woods. Instead of taking the path I had followed the previous day, this time I decided to go straight on. There was another path there, also quite overgrown, and I thought I'd see where it went.

This path was overgrown from the outset, more so than the last one. I was like a child, pushing my way through, exploring the undergrowth of a forgotten wood. It wasn't raining but it had been earlier. The rain-soaked trees brushed their damp fingers across my face and hair as I went. Before long I was soaked too but I felt better. The cool damp air was invigorating.

The path came to an end. A pile of fallen stone, deeply overgrown, blocked it. This time I was determined to see what lay beyond the boundaries of my little private world. This journey had taken on mythical significance. The wood was like my mind, cluttered and abandoned. I needed to break through the boundaries that fenced me in.

Breaking through wasn't as easy as I thought. I had to pull back the briars, which tore at my flesh, while climbing at the same time. After a few minutes I stood on wobbly legs at the top of the pile, worried in case the rocks would give way and I would tumble down. That would look good – if after the morning I'd just had I went out into the woods and broke my neck!

The pile of rocks was actually a tumbled house sitting alone and forgotten. Below me on the other side I could see a window standing alone with ivy growing in and around it. By its ornate shape I presumed this little house was once part of the manor. It was probably a gamekeeper's cottage. What a view! I could see all the way down into the valley, on to the village and beyond to the mountains visible in the distance. The beauty of the scene took my breath away. This was the kind of house I really wanted: a small house with a beautiful view. But for some reason the big one wanted me.

I stood there until I felt the first drops of rain and then I returned to the house.

Bobby had put on another pot of coffee.

"I was getting worried about you, sis."

"There was no need." I felt better after my walk.

"Of course I'm worried about you. You're under a lot of pressure."

Bobby had picked up the therapist's card off the counter and now he held it out to me. "What's this?"

I told him in a faltering voice what the detectives had

told me. Bobby was unable to take his eyes off my stricken face.

"I'm fine. It was obviously a nightmare. Perhaps I was sleepwalking. It happens."

"It does. But it is a sign of severe stress." His brow was deeply furrowed as he looked at me.

"Did you study psychology as well as engineering?" I was starting to feel angry.

"I just want to help," he said. "You have no one else."

"Don't judge me." I looked into the concerned eyes of my brother. "How long will I have you for?" I tried unsuccessfully to keep back my tears. "One day I'll get a call to say you're dead in God knows where and I'll be back here again."

Bobby reached for me but I pushed his hands away. I couldn't grow dependent on Bobby of all people. He was not dependable.

"Is that why you were living with *him*?" he asked. "Did you need someone in your life that badly?"

"Stop psychoanalysing me."

"I can't stay here and take care of you."

"Who the hell asked you to?" I was amazed at his audacity. He just turned up on my doorstep. I never asked for his help or anyone's help for that matter.

"Look," he said, "I have to go to London for a meeting about my next contract."

"Go!" My eyes blazed into his. "I'm perfectly fine, thank you."

"But I feel terrible about leaving."

"Why? If you hadn't come down you'd be none the wiser. Don't act the martyr."

Bobby's face froze in anger. He turned and marched out the door.

I heard him pound up the stairs. Five minutes later I heard him come marching back down the stairs and through the hall.

Feeling a sense of panic I ran outside in time to see him swing his rucksack into the back of his car. He turned and stared into my eyes but I was too stubborn to move. I just stood there until he turned, got into the car and drove away.

After all my brave words, now I felt abandoned. I wasn't angry with him I was angry with myself and scared of what was happening to me. Finding out that my attack was imagination had shaken me badly. I knew none of it was Bobby's fault. I was just lashing out.

The sun had gone down and the shadows were deepening and stretching over my yard. Now I was as scared of myself as I had been of the dark. Something was hiding inside of me. Something I knew soon I would have to face.

Back inside the house I paced up and down the hall, trying to control my rapidly escalating breath. This was awful. I'd angered my brother and, knowing his personality, I might never speak to him again. He barely spoke to Dad. As I walked and talked to myself my panic attack was increasing. My breath was coming in big choking gasps and I could hardly see. I sat on the bottom step of the stairs and placed my hand over my mouth and nose, trying to breathe normally. It took a few minutes but I started to calm down and my breathing returned.

Then the house phone rang.

Tentatively I picked it up. "Hello."

"You had a visitor?" The caller was back.

"I did."

"Who was he?" At least this man wasn't in the house with me or he would know already.

"That's none of your business."

"Who was he?" The normally assured and mellow tones of my caller were harsh. His anger was palpable.

"My brother, but he's gone now."

The phone went dead in my hand.

"Who is he?" I spoke out loud to the empty hall.

The phone rang again. I hesitated before answering it. It continued ringing. I picked it up but didn't speak.

"Hello."

It was Bobby. He sounded worried.

"Hi." I felt tears of relief.

"I'm sorry I ran out like that."

"It was my fault." I didn't want to harm this truce.

"No. I don't think you're crazy."

"I'm not." I wanted to tell him about the phone calls I'd been getting and hadn't reported and the shrine in the attic but coupled with what he already knew it would just make me sound even crazier.

"This meeting is only for a couple of days and then I can come back and spend some time with you. I can help you get sorted. You can move into a smaller house with your own lease and get another job. I'll be with you all the way."

I knew it all made sense. I needed someone to dig me out of there. "That sounds good. I'll be here."

"Bye, Mellie. I'll talk to you in a couple of days."

"Bye" Now I felt a lot better, and hungry.

The house settled around me. What was it thinking now, now that I would soon be leaving?

"Just a minute, Melanie." Emer Doyle had been deep in thought as Mel talked. Now she stood up quickly and, without giving Mel a chance to make a comment, left the room.

"Seán."

"Yes?" He turned from a pile of papers and the phone he'd just replaced on the table and looked at her.

"Have we got Melanie's home address yet? The one in Galway."

"Yes. 12 Ashe Way, Mount Bank, Galway."

"Right. We need to speak to her father. Are we into the house in Raven yet?"

"No. I'll come and get you when we have the warrant."

"Right. Thanks."

"Did you find out about the assault file? It should be here."

"Definitely no file here with her name on it."

"I didn't think so. She mentioned two detectives – Roe and Boland – but I knew they weren't here." She paused. "Did you run a check on her brother yet?"

"Bobby Yeats?" Seán frowned. "No. Not yet. But, you know, sounds familiar. Robert Yeats. I wonder . . ."

"What did you say?" Emer couldn't catch his muttering.

"Nothing. Just an idea."

"See what you can find."

She returned to Mel and her story.

Mel just gave Emer a chance to sit down before she resumed speaking.

CHAPTER 23

The next day I decided to call my dad and see if he'd heard anything more from Belize. I dialled the number and listened to it ringing. There was no answer. I was beginning to think he wasn't there and was just about to hang up when he answered. He was out of breath.

"Dad. What's the matter?"

"I was down the bottom of the garden."

"Why didn't you bring the cordless?"

"I forgot to charge it." He was impatient as usual. "What's up?"

"I just wondered if you'd heard any news."

"Melanie, if I heard anything I would have called you."

"Of course. I'm sorry."

"As soon as I hear anything, Mel, I'll call you." He hung up.

"Sorry for disturbing you." I was talking to thin air.

I replaced the receiver in its cradle.

For a moment I was going to pick up the phone and

ring Dad back but that would get me nowhere. I decided to do nothing. There was nobody better than my father to pursue authority on my behalf. I was never going to make him caring and fluffy. No. Let him bother the police and Belize. I would take care of myself.

I decided to go into Bantry and look up the history of the house. Why the history would make a difference I didn't know but I wanted to get to know the house a bit better. Grabbing keys and my address book off the desk, I stuffed everything into my bag and went out to my car.

It was a gorgeous day, for a change, cold and bright with deep blue skies. The drive was uneventful and almost enjoyable. I was so glad to get out of the house and see the sun.

In Bantry I parked my car in my usual spot and climbed the hill to the library. I was getting pretty hungry. Passing a restaurant as I walked up the hill a delicious smell wafted out the door towards me. I would go and get some lunch. The library could wait a little while.

The restaurant I chose to go to was very popular and always packed. It had a fusion of local and European dishes and was designed like an American diner with rows of booths. Another area had been added to the side with a space for solo diners. That was why I liked the restaurant – they didn't make me feel out of place for being in there by myself. Even before his disappearance Ryan was away a lot so it was nice to go out for lunch alone sometimes.

I sat down in the corner and waited for a waiter to come to me. A young girl in jeans and a white blouse came over with a smile.

"Are you ready to order?"

I actually smiled back. I was feeling better.

I took a second to look at the menu and then I ordered a steak. I didn't eat beef very often but when I did I enjoyed it. Ryan had stopped all red meat in the house so maybe this was a little rebelliousness now that he was gone. As I waited for the food to come out my phone rang.

I reached to answer it but the battery died. I'd forgotten to charge it. Instead of brooding about my lost call I sat back and waited for my steak.

The girl who'd taken my order walked down with my food, her smile broadening when she saw how relaxed and happy her customer was.

"You're having a good day."

"I am." I smiled and started my steak. I hadn't been this happy when Ryan was home.

I had just taken a couple of bites when I was interrupted.

"Melanie."

I looked up.

"Keith." I didn't want to talk to him. He was starting to make me uncomfortable.

"On your own?"

He could see I was. "Yes. And you?"

"Yes. I just popped in for lunch. It's my afternoon off. May I join you?"

Unable to think of a reason why not, I indicated the chair beside me. So much for solo dining.

"Thanks." He smiled cheekily and took the offered seat.

Keith was a person who took up a lot of space. He wasn't very tall, maybe about five ten but he had expansive body language. He sat with his legs wide apart and his knees kept touching me. I found myself squeezing more and more towards the wall. He always rested his elbows on things, that day one was on the lunch counter and the other on the back of his chair so he could turn sideways and look straight into my face. His features were quite chiselled and lean, as was his body. There was something a little wild and predatory about him and in the tight confines of my chosen corner I felt stifled.

"In shopping?" He raised his eyebrows in question marks.

"I'm going to the library. I was going to research my house."

"Raven House?"

"Yes."

"I can tell you about that. My mother was the house-keeper there and her mother before her. I know every corner of that house."

"Really?" I was startled and my heart beat faster when he said that.

"Yes. What do you want to know about it?"

"Just its history – the people who lived there – any scandals." I tried to sound as casual about it as I could.

"There's plenty of scandal and mystery up there. Let me order first."

He raised his arm again, touching my shoulder, to beckon the waitress. His shirt was rolled up, showing forearms which were bare and deeply sinewy.

I waited while he ordered, barely able to touch my food. Somehow Keith having a close history with my house had taken away my appetite.

"Okay then," he said. "This could take a while."

"I have all afternoon."

He leaned back and started his story.

"Raven House was built in the early 1800's. It was the

home of the Church of Ireland rector in the parish of Raven until the early twentieth century. At that time it was called Raven Glebe. The first rector, Reverend Ashe, was well known locally for his parties and high society. There were rumours he was having it away with the wives of the gentry. Then a local girl claimed that he was the father of her daughter. Because of the scandal he left the area with his wife, leaving the mother of his daughter alone. She killed herself in the river below Raven House. People around here say the house stood and watched her jump. They say it sees everything."

I tried to suppress a shiver at that. I knew it saw everything. I felt it watching me as I moved about between its walls and in the woods.

He turned to look at me as he spoke, a wide smile on his face. "What do you think? Have you seen any ghosts up there?"

I sensed that he knew I'd seen something and he was playing with me.

"No. I haven't," I snapped, wanting him to get on with the story.

For a few moments he held my gaze, his eyes appraising me. I could feel a blush spreading across my neck but I couldn't tear my eyes away. There was something intrusive but mesmerising about him. I knew I didn't like him but I didn't want him to think I feared him.

"Anyway." He flicked his eyes away, looking across the room to see if his food was on its way. "Local people say that those who live in the house claim to see the house's memories replayed again and again."

Again he paused for effect and I really wanted to slap him.

"Later Reverend William Taylor became the rector in the Raven area. He moved into Raven House with his eldest daughter Jane. She was her father's spinster house-keeper and in her thirties. But shortly after they moved in Jane fell in love with the gamekeeper on the estate. He was my great-great-grandfather. We have a long association with that place."

I looked at him as he said that. But his face hadn't altered. He still had his usual cheeky smile.

"They married in the parish church in Raven and had a happy marriage according to my granny. Gran was full of stories about the place. They lived on the edge of the wood behind the stable yard. Her father built a small house for Jane to give her privacy."

My house, I thought – Jane had lived in the house I found in the woods.

"But again it ended badly."

He obviously loved the drama of the story he was telling.

"A year after they moved into their new house Jane died giving birth to my great-grandfather, again under the watchful gaze of the old house. Her father went mad with grief."

I sat back and looked across the restaurant towards the window. The waitress had just arrived with Keith's food and he was putting salt on his steak and chips. I thought about Raven House.

On the edge of the large meadow, which stretched across below the house, the river was visible like a silver ribbon meandering amongst the trees. I could imagine what it must have been like for the mother of Reverend Ashe's baby coping in a small rural community with twitching curtains and pointing fingers. The whispers of the masses followed her to the river while the house sat quietly on its hill, watching.

Jane Taylor, another woman meeting tragedy within the vicinity of Raven House. The fate of the Raven House women filled me with an unrealistic fear. I knew it was illogical to think that the shadow of a great house could spread across the lives of its women and seal their fate but I couldn't shake the feeling of doom it brought to me.

I turned back to Keith. Somehow knowing that he was part of the lineage of the old house scared me.

He raised his eyebrows quizzically when he saw me staring at him. "What?"

"Nothing. Go on."

"Okay."

He chewed and talked at the same time. I could hear him masticating his food.

"The last Church of Ireland rector to live in Raven House was Reverend Faye. He had a wife and six children, five boys and the youngest, a girl named Emily. Herself and her dad were inseparable. Reverend Faye would visit his parishioners when they were ill and six-year-old Emily would follow behind with a small basket with a treat for the person who was sick."

I knew the next part of the story was going to be tragic because he was already altering his tone and facial expression. It was like a piece of theatre.

"Emily got sick – meningitis. She died." He picked up a large chip and held it on the fork just away from his lips, pausing for dramatic effect. "Another church member had lost a female relative in Raven Hill and, illogical or not, the house was getting the blame. So in 1920 the Church of

Ireland sold the house to a local businessman. Reid was his name. They also changed the name from Raven Glebe to Raven House. Though some old people around here still call it The Glebe. They hoped that the curse on the Raven House women wouldn't spread beyond the church community."

"Did it?"

He laughed, placing the chip in his mouth and chewing loudly. "Wait and see. The Reid family were always wealthy. They had the first car in the area, a Ford Model T, and they disappeared for months every summer for the 'Season' in London or Dublin. Sometimes my granny went with them. She started off as a lady's maid. Her name was Imelda Connolly."

I thought I noticed a hint of bitterness at that but he turned on a broad smile almost instantly.

Imelda Connolly was the name of the woman who owned the old catalogue in the cupboard. She was Keith's grandmother. I wondered if Keith could have anything to do with Elizabeth's death but he seemed too young, not much older than I was.

"How old are you?" I had to ask.

"Twenty-nine. Why?" He smiled his impudent smile.

"Curious. Go on." He couldn't have been involved. He would only have been thirteen. Just a year older than I was at the time.

"For two decades peace seemed to have come to the house. A generation of Reids grew up there, all boys. Mrs Reid remained healthy and lived to be old. Rumours still circulated about the house but it stayed silent and Mrs Reid survived the curse."

"So people were still calling it a curse?" I asked.

195

"Yes and with good reason." He laughed. "You'll be too scared to go home."

"I'll be fine," I said dryly.

He went on. "After the two elder Reids passed on, their younger son inherited the house and farm. It was a successful stud farm and Lorcan Reid was well respected nationally for the quality of his horses. It was now the forties and there was a lot of poverty in rural Ireland. But the Reids didn't seem affected by this. I don't think all their money came from horses. They had other interests abroad but Lorcan wasn't one to broadcast his business. They kept a lavish house at Raven House and threw huge parties. Mrs Reid had gained a reputation for keeping male company at the house while her husband was away. One day Lorcan Reid came home from a business trip and claimed to have found Mrs Reid dead in that corridor leading from the kitchen at the back."

My breath caught in my throat. Could that be the cause of the dark feelings I felt when I was in that corridor?

"Mrs Reid had been violently beaten about her head. The area was in an uproar. Everyone was a suspect. Police were drafted in from Dublin and Cork. Lorcan Reid held a lot of power in the area and had powerful friends in government. For weeks they scoured the area for whoever killed Mrs Reid until one young Guard decided they might be looking in the wrong direction. He started to delve into Lorcan's whereabouts on the night of the murder, believing him to be the murderer. He traced a young man, Tom Roche, who'd been having an affair with Mrs Reid. He had an alibi. His mother had vouched for him. The Garda still wasn't satisfied. He went back to Tom Roche and asked him if he saw anything unusual during the journey home. He said he'd been leaving by the stable yard and heard a car stopping in front of the manor. The Guard strongly suspected the grieving Mr Reid. He pursued the case diligently until he was suddenly transferred to a sub-station in the midlands. Neither Lorcan Reid nor anyone else was ever charged with the murder of Mrs Reid. Two years later the second Mrs Reid was introduced into the household. They had four children, three boys and one girl. She outlived her powerful husband and died peacefully in her bed. The house and farm were badly in need of modernisation. It was inherited by relatives in Boston who I think may have sold it on after doing some repairs."

"Did the little girl survive the curse?"

"I don't know. I don't know where she is now."

I made light of the conversation. "Well, I must go. Thanks for the history lesson. I hope I'm not cursed."

"I hope so too." He spoke softly and held my gaze an uncomfortably long time.

"Goodbye."

I went and paid for my food. But as I left the restaurant my heart was doing somersaults. Boston again. I turned at the doorway and looked back. Keith was smiling after me.

I got back to my car as the rain started again. The brightness of the day had been short-lived. My moods were definitely related to the weather.

By the time I was approaching my house the rain was once more coming down in buckets. Already mini-floods were creeping across the road. I spoke to the house as I climbed the avenue towards it.

"Now I know the secrets hidden within your walls."

The house didn't answer. It sat there on its elevated site silently watching my approach. It was customary now for me to park in the front. I stopped the car outside the front door and got out. In the few moments it took for me to lock the car door I was already getting soaked. I lowered my head and ran to the porch. As I stepped onto the doorstep and withdrew my key to place it in the lock I saw that the door was slightly ajar. The rain was running down the back of my neck and connecting with my skin as I stood there. Again I wondered if I had locked the house as I left.

This was crazy. The wind was starting to escalate and the door was sucking in and out according to its whims. The door was heavy but the level of wind blowing up here would soon have it battering the porch wall. Gathering my courage I entered the house.

Dripping rain onto the floor I pushed the door closed behind me and stood in the porch listening. Any presence that may have been there, was listening too, because the house was still and silent.

Every magazine article I'd ever read on how to react if you suspect an intruder is in your home always said the same thing: don't go inside. Yet that was exactly what I was doing. Somewhere in the dark recesses of my mind I knew there was a wish to face whatever was lurking in my home. Once I'd dealt with that then I could face the rest of my life.

Taking a deep breath I opened the door from the porch into the hall. It stood empty. The four doors leading off the hall were tightly closed but, looking straight ahead to the right of the staircase I could see the door to the back corridor was ajar. Did I close that? I had no idea. I hadn't gone down there at all today. Maybe I did leave it open.

I gathered my courage and walked with conviction

down the hall. I flipped the switch as I walked but the light didn't come on. The wiring in this old house must be shot – it was continuously blowing bulbs. In the corridor the cloakroom door was closed as I'd last seen it. Instinctively I reached for its handle and turned it. It didn't open. I put my hand up over it and there was the key where I'd last placed it.

Relieved, I turned to walk towards the kitchen. Then I felt my breath catch and my body went cold. Someone was standing at the end of the corridor. It was a man standing in a pool of darkness watching me. I was frozen for a moment but then I ran out to the hall and the comfort of electric light.

Should I call someone? Who was close by? Nobody. Should I go through to the kitchen from here and surprise the person? Or run upstairs and hide? I stood in the hall for a few moments and took some deep breaths. The back door was locked. The cloakroom door was locked. If there really was someone standing there they would either have to come out the way I had just come or go through the other door into the kitchen. I calmed down slightly and listened. There wasn't a sound. Why would somebody break in and just stand in the corridor watching me?

I walked to the door leading into the kitchen and listened. Nothing. I opened the door a crack. There was no sound. The kitchen was in darkness and just as quiet as the hall had been. I listened but couldn't hear a sound. No sound of fleeing footsteps.

I entered the kitchen. Cold with fear, I flipped on the light. The room was empty. The door into the back corridor was closed. I ran across and turned the key, locking it.

Then I grabbed a small sharp knife as a weapon and

held it tightly in my right hand. I took my flash-lamp from under the sink and retraced my steps to the corridor, all the time listening for any sound. As I got to the corner, ready to turn into it, I took a deep breath. Then I turned the corner. First I took a look down there without the lamp and he was still there, though not as distinct as before. Something seemed different. I switched on the lamp and trained it on the far end of the corridor. I was so relieved I lost all power in my legs and had to sit down on the ground. I'd forgotten about the old coat-stand. I never used it but it had stood there since I moved in. Then the palpitations returned. I was sure that trilby on top of it hadn't been there before.

Once more I talked to myself. Could I go now to someone and say "As far as I can tell someone left an old hat on an old coat-stand to frighten me"? No, I couldn't. I walked to the stand and took down the hat. It was just an old hat covered in dust. I was being ridiculous. I turned it around and looked inside under the rim. Embroidered on the inside was the name *L Reid*. After my earlier conversation with Keith I saw the significance of that. Someone put the hat there to frighten me, someone who might have been standing there earlier, someone who knew of my conversation with Keith. Confused and scared, I turned to enter the kitchen and the door opened freely.

I'd just locked that door from the other side.

CHAPTER 24

The corridor behind me was empty and so was the kitchen. I walked to my usual stool and sat there, too weak to do any more searching.

As I sat and absorbed what I'd experienced, the phone rang. I got off my stool, walked slowly to the phone and picked it up cautiously.

"Hello?"

"Mel." It was Dad.

"Dad! Hi."

"Did Bobby find you?"

"Yes." So my cousin Amanda was still circulating information.

"I have some news."

"What?"

"The body in Belize wasn't Ryan."

A stab of fear rippled though me. "Are they sure?"

"Yes. They identified it. It was the missing dive group guide. So Ryan is still missing."

I was right. Maybe he was still alive. I'd suspected it all along. He was walking the streets somewhere, right now, weaving his way into the tapestry of some other woman's life, remodelling her. Was he hiding from the caller? Was the caller using me to try and flush him out? Was this all some sick game he was playing with me? Maybe he really was here? Was he stalking me? Anxiety was in danger of escalating into panic. Did Ryan kill that guide?

"Mel."

"Yes, Dad?"

"Don't worry." His voice held genuine concern.

"Do you think he's here?"

"I don't know but I doubt it. Why would he be?"

"Dad, I have to go."

"Okay, Mel."

"Goodnight, Dad."

"Goodnight, Mel."

Instinctively I went to the wine rack and pulled out a bottle of wine without even looking at the label. I poured a generous glass and quickly drank it.

"*Ryan Lester!*" I spat the name out loud. I could feel his slick touch all over my life.

My life was doubly cursed. Ryan was only one part. I was there in that house, another cursed woman in a house that attracted the tragic and sat there recording all the details. I could imagine those memories like old reels of film rolling through the halls. Why women? Of course, logically I knew I was being ridiculous. Houses can't hurt people. Somehow I didn't really believe my own words.

This was all coincidence. Children get sick, women die in childbirth, lovers let each other down and jealousy can breed violent reactions in those who feel it. Why should it be any more sinister than that? Concentration! The density of tragic occurrences gave this curse story credence. Somehow my life had taken a silent crossing from the sane to the absurd.

I carried my bottle into my sitting room. The fire was out and the room was cold. I couldn't settle. Picking up my bottle, I stood up again and left the room, closing the door behind me.

Standing in the great hall, I imagined the other Raven House women passing through the front door and what they must have looked like. Through a film of wine they stood vivid and forbidding in the crowded hallway: the vicar's mistress, the vicar's daughters and the hapless Mrs Reid.

One day, would I stand amongst them? Would my ghost some day walk in the shadows of this hall? Then I had a thought. How did Elizabeth fit in here? Why did someone bring her ghost into the attics of Raven House? Was she somehow connected to Raven House also?

Elizabeth Renfield! That name didn't appear anywhere in Keith's history. Why would a girl from Boston find her way in death into an old country manor in West Cork? I was surrounded by questions. They echoed through the empty rooms.

And then I knew. Family in Boston inherited the house; those were Keith's words. Was that the connection? Elizabeth was part of the family in Boston. Was she a descendant of the murdering Lorcan Reid whose ghost left his hat in my back corridor?

That night, despite everything, my sleep was deep and peaceful but I awoke with a dry mouth and a stomach that flipped at regular intervals. Groaning, I lay back in my bed. As I did this I realised that I was still dressed. I stretched, starting as usual with my toes only to discover I was wearing my shoes.

Still exhausted, I reached down under the duvet, removed my shoes and dropped them onto the floor. I turned around in the bed and drifted back into a fitful sleep.

I awoke in the late afternoon and went downstairs to get some food. The house was exactly the same as I'd left it the previous night.

I felt lonely as I wandered the empty rooms looking through the windows at the damp dark day outside. I didn't know what was happening. Why was I rattling around with ghosts and memories, locked away from the world? The rest of the world was like flickering shadows that I couldn't quite grab onto.

A late lunch seemed like a good idea. My stomach ached for food. I got it ready, laying the table with care. I moved a potted plant closer to bring something living into my space. As I looked at my guest I started laughing out loud. I placed the palm of my hand gently against the flat leaves of the rubber plant and felt a knot in my stomach.

"I'll call you Fred," I whispered.

It's funny how laughter can turn to tears and back in seconds. How absurd I would look if anyone could see me.

I sat on my stool and started eating. Despite the trouble I'd taken in preparing my table, all I'd put together was a ham sandwich and a glass of milk. By the time I'd finished, the food had done its job and a warm feeling of comfort was already spreading through me.

I decided to go back to my room, light a fire, drag a

chair over to the hearth and read a book. Nothing made me feel happier than the pages of a good book.

Sometime towards nightfall the book slipped from my hand and the empty bottle lay discarded on the floor.

Emer Doyle's mobile phone buzzed again and moved dangerously close to the edge of the table.

"That's becoming quite annoying." Mel's brows knit and she stared at the phone like she'd like to chuck it at the wall.

"Just a minute, Melanie." Emer read the text.

Got the warrant. Galway lads on their way too.

Soon they would speak to Mel's father. It would either prove Melanie a liar or prove Ryan Lester existed.

"Sorry, Melanie. Go on."

"Fine. If you're sure." Mel's personality was changing and becoming more openly hostile at being interrupted.

Doctor Hanley was watching this closely.

An electric sense of anticipation was starting to invade the room. Everyone there was aware that they were getting closer to the truth.

CHAPTER 25

The next morning I awoke early to the sound of the telephone. I was still sleeping in the armchair by the cold fire with my neck hanging forward at a precarious angle. The pain from the struggling muscles caused me to wince as I stood and stretched. I crossed the room to the hall and reached out to pick up the receiver. Lifting my right arm almost caused me to cry out in pain.

"Hello?" I struggled to open my eyes.

"Melanie." It was Hugh.

"Hugh. Hi!"

"Were you asleep?"

I looked at the clock. It was eight thirty. "What is it, Hugh?"

"I'm still digging about your girl, Elizabeth."

"Have you found something?"

"Yes, Melanie. I know how she's connected to you."

There was a long pause. I was feeling a little dizzy.

Somehow I knew I didn't want to hear what he was going to say.

"I think I know too. Was she related to the owners of Raven House?"

"I don't know about that, Melanie. But they found the person who killed her."

Something was lurking at the back of my mind and I didn't want to face it.

"I've got to go, Hugh."

"Melanie, it's time you faced facts." He spoke in a firm tone you might use with a stubborn child.

Immediately I knew he was going to tell me that whoever my boyfriend was, that was the person who killed Elizabeth.

"Hugh, I can't deal with that right now."

"Melanie! Please. I have to talk to you about it."

"I can't."

"But you need to face things. You need to talk to someone, not hide out down there."

A loud noise was starting in my ears and I had to take deep breaths. "I can't. Not now. Talk to me later."

"I can't let you do this to yourself . . ."

I hung up the phone, cutting him off in mid-sentence, my heart breaking into tiny pieces. I couldn't hear the words. I didn't want to know for sure that Ryan had killed that poor girl, burned her car and run away. That the man I planned to spend the rest of my life with, shared my bed with, was capable of that.

Now he'd run away again. I trusted my father to find him. Dad, despite his flaws, was capable of anything when he set his mind to it and he was going to hunt down Ryan Lester.

Dad was a force of nature. He was a difficult man to live with – we could all attest to that. I opened the drawer by my side, withdrew an old photograph album and flicked through the pages. Every photograph of my mother showed a shy reclusive woman with grey hair and premature lines. Dad and Mam married in their early thirties. Bobby came along a couple of years later but it was ten years before I appeared. By then my mother was forty-five years old. People always assumed that I was her granddaughter.

Mam died just past her fiftieth birthday. She stepped from a taxi holding my hand and turned to pay the driver. He got out, withdrew her shopping from the boot and carried it to the door, then turned to walk back to the car.

Mam was lying on the path. I was sitting beside her on the ground stroking her cheek. He rushed to try to revive her but she was already dead. There was a trickle of blood on her lips. I was five and Bobby was almost sixteen.

It was all right for Bobby as he was a promising student, a bit of a protégé and an athlete. He was going to university in the States. In a few years he was gone and I was living alone with Dad.

Dad was a harsh taskmaster and ran the house like a military operation. He saw to it that I studied, ate, took sport at school and was home each night and in bed by nine o'clock. As long as I did what I was told and was where I was supposed to be, he never spoke to me.

At seventeen I too escaped to college but it wasn't as far as the States. Every weekend I was expected home with a house to clean and the week's dinners to prepare for Dad. I piled them up in Tupperware boxes in the chest freezer in the shed with a label on each so Dad could choose what he wanted.

That house was so cold on Friday evening when I came though the door. The windows wouldn't have been opened all week. A layer of dust and grime covered all flat surfaces. The sink would be full of dishes while a stack of dirty Tupperware boxes sat, waiting to be pressed into service, on the worktop.

Dad stayed out of the house until it was clean and warm. He would arrive through the door to the welcome aroma of a fresh dinner and a bottle of Harp. I could never stomach the smell of that beer afterwards. It reminded me of the ticking of the clock in the kitchen and the click of Dad's cutlery on the dishes.

He would sit back after the last bite was finished. I would get up, remove his plate and put the kettle on the stove to heat the water for tea. Though it was a quiet and in its own way a secure life, I could never muster any hope for the future. The house was always well stocked with food, my education was paid for but without Bobby I never had the nerve to dream. He did things and I waited, always waited. It was long before email so I lived for his weekly letters and phone calls.

Bobby lived life with abandon. Even the death of our mother didn't dampen that – in fact, it sharpened his need to squeeze everything he could from the world. He knew what happened when you wasted time. Bobby made me laugh and gave me the courage to dream. He promised me that as soon as I got my degree I could join him. But somehow it became harder to get away from Dad. He didn't approve of Bobby's life and he wanted to save me from his influence. I listened to Dad's lectures at home and Bobby's ranting about Dad in his letters.

Bobby never gave up on his wanderlust. When he had

his engineering degree he started his travels. I was planted in a dark house and he became a child of the world.

I was thrust from my memories again by the ringing of the telephone. It was probably Hugh trying to ring me back. There was no way I wanted to speak to him. The phone rang off and I lay there holding my stomach. It was amazing how painful stress could be. It was like someone had reached inside me and was squeezing my gut in a vice-like grip.

How could I sleep with and love someone who would watch a girl burn and just walk away? Though I hadn't had the courage to listen to Hugh actually say the words, my body knew what he meant and it was acting accordingly. I drifted into broken sleep for an hour or so but finally hunger drove me to the kitchen. There was very little left. I defrosted some slices of bread, made toast covered in a thick layer of marmalade and my usual pot of coffee.

As I took my first bite my mobile started vibrating on the counter. I looked at the screen. It was Hugh. Why couldn't he just leave me alone? It wasn't necessary for him to do anything more. All I wanted was for him to find me some information on Elizabeth and then leave it at that. People never knew when to leave well enough alone.

The house phone rang, making me jump. This was ridiculous. I crossed the room, grabbed the receiver and all but shouted "*Yes!*" into it. It was Bobby. Relief filled me. The sound of his happy voice was like balm to my ears.

"Hi, Mel! The job's sorted. I signed my new contract today. I'll be leaving on Wednesday so I won't be able to come back and see you."

"That's okay. I'll be here when you get back. How long are you leaving for?"

"It's a two-year contract."

I had to gulp back the tears that I'd been keeping in check. "That's a long time."

"I know, sis. Are you okay after your bad dream?"

"I'm fine. It was just one of those dreams. They seem so real at the time."

"Have you had any since?"

"No. And I don't get them often and never before that vivid. I'm not going crazy."

"Good."

"I'm fine, big brother. Go and bring water to the masses."

"Okay, little sis. I love you." He hung up.

He'd never told me he loved me before. The words rang in my ears. Things would get better after this. I would see to it. I promised myself I would sort everything out.

But first things first, I needed a walk. I was getting into this walking business. I locked up the house. I wanted to go and see the old house on the edge of the wood. That view had given me peace the last time I saw it. I left by the back door and crossed the stable yard, the emptiness of my life more evident than usual, but there was a heaviness also, a feeling of dread.

CHAPTER 26

Looking back from the yard gate the house seemed to be resting that day. It looked as bleak as I felt. How strange that it always seemed to reflect my moods.

I retraced my steps from the last day through the thick growth to the tumbled house on the edge of the wood. This must have been a proper path when Jane lived here after her marriage. Beneath my feet the ground was rough and strewn with the dead limbs of trees already dissolving into the ground, the cycle of nature. I could see birth, life, death and decay occur at every footstep. Tiny saplings sprang from the mulched bodies of their ancestors.

I got to the tumbled house and looked again at its ornate windows, which looked straight down into the valley. This must have been such a beautiful house when Jane's father built it. I tried to get a clear image of the floor space as I climbed the broken walls. It was probably bigger than I first thought. Part of it was buried under the trees and bushes of the forest. Keith's great-great-grandmother died here bringing his direct line into the world.

As I stood there on the wall mulling over the past, I heard the foliage rustle behind me. I whirled around, almost losing my balance on the stones. There was nothing moving that I could see. With beating heart I waited. There it was again. A rustle amongst the trees, then a snapped twig. Someone was following me. It seemed to be to my left just off the track. As quietly as I could I eased myself from the wall and stepped back onto the path. Right behind me another twig snapped.

I ran. My breath was coming in gasps and I felt pressure on my chest. Bushes whipped at my hair and scratched my face. I stumbled on until I landed on my knees in the mud. Terrified, I picked myself up and ran again until I burst through the gate and into the stable yard. The gate had one of those catches where if you pushed it, it snapped closed of its own accord. I heard it slam into place as I raced for the back door.

I placed my hand in my pocket for the key. It wasn't there.

"This can't be happening!" I wailed into the empty yard. I turned out all my pockets but they were empty. The key must have fallen out when I fell. There was nothing for me to do but to go back to the path and search.

Keeping my eyes on alert, I left the yard again, picking up a piece of firewood from an old pile by the gate. Slowly now and keeping a tight grip on the wood I inched along. I listened intently but could hear nothing. The spot where I fell was just a few yards down the path and not near the tumbled house. What if I couldn't find the key? I didn't want to think about it.

When I reached the spot where I fell I searched everywhere but there was no sign of the key. It was attached to a tiny metallic blue pocket torch so it would have been easily visible against the brown clay. When I'd searched every inch of the ground I gave up and turned back towards the house. As I did I heard the gate bang. It normally closed quickly when someone walked through. Had I heard it slam behind me when I came out? Slowly I walked towards the yard.

Just two steps from the gate a sheep burrowed its way out of the bushes and stood in front of me. Both of us were too scared to move.

Then it ambled off. I stood at the gate looking in and the yard seemed quiet and deserted. So scared my legs could barely function, I opened the gate and walked towards the house, looking around me as I went. As I got closer to the back door I could see my key, which I had just lost in the woods, sitting on the wall by the flower-garden gate. I was so scared by then that I was finding it difficult to draw a breath. I took the key, opened the door and stepped into the corridor, closing the door tightly behind me and locking it as securely as I could.

I went to the kitchen. I needed something that would work a bit more quickly than wine. I reached into the drinks cupboard and took out a bottle of brandy. I poured a small measure and knocked it back. Someone had been following me out there. I sat on my high stool and gradually the shaking in my limbs subsided. As I thought about what I should do I heard a car pull up outside my front door.

I went out to the hall and looked out the porch window. Keith again. There was no reason for him to be there. He knocked and I stepped back but he walked to the window and looked in, straight into my eyes. He must have seen the fear in them but he smiled at me anyway.

"What do you want?" I could hear my voice. Hear the fear in it. It didn't sound like me at all.

"We have to issue receipts now on payment, Melanie. My boss sent me up with one for you. I didn't have it with me yesterday." He continued staring at me and smiling.

I looked back, wondering what to do. He waved a receipt book at me. Maybe he was telling me the truth. I decided to risk it. I opened the door and stood back to let him in.

After just a few moments it felt claustrophobic to have him there. He was exacerbating my fears just by his presence but he didn't want to leave. I'd given him bad habits. I could tell by the way he stood and watched me that he expected coffee and deep down I knew that eventually he expected more than that.

"Will I put the kettle on?" He turned and walked to the kitchen to do that as I watched incredulously.

Had I given him permission to be so bold in my space? No, I hadn't.

As he filled the coffee jug I saw him looking at the brandy glass. I took it and placed it in the sink. Once more he smirked. That face was really starting to annoy me.

I sat on my stool, still saying nothing, until he sat beside me with the two mugs. I opened my mouth to speak but he interrupted me.

"See any ghosts roaming the corridors? I was wondering when I saw the brandy out."

"I think I'm getting a cold."

"There's a bit of that going around all right." Everything he said seemed to have a sleazy connotation.

"You have a long history with this house."

"I do. I practically lived up here until my mother retired when old Mrs Reid died."

"Did you guys stay in the attics?"

"We did. The ones off the kitchen." He knew about the two sets of attic rooms.

"Did you ever work here?"

"Yes." He swirled his coffee in his cup. "I did odd jobs, took care of the yard and the garden."

"So you've always lived here?"

"No. I spent some years in Boston."

"Boston." I spoke softly. Here was another link to Boston.

A little shaken, I got up to pour myself another coffee and I accidentally brushed against his thigh. I put down my hand to steady myself as I tripped, trying to step away from him. Immediately he trapped it under his, placing it on his upper thigh. I could feel the tightness of his muscles. He held it there and tried to hold my gaze.

I ripped my hand away. "What are you doing?"

"I'm being friendly."

"You're being presumptuous."

"I think you know what's going on." He smiled but his eyes scared me.

"There's nothing going on." I stood right back and glared at him.

"You're some tease, aren't you?" His voice had a breathy quality now that set my teeth on edge.

"I want you to leave." I stepped to the side, showing him the door.

He got off the chair and walked as though to pass me but at the last minute he grabbed my arm and pushed me towards the wall. He pressed his face against mine, forehead to forehead.

Finally, he pulled back slowly, laughed and turned away.

I waited until I heard him close the front door and then I ran to the hall and shut the door tightly. I saw him in his car and watched him drive away. Trembling I threw back another brandy, then standing with my palms flat on the worktop I tried to control my rapid breathing.

The ringing of my mobile disrupted my thoughts and actions. It was an unknown number.

"Hello!" I spoke sharply, fully prepared to hang up if it was Hugh saying something I didn't want to hear.

"Do you know yet who your boyfriend was?" It was the caller.

It seemed so long since I had last spoken to him. It must have been just days ago but time was blending together and I couldn't pinpoint dates or times accurately.

I didn't answer.

"Does it make sense yet?" the caller asked.

"What do you mean?" I was confused.

"Why did he come to you?" He spoke as though he were patiently guiding a slow child towards a maths-problem solution.

"Does that matter? He was playing with me until he'd had enough?" I listened to his voice closely. Was this Ryan messing with me again?

"No. There was more to it than that, Melanie."

I was getting angry and shouted, "I hate guessing games! Just tell me!"

"You'll come to it. Eventually." He hung up.

His voice was harsher than Ryan's but maybe that was

217

how he disguised it. I was so confused. Did it matter? Maybe Ryan was dead. Maybe he was living on the other side of the world tormenting someone else. The only thing that mattered now was that the caller was still watching me. Maybe he was the one watching me in the wood.

And then there was Keith. He was starting to scare me more than any of them.

"Melanie, do you need to use the bathroom?" Emer Doyle was worried about her. She'd been there for hours telling her story without a break.

"No. I'll let you know if I do."

There was palpable anger and frustration in Mel whenever they interrupted the flow of her story.

Emer whispered to the doctor but he didn't seem too worried.

"Melanie, I'll be back in a moment. I need to use the bathroom. My bladder isn't as strong as yours. I won't be long."

Mel watched her go and then turned angry eyes on the wall.

Outside the door Emer went to find Seán again.

"Hey, boss! I was just going to come looking for you. The guys in Galway have contacted us. They went to the family house. It was locked up. The front gate has a lock on it."

"Locked up? Maybe she did that when she came down here. What about her dad?"

"They're looking for neighbours who are actually in this time of day. It's one of those silent estates, they said, not a soul moving. Their house is a small bungalow. It's built back from the road. It's quite overgrown and not overlooked. They said it's unlikely anyone will have seen much of what was going on there. They're searching it now."

Just then the fax machine started working. Seán walked to the machine and pulled some paper from it. He read it as he walked back. His face registered surprise.

He pushed some fax sheets across the table to Emer. She read the sheets.

"Oh Lord!"

Seán nodded. "Exactly."

Still shaking her head Emer went back into the room and sat down. She had picked up a folder on the way in and stuffed the pages inside.

Mel looked suspiciously at the folder. "Did you bring some light reading to the bathroom?"

"We found a car damaged at the back of Raven House. It's a navy Toyota. Do you know who owns that car, Melanie?" Emer threw the question out like it was something which had just popped into her head.

"It was our car, mine and Ryan's. Why?"

Emer watched her facial expressions. Mel looked blankly back at her.

"The car was owned by Eoin Yeats, your dad. It's quite an old car. Didn't you think Ryan, the top exec, should own a better car?" Again she spoke while glancing at some papers but she was closely monitoring Melanie's reaction.

"I, eh, I maybe," said Melanie. Her expression seemed one of bewilderment. Like she'd fallen into some sort of a trap she hadn't seen coming.

"Why is the car with you? How did he get to the airport?"

"I . . . um . . . I'm not sure," Melanie said.

"Why has it been crashed into a wall?"

"I'll come to that."

"Okay, Melanie. Continue with your story. We'll come back to that later."

Mel started speaking again but she couldn't keep her eyes off the folder. Her breathing was more laboured as she spoke.

She wondered if the car was all they'd discovered or were there more secrets amongst Emer's papers.

CHAPTER 27

The eyes of the house and the caller seemed to be all around me. I turned off my mobile phone and then took the house phone off the hook. That was the only way I would get any peace. Standing up, I started to wander aimlessly around the downstairs of the house. I was starting to feel like a hamster in a wheel. But the difference between the hamster and me was choice. He had none. The little guy had to move but he had nowhere to go.

In the hall I stopped pacing and looked beyond the stairs. I walked towards the door to the corridor and opened it. A cold draught hit me. The flagged corridor was the coldest part of the house. The cold breath of ghosts, maybe.

I went down the corridor and stopped by the cloak-room door. I put my hand up, took down the key and went inside. The doorway to the stairs leading to the attic was ajar but I couldn't remember if I had left it like that. I crossed to that and climbed the stairs, going straight into Elizabeth's shrine.

"What do you have to do with me?" I asked the beautiful face. "I wish you could talk."

I opened the shutters and looked out the window. Suddenly, my attention was grabbed by a figure emerging from the shrubbery to the left, close to the wall of the house. Someone was wandering around my property. It was a man. I closed the shutters and raced across the room and down the stairs. I quietly sidled up to the doorway of the cloakroom and looked outside. The back door had a small glass panel in it to let light into that dark corner of the corridor. I could see a face trying to see in through this but the glass was frosted. I couldn't make out the person's features or whether it was male or female.

As quietly as I could I left the cloakroom and went back out to the front of the house. I stood in the centre of the hall. Upstairs in my dressing room was the best place for me but my scissors were in the kitchen. I didn't want to risk going to get them so my mind frantically tried to think of a substitute. There was a companion set in my room by the fireplace. The poker was more suitable than a scissors anyway.

I ran up the stairs just as I heard someone trying to open the front door. With my heart pounding I raced down the upstairs corridor and straight into the bedroom. I locked the door, placed the chair back under the handle and grabbed the poker.

Damn it. My phone was downstairs. I couldn't ring anyone for help. Even the landline was useless to me because I'd taken it off the hook. I was shaking. It wasn't like a shiver – it was a shake that trapped my limbs and rattled my teeth in a cycle of movement completely beyond my conscious control. I tried to bring my limbs back under my influence but they ignored my efforts. Was this the end? Ryan was here for me or else the person who came for Ryan was here for me. Who was that? My scattered thought processes tried to organise everything in my head but they were like the pieces of a puzzle thrown haphazardly into a box. I didn't have steady fingers and an ordered mind to put them in their proper place.

Hours slipped by. I didn't know how to move. The shaking had stopped and the fear had dissipated but unfortunately it hadn't been replaced by action. I was exhausted. The panic attack had sapped my body of all vestiges of energy. I sat with my back against the bed, watching the door handle. My body was exhausted but my mind was active and sharp, listening for any sounds in the house. The room was almost dark. As I sat there a light shone in the side window through the open shutter and ran along the top of the wall above the door opposite me. The beam was very strong. I stepped to the wall beside the bed and watched the beam move over and back. Then it pulled back and seemed to be moving in small but ever increasing circles on the ceiling. This wasn't a car light on the road someplace. It was coming through the side window – beyond it was just countryside. Never before had I experienced such intense fear. I was paralysed by the beam of light. I stood there transfixed as it danced on the ceiling. After a few minutes I gathered the courage to take a look. I climbed across the bed and sidled up to the side of the window. I peered around the side of the curtain. Immediately I could see that the light was shining from a point fairly close to the house. Someone was standing there, someone who knew which room was my bedroom and who knew where I ran to earlier. This person wanted to terrify me.

Whoever was outside wasn't physically threatening me but I could see that this was escalating. This person was getting bolder and instinct told me that something bigger was being planned for me. I had to get help but my phone was downstairs. I couldn't sit in the room indefinitely.

Once more I let myself out of my room and went downstairs with my ears twitching for any sound. My approach through the house was silent. I looked at the slits under the doors in the hall but there was no form of light showing there. Still without switching on any lights, I crossed the hall and slowly opened the door leading into the kitchen. The kitchen was dark also and looked empty. Opposite me the door of the scullery was open. I could see through the window of the small room that the light was gone now. It seemed to be pitch dark again outside.

I rushed to the counter to pick up my mobile phone. It wasn't there. I searched all around the kitchen. The mobile was gone. I knew it had been there earlier. I ran out and searched the other downstairs rooms. It wasn't anywhere. I didn't bother going back upstairs as I knew I hadn't brought it up with me. While I stood in the hall my eyes fell on the house phone sitting on the side table. Before I reached for it, I knew what I was going to find. I picked up the receiver. Silence. My phone line was dead.

I had to get out of there. My car keys were in the kitchen. I went back into the room without turning on the light and walked to the board by the phone where I always hung the keys. They were gone. I stood there trying to understand what was happening and then a beam shone across the dimly lit kitchen towards where I stood. It was so bright it seemed to be in the scullery as opposed to outside in the shrubbery.

Too terrified to think straight I ran back upstairs to my room and barricaded myself in. I had brought a kitchen knife up with me, having grabbed it off the counter, in case the person behind the light came into my room.

I was effectively cut off from the world.

Chapter 28

For the next couple of days my mind floated on the edge of time, never quite grasping where I was or what I was doing. Something had shifted inside of me on the day I saw the prowler outside and now I wondered where it would all end. I was vaguely aware that I was in mortal danger now but I couldn't do anything about it. Yet I knew without a doubt that I was on the precipice of change. Something would happen soon.

In the woods there was someone in the trees watching me and when I was in the attic there was a prowler combing my property – and then that awful light. I felt as though I were surrounded.

I felt the ache of hunger in my gut but was numbed and paralysed by the fear growing inside me. I couldn't leave the room. I had changed so much but that change was degeneration, the breaking down of the old world order and clearing the ground for something new. What that new growth would be, I couldn't imagine and what I was leaving behind was blocked out too. I was somewhere in limbo between those two places. But yet aware of that, aware that there was another reality I was supposed to know but yet I couldn't quite see. It was like I was looking through frosted glass. Occasionally crippled with fear I faced the fact that I probably wouldn't have the strength to effect this change. I would just break down and disintegrate.

Things were getting worse. By the end of the week or maybe it was longer, I'd stopped marking time. I couldn't get out of bed. I started sleeping all day and only managed to get up to go to the bathroom. This wasn't good. I was aware of that much but beyond that fragment of a thought, which occasionally popped into my brain, awareness evaded me.

One morning I awoke and couldn't move at all. I tried to sit up but I couldn't. I was very frightened but sleep overcame me once more.

The next thing I knew I was being picked up and carried. I tried to call out and push the person away but I couldn't. What was happening? Inside I was screaming and kicking but my passive body hung limp as I was taken from my refuge and placed in the back of a car.

Again time slipped away from me. I was aware of shapes moving about me. There were noises in the background but nothing was within my grasp. I tried to speak and reach out but my body was immobile. Then I just gave in. Whatever was happening, I let it happen. My silent internal struggle had been futile so I gave up and let myself quietly slip into the quietest place my mind could find, to a retreat it had formed from the world around it. That was the place that started to heal me. From that place the world slowly started to take shape again.

I was startled to hear Keith's voice talking to me. He was talking about Raven House, telling me about parties and happenings of people long gone from the house. Inside, in this new place, I laughed with him as he told me these stories. As my brain reached out to hear his words, I heard him describe the elegance and beauty of a Raven House that was long dead. Then he stopped talking. I slipped into silence, occasionally hearing hushed and whispered tones but always unable to grasp the words.

Frustrated with myself I tried to ask him.

"Keith . . . where am I?"

"Melanie." It was Hugh.

Once more I slipped away confused but then I heard his voice again. It was clearer now.

"Melanie!"

"Yes?"

"Oh my God! Melanie! My God, you scared me."

He was crying. I could hear him crying but I still hadn't managed to open my eyes and focus them on the room around me. I could feel him holding my hand and squeezing my fingers gently. I was trying to squeeze back but I wasn't sure if he could feel it. Then I could hear other voices. Hugh's was getting further away.

"Hugh!" I called after him in panic.

"I'm here, sweetheart. The doctors just have to look you over and make sure you're okay."

"Doctors?" Once more panic overcame me. Where had he put me? Doctors – I didn't want to be in hospital. I wanted to get my life back on track.

Gradually the room swam into focus. I could see the grave-faced doctors and the smiling nurse hovering over me. Over their shoulders an ashen-faced Hugh couldn't take his eyes off me. I turned my head and saw a drip and heart monitor. My God, how sick did they think I was?

"Why am I here?" The words came out in a croak.

"You've been very ill, Melanie." The doctor was staring into my eyes while he spoke.

The doctors continued their checks and then they walked away, leaving me alone with Hugh and the nurse.

"Melanie, we're going to give you some peace now so you can rest," said the nurse. "Press this button if you want me." She indicated a button hanging from a cord by the bed.

"Thank you," I whispered, watching her walk away before I turned to Hugh. "Is this Bantry Hospital?"

"Yes."

"How did I get here?"

"I brought you here."

"What?"

"I was so worried about you. Your mobile had been switched off and the landline was dead in your house. I didn't know what to do so I went down to check on you. Your car was there but I got no answer at the door. I decided I had to go into the house and make sure everything was okay. I didn't know what else to do."

"How long have I been here?"

"I brought you in yesterday."

Only yesterday!

"Melanie, what's going on with you? You hadn't bathed in days; you were badly dehydrated and quite emaciated."

"You could have helped me without bringing me here." I knew I was being silly. Of course he had to get help. If anything happened to me he would be in trouble.

"I've been trying to help you for weeks but I haven't

been getting through to you. Maybe hospital is the best place for you."

I flinched when he said that. "It isn't. When Bobby comes back we'll sort it out together."

Hugh had tears in his eyes. At one time we'd been so much in love but now I was the crazy woman lying in front of him in a hospital gown. For me, nothing ever matched up to what we'd had the summer we left school but we gradually lost touch after that. I hadn't even known where he lived until the day I met him on the street when Ryan was away. Up until that moment I had been mesmerised by Ryan but when I met Hugh again a spark of what we had was still there. I told Ryan I'd bumped into an old friend and even though I'd played it down, somehow he knew that Hugh was more than just an old friend. A tiny crack appeared in my relationship with Ryan that day. I still loved Ryan but I sensed suspicion on his part. The girl he had put together in Raven House was brand new. He didn't like her finding a little piece of her old life. Now he was gone and Hugh thought I wasn't able to take care of myself.

I looked into his face. It was a kind and earnest face.

"Thank you. I know you were just trying to help."

"I was."

I searched his face for a glimmer of what we once had but there was nothing there except pity, naked pity.

"Stay here in hospital for a while, Melanie. I don't think you can care for yourself right now."

His words gave me a new sense of fear. I didn't want to be in hospital. I wanted to tell him about the lights and my prowler but I held back. After my previous attempt to get police help I was wary. Dancing lights, missing phones and car keys would make me sound incompetent.

"Hugh. Go away." I turned my back on him and closed my eyes.

Hugh got up and placed the palm of his hand on my shoulder. I didn't move. I couldn't take Hugh's pity. If he thought the best place for me was *a hospital* then I didn't want him there.

CHAPTER 29

I slept deeply that night even though I was periodically woken to check my vitals. At seven o'clock the next morning the ward came alive with breakfast trolleys rattling along the corridor, cleaning staff laughing and chatting to patients while they worked their way around our beds.

One with a kind face smiled at me.

"How are you this morning?"

"I'm well." I smiled back.

"That's good, honey. You take care of yourself."

A little later the breakfast trolley came to me.

"Did you fill out a breakfast card?" The grey-haired attendant frowned at her sheet of names. "Oh." She looked up. "Nil by mouth. Sorry." She wandered off.

I was starving and felt like pulling the drip out of my arm and ordering a Full Irish. I was totally aware of my surroundings. Life in Raven House was like looking though an old film noir but here reality was strong and vibrant. Flowers and get-well cards surrounded the two

232

beds opposite me. Chairs were pulled around the beds to facilitate the extra visitors these people had.

The ache in my stomach, which had become a part of my existence, came back. Loneliness was forever lurking somewhere inside, just needing a reminder to emerge into the open. My mind wouldn't focus on the loneliness but my body couldn't ignore it. All the despair I felt was stuffed in there in the pit of my stomach.

A nurse interrupted my thoughts.

"Good morning." Her eyes sparkled and a huge smile split her tiny face. "Your blood pressure is fine now. You gave us a shock when you came in."

"Was it high?" I was looking at the figures on the monitor screen.

"No. It was dangerously low. No wonder you couldn't get out of bed. Have you had low blood pressure before?"

"Not that I know of."

"Well, it's fine now. Your heart rate is a little high this morning but nothing to worry about. Do you take much exercise?"

"No." I felt sheepish.

"None of us take enough. Start taking more walks or do some yoga and it will help with that."

"I will."

She smiled kindly at me. "You hadn't eaten for days before you came in to us. Have you had a shock recently or any major stresses?"

"No," I lied. "Really. I'm fine. I'm starving now."

"I'll remove that drip for you and we'll get some food sent down for you. Then we'll check back on you later."

"Thank you."

"The doctor will be down to see you soon."

"When can I go home?"

"I don't know. The doctor will tell you that but it shouldn't be too long."

The nurse left and I lay back on my bed. Mine was the end bed. The one to my right had the curtains pulled right around it so it impaired my view. The two beds opposite were empty now. Their occupants had decided to take a stroll after breakfast.

My body odour was becoming offensive to me. I wanted a shower. I should have asked the nurse about that because now I couldn't get anyone's attention.

About thirty minutes later my breakfast arrived. It was the same woman who'd appeared earlier. She had no trolley this time and arrived with just a tray.

"Here you go. Enjoy it." She spun and walked away before I had a chance to ask about having a shower. It probably wasn't her business anyway.

I opened my food. Scrambled eggs lay congealing on a plain white plate flanked by dry cold toast. A glass of orange juice sat there with a little paper top on it. I took the paper off and took a long drink, thinking some orange juice might sharpen my appetite, which had dulled considerably since I saw the food. The orange juice was even worse. It tasted like weak vinegar. I put it aside before it got rid of my appetite completely. I knew if I wanted to get out of here soon I needed to eat. Trying not to think of the food I started chewing.

When I finished I lay back and dozed while I waited for the doctor to come around. The doctor arrived at my bed at about eleven o'clock and woke me. He was flicking through a chart and looking at my tray. When he saw my open eyes he looked intently into my face. I didn't know whether to smile or look away.

"Well, Melanie. You're not sick. Blood tests are fine. You're anaemic and quite underweight but your blood pressure and heart rate are back to normal now."

"Can I go home?" I expected him to say no. Surely he'd want to know why I wasn't eating or getting out of bed?

"I'd prefer if you'd stay a few more nights for observation."

"No. I'd prefer to go home. I have friends who will look in on me."

The doctor looked concerned but how can you ask a woman if she has a death wish or if she really has friends? "Be careful, Melanie. You need to take better care of yourself. If this happens again you'll be back in here."

I knew I needed to be careful. Somebody had tried to frighten me to death. Someone had been doing that for a while. If Hugh hadn't come into my house and taken me to the hospital I would have died in that room. Now I knew why I was in Raven House. Somebody wanted me dead. I didn't know who but I guessed they were not going to give up. Ryan had brought me down there for a reason so, if my death was the plan now, perhaps it was the plan then. None of it made sense to me yet but I knew without doubt somebody wanted me dead. If the truth was that Ryan had sought me out in Galway then it didn't matter where I went. There was nowhere to hide. Whoever it was wanted this so badly that they were willing to travel to find me.

I lay and wondered. Scaring me to death took time. Obviously this person didn't want anyone to see it as murder. He didn't want to get his hands dirty. He could have finished me off that night at the car or any number of nights in between. I know it was stupid but I decided to go back to Raven House and face whoever it was. If my killing myself had been the plan, well, I was no longer going to do that so perhaps they would show their hand and I could go to the Guards with evidence. I knew from personal experience that without hard evidence they wouldn't believe a word I said. I was also worried about what Hugh had said about me being in hospital. I didn't want to be confined.

I didn't have any clothes. I lay back and thought. The nurse from earlier came around the end of the bed. "I hear you're going home."

"Yes."

"The doctor wanted you to stay another night or two. Why don't you stay and let us keep an eye on you?"

"No. I'm leaving but I have no clothes."

"I can get you a few things. They're not classy but they are clean and they will cover you."

"I don't care. I want to get out of here."

"Okay. You wait here and I'll be back."

I wasn't happy about wearing God knows who's cast-offs but it was a small price to pay for getting away from that place.

By two thirty I was dressed and walking out the door wearing a pair of brown trousers, a cream sweatshirt and runners. The underwear and socks were new albeit paper and more likely designed for wearing to an MRI scan. Hugh had left me money for emergencies so it was enough to get me home.

Hurrying as fast as I could, I reached the bus stop by the waterfront. I should have taken a taxi because by the time I arrived I was feeling faint and out of breath.

I stood anxiously in line at the bus stop. I had only ten minutes for the bus.

At last the bus arrived and the line started to move forward. I bought a one-way ticket to Raven.

I found a seat, sat down and tried to get comfortable. I didn't have a lot of room to stretch my legs out but despite this almost immediately fell asleep.

The driver woke me sometime later shouting "Raven!"

CHAPTER 30

On shaky legs I stood up, thanked the driver and got off the bus. Then I stood on the footpath considering my options. Firstly, I would need a taxi to get out to my house because I was far too tired to walk. There was a small hotel just across the street from the bus stop. Changing my mind about the taxi, I decided to book in and stay overnight. I wasn't strong enough yet to go home. Here I could order food and be near people until I felt better. Tomorrow was soon enough to go home. I knew I should have stayed in hospital but I hated hospitals.

I walked inside. "Hello. My name is Melanie Yeats and I'm living at Raven House. I'm having work done at the house and I need to stay someplace tonight."

"Of course, Miss Yeats." The girl was very professional. "I'll need to take a credit-card imprint."

"I came down without it. I can pay cash for tonight or go back and get it."

"That's fine." She shook her head, clicking keys to see what they had available.

"We have a room." She handed me a card to fill out and my key.

I filled out the card. "Thank you."

I made my way upstairs to my room.

The room was small and boxy with unusually heavy furniture considering the size of the space it occupied. The wall was covered in heavy floral-print wallpaper. The carpet was a deep maroon colour. This room wasn't going to elevate my mood. It wasn't dark enough to go to bed. If I crawled in there now I would still see the hideous room with its blood-coloured carpet.

I went back downstairs to the dining room. The dining room wasn't too different from the bedroom but it was large with bay windows opening out into a cheerful little garden with a brook at one end. A mock waterwheel was built on the stream. I stood in the doorway watching the other diners and waited for the waitress to come over to me.

"Can I help you?" She spoke as though I was disturbing her favourite television show.

"Can I sit in the window?" I wanted to see the garden and not a replica of my room.

"Yes." The waitress turned and walked away.

I grabbed the menu from another table on the way over to the window, assuming that it might take my waitress a while to come back to me. I watched her walk back to the counter and continue on with the conversation I'd interrupted when I came down. She wouldn't be getting a tip.

I opened my menu. It took a moment for me to figure

out what I wanted. Comfort food – Shepherd's Pie was the first item on the menu. I sat back and waited for the cheerful one to come back to me. As usual I became lost in my own world so much so that the harsh voice of the waitress caused me to jump.

"Have you decided?"

I couldn't believe it. She was actually tapping her pen on the notebook.

To be awkward I looked at the menu again and pretended to consider.

"I'll come back."

"No need." I smiled sweetly at her. "Shepherd's Pie and a glass of red wine."

The waitress turned to leave.

"Thank you." My harsh tones matched hers and for a moment caused her to jump.

She turned and met the cold stare in my eyes. Slightly shaken she walked away.

I went back to staring out the window. The garden was lovely. It was straight out of an English country village. I could picture Miss Marple out there with a blooms basket and a pair of secateurs, snipping flowers for her parlour. Just to the left of the window and almost in front of me a fat blue hydrangea bush watched the dining spectacle inside.

A dish of food appeared promptly on the white tablecloth in front of my clasped hands. I looked up at my waitress, who actually smiled.

"Enjoy your food."

"Thank you." I raised my eyebrows slightly and smiled back.

The food really was delicious. It was a dubious colour,

lacking in any great variety of vegetable but the taste was wonderful. A young barman had just dropped my wine over as the waitress was leaving. It wasn't quite to the same standard as the food but I thought perhaps the lack of sophistication that led to such tasty unpretentious food was a kiss of death for a bottle of wine.

Once I was finished my meal I pushed back my plate, satisfied. Looking back out the window I could see that the garden was getting dark. Soon I could sleep upstairs without being afraid of opening my eyes and seeing that awful carpet.

"Would you like some coffee?" A different waitress with twinkling eyes picked up my plate.

"Yes, please. A cappuccino."

"Coming up." She used a little rubber scraper to clean crumbs off the tablecloth before she left.

True to her word the coffee arrived in a couple of minutes. I was surprised. It was excellent and just as I liked it, strong and frothy. I savoured it as the last of the light left the garden and all I could see now was my own reflection. By that time I was so tired I could barely keep my eyes open. I gave my room number to the waitress when she offered the bill and then I left the dining room.

As I climbed the stairs a creak punctuated each of my footsteps. On the stairs itself a strong floral carpet covered the central portion, clipped on by old-style brass clips, but when I turned the corner at the top of the stairs I was back on that blood-coloured carpet which stretched all the way to my room door. It was the serial killer's version of "Follow the Yellow Brick Road". What kind of mind could ever think it provided an attractive look?

Opening the door, I stepped over the threshold into my

room. I turned on the bathroom light, quickly washed my face and then used a little bottle of body lotion as a moisturiser. There was a tiny bottle of mouthwash, which was an adequate substitute for toothpaste.

When I was finished I returned to my bedroom and crawled into bed. The springs were old and offered no support. The pink nylon quilted spread felt rough against my cheek. I rearranged the sheet so the spread was kept away from my skin. That was the last thought I remembered. Even though it was just eight thirty I fell into a deep sleep. Even the presence in Raven House couldn't break through. That could be faced tomorrow.

Early the next morning before sunrise I lay in bed and thought back over the last few weeks. If it hadn't been for the mystery caller I wouldn't really be able to tie all the events together. Elizabeth and the house were one side of my situation and Ryan disappearing was the other. The caller originally called and told me about Ryan's death but since then he'd made reference to Elizabeth and the house. They were all connected and he wanted me to join the dots. He'd been in my house and seen the shrine and he was playing with me. I had almost played into his hands and allowed myself to die. For the next couple of hours I lay awake staring upwards into the darkness. I wondered if Ryan was now trying to kill me or if he had already been killed and I was next on somebody's list.

With no bags to pack, I was up, showered, dressed and ready to leave in just a few minutes once the sun was up. But breakfast was included in my room rate so I ordered a Full Irish and ate heartily. After I'd finished eating I made my way to the reception desk and checked out.

Physically I was feeling much better so I decided to walk home. It was about a mile and a half to the house. I expected that even walking slowly I would still get there in less than an hour.

The day was cold but bright and before I'd gone too far I had a headache due to the strain of my eye muscles squinting against the sun. The hedgerows were high and the road winding. There wasn't much of a verge if I needed to step in from a car but the road was quiet that morning and I was undisturbed. In the trees and bushes over my head birds whistled and sang, heralding my approach to whoever or whatever might be interested.

I stopped and drank it all in – the smell of the damp hedges and the country sounds. Life was good when the sun shone. As I listened I heard a thumping sound inside the fence. A rabbit. My father had once pointed that sound out to me when I was a little girl. It was thumping its back legs to warn the world that danger was lurking. Was it me or a skulking weasel that was causing him concern, I wondered?

Finally I approached the bottom of my driveway. It was late November now and soon the trees and bushes would be bare and dead. I feared that Raven House would be a grim place to be alone in the heart of winter. The huge iron gates stood open, their massive weight buried in the overgrowth under them. They would need a lot of work done on them before they could be closed again. It looked different when you were on foot – grander in a way, as the pillars loomed over my head, but also more sullen as I was closer to the weeds and decay that had seeped into the grand old estate.

I looked upwards at the house standing on its hill. It really seemed to tower above me. The house seemed bigger and quite intimidating.

I was tired by then so I wondered if it would be easier to follow the natural sweep of the drive, which wound over and back across the hill, or to climb straight up the hill. It made the climb steeper but the walk shorter. I decided to opt for the walk shorter but only managed to avoid the first turn in the road before I decided to follow the drive instead. It was a lot steeper than when I was in my car plus with the overgrowth of grass and weeds it took a lot out of me. By the time my feet crunched through the gravel and I approached the front door I was very tired. It was time for some lunch as soon as I was in and settled.

Before I went inside, just out of curiosity I decided to look for the path my prowler had emerged from that day when I was watching from the attic. I'd never had any reason to go down there before. It was a narrow sunken overgrown path through the shrubbery, no bigger than a rabbit track, which ran close to the side of the house. Bushes and trees had spread their branches and wrapped them around the house. Before I'd gone very far the path disappeared completely but you could still push your way through the bushes. My hair was standing on end as it was pulled and tangled by the branches crossing over my head.

Finally I pushed through the last tangle of growth and found myself in a small field beyond the house. It was bordered by the wall of the stable yard on one side, the woods on two sides and a tangle of undergrowth on the other. It was a little lost field with no apparent purpose. Unless the overgrowth was cleared away it was a useless space.

I couldn't even imagine what it was used for in the old days. Maybe it was an old lawn. Perhaps the ladies and gentleman from the past had played bowls or croquet out there on a Sunday afternoon. Now it was silent and serene in its tranquil obscurity. Retracing my steps I pushed my way back out towards the front of the house.

As I moved, once more back by the wall of the dwelling house, a tight knot of bushes growing against the wall caught my eye. From this side I could see a clear space behind the bushes. I looked around them and saw a door. I pulled back the heavy greenery with my hand. There were no thorns – it was just tangles of shrubbery. The door was set into the wall of the house and was quite rotten. I turned the handle and pushed. It opened directly into a passageway extending under the house. I could feel the cold and smell dampness. I was going to need to come back out here. This passage was too dark to search now.

I left the hidden door and went around the front and on to the other side of the house. There, I looked up at the window of my room. I tried to figure where my prowler would have stood. To my left a bank of huge rhododendron bushes stood, void now of their spring finery. I could see trampled grass between two towering plants where I guessed he might have stood. From where I stood there you could see down through the fields towards the river but from the direction the light came the huge plants concealed the view. There was no way that light came from a car. It was certainly held by mortal hands. In a moment of madness I found myself saying "I hope".

Walking on I skirted the backyard and the walled kitchen garden. It had a wooden door in the wall. I twisted the handle and the door stuck on the long grass. It was obvious immediately that this door hadn't been opened in years. The ground outside the door was undisturbed.

I continued on and entered the stable yard from the back gate. I went to the back door. Hugh had left it open. It was closed but not locked. I wondered as I entered the house how Hugh had got inside to take me out.

When I got inside and closed the door behind me I got the creepy feeling that the house sighed. Was it sighing with relief that I was back?

I walked to the kitchen. In a weird way I felt as though I'd survived the house. Hugh told me I could have died but I didn't, because he got in and saved me. Maybe the house saved those it cared about and I was one of those. Maybe the house summoned Hugh. I started to laugh. Perhaps I was merging with the house.

In the kitchen I grabbed my flash-lamp and went back outside to the old door I'd found earlier. Inside the door I turned on the lamp and followed the length of the passage. A couple of doors opened off it. I flashed the light into them but they were just old storerooms long forgotten. The passageway seemed to stretch right under the house. Then I guessed its purpose. That garden was probably as I suspected a formal garden for parties and picnics. This was the servants' corridor for bringing refreshments out to the guests. I knew the passage would emerge into the kitchen. There it was – up a few steps in a narrow stairwell – a strong wooden door with a brand-new lock fitted to it. This was how someone was getting into my house and only someone who knew the house very well would know it existed.

I returned to the house and looked around the kitchen. There was certainly no doorway there, hidden or otherwise. I went into the pantry and looked around. No, there was nothing there either apart from the stairs leading up to the servants' quarters. I went into the scullery next door. Nothing. I was just about to leave when I looked at a set of shelves to the side of the little room. On an impulse I walked to that and pulled at it. It easily swung outwards revealing a door flush with the wall. This was the way into my house and where my visitor probably went that day. I shut my eyes for a second and swayed. The night the light shone at me from the scullery flashed back into my mind. That light came from inside the house and not through the window. Someone had been in the house with me!

I put together my lunch and took it out to the front step and there I sat, looking down into the valley. It was time for me to start putting steps in place to get away from Raven House. The first thing I needed was a job and then I needed to find a new place to live. I'd had my wake-up call and I wasn't going to waste any more time. I sat in the afternoon sun until it started to dip behind the mountains. Then I got up and brushed crumbs off my clothes. I needed to go upstairs, have a shower and burn those awful clothes.

After my shower and change I felt more human. To give myself something to do I started preparing dinner. Food preparation could be dragged out for hours and it helped to give form and purpose to my day. I realised how empty life would be without food. It was a simple tomato-based sauce with spaghetti but the whole meal took hours to prepare. I chopped the veggies into tiny rectangles, meticulously measuring them. As I did this I sipped my wine.

I laid the table in my usual spot and slowly ate my dinner. Fred the rubber plant was back on the counter with me. By the time I'd finished I'd also finished my first bottle of wine and without a second thought I'd opened another bottle. Fred got more talkative as I drank and fear of my prowler dissipated.

Desperate for the feeling of peace I'd had earlier, I took my wine and Fred outside again to the front step and sat there drinking, looking down at a cluster of lights twinkling in the distance. I wondered were those the lights of Raven? Were those people drinking too? Maybe they were all sitting around playing Scrabble. No, the lucky bastards were watching television, not sitting on the doorstep with a plant.

Why couldn't I get my life in order, I wondered, and get a television? Then I wouldn't need to drink. Television was drug enough for most people. As I lamented the loneliness of my life without television, I heard a car approaching. I assumed it would continue on past my driveway but no, it turned up the hill and I could hear the engine labouring on the steep incline.

Hugh.

Too drunk to care that he was going to catch me drinking alcohol when I should be drinking protein powders and going to bed with my hot-water bottle I sat defiantly on the step watching him.

He got out of his car. I stood up and waddled towards him.

Hugh stood with his head down. "What am I going to do with you?"

"I can think of something." I nuzzled my cheek against his and tried to put my arms around him. Instead he held my hands by my side and we stood like that for a moment. I was suddenly absolutely sure of what would make me feel better so I turned my face and sought his lips. For a moment he pushed me away but I wiggled my way back into his arms until he was kissing me back. This time there was no pity in his face. He too had found some of the old feelings we'd once shared.

"Since you've come this far you may as well stay." I led him by his hand into the hall, stopping to pick up Fred. He wasn't built for the great outdoors. I dumped the plant in the centre of the hall and walked towards the stairs.

"We can't get into this again," Hugh said but followed me nonetheless straight across the hall and up the stairs.

CHAPTER 31

I stretched and felt a pair of arms wrap tighter around me. For a moment my heart skipped. Who was I in bed with? Then I groaned as I remembered Hugh's arrival. He heard the groan and correctly interpreted its meaning.

"Is it that bad waking up with me?"

"Under the circumstances. Yes."

"Why."

"I was very drunk."

"Don't worry. I was safe." He showed me a box of condoms.

"They're sealed! Did you carry them with you? That was a bit presumptuous."

"They were in your bathroom and they are sealed because you fell asleep."

"Sorry about that."

"We cuddled." He corrected himself. "I cuddled. You snored."

"Thanks." I pinched the tender spot on his arm.

"I wish you wouldn't do that." He squeezed me tighter and kissed the back of my neck.

"What day is it?" I really didn't know.

"Are you serious?"

"Yes."

"It's Friday."

"So are you leaving now for work?"

"No. I'm taking the day off. I'm going to take you out for breakfast. We can go to that funny little hotel in Raven."

"Lovely." I'd had enough of that funny little hotel in Raven.

"We can go somewhere else if you like."

"No. It's fine. I'm just waking up."

"Now that you're sober we can . . ." He stopped talking and went back to kissing the back of my neck.

I kissed his arm and sat up. "I don't want to complicate things. I'm sorry."

"That's okay."

Hugh didn't sound okay.

He sat up and swung his legs out the other side of the bed. We sat like that for a couple of minutes and then I got up and went to my dressing room.

I gathered together clothes for the day and went to have a shower. On the way I saw that Hugh was lying back down on the bed with his arm over his face.

As soon as I was dressed Hugh passed me and went into the bathroom, shutting the door firmly behind him. I went downstairs with my bag to wait for him. I sat on the end of the stairs watching a dusty ray of sunshine through the porch window. We'd forgotten to close the inside door.

I could see why he was annoyed. I tried to seduce him

last night and then I fell asleep and now in the morning I wanted none of it, not when I was sober. In the cold light of day and without the influence of alcohol it just didn't seem like such a good idea. I was very confused. First I was mourning my lost love Ryan and in such a short space of time I was rekindling an old love.

His footsteps echoed down the hall so I stood up and walked towards the door.

"I have to go into work." He couldn't look at me.

"But we were going for breakfast." I reached for him.

"Sorry." He pecked me on the cheek. "I have to go." Sidestepping my embrace, he went straight out the door and climbed into his car.

I walked over and stood beside the car. "What did I do?" Though I knew.

"Nothing." He seemed really glum.

"Are you sure you can't have breakfast?"

"Yes, Melanie. I'm sure. Last night was a bad idea."

I smiled. "Nothing happened."

"They say the thought is as good as the deed."

"Did you have bad thoughts?" I tried to joke about it.

"Stop it, Melanie. It's not funny."

"Fine. Go then."

"I will." He put the car into gear and drove off.

I watched his wheels throw gravel up in the air as he sped away. A knot of fear twisted in my stomach. A deep hole was opening under me and sucking me in. What was I doing? Without Hugh I had nobody left. I ran to the top of the drive. I used to do that when I was little. Dad would drive away and I'd stand in tears and wait until he came back for me. He always did come back but I could never understand why he didn't just take me with him in the first place. Maybe Hugh was punishing me. He'd get as far as Raven and realise how much I needed him and come back.

I stood there for twenty minutes but there was no car to be heard. Then I moved back to the house and sat on the step. Still there wasn't a sound. After an hour I saw the futility in my waiting. Freezing cold, I stepped back inside, shutting the door, and made my way to the kitchen for breakfast.

After breakfast I felt even more despondent. I decided that today I would have to take steps to change my life. I suddenly had a longing to go home to Galway. That was home, not Raven House.

I pottered about the kitchen washing dishes and doing some light cleaning. Living down here I was buried. It was time for me to move on.

My thoughts were already on going home. While I cleaned I opened a drawer in the dresser and there were my mobile phone and car keys. The battery in the mobile was dead. I put the phone in my back pocket, grabbed the keys and went outside to check my car hadn't been damaged. It looked fine but I immediately knew someone else had been sitting in it recently. The seat was further back than it should have been and the mirror had been adjusted differently. I guessed that whoever had sat in here before me was considerably bigger. Feeling nervous I started the engine and drove around to the stable yard to check fuel and the brakes. The last thing I wanted was the car to crash on that steep hill. I was ready to chide myself for my overactive imagination. I drove into the stable yard and hit the brakes but the car skidded on and hit the stable wall. I hadn't been going quickly enough to cause much damage but the bonnet was crumpled and the car certainly would need a bit of fixing.

I got out and locked the door though it wouldn't be going anywhere in that state. I let myself in through the back door.

As I was going upstairs I heard a car pulling up to the house. I knew it was Hugh. I rushed back down, opened the door and ran outside.

"Thank God! I think someone is trying to kill me."

"What? Slow down." Hugh looked bewildered.

"The brakes are gone in my car."

Hugh stared. "Maybe it's mechanical failure."

"No! Someone is trying to scare me to death."

"All right. Where is the car?" He sounded weary.

"Round the back"

"Get into my car and we'll go around and take a look at it."

Silently I walked around to the other side and sat into the passenger seat. My phone slipped out of my pocket. I remember placing it on the seat beside me. Hugh started the engine and drove around to the stable yard. He stopped and got out to look at the damage.

I started talking again. "Somebody was shining lights in my window last week. They hid my mobile phone, car keys and had the landline disconnected. That was why I got sick. I locked myself in my room. I was terrified. And now this!" I pointed to the car.

"So why did you come back out here? If you were so terrified?"

He was right.

"Calm down, Melanie. Tell me everything."

Words spilled out and I told him everything, going right back to the assault outside the house, my dream during Bobby's visit, being watched and followed, everything.

My eyes stared into Hugh's searching his face for

reassurance. He looked confused and completely at a loss as to how to reassure me. His blue eyes looked down into mine. They seemed upset and earnest in their wish to comfort me.

But there was something else. He didn't believe me.

My eyes were knit in a frown as I walked after Hugh towards the house. He led me to the kitchen.

My unease was growing. Hugh thought I was cracking up. I wondered was he thinking about hospitals now.

He took charge immediately in the kitchen and went to the coffee pot. I sat and watched him refill the filter and fill the reservoir with water. What was happening to me? There were days when I couldn't remember what I'd done all day. Probably nothing and it's hard to remember the details of nothing.

Hugh had finished making the coffee and brought it to the counter.

"Don't look so scared!" he said. "We'll sort it out. As soon as we've had our coffee we'll get onto it. We'll find someplace else for you to live."

I nodded but said nothing, sipping my coffee.

I sat there nursing my cup and frowning at the wall.

Hugh was behaving as though it was all just a silly little mistake that could be sorted out. I knew he was humouring me.

"Let's go for a walk." Hugh was an active person. "It will help you to clear your head. What's out that way?" He pointed to the back of the house.

"Nothing worth seeing." I wanted to keep that little forgotten wood for me alone.

He gestured to the front of the house. "The road down below is quite narrow if there were any traffic. I don't think it's safe for walking."

"There's a wood a couple of miles away by road. We could drive there, take a walk and then have dinner on the way back."

"Excellent idea. I'll get my jacket. You get yours too. It may be cold."

I felt a little uncomfortable but I couldn't pinpoint why. In just a few hours Hugh was seeping into my life and taking over. It felt like he had an agenda.

After what happened to my car we had to take Hugh's.

"Are you okay, pet?" Hugh looked at me with a look of pity you'd bestow on a small child.

Once more that uncomfortable knot in my stomach welled up. None of this felt right. Was I uncomfortable because Hugh was providing me with a reflection of what I was really like? If I could sit across from myself now like Hugh was doing, would I pity what I saw too?

I sat looking out the window, trying to squeeze my eyes tight so my tears couldn't flow. During moments like this the sharpness and clarity of thought I possessed hurt me. It was a stainless-steel knife dissecting my soul and then showing me the pieces. Something was wrong. I didn't know if the problem lay within me or if there was a reason not to trust Hugh.

Hugh seemed to read my thoughts. He reached across and held my right hand, squeezing my fingers gently.

"I'll take care of you."

I had been aiming towards taking care of myself. Should I just lie back for a while and pass the whole mess over to Hugh to sort for me? Would I be stronger further down the road?

After just ten minutes in the car we pulled into the car park of the local National Forest. I'd driven by there numerous times but being lazy I'd never stopped. We got out and together walked towards the wooden gate leading onto the forest track.

For a few minutes we walked together in silence. We were each lost in our own thoughts. Hugh spoke first.

"We'll have you out of here soon."

"I know. I was going to do it myself when I tested my brakes."

"What were you going to do?"

"I was going to move back up to Galway. Move back into the house, get a job, get my life back on track."

"That sounds like a good idea." But he looked sad as he spoke.

"Do you think so?" I was feeling suspicious again. He still seemed to have another agenda he wasn't revealing to me yet. I sensed something, an undercurrent. I had an uneasy feeling that something else was going on and I couldn't see what it was.

"Can you trust your own judgement now?" This sounded more like Hugh, always worrying.

"Of course I can." I frowned when I answered him.

He raised his eyebrows and looked down into my upturned face. "Really?"

Again I felt a rising panic. Something very obvious was here in front of me but I couldn't quite put my finger on it.

"Of course. I made a mistake staying down here. I'm alone."

"You don't own the house so you can just pack up and leave." He leaned down and kissed me on the cheek and then hugged me tightly.

"We wouldn't work as a couple. You know that, don't

you?" I held his hand, using it to put a barrier between us. I met his gaze.

Hugh tore his hand and eyes away. He walked ahead of me down the path and stopped for a moment. I followed him.

"I'm sorry," I said. "But you know it's true."

He seemed to be having a deep struggle within himself. "Yes, Melanie, I know it's true. It's been a long time."

"What?"

"Let's just forget about it and walk." He walked and I jogged to keep up with him.

"Did you think we were going to get back together someday?" I asked.

"I said drop it!" he said, his tone elevated.

"Please." I held his arm.

He ripped it out of my grasp and spoke directly into my face. "I said leave it!"

He seemed so upset. I saw his face was snow white and he was trembling. This wasn't a spur-of-the-moment reaction. I knew he had seriously thought that we might get back together some time. Now that I'd told him that this could never happen something turned in him and made itself known to me. Something I'd never seen before.

But I was upset too. I walked in silence, keeping a discreet distance between us. I'd never meant to hurt him. I'd lost him once and now that he was back in my life I didn't want to lose him again.

The walk that we picked was a loop and it took about thirty minutes to get back to the car. We barely uttered a word as we walked. We climbed into the car and Hugh started the engine without mentioning food and I was too nervous to bring up the subject of eating. I sat back, trying to keep an eye on Hugh without turning my head. In the confined space it was obvious he was a boiling mass of emotion and it made my body tingle.

We drove towards Raven. Without asking me what I wanted to do Hugh pulled into a space outside the Raven Hotel. He got out and stood by his door, waiting for me to get out so he could lock the car. When I was standing on the street he turned and walked into the hotel, leaving me to follow behind.

As I was walking I glanced down the street to the filling station and saw Keith standing in his work overalls at the fuel-yard gate. He was staring down the street towards us. The intensity of his stare frightened me. I followed Hugh inside.

When I caught up with Hugh he gently took my hand. I couldn't understand this tenderness. It made my heart ache.

"A table for two, please," he said to the waiter, then he turned and smiled with a sweet sadness in his eyes.

We were led to the same table by the window where I sat the night I stayed in the hotel. We sat with neither of us speaking while we were handed menus and our water glasses were filled. I was too bewildered to speak. Hugh had effectively cut me out of the picture. He was looking out the window with the same sad intensity. The waiter returned.

"Do you need a moment?"

"No. I know what I want – the steak. How about you?" His voice was so tender.

I jumped. "Shepherd's Pie and a glass of wine."

"I'm afraid that's not on the menu today."

"Sorry," I stammered. For a moment my mind had turned back to the menu from my previous meal. I looked back at the list of food. The first thing I saw was Chicken Kiev.

"Chicken Kiev." I smiled and handed up the menu.

"And the wine?"

"Red. I prefer red."

"Thank you." The waiter gathered the menus and walked away.

Hugh smiled. "We can rent a DVD and watch that tonight if you like."

"No. We can't. I don't have a television."

"Oh." Again Hugh's face fell and his mind disappeared to another place. He seemed really down.

I was confused. I had rejected the idea of us getting back together so I expected anger but not this palpable sadness that was wafting across the table.

The hour dragged on. The meal tasted like rubber to me. Inside I was crying but on the outside I was carrying on the same charade as Hugh. When we'd had our coffee and paid the bill, Hugh walked to my side and pulled back my chair.

Together we walked out of the restaurant. As we passed the desk Hugh held my hand but he couldn't catch my eye.

All of this was very confusing.

Afterwards, thinking back, I wondered why I didn't see that something awful was happening. My life had been so "through the looking glass" lately that I was starting to behave like a spectator in my own world. Why was I going along with this sham? Fear and pride. I was too proud to admit my old friend was pulling away from me. I was too terrified to confront him because it was unexpected and I was afraid that this was the end.

CHAPTER 32

The drive back to the house was done in silence. When we stopped outside the door we sat in the darkness. Finally I had enough so I turned to him.

"Hugh, I think you should leave. It's not a good idea for you to stay here this weekend." I couldn't cope with the undercurrents.

He turned so quickly when I spoke that I reacted in fear and threw my head back, banging it off the window. He spoke with his face just millimetres from mine. I could smell his breath and feel it against my lips.

"I'm staying." He spoke quietly but his body language was threatening.

"But you're upset. Why do you want to stay?"

He put his hand up and grabbed my chin, turning my head towards him. "You're not safe by yourself. You know you can't cope."

"I've been doing fine." My voice rose.

"Yes. That's why you landed in hospital. Because you were taking such good care of yourself."

Was he mocking me?

I wanted to answer back but I couldn't speak. Again the feeling that something was right in front of me that I couldn't reach numbed me. Something sinister was in the dark part of my mind. It was in the shadows surrounding us, weaving itself in and out of my vision but never quite revealing itself.

"What are you looking at?" Hugh said.

"It's dark. I'm not looking at anything."

"You're looking inwards. I wonder what you see."

Was I looking inwards? I was light-headed with the stress of the previous few hours.

"I want to go inside. I want something to drink."

"You can't fix everything with a bottle."

I jumped. How did he know about my drinking? It hadn't been something I'd broadcast. Was I that transparent?

"Come on, let's go inside," he said softly.

I obeyed.

Hugh walked to the porch door and waited for me to come and open the door for him. I opened the door and stepped back.

"After you." He insisted I go first. Was he nervous I'd run off in the dark?

I walked ahead and straight to the kitchen. I was having one drink, whatever he thought. I filled a large glass of red wine and carried it and the bottle to my sitting room. He walked in and sat opposite, staring at me. I took a sip and tried to avoid his gaze but I was drawn back to his eyes. He didn't speak but just watched me, hardly blinking.

Finally he broke the silence. "Do you remember when your mother died?"

I shouted at him, "Shut up!" I could feel my eyes were blazing.

He knew I never talked about that. I wouldn't let him bring that up. Not even Hugh was allowed to go there.

"I just wanted you to think about it for a minute, that's all."

"Why?"

"I want to talk about some things with you."

"What things?"

"You know what things I'm talking about." He still spoke softly but I started shaking. "I won't talk about it!" I heard myself scream the words at him.

"You're just going to hide from your life forever?"

I threw my glass at the wall beside the fireplace and met his gaze. "I told you to shut up."

Faster than I ever imagined he could move Hugh jumped from his seat and grabbed me. Too stunned to react I sat back on the couch. At the last minute I tried to get away from him but he held my hands tightly.

"That's better. Let's have a conversation."

I nodded, unable to tear my eyes away from his.

"Do you remember you fell apart in your teens, when we were in school? That's what broke us up."

Of course I did and I remembered clearly when my mother died. But it was pushed to the furthest recesses of my mind. I never wanted to examine the memories but when they came out they were clear enough. During my years at school, I realised how completely alone I was, I just lost my grip a bit. It's very unsettling when you have nowhere to turn.

My relationship with Hugh was collateral damage. Now it hurt me to even take a look at the corner of that memory as he explored it. I knew death was there, boiling underneath, polluting my life, but I didn't want to see it.

"I was a child. What's it got to do with now?"

"You're doing the same thing now. You're burying things, trying to protect yourself, but it doesn't work. You know it doesn't work. You know the demons are still there."

Bastard! I shouted in my head, too terrified to say it out loud. I wanted him to go away, to stop dragging up my childhood when it had nothing to do with him.

He continued speaking softly to me. "Death is in your life now too and you're covering it up with booze and isolation. You need to say it out loud."

"Shut up." My voice was weaker now.

"Melanie, you were a little girl but you blamed yourself for your mother's death. She *fell*."

I was trembling. My mother had fallen but it was my fault. I was throwing a screaming tantrum and I twisted to get out of her grip as we went down the steps from the street into our garden. She lost her footing. My mother was wearing kitten heels and they slipped off the step. She couldn't right herself and hit her head on the kerb. She died instantly.

I sat there, staring at her wide-open eyes. It was just seconds since I'd been shouting up at that face and now I was looking down into it still and soft, life fading from it in front of me. I killed my mother. I never told anyone. Everyone thought it was an accident. The taxi driver had his back turned, placing our shopping near the front door. When he turned around he saw a little girl sitting on the path stroking her mother's cheek. Nobody saw me kill her but I knew I did. Later when the memories and the guilt wouldn't go away I had a breakdown. I never told anyone except Hugh. He tried to make me see it was a tragic accident but it wasn't. There are no such things as accidents and for every action there is a reaction and my life since then had been a reaction.

Hugh knew what I was thinking. He let me ruminate for a few moments and then he spoke again. "I know all about this house, Melanie, and why you're here."

"What?" A deep knot of fear gnawed at me. Now the dark thing I'd suspected to be with us was coming to the surface. His words were echoes of the voice on the phone.

"This house is up for sale. You saw that. You're squatting here, Melanie. I checked when you asked me to look into the ownership of the house for you. I spoke to the estate agent and they are not aware of you or *Ryan*."

Something exploded in me. I screamed and lunged at him, clawing my nails across his cheek. I could see the angry red lines etched into his flesh. A tiny trickle of blood escaped and ran down to his jaw. He grabbed me and pushed me back onto the couch, pressing his full body weight on top of me. I couldn't get him off me. He subdued me until he felt me stop struggling. Then he sat back on his chair.

"Why are you saying these things to me?" I said. "I'm not squatting. Obviously Ryan lied to me. I'm living here in good faith." My outburst of energy had drained me and now I sank limply against the arm of the chair.

"Melanie, I'm going to get some help for you. If you don't get out of this house you will be arrested. I shouldn't be here with you. The owners have already sent a man up here to check the house over and he guessed you were here. He rang the owner to say he thought someone was staying in the house. I have a friend in the estate agents who are selling this house. They told me that you visited them asking who owned it. They sent someone out a few days ago to take a look around. I asked them to give me some time."

"Some time for what?" I asked. I wanted to scream, to cry. What was Hugh trying to do to me? I wasn't squatting. This was my home. I moved in here in good faith. A black fear had started to close in on me but I was pushing it back. It was all lies. Everything he said was a lie. That was what I had said about Ryan and now I heard myself saying the same things about Hugh. Was anyone telling me the truth?

"Why are you saying these things to me?"

"You bury everything you don't want to face, don't you, Melanie?" His tone was soft and pointed.

"What do you mean?" I was seeing the thoughts shift and realign again in my head. This was going to be bigger. Whatever he was trying to do now was going to tear me apart. A cold sweat was breaking out on my back and my eyes were fixed on a spot above his head. I couldn't move them. My eyes were rooted in the wall. A whooshing sound started in my ears and I was sure I was going to faint.

"Where's Bobby?"

"Bobby is away." My lips barely moved.

"He's not, Melanie. Where's Bobby?" He spoke more firmly now.

"He's away. Working." I spoke a little louder.

Hugh looked sick. "Unbelievable." He muttered to himself and shook his head.

"He's away. Working." I said it louder again and then again. "Working."

Hugh pulled a folded piece of newspaper out of his pocket and threw it across to me. It landed on the floor between us. I sat there and didn't move.

"Pick it up." He spoke softly but with no room for argument.

I grabbed it and went back to my seat but I wouldn't look at it.

"What does it say, Melanie?"

I shook my head.

"Read it, Melanie, please. Read the paper, Melanie." It was like he was coaxing a child.

I opened the folded piece of newspaper and smoothed it out on my knee. As the words swam in and out of focus in front of me and realisation finally came back, the world turned black and I lost consciousness.

CHAPTER 33

When I came to he was holding my hand. I felt as though I were going to be sick.

"Melanie. He's dead. Bobby is dead."

The pain was unbearable. I sat there as rigid as stone.

"Melanie. Speak to me."

I turned to him but I still couldn't speak.

"You remember now, don't you? He died in custody."

I did. I remembered getting the call. It was the Department of Justice calling to tell us that Bobby had killed himself while in custody. He was in custody awaiting an extradition hearing about being returned to Boston to stand trial for the death of Elizabeth Renfield.

Bobby was home on one of his rare visits. The authorities somehow must have co-ordinated the arrest to coincide with this. I tried to remember the details. He'd been home twice that year. Once at the end of a contract and then as far as I could remember he'd gone on a short trip and come back but this time for a little longer. The irony of it was that the extradition order most likely wouldn't have been granted. Bobby hadn't been charged with anything, they had no DNA evidence but they did have enough witness testimony from the bar for an arrest warrant to be issued. Bobby would be going to the US to be "investigated", not charged, and our solicitor told us that wasn't permitted under the Extradition Act. But Bobby didn't wait to see it through. He died while his solicitor was seeking bail on his behalf.

My head hurt. I couldn't speak. Hugh brushed my hair back off my forehead and went to the kitchen to make me coffee. My mind held as much information as the pages had done. But around the perimeters of that, buried deeper in the recesses and folds, I knew more details and starker images lay and I couldn't face them. It was like looking at a book, knowing what the title told you, maybe scanning the blurb on the back but not knowing what lay between the covers. I wasn't ready to read the text yet.

When Hugh came back I was still sitting silent and dry-eyed gazing into space. I knew he was worried in case I was becoming catatonic.

"Here, Melanie. Take this." He held out the cup to me.

As I held it up to my mouth a strong smell of whiskey assaulted my nostrils. Lord, make me a teetotaller, but not just yet, I thought and then started laughing. Hugh's eyes opened wide in shock. Laughter was not what he was expecting.

"Are you okay?" He sounded really worried.

I nodded to put him out of his misery and drank my coffee.

"So I have to leave the house then?" I said, stating the obvious.

"Yes. On Monday a sheriff will be here to take you off the land by force if you don't leave with me."

"That friend in the estate agents must be a close one."

"She is." He looked nervous.

"She! So what was going on with us the last couple of days?" I watched him squirm.

"Don't go there, Melanie."

"Now it's all right not to go places: when it's your places."

I wanted to hit him again. He'd cleaned up the blood off his face and neck but my scratches were still red and angry.

He changed the subject. "We need to figure out where you're going to go."

"I could live with you."

He reacted like I'd scratched him again. "Melanie! Be serious."

"Who says I'm joking?" I enjoyed making him uncomfortable. Already I was pushing Bobby back into the depths of my mind.

"I know you are. But this is serious. You have to be out of here by Monday and somewhere safe. If not they will get the authorities involved."

Something about the way he said "*the authorities*" gave me pause. He was still talking in half-truths and double meanings, I could feel it.

"Are you keeping something from me?" I meant it to come out as a direct question but my voice broke and the words came out in a croak.

Hugh couldn't meet my eyes. For a few moments we sat there in silence. A deep sadness filled me. Even though I wasn't facing my troubles they were defiling every part of my life.

This was a moment of profound change and the breaking down of the old and the ringing in of the new always filled me with dread. I'd spent my life blocking out the past and had somehow never developed the ability to see the future. The future was a grey shadow, thick and murky up ahead which always rooted me in my tracks.

"When do I have to leave?" I asked.

"We need to leave tomorrow or the police will be here first thing on Monday morning."

"Are you staying with me tonight?"

"Yes." Again he looked sheepish.

"Is that why you came back? They sent you back to baby-sit me, didn't they? The owners and the estate agents or whoever you're working with."

"It's not like that."

"Oh yes, it is. You left here this morning and went to them whoever they are and told them that you couldn't deal with me. They threatened me, didn't they, with prison, maybe, unless you came back to get me out quickly and cleanly?"

"Melanie –"

I interrupted him. "You were only out here at all to keep an eye on me."

"We've been friends a long time. My loyalties are to you."

"You were going to sleep with me the other night. Was that a fringe benefit?"

"Of course not." He was getting angry now and a little embarrassed.

"What is your connection with this estate agent?" I wanted to see him squirm when he said "girlfriend".

"I do some work with them from time to time."

I knew he was lying. I could hear it in his voice and I didn't imagine it when he said "she" earlier.

"Is *she* a good boss?"

"Will you stop? What are you doing?"

I didn't know. This conversation had circled around my mother, Bobby, me squatting in the house and now my relationship with Hugh in the space of minutes and I was exhausted.

"I'm going to bed. She did say I can sleep there for one more night, didn't she?"

"Yes."

"How big of her."

"I'm going to sleep down here on the couch. Do you have a sleeping bag or extra blankets?"

"There's a bed upstairs."

"Melanie, I'm not sleeping in your bed!" He shouted it at me.

I saw red and screamed back at him, "I have one spare room with a bed in it!"

I jumped up and ran from the room, slamming the door back so hard against the wall I heard the handle stick in the plaster. It didn't matter. It wasn't my wall. I didn't stop running until I got to my room. *Their* room, I corrected myself. I started to sob.

Hugh didn't follow me and eventually I wore myself out and slept.

CHAPTER 34

I woke very early the next morning with the sick feeling of forgotten bad dreams. For a moment I lay and thought over the previous night and bit by bit it all came back. The tears returned as I realised that this was my last morning waking in that bed but it wasn't because I was strong and moving on, it was because I was being pushed. My life was like one of those nightmares you try hard to recall but the details are lost.

I showered, dressed and went downstairs. I assumed Hugh was still in the sitting room. I stood in the hall and looked at the now closed sitting-room door. I went next door instead to the kitchen.

In the kitchen I made coffee and toast and ate it sitting at the counter.

Hugh must be so angry with me. I poured a second cup of coffee and decided to go and have one more look at Elizabeth's shrine. I had decided to show it to Hugh as final proof that I wasn't *squatting* here as he'd said. I walked to the corridor and then I saw it, a small pool of dark liquid under the door. I let my eyes travel upwards to the handle. There was a dark smudge on the right side. Mesmerised I reached for the door. The dark pool was blood; I could tell when I got closer. The smudge by the handle was the same. My heart was on pause, afraid to beat.

Trembling, I turned the handle and opened the door. I stepped through the door and slipped on the blood. I found myself on my hands and knees on the stone flags. I could smell death. I tried to stand but slipped again, banging my head off the door frame. I think I blacked out for a couple of moments.

When I came to I was lying on my side looking at a mass of blood. When I pulled back I saw it was Hugh. I found myself looking directly into what was left of his face. It was almost unrecognisable.

We were both lying on the ground. His eyes were wide open and staring into mine, the white stark against the rawness of his flesh. I crawled backwards with my hands in his blood and placed my back against the wall. I stared at him.

A poker lay on the ground by his head. It was covered in blood. Pools of blood had oozed out of him and flowed across the stone floor. The blood was lying all around me and I was drenched in it.

Then I saw the knife. It was still in his chest.

I left it there. It's still there, probably with my fingerprints on it. It was the same knife I'd taken upstairs with me as a weapon the night the person was outside my house with the light.

I couldn't touch him but I was tainted with his blood.

It stuck and clung to my clothes and my body. I tried rubbing it away but it just spread against my skin.

I didn't scream or even cry. I hadn't any sounds in me. My hands and clothes were covered in blood. Nobody would believe that I hadn't done this. I wasn't that far removed from reality. But then I started to wonder, who did hurt him? For all I knew the killer could still be there, in the house with me.

Someone had been with me all the time, in step with me as I walked in the woods and wandered about the house. Their eyes were on me through everything I did. I'd felt it. But why hurt Hugh? What had he done? I'd expected it would be me that got hurt.

I stood up. His car keys were sitting on the floor by his side. There must have been a struggle. His phone was there also. I picked up his car keys, remembering my own car was damaged. I just wanted to get out of there. Whoever killed Hugh could still have been there. Hugh's car was parked out front so I ran down the back corridor and out to the front of the house, slamming the door behind me.

Everything becomes a blur after that until I got here.

PART III

BOSTON, SEPTEMBER 10TH 2007

The Brother

Bradley Renfield remembered dropping a handful of clay onto the lid of his sister's coffin. He heard it clunk onto the polished wood. He didn't cry. Grown men didn't cry. He looked around at the assembled group. It was a large funeral. Elizabeth loved a party so she would have been proud. Bradley wanted to believe that her spirit was there with them but he feared that too. He feared that she would blame him for what had happened.

At the party the night of the crash he'd seen the state Gordon was in and knew that he was angry and insecure. Everybody in the room including Gordon knew that it was the end for the young couple. Elizabeth had let it go on too long. She liked to play games but she'd outgrown that one.

Bradley should have thrown the bum out that night and Elizabeth could have stayed at the party but instead he brought the whole explosive mix to a head and got his sister killed. The last feeling he'd had towards his sister *was anger. She was too young and volatile to handle what Bradley had known would be a difficult break-up.*

Susan and Donald Renfield had stood to the side of the grave, silently watching as clay landed on their daughter. His mother was pale and drawn as she leaned against her husband's arm. They had adored their little girl. Bradley knew they would never get over losing her and they didn't. In just a few years they were both dead and he was the only Renfield left, the only one left to continue seeking justice for Elizabeth.

Everything he'd done for the majority of his adult life was to try and find the man who drove that car. He'd spent a small fortune on bribing police and hiring investigators but all his efforts were futile. It was as though the guy had vanished into thin air. It was quite likely he would never find him and Bradley knew it. It kept him awake at night and was gradually affecting his health. When the autopsy results had been made known after Elizabeth's death he discovered that she had smoke in her lungs. That bastard burned her alive and if it took him the rest of his life Bradley was going to make him pay. If he didn't, one day he would have to face Elizabeth and his parents in the next world without finding the justice he'd fought so hard for and what could he say to them?

Then the letter arrived. Bradley was sitting at his desk flicking through the post when the Irish stamp caught his attention. Intrigued, he tore it open. Immediately the child-like handwriting leapt out at him. He read through it, unable to believe what he was seeing. At first he thought it must be a joke. The story of Elizabeth's death was well known in the city and over the years his search had turned up many opportunists.

After calling a police friend in Boston he sat back and waited. Soon he knew he had enough to start seeking extradition. After all his money and efforts it took the misfiring synopsis of a young woman to finally bring him the results he sought.

The wheels of justice creaked into action. Bradley wanted to speed things up but the paperwork had to be done and they didn't want to spook their target by bringing the media into it. Extradition orders were complex and everything needed to be in order. He hired private investigators to keep Bobby Yeats under surveillance. Bobby was without a contract for his job at that time and Bradley had no idea where he would be based next. The extradition request was for Ireland and it was there it had to be served. So they needed to get the timing right. Bradley didn't want him running again and this time maybe never finding him.

The afternoon he heard that Bobby Yeats had been taken into custody for his extradition hearing, he sobbed at his desk with relief. But that relief was short-lived. In less than twenty-four hours Bobby had evaded justice again by killing himself. Bradley thought he took the coward's way out. Once more there was to be no retribution for Elizabeth Renfield.

Bradley knew now that the man who was directly responsible for killing his sister was beyond his reach but there were others who might be able to give him a sense of closure. Legal avenues had failed Bradley but there might be other options he could pursue.

CHAPTER 35

Mel stopped speaking and looked around at the police assembled in the room with her. They left out a collective breath as they thought back over her words. They weren't sure what to do with her.

Mel turned to Detective Doyle. "I need help. Can you find out what happened to Hugh?" Her imploring eyes bored into those of the detective.

"I will, Melanie, but I need to speak to you for a moment."

Mel felt that hard knot of fear she'd become so used to rise up inside her again. She couldn't speak. She just nodded.

"Melanie, as you were talking we were checking up on the details of your story. We sent the local officers up to Raven House. The front door was wide open. You probably left it open when you ran out.

"No. I definitely closed it."

"The lights were on inside. There was a light trail of blood all the way from the back corridor."

"That was where I found him. I probably trailed the blood out but I closed the door and there was no light on. That all happened in the morning – there was no need for a light." Mel was confused.

"There was a light on and by the time you came here it was late in the evening. Somewhere along the way, Melanie, you lost some time. When we got to the house we went inside and found the body of a male who we have since identified as Hugh Curtis."

"How did you identify him?" Mel knew it was a stupid question even as she asked it.

"He had identification on him," said Emer, "and we have since got someone to come and identify the body."

"Who?" Mel was curious about the rest of Hugh's life.

"His wife." Emer watched Mel's face as she said "wife".

"Hugh doesn't have a wife. He would have told me."

"He does, Melanie, and she was aware all along of your relationship with Hugh. She knew you went out together in school. According to Mrs Curtis you found him in Cork, bumped into him one day on the street and have been harassing them ever since."

"No." Mel shook her head. "No. That's not true."

"According to her it is. She was helping him with his plans."

"What plans?" Mel was more confused than ever. Then she paused. "She was the woman working in the estate agents that were selling Raven House."

"Yes."

"So Hugh thought from the minute I asked him to check up on Elizabeth and her relationship to Raven House that I was squatting there. He and his wife would have put it together. Why didn't he try getting me out before that?"

Emer smiled. "I think he was trying to but you weren't listening."

Mel knew she was right. That probably was what he was trying to do. Get her out his way without the police dragging her out.

"But technically I wasn't squatting. I went there because Ryan brought me there. He told me it was his house. I was living there in good faith."

Emer ignored that and went on. "There's more."

"What?" Mel frowned.

"This weekend he was working on the paperwork to have you committed for your own safety. By Monday you would have been institutionalised for a period of assessment."

"No!" Tears ran down Mel's cheeks and she shook her head. "Why would he need to do that? I was going to leave."

"Melanie, the phone line in Raven House has been disconnected for over a year. Mrs Curtis claims that you called Hugh constantly. She showed me a copy of their phone records. There are no calls from Hugh Curtis to you. But there are over three hundred calls in the last three months from your mobile to Hugh. We have some more checking to do on that part."

Mel's wide-open eyes were staring at a point high on the wall above Emer's head. "So why was he in Raven House?"

"He went there to reason with you according to his wife. He told her you were harmless and he could talk you out – that you would listen."

"I didn't meet a Mrs Curtis at the estate agents."

"No. She calls herself Miss Gill still for business."

Mel did remember her. "But she works in Bantry and Hugh in Cork?"

"They live between the two. It's about a forty-minute drive from both places."

"When did he seek the committal order? I mean, why didn't he just do it when I was in the hospital?"

"I don't think he was prepared. Plus you left the hospital fairly quickly."

Mel knew that was true. She'd caught him by surprise when she left. "So if I'd stayed in the hospital he would have had me committed then?"

"The application was made the day after you were brought in to the hospital."

"Why did he bring me in to the hospital?"

"Mrs Curtis said that you called him threatening to harm yourself. They thought it was an empty threat but then they hadn't heard from you in a week. They didn't want the police at the house. Hugh knows you so they went down to see what they could do. Mrs Curtis had a key to let herself in. That was why Hugh Curtis brought you to the hospital."

"He's my friend. He was worried about me." Mel was grasping for reassurance.

"Melanie. Did you kill Hugh Curtis when you found out what he wanted to do?"

"No! God. No."

The room lapsed into silence. "Will the owner of the house prosecute me?" Mel said. "Maybe I should get that solicitor now."

"That is your right," Detective Doyle said. "The owner has been contacted in Boston and he has confirmed that while the house is up for sale it has never been rented and he certainly claims not to have been living there with you."

"Boston?" Mel looked at the detective.

286

"Yes. It's privately owned by the Renfield family."

Mel had guessed that. But she said nothing.

Suddenly, Detective Doyle's demeanour changed. "Melanie, did Hugh confront you about being committed and did you hit him with a poker and stab him?"

Mel's eyes blazed. "No! I'm not capable of that."

Emer Doyle continued speaking. "We did a background search on you."

A loud noise started in Mel's ears. She could feel herself rocking with no ability to stop. She was white and silent but still rocking.

Emer changed tactics. "Your brother committed suicide twelve months ago. An extradition hearing was in progress to have an extradition order implemented to get him back to Boston for vehicular manslaughter, driving a stolen vehicle, driving without a valid driver's license, burning a body and fleeing the scene of a crime. He hung himself his first night in custody."

Mel was finding it hard to maintain her calm demeanour. She wanted to scream and lash out at them, wanted to break something, but that wouldn't help her.

Detective Doyle continued on. "Melanie, we know about your condition. We've spoken to your family doctor in Galway. You were diagnosed with paranoid schizophrenia in your last year in school. Was that when you broke up with Hugh?"

Mel nodded. "I was taking medication but when I met Ryan it got better. I didn't need to take it anymore. Ryan told me I was better and that the drugs would just keep me dopey." She looked at the tabletop. She was trying to force the information she'd just received into her brain for processing but her head was starting to hurt. Her mind was blank. "None of it was true?" She sobbed the words. "All the last few months were lies?"

Detective Doyle continued on. "You did work in a call centre for a couple of days four years ago but you left that unexpectedly on the third day – just didn't turn up. You lived alone with your father in the house in Galway. Your neighbours haven't seen you for months."

"Nobody reported me missing?"

"No." Emer had wondered about that herself. "They didn't report your dad missing either."

Mel sat up straighter and furrowed her brows. Emer Doyle watched her expression. It was like information was seeping into her brain and slowly forming a picture.

"Nobody spoke much to my dad. He wasn't well liked in the area."

"When did he die, Melanie?" Emer probed gently.

"I'm not sure." Her voice was barely audible. "He had a heart attack. I found him dead." Melanie looked up at her and the look of sheer pain in her eyes grabbed at Emer.

"Melanie, we found him too. He was in bed in your old house. He's been dead a long time. Why did you not call the authorities and let them know what had happened?"

Melanie looked stricken.

Emer watched Melanie struggle with her memories. The officers on the scene had told Emer that even though the body was quite decomposed it didn't look as though he met a violent end. He looked as though he died peacefully in his sleep. There were dead flowers around his pillow.

Melanie was speaking softly, looking at the tabletop. "He died of a broken heart. I think I broke it. It was stress. His heart coped with the death of his wife but the death of

288

his son before they got a chance to make amends was too much for it to take. A heart can only take so much pain before it just gives in to the inevitable. I killed my whole family."

Mel's liquid brown eyes turned towards the detective. They were filled with despair. A thread had been pulled and was unravelling the whole fabric of what Mel had thought was her life.

"We have no record here of your assault investigation. We checked. You did spend a night in hospital the night Hugh brought you in suffering from dehydration."

Mel couldn't get her mind in order. "I did come here."

"I'm sorry, Melanie. There are no records of that."

Melanie was stricken. She'd lost her whole family. Now she was the only one left and she couldn't even trust herself. She gulped. Her beautiful, brave, adventurous brother had stolen a car, killed a girl and run away. And look what she'd become.

"In the house, Melanie, we found numerous books on Belize. They were in a bookcase in the study you described for us. They would have given you a lot of detail on the places you talked about." She paused to let that sink in.

Melanie remained mute.

Emer continued on. "You don't have a passport, Melanie, and never have had one."

"Stop!" Then Melanie had a thought. "Why didn't the nurse stop me?"

"Stop you?" Emer looked puzzled.

"Leaving the hospital."

"There was no committal order. She couldn't legally force you to stay. You took clothes and money from the bed beside you and left."

"No. I had a conversation with the nurse."

"No, Mel. You got up and walked out the door and a small sum of money was taken from another patient."

"No. Hugh gave me money."

"No, Melanie. You took it and left."

Mel was sitting back in her chair now, her eyes firmly fixed on the tabletop in front of her, not meeting anyone's gaze.

"Hugh wasn't wearing a wedding ring." Mel looked earnestly into the eyes of the assembled officers.

"Lots of men don't, Melanie." Walter Carroll spoke for the first time, reminding Mel that there were other people still in the room.

She tried to think back over the events leading up to her running from the house but she couldn't. It felt as though as soon as she'd spoken to the detectives, once the words were out of her mouth, something closed over behind them and she couldn't look back. She couldn't examine her words and thoughts through a locked door.

"What now?" She was barely audible as she spoke.

"You're exhausted," said Emer. "We've talked through the evening and into the night. You must be starving. You have to stay with us but we will figure out what happened."

Mel took a tablet the doctor had just prescribed for her without question and followed an officer to a cell. As she walked it was like the world around her was contracting. The corridor was closing in and the roof was getting lower. She didn't want to enter the cell. The room seemed so small. But her body was feeling heavy.

As she sat down on her bunk she could feel herself relaxing and her mind slowing.

She curled into a ball and in just a few moments she was asleep. The tiny room no longer felt claustrophobic. It was just a little space for her to sleep – a cocoon.

CHAPTER 36

Early the next day Mel was back in the interrogation room in front of Detective Doyle and the same team of officers as the day before.

"Melanie, we're getting that solicitor for you. She'll be in soon. Do you want to wait for her?"

"I killed my solicitor according to you." Mel turned and looked with dead eyes at the detective.

"As soon as she arrives we'll have her step in to talk to you. She's not usually present during interviews."

"I don't care."

Emer Doyle watched Mel's face as she spoke.

"Melanie, have you been staying illegally in Raven House?"

"Yes. I must have been, according to you." Mel's expression was sullen this morning.

"Did you kill Hugh Curtis?" Emer asked.

A huge sob burst from Mel. "No! He was my friend!"

Mel sat there staring at her hands as they lay palms flat

on the tabletop. Her mother died of head trauma because of her, her brother died eaten up by his conscience, her father died of a broken heart and now she was going to be locked up because of a flawed mind. She was glad neither herself nor Bobby had ever had children. This was a gene pool which deserved to dry up.

Could she have done this brutal act? Each step of her story, even though it came from her own mouth, raised questions that she had no answer for. She was as blind to what happened as any of them. Things happened for a reason. She was brought up to believe that you reaped what you sowed but Mel couldn't understand what she had done to deserve any of this.

"Melanie, we will get you some help. You are going to a facility where we will get you counselling and sort out your medication. We'll figure out what happened." Emer had never found herself speaking so softly and with such genuine emotion to a probable murderer before. It was obvious to all in the room that something about the lost tragic woman in front of her had affected her deeply. Emer had looked into Mel's eyes as her mind struggled to come to terms with it all and she saw truth. Melanie at least believed emphatically that it was a mistake and that somehow she was the victim in all this. She couldn't have done these things.

If it wasn't for her psychiatric history and the overwhelming circumstantial evidence against her, all of them would have believed her innocent, based on what they saw on her face. But the law had to work with the assumption that Melanie had killed this man.

But there was a strange nagging doubt in the minds of all who had listened to Mel's story. They couldn't shake that doubt. Perhaps once Melanie had seen a psychiatrist and her medication had been monitored she would be more coherent and they might all get some answers.

Melanie's solicitor arrived. The officers left to give them some privacy. Mel sat looking at the table while the solicitor talked but she couldn't concentrate. All she could hear were the rambling thoughts in her own head. After a few attempts to get Mel's attention the solicitor got up and left the room to speak to the detectives.

Shortly after it was decided that Melanie would need to be taken for psychiatric assessment. She was led away from the Garda Station, head covered, flanked by her very own troop of officers, and placed in the back of a transportation wagon to be assessed by the National Forensic Mental Health Service located in Dundrum. Already she was the subject of much interest. Photographers strained their arm muscles trying to reach their cameras high enough to see into the small windows high up on the van. She would be assessed and a programme of treatment and rehabilitation would be set in motion under 4.6 of the Criminal Law (Insanity) Act, 2006, for a period of no more than fourteen days. If found to be suffering from acute mental illness she would be treated for a longer period.

None of it sank in as Mel was taken away. She was too busy trying to get her mind around the past to come to any conclusions about what the future would bring.

CHAPTER 37

The power of chemicals! Mel woke and for the third morning that week her mind was clear. Memories and feelings were flooding back into her. She wished she didn't have to welcome them but it was a two-way street. The chemicals got the memories flowing. They made her receptive to them. Gone were the days of blocking out reality. Now reality was knocking loudly on her door. With clarity came the pain of dealing with her current circumstances and her past. Her room was locked overnight, from nine o'clock onwards. Mel hated the sound of the lock engaging. Morning came with a sense of relief to have her door open again. Though there was nowhere to go it still represented a promise of freedom for her.

This morning she had a session with a therapist. She had been assigned one named Edmund Willis to assess her mental state and help her to remember as much as she could of the events leading up to Hugh Curtis's murder.

Most of the pieces were now in place but Mel knew she

wasn't going to tell him everything that had happened. But perhaps the opportunity to talk to someone about her life would be good for her.

Mel brushed down her clothes. There was no mirror in the room so she couldn't see how she looked. Her hair felt smooth as she brushed it and her face was clean but she would have loved to see herself properly. She didn't feel comfortable meeting someone without knowing how she looked. She wanted to make a good impression.

An officer appeared behind her at the door. She stood for a moment waiting for Mel to gather herself together. Then Mel was led from her room to the therapy session. As she walked along the corridor seemed too short. Mel wanted rivers to well up or mountains to rise in her path, anything that would stop her having to talk about and acknowledge the long chain of misery that was woven by her brother. Mel slowed as she approached the office door. The closer she got the more her courage was failing her. The officer with her had to urge her on.

They knocked. A friendly voice invited them in. The officer opened the door and ushered Mel inside. Then she turned, leaving Mel alone with a man in his thirties who was standing by a pine desk leafing through a folder.

The room was as friendly as his voice. A space conducive to memory, she thought wryly, looking around her. The walls were restful oatmeal, the floor was pale yellow pine varnished to reflect the sun, light streamed through a large deep window at the back of the room embedded in a two-foot thick stone wall. A rug woven from bright colours covered the centre of the room where two chairs sat facing each other.

He walked across the room. "Sit there, Melanie."

He indicated one of the chairs, the one facing the door. He took the one facing the window. Perhaps he didn't want her getting distracted. She walked to the chair and sat stiffly, her feet flat on the floor and her palms clasped in her lap.

Edmund was tall and thin with a pleasantly dishevelled appearance. He was fair-haired with pale skin and light eyes, more grey than blue.

"How are you today, Melanie?" He spoke in a soft tone.

"I'm fine." She tried to smile but lately her smile felt more like a grimace.

"Have you been sleeping well?" His pale eyes looked her over from head to toe.

"Yes. Mostly. I find it hard to go to sleep, sometimes."

"Why do you find it difficult to get to sleep?" His tone was warm like he was an old friend over for coffee.

"I can't get my mind to switch off."

"What do you think of?" He smiled encouragingly at her.

"Everything. The whole thing – the people – the dead – the fact that I'm in here."

"Is that why you used to drink?"

He was direct. Mel had to give him that.

She nodded. "I suppose so. I don't know."

"Why did you go to Cork?"

His questions seemed to be random. Maybe he was doing that to disarm her, catch her unawares. Perhaps people answered more accurately when they didn't have time to think up an appropriate answer.

"I'm not sure. I thought Ryan brought me there."

"Did you know that Raven House was Elizabeth

Renfield's grandmother's house? Her mother's family name was Reid."

"I do now but, no, I didn't know when I moved down there. How could I have?" She paused for a moment and thought back to Keith Byrne's story. "Mrs Reid, the old lady who died asleep in her bed." She escaped the curse but her granddaughter didn't.

"What?" He frowned, looking at his notes.

Mel smiled. "Nothing."

He brought her back to his question. "Do you think that's a coincidence? The girl your brother killed was a descendent of the late owner of the house you just happened to be inhabiting illegally."

"I doubt it. I keep telling you people that, when I moved in there, as far as I was concerned I was moving into my boyfriend's house with him. So obviously he knew and brought me there deliberately."

Edmund nodded as though he knew exactly what she was talking about but he said nothing.

Mel spoke first. "Do you think I'm a liar or crazy?"

"Tell me about your brother." He jumped again to another question, ignoring her comment.

"What about him?" Mel frowned. He was the last person she wanted to talk about now.

He decided to start slowly. "Did you get along?"

"Yes." Mel answered cautiously unsure where he was going with these questions.

"You were younger than him?"

"Yes. By ten years."

"You were with your mother when she died?" He was on to another angle.

"I was."

Mel's mind was struggling to keep up. Perhaps that was his tactic. He was stimulating her thoughts or maybe he was just trying to catch her off guard.

"Tell me about that."

"I don't remember a lot. I was holding her hand walking down the path to the front door. She died." Mel winced at the memories.

"Can you remember how you felt?"

"I was thrilled. Fuck's sake!" Mel angrily sniffed back tears.

Edmund sat in silence, watching Mel struggle with her emotions. Time ticked and neither spoke.

Mel broke first. "I remember sitting beside her on the path looking at her face. I'd pulled away from her. She lost her footing on the step and hit her head on the kerb when she fell. Her eyes were open. She was dead – but she was staring at me like she wanted to take me with her."

Still Edmund didn't speak. Mel's haunted eyes watched a knot in the wood by the door.

"I couldn't tear my eyes away from her. The taxi driver closed her eyes. She had to go there alone."

"Go where?" He spoke softly.

Mel looked at him. "I don't know. Wherever spirits go."

"You think that it was your fault that she died."

"It was. I was being a brat. I was screaming and throwing a tantrum. I pulled out of her grip and threw her off balance. That killed her so therefore I killed her." Mel spoke in exaggerated tones like he was stupid.

"Do you believe in heaven?"

Mel could feel her breath thick and harsh as it tried to get out of her lungs. "I want to."

"Is your brother in heaven?" He threw Bobby back into the toxic mix of memories.

"How can he be?" Mel wasn't ready to talk about that but, as he'd thrown the question at her, despite her reservations she found herself answering. She wanted him to reassure her about Bobby. He'd killed a girl, lied and then killed himself. Mel needed reassurance that he'd finally found peace.

Edmund couldn't give her false hope. He didn't know where Bobby was. "Is that what keeps you awake, wondering where your brother is?"

"What has that got to do with what happened in Raven House?"

He let her mind ponder on that without answering. He posed a different question instead. "What do you think of your brother's crime?"

"Which one?"

"The death of Elizabeth."

Mel was rocking quietly in her chair, thinking. Finally she spoke. "He didn't mean it. He told me he didn't mean it. I knew my brother. He would never knowingly hurt anyone."

"If he did nothing wrong why do you think he can't be in heaven?"

Mel shouted at him. "Because of me he never properly repented!"

"You think it's your fault he died."

"Yes."

"But you didn't take his life." He was deliberately baiting her now and she was rising to it.

"No. But I left him no choice."

"No, Melanie. He had choices. We always have choices."

299

Mel went quiet for a moment, gathering her thoughts. "I wrote the letter. It left him with no way out."

"Your brother stole a car, drove too fast, killed a girl and covered up his crime. None of it was your doing. There are consequences to our actions."

Mel was getting upset. "That's what I'm trying to tell you. His death was the consequence of my actions. He got away with his crimes. He was free until I wrote that letter."

"He wasn't free. I expect he was miserable." Edmund was trying to get Mel to concentrate on what started her flight to Cork. "Tell me, Melanie, about the night he came to you and told you his secret."

"My brother was a water engineer who travelled the world. But he was alone. Technically he lived with us. He never left home either despite all his travelling. Just like me he was trapped in that house. He didn't own or rent an apartment. He just stayed in accommodation paid for by his company or slept on the floor in a friend's house. He would stay at home with us on weekends between contracts, maybe a couple of times a year, fight with my dad and then storm off again. That trip was no exception." Mel paused to gather her thoughts.

"What about you?" Edmund interrupted. "What were you doing during this time?"

"I was at home."

"You didn't work?"

"No."

"Why not?" Edmund knew about Mel's breakdown in school. He knew about her short work life but he wanted her to talk about it. She was good at compartmentalising her thoughts. Mel had spent a lifetime hiding and he wanted to shine some light in her secret places.

"My dad needed me."

Edmund knew that wasn't quite true. "Did you ever work?"

Mel blushed. She remembered the conversation as though it were a television show, the one she'd with the police. "I worked in a call centre." She knew Edmund would have a copy of everything she'd said to the police. It had seemed so real at the time.

"For how long?"

Why did they want to make her say these things out loud? She knew they knew she had been lying. Why did she have to admit it? Again there was a silence that stretched until Mel cracked again.

"Not long."

"Why not longer?"

"I couldn't."

"Why not?"

"I couldn't take the loudness of it all."

"Loudness of it?"

"It was so loud. People talking, phones ringing, footsteps on wooden floors, shouting, televisions, I hated it."

"Is it loud in here?"

"No." Mel looked at him. Maybe he understood.

"Is that why you went to Raven House? Because it's quiet?"

"Yes. Ryan invited me. He told me it would be calm and I could finally get some peace."

Edmund frowned. He'd thrown a litany of questions at her to see what he could get her to reveal about Raven House but it always came back to Ryan asking her to go to the house with him. There was still no evidence of this

301

Ryan. The guards thought Melanie was probably down there alone. They wanted to know if Mel knew about the house prior to moving down there.

"How did you find the house?"

"Ryan found it. I didn't know anything about the house."

"You know Ryan couldn't have found it."

"I know. I made him up. That's what you lot keep telling me but, I'm telling you, it was definitely Ryan. How would I find that house unless somebody told me about it?" Mel was getting angry.

"That's what we need to find out, Mel. Somehow you found a house owned by Elizabeth's family and ran to it."

"But I never left our house in Galway except to go to the library. I can't see how I could have found a house in West Cork."

"Why were you ringing Hugh Curtis?"

"I needed help. I knew he trained as a solicitor and I knew he'd moved to Cork."

"So you started calling, asking for help?"

"I suppose." Mel's lip was turning white where she had it gripped between her teeth.

"You did uncover the Renfield's address in Boston, didn't you?" Edmund pushed her.

"I must have. I don't remember."

It was the one area that Mel was still adamant about. She went to that house after her father's death because of Ryan. The Guards were still working on that connection. If he never existed how or why did she get him inside her head? Was he just an imaginary friend for a lonely adult woman?

CHAPTER 38

The session lapsed into silence again.

"Melanie. Tell me about the letter. Why did you send it to Bradley Renfield?"

"Bobby had done a terrible thing."

"When he killed the girl?"

"All of it, drinking with strangers, stealing a car and killing her. Then he burned her." Mel's face contorted. It was a mixture of pain and disbelief. She couldn't imagine anyone treating a dead girl like that, but least of all her brother, her wonderful brother. Her stomach wrenched with pain as it often did when she was upset. She couldn't be far off of an ulcer.

"Why do you think he told you what he did? I mean, he had got away with it. In all these years there had been no evidence found linking him with Elizabeth's death."

"It was eating him up inside. He was so sorry and deep down I think he wanted to make things right. He subsequently read she had smoke in her lungs. That meant he burned her alive. He really didn't know at the time."

"He told you to make himself feel better?"

"I suppose . . ." Mel was frowning again.

A thought was hiding just inside her brain but she couldn't identify it. Something was making her very uncomfortable.

"Do you think the fact that you were in the house, alone, and never went out made it safe for him to tell you? You weren't going to tell anyone."

Mel sucked in her breath. There it was: the thought she was trying so hard to keep hidden. Bobby thought so little of his sister that he unloaded it all onto her. His sister with the psychiatric problems, who never went out, couldn't possibly reveal his secrets and she couldn't get away from him when he told her. He knew she wouldn't be able to cope with the knowledge. But he didn't care: he'd just unloaded all his guilt onto her.

She spoke quietly. "I was a captive audience, wasn't I?"

Edmund said nothing. He just sat and watched her wrestle with her thoughts.

"I remember his exact words when he finished telling me about the accident." Mel thought for a moment and then went on. "'It was a cold morning in early October, unseasonable for that time of year. I've carried that coldness with me wherever I've been since then. Even after I returned to Ireland safely a heavy stone had replaced my heart, weighing me down. One day I know I'll have to pay for what I did.'" Mel started laughing again. "He didn't pay, did he? He took the easy way out. He left me to pay."

"Do you think that was the easy way out?"

"Well, he didn't face the law. He left that to me."

"But how did he put you in this position? He died

almost a year ago. Hugh Curtis only died in the last few weeks. He had nothing to do with that. Your father died six months ago. Bobby had nothing to do with that either. Did he?"

Mel smiled now. "Of course he did. It's all connected. One thing leads to another. We all know that."

The silence returned but this time Mel wasn't going to be the one to break it.

"So you think if Bobby hadn't killed Elizabeth and then told you what he did that none of this would have happened. Hugh Curtis wouldn't have died?"

"Exactly." Mel was relieved. Now he really seemed to understand.

She had to admit that she didn't know what was happening yet. The pieces were only beginning to come back to her. They were all there in her memory but she just couldn't seem to get them arranged in the right order to tell her story.

"Right. One thing leads to another and you end up in a house in West Cork previously owned by the dead girl's grandmother."

"Yes." Mel smiled again, not because she was being sarcastic but because she knew how crazy she sounded.

"Let's go back to Bobby again. He came home on one of his trips and told you about what he'd done in 1992. Why do you think he told you that particular time?"

"I wondered about that. He was quite distressed. He'd started fighting with Dad the minute he came home. Dad went to the pub and left us to it."

"Did your dad drink a lot?

"I don't know. I never went to the pub with him. I always went to bed early."

"So you never saw him drunk." He probed deeper into the Yeats' attitude to drink.

"No. I often wondered. He would arrive in the door always just after I went to bed. I used to think he waited until he saw my light in my room before he came in but that's silly. Why would he hide his drinking from me?"

"Did Bobby drink a lot?"

Mel said. "He did. I think. I saw him drunk at least once when he was home – every time he was home. I think that used to trigger the fights with Dad."

"Kettle calling the pot black." Again Edmund decided to antagonise her. He guessed that Mel was very protective of her family and took a lot of responsibility on herself.

"What do you mean by that?" Mel asked, her eyes narrowing.

"Did you drink too much?"

Before Mel answered him she thought back to all the alcohol she'd consumed in Cork. When she lived with her dad she hardly ever drank. There was never any alcohol in the house and she didn't go out often so there wasn't much opportunity for her to drink but there wasn't a rule against it either. Even though she didn't see her father drunk she did know he was at the pub and she assumed he was drinking.

"What does our drinking have to do with anything?"

"I was just wondering what the atmosphere was like in your house. What led your brother to throw away his life and how did you end up in a house with a dead man?"

"I can't do this." Mel hung her head.

"Do what?"

"You're asking me questions, expecting me to come up with answers. We're supposed to be working towards

306

understanding what happened. But I'm not sure what's real and what's not." Mel shrugged as she spoke. "What am I meant to do?"

"We're sifting through your memories, Melanie. Some will be real and some we might have to interpret but we will figure it out."

Mel frowned at him.

Edmund could see she was deep in thought. He waited for her to continue.

"Bobby was drinking that night. The night he took the car." Mel sat back, stretched her legs out and let her hands fall down the sides of the chair, repeating the story her brother had told her. "He left the bar by himself. The sounds of laughter died a little as he closed the door behind him, the sound weakened by the heavy wood. He hated leaving a party. The next day he was coming home to Ireland. You couldn't beat a really good night out. He shook his head sadly as he said that to me. *'That's what I wanted.'* He'd spoken so softly I could barely catch the words. *'I wanted a good send-off.'* He'd found the pub by accident. I think he worked with someone who was going there and he tagged along. The night slipped by in a haze of Guinness and conversation. Everyone in that area had an Irish relative sitting on a branch somewhere in their family tree. Outside his mood slipped as he looked around the car park. He thought there would be a taxi dropping off at the door but it was later than he thought and few there drank as late as a young Irishman. Not enough to justify a taxi rank anyway. He was freezing standing there. He thought for a moment, searching through his hazy brain. He thought there was a bus stop down the road but the first bus wouldn't run for at least another few hours.

Then he saw a car parked away at the back. He looked around again at the empty car park and walked towards the car. He kept a rigidly straight line as he walked. He wanted to make sure he wasn't too drunk to drive a stolen car, proud that he hadn't lost all of his faculties. He talked reassuringly to himself as he reached the car and grabbed the lock. The door was open. With purpose, he said, he opened the car and stepped in, pulling down the visor as he did. A set of car keys hit him on the tender bridge of his nose. Even after sixteen years he remembered that silly little detail. He had a broad smile on his face as the engine sparked to life. The car had started on the first turn of the key despite the cold weather. As he pulled out of the car park a slow drizzle of rain was descending on the early morning."

Mel stopped talking, her heart breaking as she thought of her brother. How dumb. He could have gone back inside and had another pint. They'd have ordered him a taxi and the whole world would have shifted a little differently on its axis and someone else would be sitting in this room delving into their souls. She would be in Galway. And Bobby? What would Bobby be doing? Her heart ached. Bobby was on a collision course. He'd said that to her. If it wasn't that, it would have been something else.

"'I'm bad stock,' he said, his eyes sad and haunted."

"What did you say, Melanie?" Edmund hadn't quite caught the words she'd muttered.

Mel's eyes were swimming in tears. "That was the last thing Bobby said to me that night. 'I'm bad stock. If it wasn't that, it would have been something else. I was destined to crash. It was just chance what I was going to hit.'"

"Was he always wild?"

Mel nodded, too full of emotion to speak.

"What about you?"

"No. I was flat – flat and useless – until I met Ryan."

Now she'd finally said it. Once Ryan came into her life she could take on the world but he let her down badly.

"He told me to write the letter." There was total silence as she paused for a moment.

"He told me to write the letter." She repeated the words again because Edmund was looking blankly at her.

"Ryan told you to write the letter?" He wasn't sure what she meant.

"No. Bobby did," Mel answered.

"Bobby told you to write a letter to Elizabeth's brother and expose his crime, a crime for which he'd never had to pay?" Edmund sounded incredulous.

Mel nodded. "He said he couldn't live with the guilt. He wished that somehow they would find out because it must be awful living with the uncertainty."

"And you took that as him asking you to tell them."

She nodded again. "I was wrong." A gut-wrenching pain took hold of her. That letter set it all in motion. Bobby was dead because of it.

"Bobby was drinking that night?" the therapist said. "He was drunk when he said that?"

"Yes. I know now he didn't mean that. Didn't mean for me to write to them but at the time I wasn't thinking straight. I thought I was helping him by writing the letter. I thought it would help the Renfields too. I thought that once they discovered that Bobby killed Elizabeth by accident and that he was truly sorry they would get closure and we could all put it behind us. But instead I lost him."

Mel didn't want to talk after that. Her face was contorted with pain. Edmund let her go.

As she was led back to her room she turned to the officer with her.

"I can see him clearly in my head. Ryan was real."

The officer nodded in sympathy and closed the room door behind her.

CHAPTER 39

Time was never much of a concept for Melanie. She never looked at the date and sometimes whole swathes of time would slip by that she'd barely register.

A knock on the door behind her made her jump. The door was always open but it was policy to knock to give her some semblance of control.

"Yes?" She looked at the officer standing there.

"Melanie, you need to come with me. Now."

It was an officer she hadn't met before and he was quite young.

Mel turned her face back to the wall. "I'm not ready yet."

"You need to come with me, Melanie. They're waiting."

"I'm not leaving this room or going anywhere with you until you speak to me with respect. I'm not ready yet."

"Now, Melanie." He was getting frustrated.

Mel turned her eyes flashing with temper. "Get out of my room!"

He looked no more than twenty and stood there, shifting from one foot to another. "You have to come with me."

Mel turned her back on him and ignored him.

A new voice spoke. "Excuse me, Melanie. We've got to go. There are some detectives here to speak with you."

Mel turned around to see her regular escort standing in the hall. "Since you asked so nicely." Her eyes focused on the other Guard as she left the room. His nervous eyes flicked away.

They walked with her to the room she usually visited when seeing her therapist. They knocked, opened the door, ushered her inside and then left.

Inside the room she paused. Emer Doyle was sitting there with her solicitor and another detective. Emer stood up. "Melanie! How are you?"

Laura Denton her solicitor seemed to be there as an observer. She sat to the side and let the detectives do all the talking.

"I'm fine. What's up?"

"We need to talk to you."

"I guessed that." Mel was feeling stroppy with everyone. "Has someone else been murdered?"

"No. We've had some forensic results back."

"And?" Mel's temper was short.

There was a long silence. Mel was wondering where this was going.

"Hugh Curtis's DNA was found on you."

"I guessed that. I was covered in his blood." Mel wanted them to get to the point.

"But there was another blood type too," said Emer. "It was on the ground and on you. There was a quantity of blood on your back. It wasn't soaked in as though you lay in it as you described. It was a spray of drops, cast off blood, maybe from the blows Hugh received. This is unusual. Also the blood track from the living room out the front door was from another person."

Detective Doyle was watching Mel's reactions as she spoke. Did Mel know who this other person was?

Finally Mel spoke. "Who do you think it was?"

"Keith Byrne is missing."

"Missing?" Mel looked surprised.

"Yes."

Mel narrowed her eyes. "So do you think that was Hugh's killer? I mean the person who left the blood behind."

Emer smiled despite herself. She knew where Mel was going with her questions. "Calm down, Mel. I promised you we'd work this out. We're still investigating."

"I was accused of murder and locked up." She looked from one face to the other. "And now it looks as though it could have been somebody else. I think I'm entitled to get a little excited."

"We can't make any assumptions at this stage."

"You made enough assumptions before. So when can I leave?"

"It's not that simple. We have a photograph here for you to look at." She held out a photo for Melanie to see.

Mel reached out and held it in her hand. A thin man with thinning grey hair and a sad smile looked out at her.

She looked up at Detective Doyle. "Who is he?"

"This is Bradley Renfield. Do you know him? Is he Ryan?"

"No. Ryan was very handsome, self-assured. Why are you showing me Bradley Renfield?"

"His family owned the house that you lived in and now it looks as though there was in fact a third person at the crime scene so I wondered if he was Ryan."

"Well, he's not. And I didn't kill anyone. Can I leave?" Mel was speaking quickly.

"No, Melanie. Not yet anyway."

"Why? You know I didn't do it."

"You are being assessed for competency. It will take a little time."

"But I didn't kill anyone."

"Somebody killed a man in a house you were in. You were covered in the blood of Hugh Curtis. We need to do some more investigating."

"I don't know what's going on but I ended up in the middle . . ." Mel's voice trailed away. "I just ended up in the middle."

"Melanie, we still don't know if you killed anyone but nearly everyone connected to you or Elizabeth is dead. Stay here for a few more days until we work something out. I want to show you another picture."

She held out a picture to Mel.

Mel looked at the photo, her eyes lowered. A headshot of a handsome man in a very well-cut suit looked out at her. His face was held in a determined expression obviously meant to instil confidence in whoever looked at it. It was a typical corporate shot.

She nodded. "That's Ryan. Who is he?"

"He is Gordon Grant. He was Elizabeth's boyfriend."

Mel lapsed into silence again. Then she raised her eyes from the photo and looked back at the detective. "Is he missing too?"

"We haven't made contact with him yet. We still have

314

some investigating to do. Give us a little more time." Emer tried to instil some reassurance into her voice.

Mel's eyes were unreadable but somehow Emer thought this woman knew more than she was telling them.

CHAPTER 40

Two days later Mel once more was escorted from her room to meet with the detectives. She expected another interrogation. Inside, the room was a little more crowded than usual.

"Melanie." A tall blond woman threw herself at Mel and then stepped back embarrassed. Her hair was shoulder-length and looked expensive. Everything about her was polished and gleaming yet her expression was unsure, faltering. "I'm sorry, Mel. Are you okay? I didn't mean to frighten you." She looked back to the detectives for reassurance.

"Amanda. Hi." Mel looked in confusion from her cousin to the detectives, wondering what sort of sorcery they were delving in now. Was Amanda supposed to talk her into something?

Amanda was verging on the plump side these days but she was still gorgeous. Mel had always been in awe of her cousin. She was everything Mel wanted to be with all that blond hair and those dark blue eyes.

Detective Doyle stepped forward. "Melanie, your cousin has come forward and offered to have you stay with her. Due to the evidence we found at the crime scene there is a possibility that someone else was there that night. Your assessment went well so you can leave. You are still required to undergo treatment on an outpatient basis while we continue with our investigations and you must report to your local police station on a weekly basis."

Amanda interrupted, looking at Mel. "You know Donna has just finished her training. She's a psychiatric nurse."

The detectives looked at Amanda in wonder at this.

"It's okay," Mel said.

Mel had heard that Donna, Amanda's daughter, was a nurse. She hadn't known it was psychiatric nursing.

"I'm sorry," Amanda muttered.

"Don't be ridiculous. If Donna wants to monitor my drugs I don't care."

Amanda was mortified. "I didn't mean to imply that you needed monitoring. I mean Donna will be delighted to have you stay. We all will. You can stay in the guest cottage."

Mel gave a wicked smile. "Keep me out of the main house." She was only teasing. She liked Amanda's directness.

"No." Amanda looked ready to cry.

"Amanda! Stop. It's okay." Mel smiled. "I do need monitoring or they won't let me out."

The therapist was sitting at the back of the room. Mel hadn't seen him when she first came in.

Mel stepped back from her cousin. "Thank you. I'll stay wherever you put me."

The detectives watched the exchange without speaking.

Mel turned to them.

"So do I sign something?"

"It's all done. Gather your things together."

Mel went to pack.

Amanda talked non-stop all the way home. She was a teacher and her husband a cardiac consultant so they had a lovely house. Mel hadn't seen it in a long time but she guessed it would be a comfortable place to stay and they certainly wouldn't let her spend too much time alone brooding. Pat, Amanda's husband, had also inherited money so they lived comfortably in Dublin. As it was in Dublin, it made sense for Mel to stay with them.

The house was in a smart area of the city, full of old Edwardian houses. They drove up a narrow winding street and around a sharp corner. Amanda negotiated the corner and operated an electronic gate-opener at the same time.

Two large wooden gates opened inwards, revealing an expanse of lawn sweeping towards the sea. A beautiful old house stood slightly off to the right side as they entered the property. The drive swept down the side of the house.

"This isn't the house you had the last time I visited you." Mel looked around her, enjoying the view. The only sounds you could hear, beyond the occasional car on the quiet road outside the property, was the crashing ocean and the distant barking of pet dogs confined in neighbouring gardens.

"No." Amanda said. "That was thirteen years ago just after we were married. That was a little house. Pat inherited this."

"It's lovely."

"We love it too. I intend dying here." She laughed.

"Is that why you brought me here?" Somewhere between her head and her mouth Mel realised the joke wasn't very funny.

"Mel! Stop it." Amanda was annoyed.

"What?"

"It's not appropriate to say things like that."

"Why? People think I'm insane." Mel was getting angry with the only person who could genuinely help her and she couldn't understand why.

"You have challenges."

"Oh God. Amanda. Stop the schoolteacher talk."

"Melanie! Why are you fighting me?" Amanda wanted to help her cousin but Mel wasn't making it easy.

"I don't know."

"Well, stop it."

Mel changed the subject. "Where is Pat?"

"He's away on business." Amanda's face broke into a smile. "But he's fine with you being here. He's looking forward to meeting you when he gets back."

Mel was touched as Pat barely knew her.

Donna met them at the door. Melanie hadn't seen her since she was a bridesmaid at her mother's wedding, thirteen years ago. Donna was twenty-two now. She was as vivacious as her mother and reached her arms wide to embrace her cousin. Melanie tried to respond.

"Melanie. We're delighted to have you."

Mel was wondering if she'd specialised in psychoses in her nursing specialty. Maybe they brought the crazy cousin home as a case study. Another giggle started but she kept it in. She studied Donna. She was tall like her mother but her hair was short and dark brown. Her skin was more tanned. She had a beautiful smile but she had a speculative look in her eyes and Mel knew she would get little past her.

"Let me show you the house." Amanda walked along, pointing out this room and that to Melanie.

It was a lovely house. All the rooms had high ceilings, long windows and bright interiors. Amanda had a penchant for all things white. The sun and sea reflected off it in every room.

They walked to the kitchen where a buffet lunch was spread out on the preparation island in the centre of a large room. The dishes were covered in cling film.

Windows covered all of one wall, which was impressive as the ceiling in the kitchen was double the height of the other rooms. The kitchen even had a mezzanine level facing towards the sea, which was obviously being used as an office. A spiral staircase led up to it. God, what a view they must have from up there!

"Would you like some coffee with your lunch?" Donna moved towards the kettle.

"I'd love some, thank you." Mel smiled.

Amanda indicated some high stools at a breakfast bar. "Take a seat, Mel."

The view from the window there was gorgeous. It looked out onto the bay. Small boats bobbed in the distance and a couple of jet skis roared by.

"You have a beautiful home, Amanda." Mel had guessed she would have. Amanda always got the best of everything.

"Thank you." Amanda almost purred in self-satisfaction.

Mel turned to Donna. "Donna, tell me about yourself."

Donna turned her bright smile on her but her eyes burned through Mel. Already this girl was making her very nervous.

"I'm a nurse."

"Yes. Amanda told me. Psychiatric."

"Yes." Donna smiled at her mother. "I live at home still. I'm saving to buy my own place. It'll take a while. You know what house prices are like."

Mel didn't have a clue but she nodded. "Do you have a boyfriend?" She wasn't sure if you should ask that. She wasn't used to small talk.

"I do. It's early days yet."

"That's good. It's nice to have someone." Mel felt a lump in her throat but for the first time she saw Donna relax a little in her company.

"It is." Donna smiled at her. "Let's have lunch. You must be starving."

"I am. Thank you." Mel helped her cousins unwrap the food and put on more coffee.

They ate their lunch, chatting about life in general.

But suddenly Mel had a thought. "You and Pat were married thirteen years ago?"

"Yes." Amanda looked curiously at her.

"Bobby was at your wedding?"

"He was."

"You and he were great friends?"

"Yes, we were. You know that." Amanda was an only child. She and Bobby had been more like brother and sister than he and Mel had ever been. They were the same age.

"Did you know about the accident in Boston?" Mel asked.

"No. But I did notice the difference in him after that time. I just didn't know what had caused it." Amanda paused. "I should have found out what was wrong but he started pulling away from me, from all of us."

"Going on longer trips?"

"Yes."

"But you've stayed in touch over the years?" Mel was curious about the parts of her brother she hadn't known.

"We did."

"Did he visit you?" Mel wondered what Donna's impression of Bobby would have been. She wondered how her shrewd eyes would have appraised him.

"No. He rarely visited here. We spoke by telephone."

"Did you meet him?" Mel turned to Donna, not wanting to let the subject go.

"No. Well, not as an adult. I think maybe as a child I did but I don't remember him."

"He wasn't home much, Mel, as you know," Amanda interjected.

That was true.

They sat in silence for the remainder of the meal, both Mel and Amanda lost in their memories.

As they finished, Amanda stood up.

"Come on. I'll show you to your house now."

Mel couldn't believe her eyes. It was a glorious little cottage with a sea view about two hundred yards from the main house. An apple tree stood in front of the cottage, spreading its naked branches towards a latticed front window. A crazy-paving path ran from the turning table in front of the main house to the little house's front door. It was like the witch's house in *Hansel and Gretel*.

Amanda stood back and handed the key to Mel.

"It's all yours. Welcome."

Mel turned towards her cousin. "It's beautiful."

"Thank you. I hope you'll be comfortable here."

Mel hoped so too but she knew she wasn't out of trouble yet. Until certain things were sorted she would live forever under a shadow. Hugh's killer was still out there. It was a relief for her to be down here in the garden, in this little house. Maybe that would keep the others safe if he came for her again.

CHAPTER 41

Mel woke and stretched. All she could hear was the wind outside her cottage and the faint sound of the sea in the distance. Turning around she snuggled back down into her bed and closed her eyes. There were no drug trolleys rattling in the corridors or screaming from the rooms nearby. Smiling she drifted back to sleep.

When she woke the next time the wind had increased in strength and rain was being lashed against the window. Hunger pangs drove her from the bed. She ambled to the bathroom and sank into the bath she ran, daydreaming. Silence was the most precious thing to Mel. It was like a soft blanket surrounding her.

After her bath she dressed in jeans and a sweatshirt. Amanda had left some clothes for her in the wardrobe. They fit perfectly. The efficiency of Amanda was impressive. Mel went downstairs. Sitting on the counter was a flask and a basket draped with a cloth. She pulled back the tea towel and looked inside – fresh croissants, a box of chopped fresh fruit and natural yogurt. Unscrewing the top of the flask, she smelled hot coffee. She wasn't expecting any of this. There was a note on top of the basket.

"Donna will speak to you later."

Of course she would have to. Somebody needed to monitor her medication and keep an eye on her. The sad irony was that when Mel was feeling well she barely remembered how bad things were without drugs. It was so easy to let her regime slip, and with it let her mind slide backwards into darkness. Once she was there it was like crawling out of a deep dark hole and she couldn't do it alone. Poor Donna, did she know she'd been set up as the gatekeeper to darkness?

The cottage was tiny but it was perfect. Downstairs was open plan. There was a kitchenette to one side with a little seating area around a surprisingly large fireplace directly opposite it. To the front of the house behind the latticed window she'd seen on the way in yesterday there was a dining area with a padded window seat. Everything was bright and light. It looked fresh. She suspected that Amanda had redecorated especially for her. The soft furnishings were pretty and floral. Was this a therapy centre to lift Mel's mood? It was working. Already Mel felt almost happy.

She carried her breakfast to the window seat and sat down. The house was situated so that you could see the tree and the rockery from the dining area. She could imagine how pretty it would be in spring. If she was still there by then of course.

She looked around her, wondering what time it was. A microwave sat above the worktop across the room. The digital face said one o'clock. She guessed Amanda wouldn't let her sleep this late every morning. This was probably a treat for her first day.

By three o'clock the rain had stopped. Mel left the cottage to explore the garden. At the back was a kitchen garden filled with vegetable beds and surrounded by fruit trees and behind that a rain-soaked greenhouse. The front lawn ran from the cottage to the cliff-top above the bay.

A wall stretched along the cliff-top. Mel walked to it and looked across it to the sea. As she stood there a voice sounded behind her. She jumped and turned to find Amanda standing there.

Mel smiled. "Were you afraid I was going to jump?"

"No." Poor Amanda was a terrible liar.

"I love the cottage." Mel's face was lit with genuine pleasure as she looked back at her new accommodation.

"Thank you." Amanda reached for her cousin's hand and squeezed it gently. Mel froze but Amanda didn't seem to notice.

"Did you decorate it especially? It looks so fresh and new."

"It is new."

"It looks old." Mel was surprised.

"Pat's brother is a builder. He does good work. I built it as a guest house but now we have other plans for it."

"Other plans?" Mel was naturally nosy.

"Yes. We're going to give it to Donna. She's in a relationship and I don't want to be the overbearing mother. I'd like her to have some privacy."

"What does Pat think of that?" Mel didn't think many Irish fathers were that cool.

Amanda laughed. "He's not ready to let go yet. He

looked a bit green when I suggested it. But I'd rather she lived there than move away completely."

"I'll find something permanent when all this is sorted and you can have your house back. Pat will have acclimatised by then."

"Don't worry about it. Pat might take a bit of time to get used to his baby living in sin." Amanda linked her arm through Mel's. "Come up to the house. You can speak to Donna."

"Okay." Mel felt a little stiff as they walked. She wasn't comfortable with open shows of affection.

They turned and walked back to the house as the rain started again.

Donna was in the kitchen. She turned with a wide smile when they walked in.

"I've made coffee and sandwiches."

"Thanks, pet." Amanda kissed her cheek and walked to the sink to wash her hands.

Mel sat at the counter and watched them. Amanda was only a kid when she had Donna, just sixteen. It was nice to see how close they were. Mel got a pang of self-pity. She wondered now if she would ever find that closeness. She pushed the thought aside.

"I have some emails to send." Amanda grabbed her coffee and a sandwich. She walked to the door. "I'll see you later." She blew a kiss at her cousin and daughter.

Mel shook her head. Amanda was totally transparent. She was leaving Mel and Donna to *talk*.

"How are you, Melanie?" Donna was like a lot of professionals – as soon as she spoke she put on her psychiatric nurse's hat. It added years to her even though she was only twenty-two.

"I'm fine."

"Really? It's okay to talk to me."

"I'm taking my medication. Things are okay now."

Donna looked a little uncomfortable. "I have to monitor that to make sure you continue to do well."

"I know."

"You're living with my family. I have to be careful."

Suddenly the atmosphere changed.

"Do you think I killed Hugh?" Mel asked.

"I don't know. I won't take chances." Donna didn't falter. She spoke firmly, never taking her eyes off Mel.

Mel wasn't so strong. Her voice broke as she answered. "I didn't hurt anyone."

"Not intentionally." Donna finished the thought for her. "I understand mental illness, Mel. Even if it's not your fault, if you don't do as I say and take your medication regularly I will see to it that you go back." Donna didn't mince her words.

"That won't be necessary." Mel was getting annoyed that nobody had any faith in her.

"Don't get touchy about it, Mel. I have to be careful."

"I know, Donna. Don't preach at me." Mel could feel herself getting upset. "I didn't hurt anyone and I'm sick of being told I did. Even the police don't really think I did it. There was a second blood type found at the crime scene. Somebody else was there. Give me the benefit, please, of 'reasonable doubt'."

Mel didn't want to continue with the conversation. What could you do when people didn't see? She'd just have to prove them wrong . . . unless she'd wounded somebody else. Mel was afraid to voice that fear to anyone but the thought wouldn't leave her head.

CHAPTER 42

Two days later Donna drove Mel to meet her therapist. She was on her way to work so she just dropped her at the centre. After their conversation in the kitchen Mel had felt uncomfortable. Donna was wonderful but she had no faith in Mel and she wasn't even trying to hide it.

"See you later." Donna turned towards Mel and smiled. "Tell me how you get on."

"I will." Mel slammed the door and walked into the building.

It was nice to be walking to the session without an escort but she would prefer not to have to be there at all. She was a couple of minutes early so she could unwind a little before she went inside. There was a high-back chair outside the door in the hall. Mel sat down and laid her head back against the wall.

About ten minutes later a young man left the room. He was wearing runners, grey tracksuit bottoms and a white T-shirt. He stopped for a moment in front of Mel, looking at her. The therapist walked out after him. Mel stood up and the man walked on, giving a backward glance at her as he went. He reminded her of Keith Byrne. She stole another glance after him as she entered the room.

"How are you, Melanie?" Edmund turned to face her. He was wearing chinos and a woollen jumper. He was really going for the non-threatening "little ole me look".

"I'm doing okay."

Edmund directed her towards a chair. Mel sat.

"You're staying with your cousin." Edmund was reviewing his notes as he settled himself opposite her.

"Yes."

"First cousin?" He looked up at her.

"Yes."

"You must be close if she's taken you in like this." He was still fiddling with his notes.

"I suppose. She's ten years older than I am." Mel had never really been close to Amanda but she knew her and if that was what he was referring to then he was correct.

"So Bobby would be the same age as her?"

"Yes." Mel wondered where he was going with this. He seemed to be searching for something in his notes or perhaps this was some sort of method he'd developed to keep her awake. It was certainly annoying her.

"Were they close?"

"Yes. They were best friends." Mel paused for a moment. "Amanda said that things changed around the time he killed Elizabeth."

"Did she know about that?"

"No. But she said she guessed that something was wrong." Mel rubbed the back of her hand. "He started pulling away from everyone around that time but nobody could have guessed why. Could they?" She looked at the therapist for confirmation.

He didn't answer. "Why did she help you – take you into her home?"

"I don't know." Mel blew out a breath loudly. "We didn't see a lot of Amanda."

"Why?"

"She had her daughter Donna when she was sixteen. My mother was dead so I think Dad didn't want me being too close to her in case she was a bad influence."

"So he cut off his own niece."

Mel nodded. "Dad had rigid ideas."

"So he had cut himself off from family and he didn't get on with the neighbours or his son?"

"Um." Mel nodded again. "It was no wonder he was dead six months and nobody came looking for him."

"So you were isolated too?" Edmund finally got to the point.

"Yes. I rarely saw anybody."

"Did you miss Amanda?"

"I was young. I didn't see much of her after Donna was born." Mel smiled suddenly.

Edmund noticed the smile. "What?"

"I went to her wedding. My dad didn't like it. But I was fifteen then."

"Had you rebelled before that?"

"No. Bobby kept me up to date on Amanda and her family. They always stayed close. My dad just didn't want to know about her. I never liked Amanda." Mel knew she had barely known Amanda but the words just came out. Mostly she saw photos Bobby showed her or heard gossip from him.

"Why?" Finally he looked her straight in the eye.

"She was so perfect." Mel went quiet for a moment, thinking back. Amanda had been very beautiful then, but it was more than beauty. People saw Amanda. She eclipsed everybody in any room she entered. Mel blended into the shadows.

"Is she now?"

"Yes. She was always smart, pretty, with lots of boyfriends, went to college . . ." She paused for a moment. "And she and Bobby were inseparable."

"Sounds like a good role model."

Mel frowned. "I didn't see it like that." Was jealously over Amanda's relationship with Bobby the root of why she hadn't liked her? She hadn't thought about it before.

"What do you mean?" he asked.

"The gap was too wide." In Mel's eyes perfect people weren't role models. They discouraged any competition. It was a case of monopolising.

"The gap?"

"From where I was to where she was." Mel's voice was soft. "I had too much to overcome."

"Was your dad positive? Did he encourage you?"

"No. I had a psychiatric illness and no mother. He thought he needed to protect me."

"Did you feel protected?"

Mel shook her head.

"Why not?"

"He smothered me. Dad thought I was broken. He threw broken things away. If a cup was cracked he dumped it. Sometimes if a thing was expensive or of sentimental value then he would glue it back together. But he always said the same thing." Mel felt the old knot in her gut. Her

331

breathing seemed laboured like somebody was pressing on her chest.

"What did he say, Mel?"

"'Broken things are never the same. There's always a crack.'" Mel laughed. "I'm a cracked cup."

"Is that funny?"

Mel stopped laughing immediately and narrowed her eyes. "It's better than crying."

"Not always."

The room lapsed back into silence.

"Will I ever know what's real and what was fantasy from Raven House?"

"I don't know. What part are you thinking about?"

"All of it, though I suppose . . ." She hesitated. "I mean, going by past experience I can see how talking to Bobby and Dad, the phone calls and even the trip to Belize could be hallucinations or daydreams. I was talking to my family, trying to sort things out. They were dead but I was confused. Belize could have been my imagination based on books in the house. My dreams are so realistic sometimes."

"Why do you think you did it?"

Mel shrugged. "I don't know. I thought that maybe I did it to explain the photographs of Elizabeth. You know, when I found them in the attic I really thought I'd never seen them before. But after I started taking medication again I knew that I'd known about Elizabeth. I'd just blocked her out so I wouldn't have to face what Bobby did."

"Did you set up the shrine for Elizabeth?"

"No. At least I don't remember."

"Yours were the only fingerprints we found on the shrine."

Mel lapsed into silence and let her time in the house run through her mind.

Finally she spoke. "I recognised Gordon Grant in the photo the police showed me. He was Ryan so I know he existed but I can't quite organise what part was real and what wasn't. I'm not really sure how long we were down there or even what we did. We didn't go out. We stayed in the house all the time. I would occasionally go on short trips when Ryan was away. But when Ryan was in Raven, we never went anywhere. Keith Byrne the delivery guy met Ryan once or twice but nobody else that I remember. Maybe Keith knew him." It was like a light bulb went off in her head. Of course Keith knew Ryan. It wasn't just a case of paying for goods – whenever she saw Ryan talking to Keith, though they spoke in the yard or another room, they always seemed familiar with each other. Keith's family had worked for the Renfield family, Ryan or Gordon Grant dated Elizabeth so whatever Ryan was up to Keith must have known about it. Finally things made sense. She sat gazing into space. As the silence extended, questions hung heavily in the room. Did Ryan kill Hugh Curtis and where was he now? Or did Keith kill Hugh and where was Keith now? They were both missing.

CHAPTER 43

Back at home Mel lay on her couch looking at the ceiling. All evening since she'd come back she'd been battling the paranoia that usually sent her spiralling. If it hadn't been for her new medication she knew this would be a very bad time. The drugs didn't take away the paranoia but they gave her the ammunition to fight it. The authorities were waiting for a chance to prove her involvement, somehow. There was nobody left in her life except for Amanda and her family. Mel knew she was the family member from hell. Through it all her struggling mind kept letting her down.

A knock on the door brought her back to reality. She got up and crossed the room.

"Yes."

"Melanie, it's me," Donna said.

Mel opened the door. "It's your house. There's no reason for you to knock."

"Melanie, while you're here it's your space." Once

more Donna gave her the professional smile. Mel guessed she was being managed. It was good for her to have her own front door.

"Do you want coffee? I was going to make some." Mel walked to the kitchen.

"Yes. Please." Donna sat in the armchair. "How did it go today with your therapist?" Mel had taken the bus back because Donna couldn't get off work on time.

"It was good. I made a breakthrough. I think."

"That's great."

Mel handed Donna a cup and took one herself. She sat across from Donna. "You can't imagine what it's really like to make up such an elaborate tale. I invented another world."

"Lucky you. I could do with one at the moment."

Mel burst out laughing. Somebody had actually made a joke in front of her.

"I thought you had a new man in your life. Your life sounds great."

"I don't think he's 'the one' long term." Donna's professional smile slipped and Mel saw the twenty-two-year-old girl. "I want the right one."

"You're a baby." Mel couldn't believe anyone as young as Donna was worrying about finding a husband.

"I want to marry young, have my children and be young when they grow up. I don't want to be an old mother. I have my career so now it's Project Man. Mum was only sixteen when she had me and we love being so close in age."

Mel laughed but she wasn't really amused. If this little girl was on Project Man what hope was there for her? Donna noticed Mel's crestfallen look.

"You're doing fine, Mel. Let's take your medication and get that out of the way now in case you forget." Professional Donna was back.

"Okay." It was odd being treated like a child again.

"Good. I promise I'm here whenever you want to talk. You're not alone."

"Thank you."

They sat, lying back in their chairs enjoying their coffee and the quietness until Donna had to return to the house to finish some work she'd been doing. Mel went back to her latest book, the peace of the house settling around her.

A couple of hours later Amanda appeared at Mel's door.

"Come up for dinner. There's plenty." Amanda didn't come inside and just hovered on the doorstep.

"Okay. Thank you." Mel put aside her book and took her coffee cup to the sink. She washed it and Donna's cup from earlier and followed Amanda outside. They stood in the garden listening to the waves crash on the shore in the distance.

"It's so gorgeous here. You have a wonderful life, Amanda." Mel could never quite feel proud of someone else's achievements without feeling pity for herself. It always felt like the universe had denied her and overindulged others.

"I know. I feel very lucky." Amanda's voice was wistful.

"You are. Did you have a plan?" Now that things were looking a little less bleak for Mel maybe she could adopt some of Amanda's approach and find happiness for herself. She felt old sometimes even though she was only twenty-eight. She wondered if a girl with mental illness and heavily dependent on medication could ever find what Amanda obviously had.

"What do you mean?" Amanda looked puzzled.

"A life plan."

"No. All this nearly didn't happen."

"Because of Donna?"

"Yes."

"You were only sixteen." The wind blew the trees above them. Mel loved that sound.

"I was," said Amanda. "My mother was shocked. She never thought I'd get my teaching qualification. But we're a stubborn bunch and Donna was such a good little girl."

"My dad was shocked too." Mel thought back.

That was why Eoin Yeats had kept Mel so close. If a smart girl like Amanda got caught, what trouble could a flake like Melanie get into?

"You were only young. Can you remember his reaction?" Amanda hadn't really taken much notice of Mel when she was little. She was just Bobby's baby sister.

"Oh yeah. You were a cautionary tale for kids everywhere."

"How did you feel?" Amanda was suddenly curious about Mel.

"I couldn't understand it. I knew you weren't married. Dad knew you didn't have a regular boyfriend, at least none that anyone seemed to know about. I couldn't stop thinking about where you did it. Kids imagine Mammy and Daddy do it in their bedrooms. I was confused because you lived at home and I knew your mother wouldn't allow boys under her roof. I asked Dad where you did it and he nearly blew a gasket."

Mel laughed loudly but the laughter died when she realised Amanda had frozen beside her. She knew she'd embarrassed her.

Even though it was quite dark the pain in Amanda seemed to glow. Immediately the paranoia returned. Mel was mortified. She was born without filters.

"I'm sorry, Amanda. I didn't mean to upset you."

"It's fine." She spoke sharply. "You know Uncle Eoin cut me off completely? He even fell out with my mother because she told him what she thought of him for treating me like that. I never saw you. We should have been there for you. It must have been hard growing up with him as your father."

Mel ignored the comment on her dad. "Is that why you're helping me now?"

"Yes. I feel so guilty."

"Don't. It's not your fault." Mel tentatively touched her cousin's shoulder. "You stayed in touch with Bobby."

"Yes."

"Dad hated that. But he could never tell Bobby what to do."

"No. Bobby and I never lost contact." Amanda's voice held a lot of sadness.

They were quiet for a moment and then Mel spoke. "It must have been hard for you. A baby at that age." Amanda since then had made all the right decisions. That was just a minor blip in an otherwise exemplary life.

"It was." Amanda had left that place behind a long time ago and didn't want Mel to revisit it. "Dinner is ready." She walked away.

Mel watched her cousin's stiff back and quick step as she walked away. She hadn't expected Amanda to be so defensive about her past. Mel felt a pang of jealousy. Amanda and Bobby stayed in touch but she was cut off in that place alone with her father. She tried to shake the negative feelings off before she entered the house.

Inside Donna was dishing the food onto plates. Mel and Amanda sat side by side at the centre island.

"You're just in time." Donna handed the food around to everyone and sat down at the counter. A bottle of sparkling water sat on the table but no wine. Suddenly, Mel wanted a drink so badly.

Donna saw her look at the water and seemed to be able to read her thoughts.

"I thought it would be a good idea not to drink, for a change. We drink too much wine these days." She smiled at Mel.

Mel hated being treated like a child but she knew it wasn't recommended with her medication. She glanced at Amanda out of the corner of her eye. It was very obvious that Amanda could do with a drink too. Thinking about the past seemed to have upset her.

The food was delicious. Donna had baked chicken breasts in a sauce and served it with fragrant rice. It was colourful and the smell had Mel's mouth tingling. Donna had turned off the main lights and lit a couple of lamps around the room. Everything looked warm and homey.

"You're a good cook, Donna." Mel tried to lighten the moment and snap Amanda out of her forlorn mood.

"Thanks, Melanie. I enjoy it." Donna's face was split by a happy smile. She was a very beautiful girl.

Donna's smile suddenly made Mel feel like she'd been punched. That smile was exactly like another she'd seen in the past. Donna was so like Bobby. Why hadn't she noticed it before?

CHAPTER 44

As they were eating the phone rang. Amanda barely registered the sound.

"Dad's due to call now." Donna got up to answer.

The phone was in the hall and Mel couldn't hear the conversation. Amanda sat rigidly beside her, looking away into the distance. Neither of them spoke. Donna returned after a couple of minutes, breaking the silence.

"Mum. He wants to speak to you." Donna sat back down.

Amanda got up without looking at Mel and left the table.

Donna turned to Mel. "He's away on business."

"I know." Mel said. "Amanda told me – a conference."

"Yes. In Boston."

"He's in Boston?"

"Yes. He's doing some consulting in a hospital there so he's over there every few months."

"How long has he been there?"

"Two weeks. They're developing some new cardiology treatment over there. Mum just got back a couple of days before you came here."

"Amanda was there recently?" Mel couldn't keep the surprise out of her voice.

"Um. She doesn't like the long trips. She misses him. Why?"

"No reason. She just hadn't mentioned it." Mel wondered why everything led back to Boston. "Do they go there often?"

"On and off." Donna thought Mel was just making small talk.

But Mel was wondering suddenly about Amanda and Bobby. Had she known more about his business than she'd admitted? Mel suspected that they had maintained a closer connection over the years than Amanda wanted her to believe.

Amanda walked back into the room and sat down.

"Dad's in a good mood." Donna smiled at her.

"He is. The project is going well. He'll be home soon." Amanda still seemed strained as she sat back at the counter.

"That's good," said Donna. "I was just telling Mel that you're back from Boston recently."

Amanda turned to Mel. "It wasn't much of a trip. We didn't leave the hotel."

"Too much information, Mother," Donna said.

Amanda laughed. "Sorry, pet."

Donna leaned in to Mel. "A couple of middle-aged honeymooners."

Mel wasn't listening. "Umm." She wanted to speak to Amanda alone. Mel knew she was doing it again, interfering in other people's business but somehow she couldn't stop herself.

The rest of the meal was eaten in silence. Donna read a medical article while her mother and cousin gazed into space, each lost in their own thoughts. Mel couldn't get the idea out of her head that Amanda was hiding something.

As soon as she could, Mel made her way back to the cottage. Why hadn't she seen before how like Bobby Donna was? Of course it could just be your normal family resemblance but the similarities between Donna and Bobby were much stronger than the likeness between Mel and Bobby. It wasn't just physical. Even their mannerisms and expressions were similar. Mel didn't know much about genetics and didn't know if these things could pass on to more distant cousins. But instinct told her that wasn't the case here. She wondered if Pat had seen it too.

It was only eight thirty when she let herself into the cottage and sat down. She would have dearly loved a glass of wine but she didn't want to let Donna down. A cup of herbal tea would have to do instead. She put the kettle on and grabbed her book off the table. Someone had taken the trouble to stock the bookshelves with a selection of recent and popular paperbacks. Mel would have plenty to occupy her while she was there. But her mind was too distracted to concentrate on her book. Finally she threw it on the rug by the couch and lay back, looking up at the ceiling.

She guessed that Amanda would come to her. When she heard footsteps descending the path she knew they would be hers.

Mel sat up straight waiting and answered to Amanda's knock immediately. "Come in!"

Amanda walked in and stood, shifting from foot to foot, looking at Mel. Mel said nothing, waiting for Amanda to explain.

"We need to talk, Melanie."

"Why?"

"I know you've guessed. I can't have you asking questions and maybe saying the wrong thing. It wouldn't help anyone." Amanda's face and posture were rigid. She didn't look anything like the poised woman she usually was.

"I have no intention of saying anything." Mel had guessed correctly about Amanda and Bobby. She got up and moved towards Amanda to reassure her but she took a step backwards.

"Mel, you mightn't be able to help yourself."

"I'm not that bad." Mel was a little angry at Amanda's lack of faith.

"Not on medication but you made a right mess of things before, didn't you?"

Mel knew she was right. Her reaction to Bobby's confession ruined everything. That one lapse in judgement took Bobby away from both of them.

"So you think if I'm off my meds I'll just blurt out to Pat who Donna's father is?"

"Pat knows everything. I don't care about that but I won't have you tear Donna's world apart."

"Donna doesn't know?" Mel asked in amazement.

"She knows Pat's not her father. Why should she know any more than that? She thinks of him as her father, nobody else. He's always been in her life. He's 'Dad' as far as she's concerned."

"Didn't she ever ask?"

"I told her it was a boy on holiday in the area who left and I never saw him again. She just thought I was a typical silly teenager. Nobody ever thought anything else."

"I won't say anything." Mel said. "You should have told her yourself years ago."

"I know." Amanda sat down on a straight-backed chair just inside the door. "I should have but I couldn't. She would have thought that Bobby abandoned her which isn't too far from the truth, is it?"

Mel ignored that. "Did Bobby know?"

"Yes. Of course. We told each other everything."

"What did he do?" Mel was bewildered by the actions of her brother.

Amanda smiled a sad smile. "He ran away."

"He finished school and went to college. That's not running away."

"He could have gone to college anywhere in this country. Why did he have to go to Boston?"

"But if he stayed here what would you have done? Would you have wanted to be a family?" Mel was playing devil's advocate for her brother. She couldn't help herself.

Amanda flinched. "He could have supported me. He could have stayed near. People didn't have to know."

"You wouldn't have told people?"

"How could we? You can imagine the jokes around at home. We were first cousins. They'd be counting Donna's fingers."

"So he didn't run away. He made it easier." Mel still felt the need to explain Bobby's actions.

"He could have stayed and helped." But Amanda knew Bobby could never just hang around in the background. He would have been miserable and made her miserable too.

"Did you want help? Hasn't your life turned out better this way?"

"I wanted him. He was the love of my life. You remember what he was like?"

Mel did. Her brother, the reckless boy ruled by his impulses. He had a smile that would light up a room and a laugh that rang in your ears hours after the joke was told but he was infantile when it came to responsibility.

"You were better off without him and so was Donna." Mel loved him dearly but she knew that was true.

"I know." Even Amanda wasn't that blinded by love.

"You told Pat everything?" This amazed Mel.

"Yes." Something about the way Amanda said that made Mel sense there was more to it than that.

"I'm surprised."

"He loves me and Donna."

"But you said Bobby was the love of your life." Mel didn't understand duplicity.

"Don't be so naïve, Melanie!" Amanda's voice was full of anger.

"Were you with Bobby up until his death?" Mel asked.

"Yes. I was with him the night he went back and told you about Elizabeth."

"What? So you did know about Elizabeth!"

"I knew everything about him. He told me as soon as he sobered up and calmed down. He rang me. I was living at home then."

"Why didn't you tell him to give himself up? It was an accident."

"Don't be so fucking stupid, Mel. He'd been drinking, he stole a car and a girl died. He burned the car and left the scene. He found out afterwards about the smoke in her lungs. They might have charged him with second-degree murder or something. He would have been sent to prison for a long time. Donna was only young and even if he couldn't acknowledge her I wanted him to know her." Amanda was crying now.

"But he ran away anyway, didn't he?" said Mel.

Amanda nodded with tears running down her cheeks.

"You still wanted him and still made room for him in your life even after that?"

Mel asked.

Amanda nodded.

"You were married then, weren't you?"

"Yes, Mel. Legally to Pat and in my heart to your brother."

"Did Pat know that?" Mel couldn't keep the sarcasm out of her voice.

"Just assume nobody knows anything and keep it zipped," said Amanda. "Play it safe, don't say anything to anybody and then you won't get into any more trouble." Amanda smiled but it never reached her eyes. She was threatening Mel. Maybe more correctly Mel was threatening her. Mel just knowing this information was a threat to Amanda's stability.

"Trouble!"

"I've helped you, Melanie, because you're Bobby's sister and my cousin but I won't let anyone break up my family."

Mel had a thought. "Bobby was with you the night he told me about Elizabeth. Do you know why he told me?"

Amanda went pale. "We had a terrible row. I told him I couldn't bear being without him any longer. You know where he worked. I knew he would be killed out there one day and I didn't know how I could go on without him. I wanted to tell Donna and leave Pat and then finally we'd get to be together."

Mel was stunned. Amanda had money, a beautiful house and family and she'd been willing to throw it all away for a man-child who lived out of a suitcase.

"What did he say?"

Amanda closed her eyes and Mel thought she was going to fall.

"He turned me down."

For a moment she swayed. Mel was too scared to reach for her. She wanted to know what happened next. Amanda looked as though she were going to run out of the house.

"He said he couldn't live the life I wanted and wanted to know what was wrong with the way we were. I could see clearly what had been happening over the years. Bobby didn't want a wife. He just wanted me on the side. I was upset. We said terrible things to each other and I made him so angry. Luckily Pat was away at the time."

Mel realised Pat must have been away a lot. Amanda's sobs were audible now. "We knew that was the end. That was why he got so drunk and told you everything. The accident had always played on his mind and now he'd lost me too and his connection to his only child."

When she stopped talking the house became silent. Mel remembered his face the night he told her about Elizabeth. He was broken and now she knew why. He was a haunted man haunted by the crash and his tormented relationship with his father. After losing the woman he loved and his daughter he had no one to talk to. Telling Mel about the car crash was risky. She could have let it slip to somebody. He never thought she'd go to the dead girl's family. Yet he'd never told her about Amanda and Donna. Maybe a little piece of him wanted people to know about Elizabeth's death.

While Mel was thinking about what to say Amanda turned and walked out the door. Mel looked after her. What could she do to fix things between them?

Bobby was an unstable force which they had all been unable to resist or to overcome. He worshipped the "good time" and to hell with the consequences, but then there was Donna. When thinking straight Mel was a moralist. There was a moral code we all had to follow which made life easier. Bobby just did as he pleased. Mel would have thought that Amanda was like her and followed the rules but obviously not. But Amanda broke the rules and ended up with the big house, fancy husband and beautiful daughter that Mel would kill for. Yet Amanda had been willing to risk it all for the one thing she couldn't have: Bobby.

When Mel wrote that letter to Brad Renfield she'd taken Bobby from Amanda forever.

CHAPTER 45

Next morning Donna was at Mel's door at nine o'clock.

"Morning, Melanie."

"Donna. Hi."

"I've brought muffins. I went up to the village to get some."

"Lovely. I'll put on the coffee."

They sat at the dining table with the sun streaming through the window. Mel could see that there was something on Donna's mind. These weren't just random muffins. Donna had needed an excuse to come visit her.

"What happened last night between you and Mum?"

Mel was caught off guard. "What do you mean?"

"I'm not stupid. I saw her face when she came back from visiting your cottage and neither of you said two words at dinner."

"She probably has something on her mind." Mel hated to lie but she could not discuss this with Donna.

"I know she has something on her mind. What did you say to her?"

"Nothing."

"I warned you, Melanie, not to mess with my family."

"I didn't do anything to her." Mel was getting very upset and she knew it would show on her face.

Donna was visibly upset too. "You're implicated in murder. I told Mum it mightn't be a good idea bringing you here but she insisted."

Mel's chest hurt. "Your mum fought to get me here?"

"Yes. Loyalty to your family, she said."

"Your dad didn't mind?"

Donna smiled. "No. He'd support her no matter what she wanted. I won't let you hurt this family, Mel."

Mel didn't know what to say. If she couldn't stay there she might be sent straight back into an institution while the investigation was going on. There was no way to explain to Donna what had happened without talking about Amanda and Bobby and then the whole story would come out.

"Donna, I've done nothing wrong. Honestly." Mel was close to tears.

"I'll have to believe you for now but I am watching you, Mel."

Everybody was watching her. Mel couldn't turn or she might make a mistake.

Donna stood up. "I'm going to work but I'll talk to you later."

Mel watched her through the window as she went to her car. Her life was like walking through a minefield.

She got up, gathered their breakfast things and brought them to the sink. As she squirted some washing-up liquid on them she ruminated on her conversation with Donna. She placed the dishes in the rack to dry and like a child she played with the bubbles. After a time she heard quick footsteps descending the path. She dried her hands and turned to see Amanda open the door, walk straight in and stand in the sitting room shaking in anger.

"How dare you tell Donna what happened!"

"I didn't tell Donna anything." Mel's world was turning upside down around her.

"She flew out of here and straight to her car!" said Amanda.

"I said nothing. Honestly, Amanda. She was late for work."

"I don't believe you. Why did I allow you to stay here? You'll wreck everything."

"She knows nothing except that we had a fight. I'd never tell her about Bobby." Mel was panicking.

"Good." Amanda was calming down. "Pat is her dad."

"Mum. I left my phone."

Amanda turned.

Donna stood in the doorway, looking from one to the other. "What are you talking about?"

The two women stood looking at her, unable to speak. Twenty-two years of lies lay between them.

"Bobby, your brother? What does he have to do with us?" Donna turned to Mel.

Amanda was still too stunned to speak.

"Nothing," Mel said.

Amanda turned towards her and took a step.

"What about your brother, Mel?" Donna demanded.

Amanda said. "Mel! Don't."

"Don't what? What's going on?" Donna walked

351

towards Mel and looked directly at her. Her face had the scared look of a little girl.

Mel wanted to step back from them. She tried to reassure Donna. "Nothing. We were just talking about him. That's all."

"That's not all. What does it have to do with Dad?"

Amanda and Melanie could both see clearly the moment when the penny dropped and Donna understood what it meant.

"No." She looked from one to the other. "No! He was your cousin!" Her eyes locked into her mother's.

"Donna. Let me explain."

"Does Dad know?"

Amanda said nothing.

"Does he?" Donna shrieked the words at her.

"Yes."

Donna turned and ran. Once more the car could be heard accelerating away.

Before Mel could gather her thoughts Amanda crossed to her. She grabbed Mel's hair and pulled her head back painfully. She stared into Mel's eyes, her own normally twinkling blue eyes contorted with rage and fear. Amanda was taller than Mel and angrier than Mel had ever seen her. Mel tried to pull away but she couldn't break her grip. Amanda threw her against the rail of the stairs and walked to the door.

"Amanda!" Mel said. But Amanda was gone.

CHAPTER 46

Mel was too scared to follow her. It was understandable that Amanda was angry. Mel was a jinx. She couldn't go near the house; there was nowhere for her to go. Eventually she thought somebody would realise that none of it was her fault and they would come looking for her. So she sat there for the day, running the whole bizarre mess round and round in her head.

She waited until evening to act. Amanda was up in that big house alone. Mel felt so guilty. Bobby made this chaos and typically he ran away rather than pick up the pieces. Mel just stumbled into the aftermath of both of his messes yet none of it had ever had anything to do with her.

But that wasn't strictly true. Was it? Bobby confided in her about the crash and she ran to Elizabeth's brother. How could she ever have thought that was a good idea? But it had seemed that way at the time. *At the time* it seemed perfectly reasonable to pick up her pen and write to a grieving man, explain what had happened to his sister and apologise on behalf of the Yeats family.

Of course he would want to see justice for his sister and have Bobby prosecuted. Bobby couldn't bear the idea of a life in confinement. He ran out of places to run at six a.m., when there was a loud knocking on the door and a US marshal and some Irish police officers stood on the step ready to take him away. Mel still remembered the sound of the banging door and the sight of Bobby being taken away for questioning.

Within twenty-four hours they got a call to say that he had died in custody.

Now here she was again. Amanda asks her to keep quiet about her and Bobby and somehow Mel manages to let the secret out. One thing Mel knew for sure, life doesn't just keep happening to you. Somehow, she could have changed things.

It was getting dark outside. Mel looked up at the main house. It was in total darkness. Either Amanda had gone out or she was sitting in the dark. Mel had to speak to her. She rubbed the side of her head where Amanda had so roughly pulled her hair. Amanda had a temper.

Was it safe to approach her? Pat wasn't due back for a couple of days. Donna was out there somewhere. Mel decided to risk going to Amanda and sorting things out. She left the cottage. She couldn't bear the thought of her cousin sitting up there in the dark brooding.

It was a beautiful evening. The darkening sky stretched above her a deep dark blue with tiny points of light, slowly emerging. To gather her courage she walked to the garden wall and looked out at the bay. The smell of the sea and the gentle crashing of the waves in the distance helped to calm her a little.

Mel turned and walked up the path through the garden towards the side door of the house. If Amanda was inside that would be open. There was still no light on but the door opened on the first turn of the handle. Mel pushed it in and stepped into the utility room. Once more she rubbed the tender spot on her head as she crossed the small room and entered the kitchen.

The fridge door was open, casting a weak light around the room. Mel walked over to close it. She had to move around the centre island to get to it. As she manoeuvred around it her toe caught against the corner of the wood and she fell over. She hit the ground hard with her knee and for a few moments shoots of pain took her breath away. "Shit," she whispered to herself. "That was dumb." She stood up and gently moved her knee until the pain subsided.

It was very dark so she went to the wall by the fridge to turn on the light. She flicked the switch and immediately the room flooded with brightness. Mel pushed the door of the fridge and closed it.

Should she call out to Amanda, she wondered, or just go back to the cottage? Maybe she should leave and let Amanda sleep on it. Mel flicked the light off again and went to retrace her steps.

Once more as she was crossing the room her toe caught but she managed to keep standing. This time Mel knew it wasn't the counter so she reached down and felt with her fingertips to see what it was. Long hair and soft damp skin greeted her probing fingers. A scream built up inside but it came out in a gasp.

Mel ran to the light switch again. She flicked it on and turned back to the counter. Lying in front of it was

Amanda. Mel must have caught her toe in her long hair, which was spread behind her along the tiles.

Her beautiful face was a mess of blood. Mel moved further around the counter to move away from the horror in front of her and once more stumbled, landing on her butt with her hand grabbing thin air to steady herself.

Mesmerised, she couldn't take her eyes off the body in front of her. Amanda had often stood at the counter with her back to the garden door. She had a bank of family photos on the wall opposite and liked to stand and look at them. Melanie guessed she was struck first from behind. Her eyes darted around the room. A few yards from Amanda lay a baseball bat that used to hang on the wall above the desk in the corner.

Mel gasped. A flash of a violent image played itself out in her mind. The sound of a body being struck, gasps, shouts, the sound of the knife penetrating flesh. Images played across her mind like flicking through a digital camera. At first the images were blurred and surreal then they started to gain form and structure. The sounds went from background noise to a crystal clarity that took over her mind. Mel could hear sobbing, but realised that she was the one crying.

Mel had seen Hugh murdered. She'd pushed the images back into the recesses of her mind but here looking at Amanda it all came rushing back. It was like watching a graphically violent movie playing in her head.

Mel had got up to go downstairs but halfway down the corridor she'd heard the sound of fighting. She ran back and got the knife she'd brought upstairs for protection. She ran downstairs. At the bottom of the stairs she listened. The sounds were coming from the back corridor.

Mel gripped the knife tightly and made her way down the hall, her heart thudding against her breastbone.

What she saw shocked her to her core. A stunned Hugh could barely remain standing. The intruder had the advantage in strength and violence. Hugh was knocked to the ground and his opponent wielded a poker as he battered the now prone body. He alternated between kicks and blows with the poker as Mel ran screaming towards them holding her knife. She thought she'd managed to hit him somewhere with the blade but he turned, hitting her once, knocking her immediately to the ground as he took the knife from her. Mel's head hit the wall and she lay there dazed.

Hugh was long gone and his shell of a body was on the ground but the attacker continued to hit him. He had Mel's knife in his belt. It all happened so fast. He started using the knife. She could see he was crazy. The blood spray spread as far as where she lay. Terrified, she couldn't look away, assuming that any moment he would reach for her. There was no way she could fight an attack like that. Hugh was tall, athletic and very fit and if he didn't stand a chance against the intensity of the attack she certainly didn't.

This was how she was going to die. She remembered thinking that so clearly. But the violence seemed to sate him and he sat back almost peacefully against the wall. That was when Mel acted. Hugh's keys were on the ground a few feet from his lifeless body so she grabbed them up and ran. The intruder's laughter followed her down the hall. She could hear his voice getting closer as he got up and followed her.

Outside she ran to Hugh's car and opened it, her hands shaking violently. As she fumbled with the engine she saw him standing in the doorway. Then he ran towards her. But the engine sparked to life and she remembered driving off before he reached her.

The next clear memory she had was sitting in the car outside the police station in Bantry.

Now, here she was again in another house and with another body. It was all going to happen again. The police would be called and now they would lock her up forever. But why? Mel knew who did it but she just couldn't understand why. Was the ruination of her the end game? Guilt consumed her. If she'd only been able to convince them that it wasn't her who killed Hugh, Amanda would still be alive.

Mel couldn't stay there and let it happen again. At the very least she would be charged as an accessory. Mel had little faith in the legal system. This time there was no way out of this. She would go away for a very long time.

Working now on autopilot, she jumped up from her position against the wall and crossed the room. Tenderly she touched the back of Amanda's hand. "Goodbye," she whispered. She ran from the kitchen through the back door and stood in the yard. Had she blood on her? She didn't think so.

Someone would call the police before she'd got very far. Could she go through other back gardens? She didn't know. The walls were high and certainly some of them had dogs. She'd heard them barking at times. The beach. She would try that. Mel ran blindly to save herself.

Whipping around, she ran to the garden wall. Since she'd arrived she hadn't seen anyone going down there but there must be a path. Well, maybe not, she thought, suddenly grabbing the sides of her head to control another onslaught of images.

She ran along the wall and at the other end from her cottage she found a wooden gate. Mel tried to open it. It didn't budge. She shook it but it held fast. Then she felt a bolt at her side. She pulled that back, opened the gate and stepped through.

As her feet touched ground on the other side of the gate a powerful arm reached out and grabbed her waist, pulling her back towards him. Mel screamed but he clamped a hand roughly over her mouth. This was it.

CHAPTER 47

There was a path beyond the garden gate, which was quite steep, leading downwards through the trees towards the water. You could see the water over the treetops.

He pushed Mel forward. They descended the path with him holding Mel steady as her feet stumbled on the cobbled walkway. The sea got louder as they approached. The path became less steep as they got closer to the shore.

They stepped off the path onto the beach. The waves crashed and broke, with spray hitting them in the face. He pushed her onwards, stumbling over the rocks closer to the water.

Then he stopped. They were standing on a large slippery flat rock beyond which lay deep water. Was he expecting her to just walk off the edge? Probably he did. If she'd died locked in her room in Raven House it would have looked like she'd killed herself, if she'd crashed down the hill it would be a tragic accident now, if she jumped off these rocks, the whole world would believe that she had a psychotic break, killed Amanda and committed suicide just like her brother had done.

Edging forward she looked at the water. It would make things easier if she followed Bobby. There was little for her here. If he let her live she would be locked up for the rest of her life. If she didn't jump of her own free will he would probably push her. Mel was a strong swimmer. It was the only activity she ever got involved in as a child. She'd been a lot better than Bobby, Mr Water Engineer, had ever been.

For the first time she turned and looked at his face. She hadn't needed to do that before then. She'd known the minute he stood behind her who it was. Keith had killed Hugh and now he'd come for her.

He smiled at her though the smile only moved his mouth. His cold eyes remained untouched.

Mel pinched herself. "Why? Why kill my cousin and Hugh? And why drag me into it?"

He was crazy. Mel could see it on his features. There was no humanity there, just a cold speculating stare.

"Let me tell you a story, Melanie. Once upon a time there was a little boy named Keith. His family had always toiled at the big house. One day his grandmother told him 'This too will be yours'. Yes. One day the little boy might also fetch and carry for the Reid family. Then the little boy fell in love. A beautiful girl came to the house to visit her grandmother. Yes. That little girl was Elizabeth Renfield. She charmed the little boy. They played together and even though she was older she always had time to spend with him. One day he told himself he would marry the beautiful Elizabeth but four years later she was killed in a senseless crash in Boston. The little boy would never see Elizabeth again."

Mel couldn't believe her ears. Elizabeth's memory was threaded through all of them.

"So the shrine was yours?"

He nodded. "Before Gordon brought you down there I took care of the house. Bradley hired me as the caretaker."

"You know the family well?" Mel needed to keep him talking so she could figure out what to do.

"After Elizabeth died I wanted to be as close to her as I could so I asked Bradley for a job in America. I'd known him too as a youngster when he would stay in Raven Hill."

"You went to Boston?" Mel could feel the mist from the waves as they talked.

"Yes. I worked there for ten years until something amazing happened." He laughed. "Bradley got a letter."

Mel felt sick. Her letter.

"Bradley had me working in the house and we often talked. He knew about the loyalty my family had shown to his and he knew how strongly I felt about what happened to Elizabeth."

Mel stepped back and felt with one toe as he spoke. She was close to the edge of the rock.

"Bradley was so excited. Finally they would get some closure for Elizabeth. He got things moving to try and extradite Bobby Yeats but we all know what happened, don't we? The coward opted out again."

Mel needed to know why they brought her into it. "How did I end up in the middle of it?"

He laughed. "That was Gordon's idea. He was nearly as guilty as your brother when it came to Elizabeth's death. Bradley had him under his thumb in so many ways. He never let Gordon forget that if he hadn't let Elizabeth out of the car then she wouldn't have died. Bradley sent

Gordon to Galway to find out more about you. They're American. Someone has to pay. He thought since they couldn't do things through the criminal courts now that Bobby was gone, perhaps they could get your family through the civil courts. I tried to explain to him that civil litigation wasn't going to work here. Gordon was on a fact-finding mission initially, even though being a lawyer he knew it was a wild-goose chase. Then Gordon and myself hatched a plan together. We would get retribution for Elizabeth. He would take you down to Raven and we'd make you pay. But Gordon couldn't go through with it. He went soft on me and thought I should forget about revenge. Somehow he fell in love with you and wanted no part in killing you. So I took over."

Mel's heart jumped. Ryan had loved her. "Where is Ryan – I mean – Gordon now?"

Keith laughed. "Who knows? Coward took off."

"Why take me to Raven House?"

"We wanted to let the curse get you. We thought it would be *poetic*." He started laughing. "It nearly did."

"Like it got Elizabeth?"

He looked beyond Mel into the darkness and frowned as his haunted eyes looked out over the sea. Then he looked back at her and the insolent smile he used on her in Raven House was back.

"I can see why Gordon wanted to play with you." He reached out his hand and ran his finger slowly down over her breast.

Mel sucked in her breath. She couldn't step back any further. There was no space.

"Why did you kill Hugh?"

"I had to. He heard a noise and went to investigate. He

thought I was someone breaking into the house. I could have got him to ring 'Miss Gill' to vouch for me. She works with the estate agents selling Raven House and we'd met in the past. But I didn't want him telling you he caught me wandering the back corridors. Even you would get suspicious at that."

Mel was shaking. Her mind was jumbled and she was finding it hard to separate things that may have happened and all the things she'd convinced herself were lies.

He stopped talking and the only sound was the sea.

Mel's pulse was racing. Now was no time to fall apart. By now she was so close to the edge that her heel was actually hanging over fresh air. The surface of the rock was slippery. His body was uncomfortably close to her.

Minutes ticked by and the tide seemed higher on the rocks. Nobody spoke or moved.

Mel guessed this wasn't just about his lost love Elizabeth. He was psychotic. He enjoyed the killing. But it wasn't just the killing. He enjoyed torture. The story of Elizabeth's death just gave him a reason to start. Keith was the cat to Mel's mouse.

Mel looked around her for any way of escape but there was none.

He started to laugh. It was so quiet now she could hear the little puff of air he exhaled through his nose. Mel waited, her eyes closely watching his as they flicked about over his dark memories. She wanted to be sick.

Keith moved a little closer to Mel. "Gordon letting Lizzie out of the car that night started an odyssey. We became the navigators. You were part of the journey with your letter."

"What do you want from me?"

He smiled. "You and me have come to the end of our journey. You should have died that night in Raven House. The Guards would have found two dead bodies. But I couldn't kill you the same way it had to look as though you killed Hugh and then killed yourself. I was going to put you in the car and use the exhaust fumes."

"Why did you kill Amanda?" She had to know that before he killed her.

"I overheard your conversation."

"Why would our conversation make a difference?" Mel's brain slowly tried to catch up.

"She was Bobby's woman. He had a family. It seemed like justice that I would take from him what he took from us."

Fear gripped Mel. Donna. Had he heard about Donna? He didn't say and, if she asked and he hadn't heard that part, then she'd be telling him.

"You went to the Guards. I wasn't expecting that. They locked you up and I couldn't get to you but once you were back here it would be easier. But I wanted it to look like you took your own life. Perhaps an overdose."

He was insane and there was no way for her to get past him. He was blocking her path and he was the stronger of the two. If she stood there for too much longer he would put whatever plan he was hatching in his head into action and she wouldn't be strong enough to get away from him. Mel knew she couldn't let him win. There were just inches between them. At that moment he just seemed to be enjoying the spectacle of her terror. This was the end for her if she waited for him.

Desperately she tried to think of a way out. The only thing she could do was to take him by surprise.

Without thinking Mel turned and dived off the rocks. She hit the water between two outcrops, praying that there was nothing underneath that would catch her. As she surfaced a shout rang out over the sound of the sea but she couldn't catch the words. Tossed by the waves her shoulder scraped painfully off a rock but she tried to stop the panic. At least if she died now it would be as the result of her own actions and not his.

The tide was going out. If it had been going in she would have been battered on the rocks. It wasn't so rough and as soon she was away from the rocks she could swim. Keeping her head up a little she could see the lights of the houses along the coast. What could she do? He might walk along the shore and wait for her to come in.

Mel swam towards an outcrop of rock. Her body was aching and her strength was nearly gone but she got a hand onto a rock. The currents immediately grabbed her and swept her sideways breaking her grip. Mel had almost given up when she was swept onto the sand just past the outcrop. She dragged herself up and lay on the small beach with her chest heaving. Geographically she hadn't gone far. She had only been in the water a short while. It wasn't the distance that wore her out; it was fighting against the currents.

What could she do? The cold was drilling into her bones and her head was pounding from the exertion in the icy water. She moved a little further up the beach and sat between two rocks to try and keep the worst of the cold wind off her. A light drizzle had started and the wind was picking up again. She strained to hear any movement beyond the wind. At any second Keith could get to her.

It was very dark. The lights from the streets and houses

above were hidden from the beach. Mel looked to her right and saw a long stretch of sandy beach. She could walk along it but where would it take her? As she ran her mind along her options she saw a small light appear around the headland to her left. It was bobbing along like a torch on the beach. He must be following her. Too exhausted to move she pulled herself further between the rocks and kept her head as low as she could. The light swept the ground as it moved. It was only inches from her toes and then it was moving on along the beach.

Mel couldn't stay there. If he was the one behind the light, then he could come back along here at any moment. Keeping as far into the shadows as she could she moved up the beach. Just about fifty yards away a wooden gate marked a path up off the strand to a house above.

Mel went straight for this, trying not to send stones skidding in the dark. She had just made the gate when she heard a sound. He must have switched off the light and doubled back. She could hear stones skittering as his footsteps gathered pace.

Opening the gate she ran up the path, moving as quickly as her tired body would allow. Like the one they'd come down earlier it was quite steep at the beach but started to level as it got closer to the garden above. Mel could hear distinct footsteps now, not far behind her.

The path blended straight into the garden. Unlike Amanda's garden there was no garden wall bordering it. Instead it just sloped down towards the trees and then the beach. When Mel got onto the lawn she ran across it with, her lungs bursting for air. She had no idea where she was going or what she was going to do. The house above was in total darkness. Banging on doors would just waste valuable seconds so she ran onto the driveway and towards the road. Luckily the gates leading onto the road weren't locked.

As she approached it she could hear sirens in the distance. Sobbing, she weighed up her options. Either turn back and bump into him or go forward and meet the Guards. She feared he was mere seconds behind her and gaining quickly. She ran on through the gates and straight onto the road.

Mel appeared on the road directly in front of a squad car, which swerved to avoid her. The car hit the kerb and turned over on its side rolling through the open gates of the house and into the driveway. A horrific scream came from the impact. Mel could hear screeching brakes as other cars skidded to a halt and officers jumped out.

Mesmerised, Mel walked back towards the car, which was on its side with its wheels spinning in the air. She could see steam hissing from a broken pipe. An officer grabbed her, pulling her away. As she turned she saw a body under the car. The Garda driver and his partner were still inside. One of them was crawling through the top of the car, shouting to the other one still inside. The man she could see under the car wasn't moving.

Giving backward glances over her shoulder towards the wreck Mel was led away amidst flashing blue lights and sirens.

CHAPTER 48

Mel was placed in the back of a squad car wrapped in a space blanket. As she sat there the rain got heavier. Little rivers ran down the screen in front of her eyes, the droplets reflecting the flashing blue lights. As she watched, officers milled around the car, checking their colleagues were okay and trying to see who was under the car. There was no way to do that without moving it. They were not sure if he was dead but she was alive. Melanie had faced the monster and won.

Two officers got into the front of the car she was in and started the engine. A description of Mel had already been sent out before the accident so it had been her they were coming to find. She was brought to the station amid as much fanfare as they could manage, with sirens and lights all the way.

Immediately on arrival she was cautioned and offered a solicitor. She just shrugged and turned her face away so they held her to wait for the detectives to arrive. Mel sat quietly in an interrogation room, almost the same as the one she'd been held in previously. She wondered if they came in just one standard design.

Two detectives came to speak to her now.

They were both men in their forties. One was fair and small while the other was tall with dark hair going salt and pepper grey. The small one spoke first.

"Hello, Melanie. I'm Detective Morgan and this is Sergeant Clancy. "

Mel nodded and smiled weakly.

"You know about your cousin's death?"

She nodded.

"Do you know what happened to her?"

"Keith Byrne killed her." Mel looked vacantly past Detective Morgan's head.

"Who?" Detective Morgan asked.

"The man in the crash."

"Do you know who he was?"

"He's from Raven in West Cork. You probably know there is an open murder down there. I'm a suspect but there was a second blood type found at the scene. It wasn't mine and I'm sure you will find that it matches Keith's."

"Really?" He didn't seem convinced. "Do you know why he was chasing you?"

"He wanted to kill me next."

"Okay, Melanie. You wait here." Detective Morgan left the room.

Outside Morgan walked to the squad room and sat down. One of the investigating team came over to him. "They've moved the car."

"And do they have an ID on the victim?"

"Keith Byrne. He had ID on him."

As they talked a fax came through. It was Mel's story from the first night she walked into the station in Bantry.

"What a mess!" Detective Morgan flicked down through the transcript and then went back to Mel to hear the rest of her story.

Melanie found out that shortly after she left the house Donna had come home. It was she who had found Amanda's body. She'd immediately called the police. Mel's heart broke into little pieces when she heard that. She knew that the first thought which would have entered Donna's mind was that Mel had done it. She'd killed her mother and it was her fault for letting her stay in the house with them. Donna knew mental illness. She knew the consequences of a mind that couldn't be trusted.

Even though Mel didn't kill Amanda, it was as a consequence of her being in the house that Donna had lost her mother. That would be difficult for her to forget. Mel tried contacting her but Donna wasn't ready to talk to her and she worried that she never would.

CHAPTER 49

The only place Mel had to go was back home to Galway. It wasn't going to be easy. By now she was national news. It didn't really matter where she went as the media had saturated every home in the country with her image and her story but at least Galway was familiar to her. Mel didn't intend on staying there long term. She just wanted to get the house sorted, sell it if possible and move on. If she could organise her finances she thought she would have enough to buy a property in another part of the city.

When Mel got to the house the palpitations started. She stepped into the garden on the same spot that her mother had fallen and died. Standing on the step she looked at her family house. It looked small and dead, dwarfed by the encroaching foliage. The hedges and shrubbery had grown wild and the lawn was almost up to the level of the windows. The paint on the walls was a dull grey. The paint on the front door was peeling. A window at the side of the door was broken but some well-meaning person had nailed a piece of wood across it. A padlock had been placed on the door but the local Guards had made sure that it was clipped open before she got there. Mel didn't remember the house being this worn and sad.

Mel pushed the door and walked in. This was the doorway where she last saw her brother alive. Flanked by officers and crestfallen, they had taken him away. Stepping inside, she immediately saw the hall was musty and the house smelt old. She felt the stirrings of panic taking control of her whole body and she wanted to turn and run. If she had any other option she would have gone. But she had to do this – lay to rest the ghosts of her life.

Closing the door behind her, she started to walk down the hall. It seemed to get narrower and more restricted as she passed the room where her father died. Her lungs were straining against the mould and dust blowing around the house but a few spores were nothing to the ghosts and memories she saw floating through these rooms.

The kitchen door was open at the end of the hall. Mel could see that the room was exactly the same as it had been the day she decided to follow the smooth-talking Ryan Lester to Cork. The tea towel was folded on the rack exactly where she put it that day just as Ryan's face appeared at the back window in front of her. A cobweb spread from it now to the dish mop sitting in a stone jar on the window ledge. She stood in that spot and let the past wash over her.

Her mind flashed back to when she saw Ryan and her face split into a broad smile. Ryan had come around the back of the house to surprise her as she worked. Walking to the back door, she'd invited him in. Their relationship was still new. They'd only known each other a month. He wrapped his arms around her and held her close. She could remember his smell and the feeling of his warm breath against her hair. Mel looked up into his face and saw her future and she never doubted it was secure. His eyes crinkled and shone as he talked to her about his house in Raven, West Cork. It sounded wonderful.

Mel held her breath and then he said it. "Come with me. Live with me in Raven."

Mel had jumped up, wrapping her arms around him. "When?"

"As soon as you like. I'm going away for a couple of days. I'll come back for you."

Mel was ready and packed, waiting for him when he arrived. She'd already said goodbye to her dad earlier, believing she would never see him again. This was going to be a new life away from this dreary little house. Mel closed the door behind her and never meant to look back.

Now, she stood at the sink looking into the garden. It looked a lot smaller with the tall grass blowing in the breeze. She noticed the shed had a new lock on it too.

This house was never comfortable and it would take a few days to get it habitable. The detective who sorted out the locks and keys for her had also given her sufficient money for essentials from a hardship fund. She would have to look more deeply into her finances. Her dad would have left her something and probably Bobby – though now that she knew about Donna, perhaps not. She wondered if he had made a will. All those things she would see to later.

Mel had been let out this time without restrictions but

she was still going to visit a psychologist in Galway. Edmund Willis in Dundrum had recommended him. She'd been through a lot and knew she couldn't put it behind her alone. Edmund gave her hope. Through his guidance she realised she could have a good life once she'd said goodbye properly to her old one. Mel's psychotic break came as the result of an accumulation of tragedy. It was the perfect storm of events: the shock of Bobby's story, his suicide, her father's death, the residual guilt left over from her mother's accident and the disappearance of Ryan. Such a storm centre, thankfully, was rare in anybody's life and now Mel had help to leave it behind.

When the guards found Keith Byrne's body under the car they believed her story. The clothes he was wearing that night were covered in Amanda's DNA and fibres from his clothes were found on her body and in the house. There was no cast-off blood on Melanie's clothes. Any blood on her hands and shoes was lost in the sea. Keith's blood matched the blood found at the scene of Hugh Curtis's murder. There was no reason to hold Mel any longer. There wasn't enough evidence against her for a trial.

The Gardaí wanted Ryan (it was still difficult for Melanie to refer to him as Gordon Grant) for questioning but he appeared to have vanished. While there was no evidence that he committed any crime, he was an accessory before or after the fact, or perhaps both. Either way he'd lured Mel to Raven and he was an accomplice, unwitting or otherwise to what happened next. All they needed was to find him and then she supposed she would have to testify against him. She wondered did he know that.

Mel left the kitchen and made her way to her room. Nothing had been touched. It didn't seem like her room anymore. She'd grown up a lot over the last year. This room seemed like the room of a child. Mel realised that was what she was, before Ryan took her in hand. Looking around her she could see each stage of her life displayed around the room from babyhood to womanhood.

The bed seemed damp. She placed her hand on it. It was definitely damp and cold to the touch. This wasn't going to be forever. Soon, when she had everything sorted, she could get out of there and leave this part of her life behind. It wasn't going to take long more.

Mel had a small bag of provisions with her, which she'd picked up earlier so she unpacked this and put on a pot of tea. Sitting at the kitchen table she was amazed at how quiet it was in there. She realised she brought isolation with her. While she sat deep in thought the light faded from her first day back in Galway. Her haunted eyes looked around her and thought this was the house that wouldn't let her go.

"No." She spoke out loud in the darkness. "No."

Edmund had warned her that this might happen. Mel's life could be anything she wanted it to be if she could dig herself out of the quicksand of the past. Finally the light faded completely and she moved from the chair where she'd sat for most of her life and washed up her dishes.

Still not comfortable with her freedom she brought a knife from the kitchen and laid it on the nightstand. Despite her surroundings, she slept fitfully.

Some hours later Melanie awoke. The room was dark so she switched on the bedside light and got out of bed. She reached for the knife and, holding it by her side, walked to the door. The hall light didn't come on when she flicked the switch. Tomorrow she would have to change that bulb. Mel was thirsty and needed to use the bathroom. She missed having an en suite. Carrying the knife she walked to the kitchen and placed it on the counter before getting herself a glass of water. Standing at the sink she sipped it slowly.

Picking up her knife again, Mel walked to the kitchen door. The door was closed. It always swung closed of its own accord. It was annoying if you were carrying something and you needed both hands.

Mel reached for the handle but the door was pushed in before she could touch it and a dark shadow filled its space. Mel stepped back into the shadows until she felt the edge of the worktop behind her back. Then quietly and swiftly the shadow crossed the room towards her.

Somewhere in her heart she'd known it wasn't over. She knew she should have felt fear but she didn't.

Her knife was still in her hand. The shadow stopped halfway and stood watching in the darkness. Mel felt the blade of her knife pressed against her buttocks.

"What are you doing in my house?" she demanded.

"You've spent the last few months in mine."

"I was invited." Mel spoke with as much bravado as she could.

"I heard there's a great big question mark over whether your memory can be trusted."

Mel squirmed in the darkness and her fingers gripped the knife. Her memory of her time in the house was a blur and even now she could hardly decipher what part of it was true and what was fantasy but people had died – that was true enough. This man was responsible for their deaths.

He started laughing. "Are you trying to figure out if I'm really here?"

She was.

Silence returned to the room, broken only by the ticking of the clock. That was some battery, Mel thought. It was at least a year old. She realised he'd moved a step closer, shuffling very quietly in the darkness.

"Stay back."

He laughed again and this time he obviously moved a step closer. "What are you going to do to me, Melanie?"

Mel shifted her position a little, moving the knife out from behind her. She hadn't seen his face, just his murky outline as he approached but she knew who it was. Keeping her eyes fixed on him she moved sideways, a little more out of his reach.

"Stop moving. There's nowhere for you to go. There's a padlock on the outside of that back door."

She froze for a moment. "Is Ryan dead?"

He avoided the question. "He fell in love with you." He spat these words in hatred. "He loved me?" Mel whispered. "So you killed him?"

"No. I haven't killed anybody. Keith did all that. A faithful servant just like all his family before him."

Mel smiled in the darkness and wished Keith could have heard those words. They wouldn't have brought him the pleasure that Bradley meant them to bring.

"So Keith did it?"

He didn't answer but he didn't have to. Mel knew he must have.

"So that was why Ryan left me?"

"Well, it's hard for a dead man to play lord of my manor, with you."

"What do you want from me?"

He seemed to be thinking, struggling with the thoughts he was mulling over in his head.

378

"There was a plan. I was to be the head of the family. Elizabeth would marry. My parents would retire and I would be at the helm of Renfield industries. There should have been Fourth of July celebrations; weekends in the cottage on the Cape, Thanksgiving and Christmas but Bobby Yeats stole all of that from us. Elizabeth died. My parents died a short time later."

Melanie spoke softly. "You could have married."

"No. How could I?" His body seemed to shudder. "I couldn't let her death pass and not do something about it. Somebody had to pay. Somehow."

Mel's eyes darted around the room, assessing her situation.

"But why do I have to pay? Why did Hugh Curtis or Amanda have to pay?"

"That was Keith. They were a mistake."

"Bobby killing Elizabeth was a mistake."

"He burned her to death. That was no mistake."

He was sobbing now in the darkness.

"I lost my family too. I'm the last one left." Mel's voice was soft and coaxing. Keith had done the killing. Maybe Bradley just needed to talk.

Bradley crossed his arms and gripped his shoulders like he was fighting great pain. He shouted into the shadows at her.

"You're not going to seduce me! I'm not Gordon!"

Mel jumped and gripped her knife tighter.

That was the moment when he made his move.

His body pushed against her, pinning her to the worktop. He didn't have a weapon but his hands were up and around her throat and he was surprisingly strong for his slim build. As she gasped for breath, Mel's arm shot up and the blade in her hand penetrated upwards into his abdomen. She pushed hard at the blade and the pain caused him to scream. She used the opportunity to wriggle sideways, twisting and turning the knife and then letting it go. His body fell downwards on to the floor. He tried to drag himself back up but he slid into a semi-reclining position against the cupboard door.

Ignoring his moans, Mel went to the other side of the room. When she flicked on the light switch, the glow turned the dark shadowy world where she'd just fought the fight of her life back into a dusty old kitchen and the monster who had just tried to strangle her was a beaten and dying man.

"Why?" she asked him.

Blood was bubbling through his lips and she knew he was mortally injured. His lips were moving but she couldn't hear him so she walked closer.

"Retribution."

Mel sat on the chair by the table.

"Was it worth it?"

Silence.

"I wanted to make peace," she said. "Bobby was sorry – it was truly an accident and now three people are dead – and look at you."

Once more he tried to speak. Mel moved a little closer.

He coughed blowing a spray of blood onto the lino. Then he tried to speak again but by now his voice was very faint.

Mel got a little closer.

"I loved her." His life was fading in front of her.

"I know."

Mel sat back in her chair watching his eyes as the light

died in them. She sat and watched him until she knew he'd gone then she walked down the corridor to her room.

Mel picked up her new phone and dialled 999.

"Hello. Can I have the police, please?"

She waited to be connected.

When someone answered she started speaking quickly, her anguish genuine. "This is Melanie Yeats, 12 Ashe Way, Mount Bank, Galway. I just killed an intruder. Please come quickly."

Mel hung up and waited for them.

It only took ten minutes for the Gardaí to gather in a whirr of blue lights outside her gate.

Mel had been through this before. She sat wan and sad as the crime scene cops did their job. Then she went with them to the station to give her statement. This time there was no doubt she'd killed someone, a man who invaded her home in the dead of night, a man who wanted to do her harm. They saw the damaged lock on the front door.

That was the first and only time she met Bradley Renfield in person: the night he came to her house to kill her. Somewhere in the course of his life Bradley had closed off any other avenue except revenge: *An eye for an eye, a Yeats for a Renfield.*

Mel couldn't get the image of Gordon (she'd finally come to terms with no longer calling him Ryan) out of her mind. Did Keith kill him too? Questions were still unanswered. The Guards had investigated and all they knew of Gordon Grant was that he'd been in Ireland on a number of occasions the previous year but they couldn't place him in Galway or West Cork and he'd left the country prior to the murders of Hugh and Amanda. He was no longer a person of interest to them.

Mel had to find out more so she went to her local library and Googled the Grant family. At first she couldn't find anything. She found herself spending hours online searching and researching every avenue she could think of, even going state-by-state looking for any Gordon Grant listed.

Then she found it. There was a listing for Gordon Grant, winner of a sailing regatta in Boca Raton, Florida. Mel opened the link and there was her Ryan standing on a dock holding his prize aloft for the camera. He was suntanned, windswept and had a bright smile which grabbed at her heart.

Now that Mel had a starting point she found out lots more about Gordon Grant. It didn't take long to find an email address and then a number and in a short time Mel had Gordon on the phone.

It was strange hearing his voice after all this time and at first she could hardly speak.

"Ryan, I mean Gordon. It's me." There was a long silence.

"Melanie?"

"Yes."

"Why are you calling me?" He sounded angry.

"I needed to speak to you. To know what happened."

"Damn it Melanie." Silence. "How did you find me?"

"Does that matter?" Mel's courage was rapidly evaporating.

"Melanie, the last I heard was that Keith and you had been together."

"What?" Mel wasn't expecting that.

"He told me you slept together. I was coming back but I couldn't after that."

"He lied to you. I never laid a finger on him. Haven't you heard what's been happening here?" Mel asked.

"No. I haven't spoken to him since that night. I left for work and told Keith I wanted nothing to do with any more revenge. I rang him to talk and he told me you and he had been together. I couldn't come back after that."

Mel let his words run through her mind. Was he telling her the truth?

They talked for a long time.

Bradley had told her that Gordon loved her and so had Keith. Mel knew now he had loved her. They had told her the truth. And if Gordon loved her she was willing to give him another chance.

"I'm coming to Florida to see you," she said. "I've never travelled. I need to get away."

"Why not Belize?" He asked. "We can really spend some time together."

Mel was thrilled.

Now, a month later Mel stood at the airport in Atlanta, travelling to Belize on her first ever passport.

EPILOGUE

A Sailboat a mile off Boca Raton on the
South East Florida Coast

Gordon's wife had left yesterday to take the kids to Monterey in California to visit her parents. Gordon and Sandra had been married for six years and now had two small girls: Brooke, aged three, and Katie, two. The couple each had their own passions and they rarely mixed. Gordon loved the ocean wind in his face and she loved the restaurants, galleries and symphony in Monterey. She was a West Coast girl to the marrow of her bones. So for three weeks every summer she migrated to Monterey and he went south to Mexico, usually docking in Puerto Morelos just South of Cancún. They had often joked that this was the secret of their successful marriage. They were happy together or apart. That had come in useful during his time in Ireland. He did travel extensively for work but he was always careful about receipts and any items left in his bag or pockets so Sandra wasn't suspicious.

His boat was the real love of his life and it was only

aboard this forty-foot floating dream that he was truly happy. It was funny how one man's misfortune could further another's happiness. Gordon had recently bought the boat after it had been repossessed from a former Lehman Brothers director when the recession really started to bite.

That was the one real part of himself he'd given to Melanie: his love of the sea. Now that was coming back to haunt him. She'd traced him through it.

He'd wondered what that girl understood and what she invented. When he stayed with her in Raven House she often talked of her brother Bobby and what he might be doing on his travels when, unknown to her, Gordon knew all along about the suicide. Melanie never seemed to be lying. She really seemed to believe her own stories. It got a lot worse after he encouraged her to give up her medication. The change in her was dramatic.

After Elizabeth Renfield's death in Boston, Gordon's life became a living hell. Bradley Renfield and his family had tried every way they could to make him pay for what happened to Lizzie, finally driving him out of Boston for good. This was when he moved to Florida. For a time Bradley seemed satisfied with this. Out of sight out of mind, he supposed.

Then Gordon met Sandra Russell. But Melanie could bring that down around him like a small shack in a hurricane. Gordon had never discussed Lizzie with his wife. She certainly didn't know about Mel. Sandra's family had all the money and her father had made him sign a pre-nup. If they divorced he got nothing.

So Gordon knew he had a problem when Melanie suggested coming to Florida.

It would have been simpler for them all if she'd died in Raven. Keith was a moron. It was meant to happen cleanly, an unfortunate accident or death at her own hand but nobody else was meant to get hurt. After he left to return to Sandra, Keith had killed two people and then got himself killed too. Gordon brought Melanie to Raven but he knew he couldn't kill her and he told Bradley that. It was always supposed to be Keith. But now she'd forced his hand. He had to tell her on the phone he was jealous of Keith. It was the only reason he could think of that made any sort of sense.

What a disaster! He still couldn't believe she'd found him. That girl was tougher than anyone ever gave her credit for and now she was on her way to Belize to be with the man she loved and thought loved her in return. He couldn't tell her about his wife. He'd seen what Melanie was capable of.

Gordon turned his face into the warm wind as he trimmed his sails. He had cared for her but not in the way that she loved him. He knew that once she'd figured that out, she would destroy his world. After dispatching Bradley so neatly and then forcing him to make contact with her, he saw her from a different angle. Melanie was dangerous to him.

No. He would sail to Mexico as he did every year, sort things with immigration and leave his boat docked in Puerto Morelos. He could get transport locally which wouldn't leave a trail and he would travel on to Belize where he would meet with Melanie.

Gordon pushed the tiller leeward trying to make the most of the wind making his sails billow. He knew she was excited to be finally seeing all the places he had told her about, to finally see for real the island she'd so often travelled in her head. She was a strong swimmer and he could see them diving together, maybe out on a boat searching for manatees.

Things can go wrong in the water. The ocean is a very dangerous place. Melanie Yeats was going to meet death in Belize and this time there would be no escape.

But, as Gordon concentrated on the task at hand, he knew in his heart that he shouldn't underestimate Melanie Yeats.

THE END

An Interview with
Ellen McCarthy

1. **Your plotline includes many twists and turns that keeps your readers on their toes. How did you work out the complex structure of *Silent Crossing*?**

I never plot a story completely before I start. Normally I would have a character clearly set out in my mind and then that character just develops as I write my story. The element of surprise is greater for me that way. In *Silent Crossing* I developed the main characters before I started writing the plot. Once my first draft is completed I start to do a lot of re-writing. At this stage I weave in the story and this is probably what makes the structure more complex.

2. **Are you influenced by contemporary media like film and television? For example, by the current taste for intricate plots in films like *Memento* and *The Usual Suspects* and TV shows like *Without a Trace* and *Law & Order*?**

Hour-long shows like *Law & Order* are often too short and rushed to fully develop characters and provide a satisfactory solution to the drama but I do love a good thriller. *Mystic River*, the Dennis Lehane novel, is a good example of a book plot that transferred well to movie media.

I like to read the book first and then watch the film before comparing the two approaches. Usually I prefer the book and think as a writer the flexible length of a novel gives more scope to tell the story. While I'm not influenced as such by movies, a good thriller is an excellent manual on how to build suspense and keep the reader guessing.

3. **Why are you drawn to writing suspense books in particular? Do you feel they are more rewarding to write than other types of novel? Would mystery novels be your read of choice?**

Suspense writing has always been my main area of interest. Creating mystery, piecing together the plot and developing the character feels like working out a puzzle. The most rewarding aspect for me is to bring the reader to the end of the book and then surprise them. The key challenge is to avoid predictability. For that reason thrillers are always my first choice for reading.

4. **Your books are very atmospheric. The settings in your novels are crucial to the overall tone of the book. Why do you think this is?**

In my first novel *Guarding Maggie* – Maggie's lost youth

is mirrored in the decay of her farm and surroundings. The setting is also important in *Silent Crossing*. Melanie is hiding from the ghosts of her past and this is reflected in the old house and its tragic history. Gothic storytelling has always heavily influenced me and I think this genre, more than any other relies heavily on atmosphere.

5. **You appear to have an affinity for country life. Why is this? And why do you choose country settings for your novels?**

My childhood was spent in the country. In the countryside there is so much scope for atmosphere, with long narrow roads, forgotten farms, mountains and the unpredictable weather. The country setting allows me to take the comfort zone of quiet isolation and twist it into something eerie. If something frightens me, I hope it will also scare the reader.

6. **Your leading characters tend to be extremely vulnerable women either in terms of their geographical isolation, their temperament or both. From a sociological point of view, do you feel women are particularly vulnerable at this point in time?**

I'm not a particularly fearful person but I'm aware of danger. I think that all people are vulnerable in some way. Vulnerability can be measured in both emotional and physical terms. Women are often physically weaker and sometimes isolated in the home. For these women even their home can be a dangerous place. In my writing I like to analyse frightening situations and incorporate them into my novels.

7. Do you have a favourite character in *Silent Crossing*?

Bobby. He was the most interesting because his actions touched so many people. I can't say more than that or I'll give too much away.

8. In *Silent Crossing*, what character & scene was most difficult for you to write?

The most difficult scene was the very first scene I wrote which was subsequently changed. As the story developed the scene didn't work because my character changed as the book progressed. Writing a plot for me often leads to excess scenes that will be cut later. I haven't had a problem with writing any of my characters. It's not me I'm writing about.

9. Can you (without revealing the plot!) explain how you thought of the title *Silent Crossing*?

Before I started the book I had the title *Silent Crossing* in my mind. As the story developed I knew my characters were going to face choices and make tough decisions that would change their lives drastically. In just a split second your life or the lives of those you touch can take a silent crossing to a different place. Their lives may never be the same again. Sometimes one decision can affect generations to come.

10. **You have an Honours degree in Literature and Sociology. Do you find that your academic background has influenced your writing?**

I deliberately studied Literature and Sociology to prepare myself for writing. I knew it would take a lot of work and luck to put what I learned into practice but I was ready for the challenge. Sociology changed the way I looked at society. It made me more analytical and curious. Unfortunately in life there are not always clear-cut answers. A question often just raises another question. I don't try to give definitive answers as there are always multiple points of view. During my literature courses I examined the works of great writers with the guidance of tutors. Reading these texts with the benefit of study manuals allowed me to see how these writers structured their work. Reading is a huge benefit to any writer.

If you enjoyed *Silent Crossing* by
Ellen McCarthy, why not try
Guilt Ridden and *Guarding Maggie* also
published by Poolbeg?

Here's a sneak preview of Chapter One of
Guilt Ridden followed by
Chapter One of *Guarding Maggie*

ELLEN McCARTHY

Guilt Ridden

CHAPTER 1

Amy watched her polished reflection divide into two as the elevator doors opened. Smiling widely and allowing her eyes to flick casually across the expectant faces lined up inside, she stood at the front of the car with her briefcase casually hanging by her side. Amy continued to smile to herself, knowing everyone in there had their eyes glued to the back of her shiny blonde head, delighted to have been in her line of vision first thing in the morning. They were obviously a bunch of new hirelings.

This was Amy's good deed first thing in the morning. Play the game and let the people feel important. In a blue-chip corporation like Helfers the illusion of opportunity was very important. By using the elevator, at least once a week it was possible to ask Amy Devine, the vice-president herself, how her weekend had gone or if she had any plans for next weekend or just simply to moan about the traffic. The play at camaraderie was good for morale and made everyone feel as though they were on the same level, even though the elevator went one floor above all of them. And if Amy herself were ever to step through the glass ceiling and into the shiny Helfers building in New York there would be a whole new elevator to ride.

When the doors closed behind her on the top floor, she walked down the hall to her corner office with both the Irish and United States flags waving cheerfully in the breeze outside her window. The illusionists just kept on performing for the company crowd. Amy had heard through the corporate grapevine that there might be some rerouting of operations through south-east Asia, but still those flags danced in the breeze announcing Helfers' special relationship to the people of Dublin, providing a sense that if they only had a parking space where they didn't have to keep moving and outwitting the parking attendant, life would be perfect.

Just exiting her office as Amy approached the door was a man she had never seen before, carrying a basket of mail. Amy flashed her bright smile on him, causing him to take the corner a bit too sharply and bang his elbow. A word pushed itself to the surface automatically but she barely caught the initial "F" sound before he swallowed it. His bumbling attempt at regaining his composure could take a while so Amy broke the ice.

"Anything interesting in there for me?"

"In here?" The poor man looked into his basket.

"I presume you left whatever it was in my office when you were in there."

"Of course."

By now he was an etching in mortification and Amy genuinely felt sorry for him. "Miss Devine," he added hastily.

"Oh, please! Call me Amy." She held out one of her long white hands.

He tried to form the word but he couldn't – he just held out his hand and limply gripped hers.

"Thank you, Kevin. How are things in the mail office?"

"How do you know who I am?"

"Your name tag – and you're carrying the mail."

By now poor Kevin looked close to death.

"Very good! Well spotted!" He gave a short laugh, a last attempt at confidence.

"That's how I got the corner office, Kevin. See you tomorrow."

Amy entered her office and Kevin gratefully took his leave.

The outer office was empty. Amy walked past her assistant's desk and opened the door to her own office.

You could set your clock by her assistant's routine. Two minutes later, after Amy had turned her swivel-chair and sat with her face towards the bright blue sky, he came in with a steaming mug of coffee and the opened mail. A coffee pot and a silver letter-opener were just another opportunity to perform in this equal opportunities company. Greg Bannon stood a moment and, in his slightly camp way, discussed his latest crisis and the traffic jam he found himself in on the way home yesterday and then left Amy to her reading.

Weary and bored after five minutes, Amy gratefully reached the last envelope. It was a large brown manila stuffed full of paper. There was no sender's name and address on the back. She turned it over and looked at the front. It was marked personal. Amy pulled out the sheaf of papers and laid it on her desk.

Written in bold black lettering across the front of the top page was a single word: *RUTH*

Amy's heart gave a jump.

A typed single sheet of paper fluttered out when she shook the envelope. No stamped addressed envelope enclosed.

She picked up the paper and read it and suddenly her carefully groomed and manicured life came tumbling down around her.

Dear Miss Devine,

I know this manuscript will come as a surprise. I'd meant to send it to you a long time ago after Ruth's death but it took longer than expected to compile. You were working in Marlow Publishing at the time. I was disappointed to hear of your move but I'm sure you still have plenty of contacts in that area.

I know Ruth's story has appeared many times in various collections over the years but this one is different. This is the definitive account of what happened. I have collated most of the data I gathered on Ruth and am presenting it to you in rough book format. I've used newspaper articles, her own diaries and my personal knowledge of her in my writing. Ruth was a compulsive chronicler of her life and the world around her. Her diaries were like vast essays detailing the most minute details of her daily activities and were indispensable in my writing of this manuscript. Coming to know her as I did, I suspect a certain level of graphorrhoea: her need to write was compulsive and abnormal and she consumed vast amounts of paper, spewing her thoughts and feelings on to the page.

Occasionally I have used some creative licence in order to protect some things that perhaps should remain a secret even from you. Also I must insist that you don't contact any outside groups until I've finished my story, otherwise I won't be able to tell you what really happened to Ruth. I need to know I can trust you so I haven't revealed the whole story here.

I hope you enjoy reading our story.

It was unsigned.

Amy pressed the button on her desk and called for more coffee. Marlow was a publishing house in the UK and New York. After college Amy had worked for them but only from the business side of marketing and advertising. She had never been close to the area of publishing and editing. Still, she was sure this was just somebody's crude attempt at getting a publishing deal. Someone who thought her personal connection to Ruth Devine might help them. It was distasteful and already she disliked this writer.

She turned to the back page of the manuscript and saw the words *To be continued.* Whatever he had to say was coming in instalments.

Once her assistant had brought the coffee and left the room, she turned her chair away from the sun and placed the manuscript on her desk.

Feeling sick at the prospect of re-entering this area of her life she started reading.

Ruth was back in her life after fifteen years.

I watched the involuntary swallow and the barely visible arching of her stiff back as Ruth took a sip from her coffee, her eyes riveted on the newspaper before her. "YOUNG WOMAN FOUND DEAD IN DUBLIN." The headline stood out in bold on the front page. I had my own copy open on the canteen table in front of me as I followed the progress of her eyes down the page.

An eighteen-year-old girl had been killed in Bushy Park near her home in the Rathfarnham area of Dublin. The middle-class suburban neighbourhood was *"reeling from the shock of the murder"*.

Newspapers always make these generic statements, don't they?

The dead girl was a student at Waterford Regional Technical College, now known as the Waterford Institute of Technology. Her name was Sinéad Daly. She and Ruth were in the same class in college. There were thirty-three students in that class and Sinéad was one of the younger ones. Her group hung around in a gang of about ten. I would see them in the canteen or outside the college. They talked the most and wore the most make-up. The extended group contained about eight boys – the groupies, I always called them.

Sinéad had been out of college all that week and had missed her exams because she was sick. Sinéad was always sick when something important was happening in class.

I watched Ruth's face as she scanned quickly through the main details of the article. Her intensity was visible from across the room.

Sinéad left her home Monday afternoon to pay a visit to a friend. The gardaí were appealing for witnesses who might help shed some light on her whereabouts between then and early Tuesday morning when they found the body. The friend, not named in the article, told the gardaí she never arrived as they had planned, though she did call. Sinéad said she had something else on and would see her later. She received the call at six o'clock on Monday morning.

Ruth saw the story on Wednesday.

The body was found on Tuesday morning by a passer-by on the way to work. The coroner's report wouldn't be published yet but a source said she had been dead some hours when she was discovered.

The newspaper showed a photo of the path where they found her. It was next to an oval depression at the base of a small waterfall. At the angle the photograph was taken you could see the waterfall as it fell down over a collection of rocks into the basin. From there the water ran into a gully and onwards to where the picture didn't show. It was odd for me seeing it isolated like this in a grainy black and white image. It made it sort of surreal.

I could see that Ruth was hooked on the story. She was fascinated by murder and here was one in her world. Someone she knew. Something she could really let her imagination work on.

Steam rose from her coffee in a steady stream and her eyes wandered up after each wisp until it faded. It was too hot to drink so she just dropped two sugar lumps into the cup and played with the plastic spoon. Her eyes wandered around the room, unable to focus. There were few students in that morning, just a small spattering through the tables, but the place could have been empty for all the notice Ruth took. I felt my breath quicken as she glanced in my direction but we never made eye contact. Ruth was too preoccupied. One of her classmates was dead. Murdered. This crime was so real for her.

As I watched her finish reading the article and saw the drooping angle of her shoulders, my face broke into a smile. Over the months since she'd started in the college I'd watched her read her newspapers and crime novels, always alone, and though it hadn't been my original intention, here she was now, reading my story. My murder was in there on the printed page, staring up at her, teasing her into its depths.

We'd arrived two minutes apart that morning and I saw her buy *The Times*. It seems like an odd paper for a student to buy but she bought it for the crosswords. I passed by her chair many times and saw her engrossed in them and oblivious to her surroundings. Ruth was never a conventional student. I'd already seen the headlines so I was really excited about seeing her response. You know yourself in your line of work how satisfying it is when you get the validation you deserve for a job well done. She hadn't noticed the story on the cover then. I watched her with anticipation walking down from the counter to her usual table. The story took up three-quarters of the page. I suppose nothing more exciting had happened that day.

To be truthful I hadn't really expected her to be in college. It was the last day before the Christmas holidays. Most students wouldn't bother turning up.

But then Ruth was different. Wasn't she?

She was beautiful in a delicate way. She always

wore jeans and bright jumpers, never skimpy or revealing clothes. For some reason her clothes were always a size too big like she needed to grow into them. I knew she had a beautiful body. Don't get me wrong, I'm not a pervert, but I'd seen it through a window at her house once. She hadn't bothered to close the curtains because you would have to be standing in her garden to see her. Isn't it funny how people get so complacent about the security of their own patch?

I loved her from the first moment I saw her. That was such a long time ago. Our lives had gone through many changes since. Ruth always had so much grace and energy. But you wouldn't have known her then. It was after you left. For many years our paths had taken different directions but when she went back to college they merged once again.

I really wanted to introduce myself in September but I couldn't. She didn't recognise me even though I followed her every move. I discovered the time she came to college and soon had most of her timetable figured out. I knew when she had lunch and when she went home.

Often she would sit gazing over the sea of canteen faces but her gaze would never alight on any individual for long. Many times I wanted to catch her eye but I never had the courage. Not then anyway! In my heart I was afraid of what she might see. It was too soon to share any of that.

After a few weeks I found out where she lived. That was easy. The bus left every day from outside the college and stopped almost outside her door. I would step off behind her and casually follow her up the road. At every step I'd watch the little curls at the back of her neck bounce and convince myself that any second now she'd turn around, but she never did.

I yearned for her but I feared rejection so I was content, for then at least, to watch and wait. She would see me when the time was right.

Shortly after that I had the perfect opportunity to meet her again and tell her who I was but in the end I was just too frightened of rejection. It was one afternoon as she returned from college. She got off the bus and dropped her wallet. I picked it up and ran my hands over it and held it to my nose, smelling the brocade cover. It was like a trace of her still clung to it.

I stood in the phone box across the road from her house, holding the wallet in my hand, and watched her front door. You, of course, must remember her house, a small mid-terrace lacking in pretension. The door was painted in red gloss. The windows flowed with wooden flower boxes turning a bit wild. It looked like a little house all dressed up but just not quite getting it right.

When she was a little girl she was just like that house, all dressed up with her toes turned in and a shy smile on her face. Ruth looked like she raided the rag-box for clothes when I knew her. But she was such an individual. Her brown hair was always a mess and badly needed combing. I used to feel myself getting hot fantasising about combing it for her. In those fantasies she would sit on my knee facing away from me and when I finished she would lean back against my chest. I would wrap my arms tightly around her tummy and feel my strong muscles protecting her small body. I imagined her whole abdomen would fit in the palm of my hand. My hands are large but how would you know that without me telling you?

I realised she lived alone – at least I never saw anyone else there. The only visitors were her family. Her mum came once a week and sometimes her dad. Sometimes friends would visit, but not so often.

I stood there in the phone box that afternoon for half an hour, though I knew it was dangerous for me to hang about during daylight, until I saw the red door opening. Ruth came out and hurried around the corner to the shop. Two minutes later she came running back and crossed the street towards the phone box, directly towards me. I put the telephone receiver down and, pulling up my hood, exited the phone box. I held the door for her but she went into the box without looking up, just muttering "Thanks."

In the phone box she spoke while looking up the road towards the school. That road was so quiet and sometimes very lonely. Maybe she turned towards life. This thought made me love her even more. I hesitated for a second, watching her dial as young people played basketball in the schoolyard.

When I was sure she'd started her conversation I crossed the street and dropped the wallet in the letterbox. I didn't have the courage to leave a note. I just didn't know what to say.

As I'd waited in the phone booth I'd looked through the wallet. Inside was a photograph of two little girls. I recognised Ruth and the little blonde girl was you. I took the photo and put it in the pocket of my shirt. I could feel it next to my heart as I walked away from her door that day. It crinkled against my skin like it was whispering to me that I had a little piece of her now. I still carry that picture with me. Ruth is a shadow now but you are as vibrant as ever.

That was a good day. Somehow touching her stuff and looking into her inner world like that brought me closer to her.

Ruth! Often I found myself just saying her name over and over. I would repeat it to myself as I went to sleep.

I apologise. I've gone way back in my story. That morning, the morning the story appeared in the paper, I picked up my bag and followed her into the corridor when she went for her class. I was in a different class, different course in fact, but we shared the same corridor on Wednesday. She was already out of sight when I exited the canteen. I wound my way through the hall and could almost smell her as I approached her classroom door. The lecturer was late that day so the door was still open as I went by. I turned my head slightly and there she was at her desk, her head down, rereading the article. Around her the class was in an uproar. They were all talking about Sinéad. Many students had only found out that morning in class. She made her last public performance on the front page of the national newspapers. I smiled again, continuing on to my own class, nodding to people as I passed them. Of course all classes were subsequently cancelled that day. It was all thanks to me! Life was good and I knew then that it would only get better.

ELLEN McCARTHY

Guarding Maggie

CHAPTER 1

Maggie sat with life pressing heavily on her shoulders. There was no point in lighting the fire. She would be going to bed soon. A roaring fire was a waste at this hour. She gave a jump, splashing tea over her wrist as a sound broke the stillness. Betty the tabby, attracted by the movement, jumped onto her knee.

The sudden disturbance in the dead of the night frightened Maggie. Her brain had slipped into a trance. The sound she'd just heard must have been the wind – it had whipped up to make quite a noise in the last few hours. Up here by the mountains its howling could be akin to shrieking voices as it beat against the eaves and echoed down the chimney pipe.

Pascal hadn't come in yet.

For a moment a silent tear slid down her face but she brushed it off. She had to be strong now. She couldn't lose control.

Maggie pushed the chair back from the table, clasping

Betty to her heart. The cat stretched out, her soft feet briefly exposing her tiny claws to grasp the wool of Maggie's jumper in a loving grip. She started to purr and tenderly rubbed her cheek against Maggie's face. The loving gesture again brought a wave of emotion to the surface. For a moment the woman and the tabby cat held each other in an intimate gaze; two old friends sharing the night, their hearts filled with love.

Maggie held the cat close and rose painfully. Her bruised hip ached and she knew if there was ever a time to act it was now. Life could be different if she could spend it with Tommy. She eased her body into the rocking chair by the fire. Gently she guided the chair into a rolling motion and watched the slanted eyes of the cat get smaller and smaller until the purring turned to gentle snores and the gripping claws withdrew. She mustered all her courage. Invisible bands were constricting and gripping her, stopping her from lifting the phone. Pascal was due back soon. Would she have the strength to tell her news before then?

She glanced back at the clock. A quarter of an hour had passed since she'd spoken to Reeney and soon she would have to do it. She hoped she had the nerve. The rocking of the chair was getting more agitated as she wrestled with her courage. America was five hours behind so it was the perfect time. The rest of the family were together having dinner in New York and she was going to tell them about Tommy, tell them right now if she could get her fear under control. Some of them would understand, some would disapprove but, once they all knew, Pascal would no longer have a hold over her. She would be free to go and spend time with Tommy if he still wanted her.

Again a thump rocked her heart. It had been doing that a lot tonight. These palpitations were just a reminder to her that she was still alive. She needed those from time to time. She gently lifted the sleeping cat and placed her on the warm cushion of the chair.

Maggie moved her stiff bones towards her bag and pulled a little wallet out of the middle zipped pocket. Inside was a small book where she kept her phone numbers and her reading glasses. She held them in her slender fingers as she took them back to the chair. Betty saw her coming and bounced off. She knew from experience that Maggie was gentle getting out of the chair but had a habit of sitting on her when she came back, so she decided it wasn't worth the risk. She sat on the hearth with her slanted eyes looking through the stove door at the dying embers.

Maggie put on her glasses and opened the book. Flicking the pages she turned to Brian's number. Her own brother and she couldn't remember the last time she'd spoken to him. Pascal would call him from time to time but Maggie only ever answered the phone the odd time he called here. But tonight she had to make the move herself, for Tommy, her little Tommy. The best day of her life had been that first day when he stepped out of the car in the yard and introduced himself to her.

She'd been baking in the kitchen all morning when she heard the car pull up outside. She already had a tray of scones cooling and was about to take out the brown loaf, which was just nicely crisped on the outside. She had two rhubarb tarts to go in after the bread came out. Maggie always overdid the baking, giving some to her neighbours as gifts. She came from a large family and she'd never adjusted properly to it being just herself and Pascal. All that week her neighbour Dolores Blaney, who lived in the next farm over from theirs across the mountain, had men in helping out with some land reclamation. Five extra men, on top of the three she already had in the house, ate a lot of food so Maggie was glad to help out.

Sheila barked. That was nothing unusual. Sheila did a lot of that but this time she continued on unabated. Maggie marched to the door to order the old dog to the barn but stopped in her tracks. Sheila was walking circles around a strange man. He'd driven up in a big car – people-carriers she believed they were called. The back was full of cases. He was leaning against the opposite side of the car, gazing around him at the yard.

Maggie watched him for a few moments without speaking, thinking there was something familiar about him but she couldn't quite put her finger on it. He didn't look particularly aggressive. He looked a bit overwhelmed. Then he turned and looked into her eyes. Again she got a strong sense of the familiar as she looked back into his face.

He was very handsome. His skin was tanned and his eyes from where she stood looked like brown orbs. He smiled at her. It was a shy smile that lit up his face. He had an intense gaze and Maggie found herself blushing. Being sixty years old, this wasn't something that she experienced often.

"Are you Maggie?"

She nodded.

"My name is Michael."

He walked towards her and extended his right hand. Maggie wiped her buttery hands in embarrassment on the front of her apron. Then she took his hand in her own trembling one. She had to pull her hand away as he held on, looking into her eyes. Now that she was close she could see that they weren't brown – they were hazel like her own and swimming in tears. She wanted to ask him why he was upset but she didn't know how to broach the subject without embarrassing them both. She felt no threat, even though she'd never laid eyes on him before – Pascal was around somewhere and there was always a neighbour passing by. Contrary to what the townspeople thought, there could be a lot of foot traffic in the country. Without hesitation she invited him in and offered him some tea. Like a little boy collecting for the local GAA draw he followed her meekly into the house.

"Sit down there." She gestured towards the two-seater couch by the fire.

She wet the tea and got a tray ready with a plate of scones, butter and jam and a piece of the tart she'd made yesterday. While she worked at the kitchen table she had her back turned to him but she could still feel his eyes on the back of her neck. As she turned around she was amused to see Eddie Molloy, her neighbour from down the road, taking sideways glances at the strange car as he crossed her yard to the upper gate. Eddie had land taken up there where he kept some cattle so he was a regular passer-by. He walked up every day to a hide he had there for hay. He fed them the hay and when the hide was empty he drove up on the tractor to replenish his supplies.

He had a smallholding that was doing okay but he didn't have enough grazing close by for his cattle. He needed that, especially in the winter, to feed them.

Maggie crossed the room and placed the tray on the low table by Michael's side. He drank some tea, then munched on his scone, never taking his eyes off her face. He seemed to be having a struggle with words. He appeared on the verge of speech more than once and then he went back to chewing and watching Maggie with the same unwavering gaze. Maggie used that opportunity to go back and put the finishing touches to her tart and place it in the oven. When that was done and the bread was on the wire tray she went and sat in the chair opposite him.

"It's about time you told me more than your Christian name, isn't it?"

He nodded. "My name is Michael Reynolds. I've come from Boston to see you."

"You have?" By now her curiosity was at boiling point but she didn't want to rush him. "How do you know me? Are you a relative?"

Like most Irish families the Breslins had a smattering of American relatives and they often came knocking on the door looking for their roots. The old stone walls in Ireland were like a call from the mother ship for them. A pilgrimage they all had to make at least once.

As she sat now in the dead of the night, thinking back, the impact of his next words still hit her like a clenched fist.

"Maggie! I'm your son. I've wanted to meet you for such a long time."

Maggie was glad she was sitting. If not her legs would surely have given away. For a moment she looked around her, confused, trying to formulate her thoughts.

"Are you sure?" was all she could come up with.

"I wasn't! Not until I met you. But I am now. Instantly I felt like I recognised you. Didn't you feel it too?"

Maggie had. She knew now that was what she'd felt. He had her eyes and he had a look of Pascal when he was his age, the shape of the brow and the earnest expression. But the boyish smile and the easy charm, those belonged to

417

someone else. Someone she wouldn't be able to give him much information about.

"Tommy!" she said almost to herself. "My little Tommy!"

"Tommy!" he repeated, looking puzzled.

With a break in her voice Maggie explained that Tommy was the name she'd chosen to call him the day he was born but she'd never been given the opportunity. Like a stab wound, the pain of separation still burned in her. She'd felt stretched all these years as if the child she'd had to let go still had a grip of her and was tugging at her from a great distance. She hadn't realised that distance crossed the Atlantic.

The brown-haired man sitting in her kitchen suddenly stood up and reached out his arms awkwardly. She stood and stepped towards him. Shyly she returned his embrace and felt his hot tears wet on her cheek.

A sharp voice broke the moment. "What is this?"

Pascal her brother stood in the doorway, his dark shape blocking the light. His face was hardened into a frown and his eyes were like granite in his wrinkled face.

Pascal was the eldest son. He had inherited the farm when their father died. He'd been twenty years old at the time. Maggie was just a baby then and he'd been the only father figure she'd ever known. He was father, brother and provider all in one and he was the tie that bound her to pain all these years. His presence was like a band of iron constricting the house, even now at eighty years old.

Pascal had been the head of the household since the death of their father and neither Maggie nor her mother before her death had ever disputed this. Sometimes Maggie questioned it in her own mind but life hadn't produced many alternatives. A suitable husband hadn't come along since her return to Donegal and she hadn't wanted to settle for less;

she'd known passion, brief as it was, and somehow she could never see that in the men around her.

Life just settled in, enclosing her. Gradually she succumbed to the weight left behind by the residue of her dreams and hopes. By the time the sixties came around for Maggie, her mother was in ill health and it was her place to take care of her. Pascal had the farm and the stock to look after. Áine Breslin's life ebbed and with it went Maggie's youth. For the last ten years it had just been her and Pascal.

She knew him and his ways. She knew how to get around him when he suffered the dark moods that sometimes rendered him almost motionless for days, days when the farthest he'd venture was the opposite side of the yard where he'd lean on the edge of the open gate and look down the lane ruminating on the past. Maggie knew him and never questioned their roles. It had always been so. Even in her own mind she didn't have a satisfactory answer as to why she put up with it. He was her brother, her family, beyond that she didn't explore it in any more depth. She learned to live within a confined space and the outside world fascinated but terrified her. Up until now there had been nothing abroad to tempt her out.

Michael was oblivious to the politics of the house but natural wariness made him leave the explanations to Maggie.

"It's Tommy, Pascal, he found me." She smiled hopefully at him. Hoping for some reprieve from her lot of the last forty-five years, hoping for some pity at this stage of her life. But none was forthcoming.

Pascal stood back stiffly and gestured to the open door. "Leave, please."

"Mr Breslin!" Michael pleaded.

But it was obvious pleadings would fall on deaf ears. Michael, being a diplomat, thought best to leave it for now. He thanked Maggie for the tea and walked slowly to the door. He turned back in the doorway, his hazel eyes fixed on her as if afraid he would never see her again.

Maggie wailed.

The sound surprised both of the men and they stood looking at her.

"Pascal, please!" she begged.

Pascal walked to the table and sat down. "Say your goodbyes. He's not welcome in this house."

Maggie clutched at the small concession her proud brother had granted her and ushered her son out the door.

They stood in the yard facing each other but Maggie couldn't look above his knees. The buildings and walls felt like they were gathering around, squeezing her in and keeping him out.

Michael's voice broke into her thoughts. "I'm going to write to you. He can't stop you reading a letter. I'll be in the town for another week. Meet me in Letterkenny. We can have dinner and I'll tell you about your grandchildren."

"My grandchildren!" Maggie's eyes finally rose to his and opened wide in her lined face.

"Yes, dear. You have two grandchildren: a boy Darren and my baby Trudy. Darren is twenty – he's in college and will be going to medical school soon – and Trudy is seventeen – she wants to study law. I knew you were my mother when I saw you, you know. Trudy is very like you." He leant down and kissed her cheek. "I'm staying at the Beachwood Hotel. Call me when you're in town."

He climbed into his car and drove out of the yard. As he passed her she noticed again the luggage in the back. He must have come here to Cooleen to find her before he even went to the hotel to unpack. Her heart leapt. That made her feel very special. Slowly she turned back to the house, her movements robotic with her thoughts speeding down the road in a rented car.

She'd expected an argument when she went back inside but Pascal presumed the subject was closed.

"Is there any tea in the pot? I'm starving."

She bustled around cutting bread and getting his tea. Life was too short for complacency but Maggie's life got shorter every day. Inside, she knew silence was the reason she lost Michael. Silence allowed him to be taken from her, kept her locked up here all her life and took her life away from her. Pascal had to preserve the silence; inside silence you could hide so much. When everyone knew, Pascal couldn't keep them apart. She knew she had to act now and take back the years he'd stolen. Her first step would be to break the silence.

POOLBEG WISHES TO
THANK YOU

for buying a Poolbeg book and will give you
20% OFF (and free postage*)
on any book bought on our website
www.poolbeg.com

Select the book(s) you wish to buy
and click to checkout.

Then click on the 'Add a Coupon' button
(located under 'Checkout') and enter
this coupon code

CAUEA15165

POOLBEG (Not valid with any other offer!) POOLBEG

WHY NOT JOIN OUR MAILING LIST
@ www.poolbeg.com and get some
fantastic offers on Poolbeg books

*See website for details